I0717921

Harriet pushed aside her bowl and folded her hands on the tabletop, the epitome of calm and propriety. "If you are worried that I am trying to spring the parson's mousetrap on you, my lord, I assure you that is the farthest thing from my mind. I already have an intended groom."

Just the tiniest of lies, since Sir Percival hadn't actually proposed. Yet. But he would. Just as soon as she had a dowry. He'd almost as much as said so.

Sheffield still didn't look convinced. She pressed on. "My brother won't be able to accompany us, but Betsy, my maid, will be aboard, so we will be properly chaperoned at all times." And Gabriel would make certain Mama thought Harriet was visiting Aunt Elizabeth, and that Aunt Elizabeth thought Harriet was at home with Mama.

No one would know she had been gone until after she returned. And she wouldn't have to wear breeches to carry out her plan.

Gaining her dowry, and Sir Percival, would be worth suffering through two weeks at sea in Sheffield's company, on board his ship. The end result would be worth any temporary discomfort.

Sheffield leaned even closer, a twinkle in his eyes, his bare index finger idly stroking a design on the back of her hand. "Admit it, Miss Chase," he said, his deep voice soft and slow, as much a caress to her auditory senses as his finger on her skin. "You want to go on an adventure before you settle down as a respectable matron."

First edition

ISBN: 978-1-955613-04-0 E-Book
978-1-955613-10-1 paperback edition

Cover art by Daniela Colleo, StunningBookCovers.com

The Viscount's Hidden Treasure

Scandalous Ladies Book 4

A Lighthearted Regency Historical Romance

Shirley Karr

Dedicated to my readers who became fans who became friends, who patiently (and sometimes impatiently) kept asking, and waited all these years for me to finally finish Nick's book.
Thank you for your support!

Chapter 1

Brixham, Devonshire, England
October 1816

"I can't do it." Harriet Chase stared at the dark brown woolen breeches spread out on her bed, starkly contrasting with the colorful patchwork coverlet.

"Yes, you can." Her younger brother Gabriel perched on the edge of the bed and leaned back on one elbow, patting the coarse fabric. "You just slip one leg in, then the other, and pull them up. I do it every day."

Harriet bit her bottom lip. How had it come to this, things sunk so low? Bad enough the economies they'd already made. Madame Zavrina, owner and headmistress of Torquay Academy for Ladies, couldn't have picked a worse time to pass on. How could someone so fastidious about proper behavior have been so foolish as to not have a will and make provisions for the continuation of her school, not to mention continued employment of all her teachers? Without Harriet's income as a teacher, modest as it was, her family had already been forced to dismiss all their staff except two maids.

But wearing men's breeches? Even if they did belong to her adolescent brother.

Madame Zavrina would roll over in her grave. At some point in almost every class, every day, every one of the teachers—including Harriet—had pontificated on proper behavior for ladies of quality. Wearing breeches most certainly did not qualify as proper.

"Want me to step out? I can pop into the hall, make certain Mama's still in the parlour."

"No, I don't think that would help." Harriet lifted the fall of the breeches and fingered one of the horn buttons. The garment wasn't entirely foreign to her—she had sewn them for Gabriel last year, after all. But the thought of pulling them on, between her legs, wearing a masculine garment... She let go of the button.

Gabriel smoothed the fabric. "They're not that different from the drawers Amber Barrow-Smith wore under her gown to the assembly last week."

"Yes, and did you see that no one would dance with her? No wonder she was expelled from the Academy last year."

"There was Reggie Dwight, and Sir Stanley Danielson, and Lord Walcott." Gabriel counted them off on his fingers. "They each claimed two dances with her."

"Rakes and rogues, all of them." Harriet waved her hand and began pacing. "Not a marriage-minded man among them. They only danced with Amber because they thought she was fast. They thought they could steal a kiss from her."

Gabriel nodded. "Reggie planned on trying to get more than a kiss. I heard him in the card room."

"My point exactly. Someone as honorable as Sir Percival would never dance with a girl he thought was fast." Harriet paused to shake her finger at Gabriel. "And what, pray tell young man, were you doing in the card room?"

Gabriel joined Harriet in her pacing. "You think Sir Percival wouldn't come up to scratch if he found out you ever wore breeches?"

Harriet rubbed her temples.

Gabriel waved toward the window, gesturing at the road leading downhill to the harbor and the open sea that lay beyond, away from the world she'd always known. "Well then, how do you expect to make this grand trip? You can't go to Spain by yourself dressed like a girl, even with a maid." He let out a gusty sigh and rested his hands on his hips. "I guess you'll end up staying in this tiny village for the rest of your life, an ape-leader. A spinster like Miss Galloway. Except Miss Galloway won't be picking oakum with us in the poorhouse after they turn us out when we can't pay the mortgage next month."

Harriet stiffened her spine, her chin jutting out. She spun away from the window, a sharp rebuke on her lips, when she noticed the twinkle in Gabriel's eye. How often had he goaded her into doing something outrageous with just this kind of teasing?

She wagged her finger at him, and he ducked his chin. Turning back to the window, she stared out at the harbor, absently fingering the H-shaped pendant that hung on a silver chain around her neck. She'd worn it every day since Papa had sent it home five years ago, accompanied by a cryptic note that said it was the key to her future, and a map he'd drawn that purported to lead to a treasure he'd hidden while on leave in Spain.

A key to a bank box would have been more helpful.

In the distance, the tide had turned and ships were heading out to sea, their sails filling, nimble sailors climbing aloft to unfurl the topsails. If she couldn't even bring herself to try on her brother's breeches, there was no way she could disguise herself as a cabin boy to earn passage to Spain and retrieve the treasure Papa had hidden during the war. If she couldn't get the treasure, she'd have no dowry. No dowry, no marriage, no paying the mortgage. With so many unemployed sailors and soldiers now home from the war willing to do any sort of work, she and Mama hadn't even had any luck taking in laundry to help earn money. The thought of living at the poor house made her shudder.

If Papa hadn't died, he would have retrieved the treasure himself. There'd be no need for Gabriel to leave school and begin an apprenticeship with the cobbler to keep him from seeking work on a fishing boat, no need for Mama to give pianoforte lessons despite her aching arthritic fingers, no need for Harriet to tend fishing nets with other women from the village, and they certainly wouldn't worry about even having a roof over their heads.

If Harriet had a dowry, Sir Percival Finlay wouldn't hesitate to propose. As Lady Finlay, she could provide a proper education for Gabriel so he could one day earn enough to support a wife and family, take Mama to the healing waters of the Pump Room in Bath, and make certain they all had a home.

If she had a dowry.

She had to go get the treasure.

But how?

"How are you going to get to Spain?" Gabriel flopped back onto her bed, his fingers clasped behind his head as he stared up at the water-stained ceiling. "And even if you do find the treasure, don't forget only half of it is ours. The other half belongs to Lord Sheffield."

Their father's dearest friend, who had perished in the same battle as Papa.

And what of his heir, Nicholas, the current Lord Sheffield?

Despite the close friendship of their fathers, Harriet had only met the current Lord Sheffield once, seven years ago. She'd been visiting her friend Marianne in Bath. Marianne's family had taken in their cousin Charlotte after Charlotte's mother died. As a friend of the family, Sheffield had arrived to escort Charlotte to her brother. On his ship.

Harriet stopped pacing.

Half the treasure rightly belonged to Sheffield.

And Sheffield had a ship.

He'd looked every inch the pirate, with long black hair tied back in a queue, gold hoop earring, tanned skin, and a rolling swagger from time at sea. All he'd lacked was a cutlass and eye patch. Rumors swirled about him like the capes of his greatcoat—that he'd killed dozens of men as a privateer during the war, and bedded more than a hundred women before his twenty-first birthday. Harriet doubted there was time for him to have accomplished both feats, but with his roguish smile and chilly blue eyes, there might be a drop of truth to the gossip.

Could she trust such a man? A privateer was just a pirate with a license. She'd have to trust him with her life, her safety, her half of the treasure. Such doubts had kept her from enlisting his aid before, but the mortgage due date had seemed such a long way off, and Harriet's salary as a teacher would have made it attainable. But not now.

Harriet took a shuddering breath and steeled her nerves. "You're going to escort me to London, and there I'm going to persuade Lord Sheffield to give me passage to Spain."

Chapter 2

Nicholas Langston, fifth Viscount Sheffield, gave up trying to find a comfortable position in his unpadded oak chair, rested his elbows on the desk, and contemplated the view in his father's study. Correct that: *his* study. Everything that had belonged to his father now belonged to Nick. The other nine straight-backed armless chairs, still set in a circle for a prayer meeting, and the floor-to-ceiling bookcase filled with religious tracts and improving works, all reeked of his father's sensibility.

Nick wanted to toss it all out to the street.

But as with every other time he'd arrived in London and reluctantly come to the townhouse to deal with his steward's frantic requests, it was too late in the day to make the servants implement the changes. He wanted to see the stuff carted out in person. He'd stop just short of making a bonfire of it. Let it be grabbed up by beggars.

Nick had inherited everything he was going to by the age of twenty-one, a heady experience ... until the full weight of the accompanying responsibility made itself known. The livelihood, not to mention quality of life, of so many people here in London as well as at the properties connected to Langston Hall in Dorset relied on the decisions he made, from this very desk.

His friend Alistair would likely spend most of his adult life waiting to receive the fullness of his inheritance. He was in line to be a marquess and a duke once his father and grandfather popped off. Fortunately, Alistair seemed in no hurry to move beyond being Viscount Moncreiffe, and was currently off enjoying his honeymoon.

Their friend Tony would never be elevated above Mister unless his brother, the Earl of Sinclair, died without issue. As Sinclair had entered into a scandalous love match early this summer, the chances of that happening diminished daily. Tony had married just a couple months ago and was busy setting up a business enterprise with his bride.

Which left Nick at loose ends.

The bank drafts signed and enough other matters dealt with to appease the steward for the day, Nick hurried out of the oppressive room and toward the front door.

"Shall I have your bed chamber prepared for later tonight, my lord?" The butler held the door open. Two carriages rattled past on the dark street beyond, lanterns casting fast-moving shadows.

"No, Alfred. I'll be returning to the *Wind Dancer* as usual."

"Very good, my lord."

Was that a hint of disappointment in the old retainer's voice?

No matter the fellow had served the family since Nick was in short coats and had shown a young boy many kindnesses, Nick wouldn't stay in his father's house a minute longer than necessary.

He put thoughts of his inherited properties out of mind and headed for Lord and Lady Hartwell's ball at the Argyle Rooms. To many sticklers in the *ton*, Sheffield was an upstart, as his title only went back a century and a half, but it still opened plenty of doors for him. Hartwell liked his liquor and only served the best, and Lady Hartwell was open-minded enough to invite an interesting mix of guests.

Within the hour he'd done the niceties and was enjoying a glass of champagne, determinedly ignoring the row of wallflowers and optimistic duennas. His two closest friends may have recently stepped into the parson's mousetrap, but Nick had no intention of following them. The lovely widows winking at him over the tops of their fans, however, were another story. With which one would he pass the night? Or at least a diverting hour or two.

The lovely Lady Slavin was particularly agile, he recalled, and looking fine as five-pence tonight in a deep blue dress cut so low her ample breasts seemed in imminent danger of tumbling out. She gave him a knowing smile as he slowly raised his gaze from her cleavage to her face. He stepped around this flirtatious couple and that one, making his surreptitious way around the room. With a tilt to her head, Lady Slavin headed toward a handy, dark alcove.

Smiling in anticipation, Nick sidestepped the Marquess of Penrith just before the gent upended the punch bowl over the head of his father, the Duke of Keswick. Orgeat punch drizzled through the duke's white hair and dampened his elegantly tied cravat.

Matrons nearby gasped in shock, but Keswick remained unfazed. It had likely happened several times now, since Alistair, the family peacemaker, was off on his honeymoon, no longer at hand to cool his relatives' flaring tempers.

Penrith casually handed the now-empty crystal punch bowl to an open-mouthed footman. Ignoring the pointed stares of disapproving matrons, he slung an arm around Nick's shoulders as he passed. Nick caught the eye of Lady Slavin, still many feet away. She hunched a shoulder and turned her back. Ah, well. She was not much fun if she was in one of her moods. Nick allowed Penrith to steer him toward the card room.

"So, m'boy," Penrith began, giving Nick a slight shake. "Seen your uncle lately? I can't win back my blunt if he doesn't come to the club."

Nick glanced over, unsurprised to see Penrith retained not a trace of the anger that had led to the punch bowl incident. "No, sorry, haven't seen Uncle Zach since I've been in Town this trip. Probably found himself a new mistress and doesn't want anyone to steal her away. Again."

"All's fair," Penrith said with a grin. "Yvette was truly lovely, far too good for a reprobate like Zach."

They passed a row of giggling husband-hunters, their fans and eyelashes fluttering flirtatiously. Nick quickly averted his gaze lest they mistake him as willing prey.

"You know what you need, boy?" Penrith winked at one of the chaperones, who blushed furiously. "You need to find yourself a girl." Penrith pointed Nick's chin toward a heavily rouged woman standing near a potted palm in the corner, her dampened skirts clinging to her generously curved hips and thighs. "That one looks ripe for plucking."

Nick lifted his chin free, determinedly headed for the card room and its brandy. Whisky would be good, too. "Thank you, no."

"You prefer boys? I know this private club that caters to—"

"No, that's not necessary. What I want is—"

"Time to go," Penrith abruptly said, and disappeared into the crowd so fast Nick almost thought he'd imagined their bizarre conversation.

"—a glass of brandy," he said to the now empty space at his side.

Lady Hartwell suddenly stood in his path, a young woman at her heels in the international sign that meant danger to bachelors. Ah. Wonder if Penrith was avoiding the chit, or their hostess?

No doubt Lady Hartwell's strained smile was from having to perform this introduction as part of her duties as hostess, when her own plain daughter had stirred nary a whiff of interest among eligible men during the Little Season. But Miss Hartwell had little to fear in the form of competition from the little brown wren at Lady Hartwell's heel.

"Lord Sheffield, may I introduce you to Miss Harriet Chase?"

The name sounded vaguely familiar. Nick narrowed his eyes, fairly certain he'd never bedded the plain sparrow before him.

With the social niceties performed and the string quartet beginning to saw away on another tune, both ladies looked at him expectantly.

Nick cleared his throat. "Would you honor me with this dance, Miss, ah ..."

"Chase," she said with another vapid, polite smile.

"Miss Chase." Nick held out his arm, Miss Chase took it, and Lady Hartwell sailed off in a swirl of skirts, hostess duties done.

"You don't remember me at all, do you, my lord?" Miss Chase said as soon as they'd taken their places on the dance floor.

A waltz. Nick mentally winced but kept his expression polite. Should he remember her?

"That's all right," she continued after barely a beat. "You were there to collect my friend Charlotte and take her to her brother. I doubt you had a thought to spare for two schoolgirls in the background."

"You're a friend of Charlie's?"

She nodded, and Nick relaxed a tiny bit.

His relief seemed premature as she lowered her voice and angled closer to him. "I have a proposition for you, my lord."

Nick leaned away. "I'm very flattered, miss, but I don't bed wenches fresh out of the schoolroom."

Twin spots of color bloomed high on her cheeks. "Allow me to rephrase that. I have need of your help to retrieve something that belonged to my father. And to yours."

Ah, now Nick knew why the chit's name seemed familiar. His father had served as a naval officer with a Chase. Sitting around the dinner table during the viscount's leaves at home, the tales of adventure and Royal Navy's glory at sea always included Giles Chase. The gunner's mate had saved the viscount's life early on in their service in His Majesty's navy, and they'd been inseparable chums ever after. Even died together.

"What is this something to be retrieved, and from where?"

Miss Chase smiled. "Treasure. Something our fathers won in a card game but which was too large to bring back on their ship, so they hid it in Spain and planned to go back for it after the war." The words tumbled from her lips, faster and faster. "I need your help to get to Spain—we can take your ship—find the treasure, then split it since it belonged equally to both our fathers. And since they're gone, it now belongs to us. You and me. Jointly. You'll have to front the expenses until we get the treasure, but I'll repay you half out of my share as soon as we have the treasure in hand. Do we have an accord?"

Nick stopped in mid-step and cocked his head to one side. "You talk really fast."

Harriet felt like stamping her foot. "Do we have an agreement, my lord? You help me retrieve what belongs to both of us, and I'll reimburse you for your expenses in getting the treasure."

He continued to stare at her with his head tilted to one side, as though she were an interesting bug under a magnifying glass.

"My lord?" Good heavens, had she misjudged how much he'd had to drink? He hadn't seemed foxed. Just imbibed a glass of something or other to get through the social event bachelors were supposedly loath to attend. Though the pot boy Gabriel had questioned earlier tonight had said the viscount had left for the ball in a pleasant mood, which for many men meant they had been imbibing liberally.

"Balcony," Lord Sheffield suddenly said, and took her by the hand, striding for the double doors.

Several heads swiveled to watch their progress. "My lord," Harriet hissed, unable to withdraw her hand from his large grasp. She kept her expression polite but tried to dig her nails through both their gloves and into his palm.

"Ow. What?"

Candlelight glinted off his gold hoop earring as he finally turned and looked down at her. Some of the rumors and stories she'd heard about him—dangerous stories—suddenly seemed much more plausible.

"I can't rush out onto the balcony with you," she whispered.

It took him agonizing seconds to reply. "Oh, right." He glanced to the left, then the right. "Where's a big potted palm in a dark corner when you need it?"

Harriet glanced around the ballroom, barely noticing the famed décor of the Argyle Rooms as she searched for somewhere they could talk in private.

Lord Sheffield hauled her into his arms and resumed the waltz. Under cover of the movement of the dance, he nuzzled her neck. "Tell me more about this treasure," he said, his lips brushing her ear.

Harriet barely heard him, what with the humming down her spine from his warm breath stirring the fine hairs on her nape.

Treasure. She cleared her throat. She opened her mouth to speak but became aware of the heat from his hand on her waist, his other hand engulfing hers. He'd reportedly killed at least three men with those hands. Maybe dozens.

"Miss Chase," he whispered.

She stared into his intense blue gaze, which didn't seem all that frightening just now. This must be the look he reserved for the scores of women he'd supposedly seduced.

She wasn't going to be one of them.

"My father sent home a map to the treasure. In his letter he said he'd go back after the war, along with Sheffield, to bring it home. I'm surprised you haven't gone after the treasure yourself before this." A frisson of fear raced up her spine. Perhaps he had already found the treasure, and had no intention of giving any of it up?

"But they didn't come home." His murmured reply took her by surprise.

The naval officer who'd delivered the news said there hadn't been enough remains to put in a box after the ship went down with all hands aboard, victim of an explosion in its powder room during a battle.

"Why now, Miss Chase? They've been gone for five years, and we've been at peace almost two. What makes you want to go find the treasure now?"

He could be playacting, but she doubted it. He hadn't found the treasure, she was sure. Almost.

She lifted her chin. "Frankly, I am in need of a dowry, and my family's half of the treasure will provide it."

Sheffield whirled her around another couple. "Fair enough. Give me your direction, and we'll discuss this in greater detail tomorrow. In privacy."

The waltz ended.

Harriet gulped. "I'm afraid our townhouse is still at sixes and sevens, not fit for callers yet. Perhaps we could meet at Gunter's to continue our conversation? At three?"

"Have you a sweet tooth, Miss Chase? It's getting a bit late in the year to enjoy an ice." He flashed her a charming smile that made her knees feel decidedly weak.

"Until tomorrow, my lord."

* * *

"So you're saying you don't trust me, Miss Chase." Viscount Sheffield seemed to crowd her despite being seated on the far side of their table.

Harriet resisted the urge to push her chair away from the table. No one in Gunter's seemed to notice that the viscount was so close to her, head bowed toward hers in intimate conversation. Gabriel and her maid Betsy sat at a nearby table, oblivious to her discomfort, caught up in watching the activity on the bustling street outside. "I never said I did not trust you."

"But you won't give me the map."

"It was my father's. Didn't your father send a map home to you or your mother, like mine did?"

Sheffield's expression clouded. "He did not." Sheffield drained his coffee cup before setting it down with a thud. "If you won't give me the map, how in blazes do you expect me to be able to find this treasure and bring you back your share?"

"I don't."

His brows rose. Thick black brows, as black as his long hair tied back in a queue, which perfectly set off his chilly blue eyes. Light glinted off his gold hoop earring.

Her ice eaten, Harriet clutched her empty bowl with both hands to keep from shivering. "I intend to go with you."

He didn't snort or scoff, as she'd expected. Just stared, his blue eyes boring through her as though he could see the graying, frayed chemise beneath her best blue morning frock.

"Have you ever even been aboard a ship, Miss Chase? It will take us a week or more to sail to Corunna—each way—and then the time required to find the *iglesia* referenced on the map. The *Wind Dancer* is built for speed and carrying cargoes, not passenger comfort."

"I was born aboard a ninety-eight-gun ship of the line, my lord, and spent the first four years of my life at sea. I will not be complaining about life aboard a civilian vessel while we are at peace."

"But now you are not a child in the care of your parents."

"You mean I am a young woman who must have a care for her reputation? Or are you more concerned about how having an unmarried woman aboard your ship will affect *your* reputation?" She pushed aside her bowl and folded her hands on the tabletop, the epitome of calm and propriety. "If you are worried that I am trying to spring the parson's mousetrap on you, my lord, I assure you that is the farthest thing from my mind. I already have an intended groom."

Just the tiniest of lies, since Sir Percival hadn't actually proposed. Yet. But he would. Just as soon as she had a dowry. He'd almost as much as said so.

Sheffield still didn't look convinced. She pressed on. "My brother won't be able to accompany us, but Betsy, my maid, will be aboard so we will be properly chaperoned at all times." And Gabriel would make certain Mama thought Harriet was visiting Aunt Elizabeth, and that Aunt Elizabeth thought Harriet was at home with Mama. No one would know she had been gone until after she returned. And she wouldn't have to wear breeches to carry out her plan.

Gaining her dowry, and Sir Percival, would be worth suffering through two weeks at sea in Sheffield's company. She fingered the silver pendant on the chain around her neck. The end result would be worth any temporary discomfort.

Sheffield leaned even closer, a twinkle in his eyes, his bare index finger idly stroking a design on the back of her hand. "Admit it, Miss Chase," he said, his deep voice soft and slow, as much a caress to her auditory senses as his finger on her skin. "You want to go on an adventure before you settle down as a respectable matron."

Harriet tried not to smile back at his conspiratorial tone, the laughter in his eyes, or shiver from the frisson of pleasure tingling down her spine at his touch. Here was the rogue who'd supposedly seduced dozens of women. She saw why they'd succumbed to his charm.

Forewarned was forearmed. She would not be counted among his conquests. She was saving herself for Sir Percival.

"I want to retrieve my family's share of the treasure. Nothing more, nothing less. If there were any other way to accomplish this, I would not leave my home in Brixham."

Sheffield gave a slight harrumphed and sat back.

"How soon can you have your ship and crew ready to sail, my lord?"

He shrugged. "A week, maybe less. If we don't leave soon, winter storms will make the crossing more..."

"Dangerous?"

"Interesting." He grinned, showing white teeth against tanned skin. They weren't boring, perfect teeth—a small chip on one side tooth accentuated his canine teeth, lending him a wolfish air.

Harriet suppressed a shudder. "Can you be ready in less than a week?"

"Why the hurry? If we don't go now, it will still be there come spring. If it's still there at all. It's already been five years since our fathers hid the treasure. We'll be lucky if gypsies haven't found it and made off with it."

Harriet shifted in her seat. "There's something I haven't told you yet."

Sheffield narrowed his eyes, banishing all traces of humor. "I'm listening."

She cleared her throat. "Someone broke into our home a few days ago and rifled through my father's effects, all his correspondence. Mother thought it was boys from the village hoping to read gory tales of the war. I'm convinced it was someone after the key that's mentioned in one of Father's letters. The map was gone and they stole all the keys in Papa's desk, even the key to my music box, as well as the housekeeper's spare key ring."

"We don't need a key. If it's a locked chest, a pistol can take care of the lock. But if the thief stole the map, how are we to find the treasure chest in the first place?"

Harriet tapped a finger to her temple. "I spent many hours studying it over the years since Papa sent it home. I have drawn a copy." She rested her hand on Sheffield's forearm. "My lord, we need to go get our treasure before the thief claims it and it's lost to us forever. Whatever this treasure is worth, it might be a paltry sum compared to your family's fortune, but my family has great need of it."

He glanced at her hand on his arm. She quickly withdrew it.

"Let me hazard a guess. The dowry for you, and education for your brother."

Harriet blinked.

Sheffield abruptly straightened. "Give me your direction, and I'll have one of my men come in two days to collect you, your maid, and your baggage."

Harriet shook her head. "There's no need to trouble yourself or your men. Give me direction to your ship's berth, and Gabriel will escort me."

Sheffield tilted his head to one side. Could he see how worn her dress had become, how she'd had to mend her gloves? "Need to leave your lodgings and come take your berth on the *Wind Dancer* right away while we're provisioning?"

Harriet almost sighed in gratitude. He didn't need to know she'd been unable to sleep in their hotel room—the only room they'd been able to afford and still have money for food—because of the mice that scurried across the floor as soon as the candles were doused. Never mind the little creatures sharing the mattress with her and Betsy. A canvas hammock on the ship now seemed like a heavenly place to sleep.

"Yes, thank you. That would be most agreeable." She called Gabriel over, and within minutes they had directions to what would be her new home for the next fortnight.

Other than her room at the Academy, she hadn't had a new home since she was four years old.

And this home could sink.

The dowry, she reminded herself. A roof over their heads. Just keep thinking of the reward that awaited her and her family for taking these risks.

Chapter 3

"I don't know about this, miss," Betsy said as two sailors set down their trunk and portmanteaus in a cabin aboard the *Wind Dancer* the following morning. The men slid the door shut as they left, and Betsy grabbed for the wall as the ship subtly rolled to starboard.

"Nonsense," Harriet said with forced brightness, widening her stance and bending one knee to remain upright. She hung her cape on a hook and refused to grab on to it for support. "This will give us time to adjust to the ship before we set sail. Find our way around, know where everything is." Learn how to not fall on our arse, she silently added, as she shifted her weight again to keep her balance.

Flashes of memory from her childhood came to her, of running and playing on a ship's rolling deck with ease, but once ashore continually falling down as though it was the land that pitched and rolled, not the sea.

Betsy looked a tad green about the gills, though Harriet was sure it was just the lighting. Her own stomach's current distress was merely a disagreement with the lumpy, stale porridge they'd had for breakfast at the hotel. It would soon pass. She resumed her inspection of their new quarters.

Given the flat back wall, they must be at the stern of the ship. How lucky for her that the brig had such a nice passenger cabin, since Sheffield had said he normally carried cargo rather than passengers. She'd expected to be bunking in the hold instead of a cabin above the water line. Daylight filtered through the two small windows above the single bunk against the far wall.

To get to the bunk, one had to step around a table with four chairs. Off to the left was a wardrobe, a companion piece to the slant top desk on the opposite wall. Beneath the scratches and worn spots from decades in service, Harriet recognized the well-made lines of Chippendale. Last year, Madame Zavrina had been thrilled to find a Chippendale secretary at a used furniture merchant, at a price that would have paid Harriet's salary for months. She gave it pride of place in the parlour to impress visitors.

Wait. A desk, in a passenger cabin?

With growing unease, Harriet peeked in the wardrobe, and found it filled with shirts, folded trousers, and other masculine garments. Ignoring Betsy's complaints about the ship's constant motion, Harriet stepped over to the desk and opened the slant top.

Quill and ink, compass, sextant, and a leather-bound book. The ship's log.

Oh, good heavens, they were in the captain's quarters!

"Come along, Betsy," Harriet said, sliding the door open and trying to calm her pounding heart. "We won't be staying here."

"Thank the good Lord above," Betsy muttered, and fell into step behind Harriet.

They pressed back against the wall to make room for crewmen carrying crates of foodstuffs to the galley, and climbed to the top deck in search of Sheffield.

He and his first mate were on the quarterdeck, directing men who were hauling on ropes, which controlled a cargo net filled with barrels, crates, and bundles of hay swinging overhead toward the open hold.

"Lord Sheffield, there's been some mistake," Harriet began. She started her next sentence but gave up when the crew's singing, a chant really, drowned out her words.

"*Heave away, haul away,*" they sang as they worked in unison, and the full net quickly descended into the hold, disappearing from sight.

Sheffield turned to her. "You were trying to say something, Miss Chase?" The early morning sun was at his back, glinting off his gold earring, shrouding his face in shadow so all she could see clearly was his large form, draped in a caped greatcoat against the October chill.

Ah, yes, she had come up here for something. What was it again? "Your men put my things in your cabin by mistake."

"No mistake. It's either there or put you in the hold with the goats." They both turned as three men walked up the gangboard, each carrying a dwarf goat. Very unhappy goats, judging by their loud bleating, especially considering the animals' diminutive size.

"But if I'm in your quarters, where will you sleep?" Oh good heavens, he didn't mean to share, did he? There was only one bunk, and it was already going to be a snug fit sharing it with Betsy. "With the goats?"

The first mate laughed. Sheffield stared at him, and the mate quickly turned the laugh into a cough up his sleeve.

"No, Miss Chase. I will hang a hammock with the crew."

A shout came from the hold, and the empty net swung up and out, back over toward the dock, where men waited by stacks of crates and barrels to load the net again.

"In that case, I'll leave you to your work." She gave a slight curtsy and headed for the aft hatchway, out of the crew's way.

Sheffield gave a slight bow, one corner of his mouth curved up.

The loading went on for hours. When darkness fell, lanterns were lit abovedeck and on the dock, the flickering lights making shadows dance on the cabin walls. Betsy and Harriet settled in as much as they could, hanging garments on hooks to get the wrinkles out, and set about cleaning and scrubbing the cabin, which was not nearly as dirty as she'd expected.

Eventually the scent of food wafting from the galley drew them out of the cabin. The ship's cook had completed stowing foodstuffs and now had a kettle bubbling on the brazier. As they entered the fo'c'sle she caught a glimpse of broad shoulders and greatcoat turning the corner, heading topside with a steaming mug.

"Smells delicious." Harriet smiled at the cook, a swarthy Italian. "What is it?"

"Is best not to ask, *signorina*," he said with a suggestive lift of his thick eyebrows, ladling a bowlful and handing it to her, then another for Betsy.

"Especially best not to ask when we've been out to sea for a bit, miss." The newcomer, whom Harriet recognized as the first mate, dipped a ladle to fill his pewter mug with soup, then sat at the drop leaf table to drink it. "Luigi here can get a bit creative, if'n you know what I mean." He took a swig of soup and winked at Betsy, who tittered.

Harriet briefly debated the proper thing to do, which would be to carry their meal back to their cabin. It's what Sir Percival would expect.

Actually, Sir Percival would have expected her to wait in the cabin until Betsy brought her a tray.

Harriet turned partway back toward the passageway. Betsy, however, had already seated herself across from the sailor, her soup untouched, and begun questioning him about the tattoo visible on his forearm. Shockingly, not only had he removed his coat, he'd rolled up his shirtsleeves as well.

Equally intrigued by the design and the explanation—involving savage natives, sharp sticks, and octopus ink—after a slight pause Harriet sat beside Betsy and dug into her meal.

"I'm Thaddeus, by the way," the first mate later said, refilling his mug. "But everyone just calls me Jonesy."

"Pleased to make your acquaintance, Mr. Jones." Should she stand up and curtsy or hold out her hand under the unusual circumstances? Madame Zavrina had never included in her instructions the proper way to greet common sailors. Jonesy tugged on his forelock, raised his mug toward Betsy in salute, and silently headed topside.

The loading continued long past dusk, the men working with a seemingly endless stream of chants and songs punctuated with shouts and swearing. Betsy mended hems while Harriet pretended to sew, darning the same stocking for hours, listening to the work going on, until it grew too dark to sew even with a lamp hung above the table, and they turned in for the night.

* * *

Something had changed. Harriet opened her eyes and looked about the cabin. Gone were the flickering shadows cast by the lanterns on the dock, filtering through the tiny windows above the bunk. Complete darkness engulfed the cabin. Silence reigned, broken only by the gentle creak of wood and ropes.

Harriet sat up, and then grabbed the edge of the bunk as the ship rolled, more than when they'd first boarded.

They were underway!

Her heart pounded. They were on their way! After so many months of worry and yearning, so many sleepless nights, she was actually, finally, really on her way to collect the treasure, get her dowry, and get on with the rest of her life. Sheffield must have kept his crew working around the clock in order to leave with this turn of the tide. How fortuitous that he fell in with her plans so readily.

She lay back, ignoring the snores of Betsy beside her, and pictured what form the treasure would have. Gold, silver, and precious gems? No, Papa would have carried home small things like that. Priceless paintings or other large works of art? She drifted to sleep with a smile on her face, lulled by the gentle rocking of the ship as they sailed down the Thames, toward the English Channel, Spain, and her future.

* * *

Nick stood on the quarterdeck beside the tiller, keeping a gentle grip on the weathered wood as they sailed toward the mouth of the Thames. Following the signal from the bow lookout, he steered slightly to starboard to avoid ramming a couple of skiffs whose occupants were too busy rowing upriver to notice the ship bearing down on them, then back to port to stay in the main channel. It felt good to be on the water again, on the deck with a slight roll under his feet. Even if they were still in the tame waters of the Thames, they were headed to sea. To adventure. To *something*. If the breeze stayed fresh they'd be in the Channel by morning, and Spain was less than a week away after that.

Before Miss Chase had entered his life with her quest, since the war had ended and the Crown no longer needed his services, things had become so boring he'd considered drastic measures like transporting goods for money. The *Wind Dancer* had started her life, after all, as a smuggling vessel. Grandfather had loaded her with silks, brandy, tea, and who-knows-what other contraband, to restore the family coffers and stock the cellar.

Nick had refused to join the Navy, refused the midshipman's position his father, Adam, had arranged and tried to force him to accept. Using *Wind Dancer* to capture enemy vessels and pilfer their cargoes as a privateer during the war had seemed a more fitting way for Nick to carry on the family legacy interrupted by his self-righteous father.

Within the fortnight Nick would have the treasure Adam had taken such pains to hide from him, to deprive him of. It wasn't enough the pious hypocrite had donated most of the estate's cash to a slew of charities and the church, leaving little for Nick to inherit. What else had Adam kept secret from him, tried to deny him? Well, Nick would show him. He'd find that treasure with Miss Chase and thoroughly enjoy spending every single penny Adam hadn't wanted him to have.

"Anything amiss, Cap'n?"

"What? No, everything's fine." Nick loosened his white-knuckled grip on the tiller and patted his second mate on the shoulder. "The stars are out, the moon is bright, we've a fair wind, and we're off on a quest for a damsel in distress. What could be better, eh?"

The crew knew only that they were transporting Miss Chase on her search for something bequeathed by her dead father. No whisper of the T word.

Instead of pious charities, Nick knew several whores who'd appreciate a donation from his share of whatever treasure they found.

That should make his father roll over in his grave.

"Care to share the joke, Cap'n?"

"Not yet, Bos'n. Not yet."

Chapter 4

Pleased with the excellent time they'd made coming down the Thames, Nick stopped at the mouth of the river in Gravesend long enough for the bumboats to come alongside and let his crew make last purchases of fresh fruit and other luxuries before heading out to the Channel. They also brought aboard the ship's surgeon, who'd been visiting his family.

Now a day out to sea, with England no longer visible, their progress slowed as the wind seemed to take back what it had so freely given on the congested river. Nick took a deep breath of the freshening breeze. Rain was coming. On the open sea, with nothing to slow down the billowing storm clouds blowing their way, they would soon be diving bows under, his crew getting soaked.

How would a novice sailor like Miss Chase and her maid handle rough seas? Nick had already done the hauling-them-back-from-the-rail bit when a previous passenger, carrying valuable intelligence on French battle plans, had become seasick two days shy of Dover. It took the crew a week to rid the fo'c'sle of the stench, not to mention Nick's sore arms from keeping the spy from falling overboard.

Miss Chase was petite, but her maid was as big as an outhouse. Time to check on them. Besides, he hadn't seen either of them since before they'd cast off in London. Luigi reported Miss Chase had fetched their food, citing the maid's seasickness. The little brown wren had passed him his logbook and other supplies around the edge of the door as if afraid of passing contagion to him. Or catching it from him.

His cabin probably stank to high heaven by now.

He signaled to Bos'n that he was going below, and went to check on the damage.

"We're fine," came Miss Chase's reply through the door. "No need to trouble yourself on our account, Captain."

"It's no trouble at all." Nick forced a smile into his voice. Just what were they doing in there they didn't want him to know about?

"Really, there's no need to bother about us."

The chipper tone in her voice sounded just as false and forced as his own, setting off alarm bells. "Really, Miss Chase, I insist. I hope you're decent." Without giving her any more warning, he pushed the lever to open the door.

Locked.

What in blazes were the chits doing, locking him out of his own cabin?

Of course. Protecting themselves against his ravaging crew. He should have thought of that himself, not that he had any worries about the crew on behalf of Miss Chase. His men knew better than to crap in their own nest.

He heard scurrying sounds from within the cabin as he fished the small ring of keys from his waistcoat pocket and opened the door.

Miss Chase stood at the head of the bunk, her cheeks flushed, bosom heaving against her décolletage. He admired the view a moment before realizing her hands were tucked behind her back.

His alarm bells were still ringing. "Are you feeling well, Miss Chase? Most people become acclimated after three days or so at sea."

"I am fine, thank you, as I said. It is poor Betsy here who is having a tough time." She gestured at the maid curled up on the bunk, then quickly put her hand behind her back again. The maid was completely covered by the red and black plaid wool blanket, with not even the top of her head visible.

Aw, crap. All he needed was the maid casting up her accounts on his blanket and mattress. He patted the lump near what might be her shoulder. "You'll feel better if you get some fresh air. Up you go." He reached for the corner of the blanket, only to be blocked by Miss Chase.

"Really, Captain, Betsy is too ill to walk. We'll just stay here."

Nick narrowed his eyes. "I'll carry her," he ground out, and flung the blanket back.

Instead of the sickly maid, there were just more blankets, molded into a vaguely human shape.

Miss Chase nibbled on her bottom lip.

"Where is your maid, Miss Chase?" Nick felt the pulse beat at his temple. There could still be a simple explanation. The maid being off diddling with one of his crew wasn't the most disruptive thing a passenger had ever done but an annoyance nonetheless.

No answer was forthcoming.

"Miss Chase, where is your maid?"

Miss Chase shuffled her feet and glanced around the cabin, then looked at him and opened her mouth.

He held up his hand, stopping her before she could speak the lie. "The truth, Miss Chase."

She took one deep breath, which did interesting things to her décolletage, then another. Nick forced his gaze upward to her eyes.

"She went ashore with one of the bumboats at Gravesend."

"And forgot to come back?"

Miss Chase pursed her lips. "She went to stay with her sister until I return. She was sick all the way down the river. It would only have become worse when we sailed out on the open water. I didn't want her to suffer the entire voyage." She tapped her finger to her bottom lip. "I wish I'd remembered that *mal de mer* usually gets better after the third day. She might have been able to manage after all."

An unwed young woman, of respectable lineage, alone on his ship? In his cabin? Nick headed for the door.

"Where are you going?"

"To turn the ship around and dump your unwed arse off with the nearest chaperone."

"No! You can't do that!" There was an edge to her voice as she stepped forward, her progress impeded by bumping into the table.

"It's my ship. I can do anything I damn well please with it."

"You can't take me back! What about the treasure? I'm the only one with the map." She flattened her palms on the table, leaning toward him. "You can't find the treasure without the map."

"No treasure is worth the parson's mousetrap." Nick had his hand on the door handle. "I'm disappointed, Miss Chase. I didn't take you for a liar."

"I am not a liar. I told you I have plans to wed another. I have no interest in you, other than as a means to retrieve the treasure to which we are both entitled."

Nick tilted his head back and looked at her through narrowed eyes. "Not trying to trap me into wedlock?"

"My, aren't we puffed up with our own consequence." Miss Chase sat on the edge of the bunk, her hands primly folded on her lap. "I concede that your title, lineage and form may appeal to some women, but I have other plans. I am only interested in my share of the treasure. Since other parties are also interested in retrieving the treasure, we must make haste. I'll make do without a maid. There is no time to turn back and get another."

Now that she'd pointed it out, Nick noticed how wrinkled her gown was, as though she'd been sleeping in it. Silly nonsense, this fashion of women wearing clothes they couldn't get into and out of on their own. Although there had been many occasions when Nick had happily helped a woman out of her clothes.

Miss Chase coughed.

Nick looked up from her bosom, startled to realize he'd been imagining what Miss Chase looked like out of her dress. Did she know that's what he'd been thinking?

Never mind. The chit said she had another man in mind for her matrimonial plans. Or at least that's what she claimed now, when no one knew where she was or in whose company, and that she was alone. With him.

Or did they?

"Let me make this painfully clear, Miss Chase." He drew himself up to his full height, folding his arms over his chest. Green sailors had been known to wet their drawers when faced with The Sheffield Stare. "I take no responsibility for your reputation. It is entirely in your hands. Should a scandal arise from you traveling alone, I will not be doing the gentlemanly thing. We will not be marrying. Am I clear?"

Her cheeks flushed bright red, but otherwise she seemed unfazed.

Damn. He was going to end up taking the chit all the way to Spain. Unaccompanied.

Harriet fought to keep her body perfectly still, to not betray her pounding heart, or blink before Sheffield's stare. He expected her to be a milk-and-water miss, afraid of her own shadow, at least where her reputation was concerned.

Normally, she would be.

But her future was at stake here. To turn back now meant a life of certain drudgery, for Sir Percival would never marry her without a dowry. And she had Gabriel and Mama to worry about.

If word got out and there was scandal, would Sir Percival accept her then, even with a dowry?

Probably not.

But if she had the treasure and marriage was no longer an option, she would be fine. Just move to another village where no one knew of her scandal and set up housekeeping with Mama. She'd be a spinster but one with a roof over her head.

If they didn't find the treasure and there was a scandal... It did not bear thinking on.

Sheffield could turn the ship around now, and she could still return to her quiet little life of desperation, unscathed.

Should they turn back? Was the risk of going forward worth the potential reward? She considered the worst that could happen, and the best.

"I understand, Captain. I take full responsibility for my reputation. How soon do you think we'll reach Spain?"

The slight lift of Sheffield's eyebrow was the only reaction to her declaration. She couldn't even tell if it was surprise or loss of respect, or some other emotion entirely.

"Depends on the storm that's about to blow through." He headed for the door. Harriet shook out her skirts and followed close on his heels.

He stopped so abruptly she collided with his back. His very broad, very tall back; she couldn't even see over his shoulder. She grabbed his elbow to keep from toppling over.

"Where are you going?"

"To get some fresh air, of course. I've been cooped up in here for three days."

He grunted. "Watch your step. Don't want to fish you out of the water."

She nodded. "Why did you stop?"

He smiled, with a crinkling of his deep blue eyes and a lift to his eyebrow. "Because." He patted her hand, which, to her dismay, was still gripping his forearm.

She let go as though his sleeve was afire. As a grin spread across his handsome, chiseled features, and he stared at her with a gleam in his eyes, she heard alarm bells in her head. They sounded suspiciously like the bells that had called her students to class at Torquay Academy for Ladies.

She gathered her wits and squeezed past him. She could feel his stare between her shoulder blades, but the prospect of fresh air for the first time in three days helped keep her steps sure and steady.

Until she reached the top step and felt the wind. A sudden gust whipped at her hair, stinging her cheeks, buffeting her skirt until she could barely move her legs. She grabbed the hatch cover to keep from toppling backward. The wind on the Thames had never been this strong.

Just as suddenly as it appeared, the wind abated and Harriet stepped to the side, allowing Sheffield to emerge from the hatch. He'd left his hat below, and the breeze ruffled his hair, swinging the long queue across his back. The air crackled with tension.

No, wait, that was the sails, filling and emptying as the breeze abruptly shifted. Harriet shook her head and hurried to the rail, holding on firmly. With her face turned into the wind, she watched the bow slice through the white-capped waves, taking her closer and closer to Spain. To her goal.

Soon she realized the wind was from just off the bow, not the stern. Rather than the wind hurrying them along, it was slowing their progress. At this rate it would take weeks to get through the Channel and across the Bay of Biscay. Harriet made her way aft to the tiller where Sheffield now stood, his hand possessively gripping the weathered oak beam.

"How long do you think it will take us to get to Spain with this wind?"

Sheffield stuck his index finger in his mouth, then held it up as if just noticing the breeze. Harriet propped her hands on her hips and tapped one foot. He grinned. "With this storm, we're lucky we're not moving backwards. We'd make excellent time if you wanted me to steer for Dover."

"Don't be ridiculous." Her future depended on reaching Spain before the thief did. "I'm sure you'll do your best to get us to our destination in a timely manner."

"Yes, Miss Chase."

Harriet chose to ignore his sardonic tone and turned back to the bow, looking for a spot out of the crew's way where she could hold on securely yet still have a good view to observe the workings of the ship. A coil of rope near the base of the foremast made a passable cushion. She folded her legs tailor-style and tucked her skirts out of the way.

Crewmen came close to her position and swung over the railing to climb the ratlines. She hadn't even heard the command to take in sail. Sheffield was only thirty feet aft, but the wind ripped his words away. She tilted her head back, way back, to watch the sailors nimbly climb up high above the deck then work their way across the footropes, moving as confidently as she would step between rows of vegetables in her garden.

They stood barefoot, two men on either side of the mast, balanced on a narrow rope twenty or more feet above a deck that now lurched almost as much as Harriet's stomach did at the sight, as they furled the sail and tied it up. The evidence before her eyes proved it was a task that became easier with practice, but how in the world did they bring themselves to climb to such incredible heights the first time? Or the second? Harriet shook her head in disbelief.

Too soon, her eyes burned from the wind and her fingers and toes felt like icicles. Much as she needed to get out of the weather, she loathed spending more hours alone in the cabin. She'd already explored and cleaned every inch of the tiny space several times and mended every article of her clothing until some items were more thread than cloth. She had never thought she'd miss Betsy's chatter.

Jonesy, the first mate, rang the bells indicating the start of first dog watch. The men just completing their watch made their way below, where Harriet knew Luigi had their evening meal prepared.

So early in the voyage, they'd still have fresh food, not the salt beef and hardtack they could expect later. After their meal, they'd probably play music and tell ribald tales in the two hours before going back on duty, as she'd heard them do yesterday. The men on both watches followed the same pattern. The rough voices, mixed languages, and broken grammar of the tars was a stark contrast to the silly twitterings and giggling of the girls at the Academy that she'd been surrounded by for four years.

Dare she join them? Sir Percival, and especially Madame Zavrina, would expect her to retreat to the privacy of the cabin and not consort with common sailors.

Sharing a meal aboard ship wasn't consorting, was it?

"Good evening, *signorina*," Luigi hailed as soon as she ducked into the fo'c'sle mess.

"Good evening," she replied, glancing at the men already seated on benches around the drop-down table. As soon as they finished, the benches and table would be folded back up against the bulkhead, out of the way, until the next watch came below. She sniffed but smelled only hemp rope and damp wood and hardworking men, all overlaid with a tinge of salty sea spray. Not a hint of cooking food. They were eating something, though.

Jonesy stood up from the table as she entered. The three other sailors nodded and tugged at their forelocks but didn't rise. In answer to her unspoken questions, Jonesy held up a plate with tiny brown lumps in some kind of sauce, and two lighter colored lumps. "When it blows like this we get beans and ship's biscuits." Ah, that's what ship's biscuits looked like. Even she could bake biscuits that looked more appetizing.

"No, no, *signorina*," Luigi called, hurrying over. "You no eat cold beans like a tar. The Old Man, he has warm stew."

"And hot coffee," Jonesy added. "He'll probably share if you get there quick."

Old man? "You mean Tucker?" Why would the old sail maker get preferential treatment?

"Nay, missy, the captain. He's in his quarters."

Harriet nodded her thanks and hurried to the captain's cabin, blowing on her icy fingers to warm them.

She paused at the closed door. Should she knock first? She'd been staying in there for the last three days. In some respects she was entering her own quarters.

"Enter," was the reply to her knock.

Sheffield stood as she closed the door against the draft billowing down the passageway. The table was set for two, her bowl of stew cooling, his bowl half empty already. "Was wondering how long it would take you to find the food." Grinning, he sat down without waiting for her and resumed eating.

She gravitated to the small brazier and held her hands out to its warmth, ignoring the slight spatter of rain coming in the open window. "I thought I should eat in the fo'c'sle."

Sheffield shook his head. "With any luck, we'll reach Spain long before you have to eat cold beans and hardtack." He took another bite. "What?"

"I was just wondering why they called you an old man. I know for a fact you're not a day over twenty-seven."

"Twenty-six, but every captain is referred to as the Old Man." He shrugged one shoulder and gave a wry smile. "Or worse." He pushed the silver coffee pot her way when she sat down. "This is the best it's going to be today so drink up."

Harriet poured and took a sip. And spat it back out. Sheffield thumped her on the back while she coughed. "This vile, bitter stuff is the best?"

"At this point, yes. It will get even more bitter the longer it stays on the coals."

Harriet quickly took a bite of stew to cleanse her palate. Not as good as what they'd had at the beginning of the trip, though still edible. Undoubtedly better than cold beans.

Sheffield stood, taking his empty bowl with him. "Drop your things off with Luigi when you're done. See you in a few hours." With that, he was gone.

Harriet ate her stew before it got any colder and tried not to sulk. Of course Sheffield couldn't stay at table with her like a gentleman. They were not at a country house party, though she did feel like an unwelcome guest. He was going back on deck in that storm, getting soaked and chilled while she stayed dry and relatively warm. Alone.

He'd probably want to come warm himself by the brazier before turning in, wherever it was that he'd been sleeping, so that was something to look forward to.

How pathetic. She missed Betsy, if only to have someone with whom to chat. In whose presence she felt comfortable. Betsy never seemed to take up all the space and air in the cabin, as Sheffield did.

Just then Harriet noticed the coiled rope and canvas hanging on a hook by the door. That hadn't been there before, she was sure. They must be storing it there to keep it dry during the storm.

The bells rang for the second dog watch. After finishing her rapidly-cooling meal, Harriet made her way forward to the galley and dutifully gave her dishes to Luigi. What did he do, dunk them in a net overboard to clean them?

Ignoring the outraged voice of Madame Zavrina in her head, Harriet perched on a barrel rather than retreating to the cabin and listened to the sailors tell tales after their meal. Drawn from their varied backgrounds in the navy, piracy, and fishing, the stories were much tamer than she expected. The most ribald involved a drunken bos'n who fell overboard and was rescued in a fishing net.

At last Harriet no longer felt chilled, as the body heat from five sailors in close quarters warmed the space. They were snug and dry here, though the ship moved more violently beneath her feet. Must be particularly nasty on deck, with no protection from the weather.

The watch changed again, and the men who came below were soaked and shivering, their lips blue. A couple spared her a glance, but they all began changing out of their sodden garments and hanging up hammocks, heedless of a female presence. Harriet beat a hasty retreat to the cabin and prepared to spend the fourth night in a row trapped within her sturdy and now sadly wrinkled brown woolen gown. She was sure Sheffield would happily unbutton her gown, but she wasn't sure he'd stop there ... or if she'd want him to.

***

Harriet sat up, immediately wide awake. The cabin was still pitch dark, and the ship still lunged up and down with every swell as rain pounded the deck and waves battered the hull. But something was different.

Snoring.

Someone was snoring. Inside the cabin.

Harriet swung her legs over the side of the bunk and clutched the blanket to her chest. Had one of the sailors come inside the cabin to escape the storm?

There, by the door, suspended a few feet above the floor. A shape that hadn't been there before.

Still clutching the blanket to her chest, Harriet crept forward, around the table. And tripped on her blanket. As the ship lurched toward the bottom of a swell, Harriet pitched forward, straight into the mysterious shape.

A warm body.

Sheffield's warm male body.

"Ho there, you scurvy d—" He bolted upright, wrapping his arms around Harriet. "Well, hullo."

Harriet tried to pull back and straighten up but Sheffield's hold didn't loosen. Perhaps he was concerned she'd fall down, given the precipitous angle at which she leaned against his chest. "What are you doing in my cabin?"

"My cabin, Miss Chase." Did his fingers just stroke her nape? His middle-of-the-night voice was an intimate, deep rumble.

"Yes, but..." The rough material beneath her fingers, beyond his shirt, must be a rope. The coil of rope and canvas she'd seen hanging by the door was his hammock. That meant... "You planned this? To sleep with me?"

"Sleep, yes, and I was doing it quite well until you started fondling me." She felt his chest expand as he took a breath, and heard a smile in his voice. "Feel anything you like?"

She jerked backward and he loosened his hold just as the ship lurched again, and she fell to her knees. It took a moment before she was sure which way was up.

The hammock creaked as he must have leaned over the edge. "You all right down there?"

"Yes, I'm— Ow." Trying to rise, she'd bumped her head against him as the hammock swayed. Just which part of his body she'd bumped, she didn't want to know. At least in the total darkness he couldn't see her blush. His hand landed on her head, patted her, then skimmed down her shoulder and upper arm. Before she could sputter a protest at being manhandled so, he leveraged under her elbow until she stood upright again.

She followed the edge of the rope to where it looped over the hook in the bulkhead. She should be safe here. "I am fine now." She cleared her throat. "Thank you for your, ah, assistance."

"Happy to offer you, ah, assistance any time, Miss Chase." The rope creaked, the hammock swayed. Sheffield sighed.

The blasted man was at his ease, in her quarters, apparently going back to sleep. Just like that. "You can't stay here," she blurted.

"My ship. I can sleep wherever I bloody well want. And since you're here alone, with no chaperone on a ship full of men, I want to sleep here." She heard the ropes creak and his voice moved as he must have risen up on one elbow. "Do you need help getting back into bed?"

Images leaped to mind which she ruthlessly tamped down "I— No. No, I do not need your assistance getting into bed." She cast about for an alternative, but there was nothing for it except to go back to the bunk, cover herself head to toe with the blanket, and wait for the interminable night to be over.

Clearly there would be no more sleep for her that night. Not with Sheffield at his ease just steps away. Breathing. Taking up all the space.

* * *

Nick opened his eyes as the dim grey dawn peeked through the window above the bunk. His hammock swayed violently with the force of the storm battering the *Wind Dancer*. He'd come below at midnight with the larboard watch to get dry and catch a few winks but now he needed to get back on deck. Make sure everyone had a safety rope, check on the masts and sail configuration, and a dozen other details that Jonesy and Bos'n were perfectly capable of handling but which Nick still felt compelled to check for himself.

He swung his legs over the side and stood, holding on to the rope for a moment while he got his bearings, and glanced at Miss Chase. She had curled onto her side in the bunk, one bare foot and calf hanging over the edge—a precarious perch with the swells they were cutting through. If he rolled her to her back and covered her up, would she appreciate his thoughtfulness? She'd probably lambaste him again.

She already had a poor opinion of him. Yesterday he could have told her he intended to sleep in the cabin, but he had thought he'd be in and out without her even knowing. He'd never expected to be awakened by a sudden lapful of warm female in the darkness. He hadn't intended for his hands to wander as he helped her up. It seemed they had a mind of their own when encountering a female form.

He should leave her be. Let her learn the hard way how to sleep—or not sleep—on a rolling ship. Minor bruises now might save her serious injury later.

He coiled his hammock, put on his greatcoat, braced himself for the elements, and went up into the storm.

* * *

Harriet woke up as her hip and elbow and other body parts abruptly connected with the deck, after being dumped out of the bunk by the ship's motion. The deck tilted at such a steep angle, surely they were in danger of flipping aft over fore and sliding under the surface straight to the bottom of the sea. Weak daylight filtered through the window above the bunk. How had so much time passed? It was only a moment ago she had closed her eyes. Suddenly the ship began climbing the swell, and Harriet had to grab onto the bunk to avoid slamming into the bulkhead.

Much more of this, and she was going to lose the meager contents of her stomach. Going up on deck was out of the question, but perhaps if she went close to the hatch and breathed some fresh air, it would restore her equilibrium.

She quickly pinned her uncombed hair up into a bun to keep it out of her eyes, then stumbled to the gangway, holding onto the table, a chair, the door jamb, anything to keep her balance as the ship crazily pitched and rolled.

Men shouted above deck, their words torn away by the wind, an occasional body visible as he hurried past the opening, leaning into the wind, attending to something urgent. Rain pelted down the opening along with blessed fresh air. Ignoring years of training from Madame Zavrina about the proper way for a lady to stand, Harriet spread her feet apart, braced for each change in pitch, and gripped the handrail of the steep staircase with both hands so the rain would not loosen her grip. Ah, much better.

More shouts, an ominous rumble, and something rolled past the open hatch above.

A cannon.

One of the cannons was loose on deck.

Rolling back and forth, it could tear a hole through the side. Would that let enough water onboard to sink them? Harriet had learned to swim in the calm bay at home but doubted she, or any of them on board, could survive long in the roiling sea.

The ship climbed another swell as it rolled to port, and the cannon rolled back—and stuck, one wheel splintering the top step. Something metallic broke off the carriage and bounced off her shoulder as it fell. It clattered to the deck at her feet and rolled into the shadows.

Harriet looked up again. If the cannon fell, it could punch a hole right through the bottom of the ship.

Without another thought, she raced up the steep staircase, half-expecting to be crushed any second.

The face of one of the sailors was visible in the opening—Jack, she thought his name was—as he frantically grabbed for the cannon. At such an awkward angle, his hands, slick from the rain, could get no purchase.

Harriet reached up, pressing up on the cold iron. Chilly rain beat down on her head, streamed in her eyes, and ran up the sleeves of her woolen gown, soaking her chemise. She pushed and stepped one step higher on the ladder. The wheel dug into her shoulder, threatening to crack her bones.

"Push harder, Miss!" Jack shouted. "Give it a shove!"

"What do you bloody well think I'm doing," Harriet muttered, and pushed with all her might. Just as she despaired of budging the cannon, the ship crested another swell. The canon shifted a fraction, and she and Jack were able to nudge it back from the brink. She scampered up the remaining steps and helped Jack roll the cannon and shove it up against the starboard gunwale where it belonged. On rings nearby were the broken rope, frayed ends flapping in the storm. Jack threaded one broken rope through a ring on the carriage, but it was too short to tie off.

"Hold it here, Miss," he shouted above the gale. After she nodded, Jack went to retrieve a longer rope to secure the cannon in place, bent almost double against the wind.

The ship rolled to starboard, the deck nearly standing on its side. The mouth of the cannon was engulfed in water, the top of the gunwale terrifyingly close to the tops of the waves. Jack grabbed the quarterdeck railing as a wave threatened to wash him overboard. Harriet's wool dress was soaked, she was chilled to the bone, and salty ocean spray stung her eyes. Despite her hands going numb, she kept her grip on the cannon's rope, keeping it taut.

The ship rolled back, the deck leveling out. She turned her head out of the wind to take a deep breath without the rain slapping her face. Sheffield and another crewman each had both hands on the tiller, rain streaming down their faces, struggling to steer the ship. Jonesy used hand signals to the crew rather than trying to shout over the gale, a line tied about his waist securing him to the quarterdeck railing.

The deck continued to roll to port. Harriet's stomach plummeted. Jack shouted something, his words indecipherable over the rumbling roar of the storm. No, the rumbling was the wheels of the cannon carriage. The rope ripped out of her hand as the carriage rolled across the deck and kept going, directly toward the port gunwale, picking up speed.

Just as she was certain it was going to bust through and push the port cannon overboard, the ship began to roll back to starboard. So did the cannon.

Jack had managed to tie one end of a rope to the mainmast and now lunged toward the cannon, frantically trying to thread the new rope through a bolt on the moving carriage. As Harriet stepped back to get out of his way, her feet slid out from under her on the slick deck. She landed on her rump hard enough to rattle her teeth.

Jack couldn't thread the rope through the bolt, and the cannon was picking up speed as it rolled toward the side of the ship. Harriet felt herself moving with it.

Her skirt was caught on the rear wheel. Her sturdy wool gown, the best she owned, was tangled on the rear axle of the cannon carriage that was about to crash through the side of the ship and sink to the bottom of the English Channel.

Perhaps the ship would roll the other way first. Like it had just moments ago.

Frantically she yanked on her gown, trying to untangle the dense wet fabric from the axle. It wouldn't rip and it wouldn't come loose. Damn those double-stitched seams. Why had she insisted on making the dress so sturdy? Any London lady's gown would have torn at the slightest tug. She scrabbled for anything to dig her fingers into to stop her slide or divert the cannon's direction. The rain-slicked wood offered no purchase, and the cannon aimed unerringly for the gunwale.

For a heart-stopping moment she paused in her slide, her arm nearly ripped from its socket as Jack grabbed on to her wrist, the muscles in his neck bulging with the strain.

But the weight of the cannon and the sturdiness of the wool skirt won out. He lost his grip on her and fell back on the deck, his face a mask of horror that must match her own as the cannon smashed into the gunwale and rolled overboard.

As Harriet slid through the gaping hole, she grabbed the rope that had once lashed the cannon in place. The cannon fell off its carriage as it tipped over the edge and plunged into the sea, but the carriage itself was still caught on her skirt.

She plunged into the cold sea, her hands burning as she refused to let go of the rope, and the carriage dragged her down, down, down.

Chapter 5

They'd passed the worst of the storm. The rain still whipped at Nick's face, the wind tried to snap *Wind Dancer's* masts like kindling, and waves threatened to swamp the decks ... but the weather was turning.

They still might sink if they couldn't get the starboard gun held fast. Nick saw when the line lashing it in place broke. Jack jumped to it before Jonesy had a chance to give an order. Other hands would have helped Jack but as the ship dove bows-under again, the jib boom snapped.

Nick was about to have Bos'n leave the tiller to give a hand when Miss Chase's head popped up from the hatchway, and she helped Jack heave the gun back from tumbling down the ladder.

Bos'n could handle the helm. Nick shrugged out of his greatcoat and shoved it into the maphouse. He checked that his safety line was secure, one end tied around his waist, the other to the starboard railing, and left the tiller to ... to what, chastise Miss Chase for leaving the safety of the cabin? Thank her for possibly saving the ship from sinking if the gun had fallen down the open hatch? Nick grabbed onto the railing as a wave swamped the quarterdeck again. Jack and the others should have seen to the gun themselves. Should have checked the rope for wear and replaced it before they even set sail from London. A rolling deck in a storm was no place for a loose gun—proven again as they rolled to starboard and the gun smashed right through the gunwale.

Oh hell. Her skirt was tangled on the carriage axle. Miss Chase couldn't hold back the gun, and Jack couldn't hold Miss Chase.

Nick's stomach twisted as the gun plunged over the side, dragging Miss Chase across the deck and into the sea.

He leaped past Jack and leaned over the rail. Thank God for her stubborn nature. Below the churning surface he could just make out her pale hands clinging to the tattered rope. He grabbed with both hands and heaved, planting his feet against the bulwark for leverage. The rope didn't budge. No telling if it would break again. She remained just out of his reach.

One of her hands let go.

Nick dove in, as deep as the rope around his waist would allow.

He grabbed a flailing ankle, narrowly avoiding being kicked in the head, and felt for the bottom of her skirt. He yanked and twisted but couldn't untangle it from the carriage, nor rip the wet wool.

He kicked hard toward the surface, keeping one hand in contact with her body as he rose through the water. If he was beginning to run out of air, being pummeled by the sea as he was, surely she would go limp and let go any moment. Her long brown hair swirled in the water, hiding then revealing her eyes, wide with fear and disbelief. The carriage was dragging her down. Her hand slipped farther down the rope. At least it was calmer below the surface than it was above, the water eerily quiet after the roar of the storm, the buoyancy gifting him a scant few seconds to save her.

Just shy of breaking the surface, he grabbed his knife from his boot. Without thought for her delicate sensibilities but cognizant of her delicate flesh, he felt for the neckline of her gown, inserted his knife with the tip pointing down, and sliced the fabric.

Under the strain of holding her, himself, and the carriage, her rope broke. For a few heartbeats they floated free, slowly drifting down. He grabbed her wrist, the only body part he could reach before the water tore them apart, and held tight as his safety rope suddenly grew taut and yanked him forward and up, the ship pulling him along.

She retained enough sense—and trust—that she let go of her broken rope and let her now-gaping gown slide off one shoulder, threw that arm around his neck, and shimmied until her gown slid off the other side.

Freed of the dead weight at last, she clung to him as they surged up to the surface and gasped for air. When their heads broke through the waves, Jack and others began pulling on his safety line, hauling them toward the ship. Ignoring the waves slamming into them and the wind whipping water in his eyes, Nick kicked and stroked, his arms free because Miss Chase was clinging to his front like a limpet. Both her arms were wrapped around his neck, her legs around his waist.

In any other circumstance, this would be erotic.

Despite the chill of the stormy Channel water, his body heated everywhere she made contact with him. Without her sensible wool gown, which had sunk out of sight with the gun carriage, she was now clad in only a thin muslin shift, tangled and hitched up around her waist. Soaked with seawater it must be so sheer she might as well be naked. Too bad he couldn't take the time to confirm or appreciate the view. He was too busy trying to keep them alive.

After what seemed hours of being battered by waves, many arms reached down and hauled Miss Chase out of the sea, then helped Nick climb up onto the deck. The two of them lay side by side on their backs for a moment, shivering and gasping like landed halibut. He tried to slow his breathing and vaguely heard cheers for the successful rescue.

They'd just cheated death.

As a privateer during the war, he'd done that on a fairly regular basis. Mother Nature or Father Time or Whomever would usually grant him one boon, one miraculous escape, per voyage, and they'd just used it up. He sincerely hoped this storm was as exciting as their little trip to Spain would get.

The cold rain pounding down soon had them on their feet again. Her muslin shift did indeed seem to disappear where it plastered itself to her damp flesh. Very chilled flesh, with snug little curves in all the right places. Her small but perfectly shaped bosom heaved as she tried to catch her breath.

Just as Nick realized every man on the ship was taking in the same delicious view he was, and before he could roar at them, Jonesy had the presence of mind to appear at his side with a wool blanket. Nick yanked it from his first mate's hands and swung the blanket over Miss Chase's shoulders. He brought the ends together in front of her chest and held it there until her icy fingers took hold.

With reluctance he brought his gaze up to her eyes. What would he find there? Hysteria? Anger? He braced himself.

She swiped at the wet hair hanging in her face then shook her head, flinging droplets everywhere, her long hair a tangled mess unfettered by even a single hairpin. She laughed. She whooped. Breathy, full-throated laughter without a hint of restraint.

Nick braced his hands on her shoulders. Well, laughter was certainly better than screams or hysterical tears. Still cautious, he tipped her chin up. "Are you all right, Miss Chase?" What a banal question. She'd nearly died just now. Nick mentally kicked himself.

She nodded, a huge smile lighting her face. She grabbed his soaked cravat and tugged. He bent down, perfectly willing to let her whisper in his ear. Instead she planted a chilled kiss on his cheek, close beside his mouth. He had the feeling she would have kissed his lips if not for the damn sailors surrounding them, watching them. "Thank you," she shouted loud enough to be heard over the storm.

And just like that, she made her way down the hatch, safely below decks and out of the storm.

Nick watched her disappear, then snapped his mouth shut. "What are you lot looking at?" he shouted at the gawking sailors. "Haul to braces! Secure that boom!" Sailors scampered to follow orders. Chang and Dieter, the carpenter, began nailing boards to block the hole in the gunwale. Nick nodded his approval. One stormy swim per voyage was quite enough.

Later he'd mourn the loss of the gun, a cannon that had been a fixture on *Wind Dancer* longer than he had. Would the treasure be worth enough to cover the cost of a replacement? If they could even find the treasure.

He staggered across the rolling deck to check the portside gun. Once satisfied it was secure and the rope in good condition, he made his way fore to check on the broken jib. The sail had already been taken in and stored below, and Winston and Tucker were busy taking care of the loose lines. He'd probably have to put in to port before they could repair the damage, though perhaps Dieter could work his magic. The loss of a few square feet of canvas wouldn't slow them appreciably, but added to the delay caused by the storm, would the thief make it to Spain and find the treasure before they could get there? The *Wind Dancer* had as much canvas unfurled now as he dared carry in this weather.

What other damage had the ship suffered? In leaving London so hastily, had they missed replacing any other worn or frayed lines? Nick was busy inspecting the foremast and yardarms when Jonesy made his way from the quarterdeck.

"Might I suggest m'lady needs your help with her gown," he shouted into Nick's ear.

Nick grinned. Smart man, his first mate, appealing to Nick's base nature rather than telling him he was being an overprotective idiot and to go below to get warm.

Only when he was below deck with the hatch closed, cutting off the howling wind and pounding rain, did Nick realize he was chilled to the bone. That chattering noise might even be his teeth. The sharp pain around his middle every time he inhaled could be a fractured rib or two. He shook his head. Such foolishness, diving into the stormy sea to rescue a woman he barely knew.

He knocked once on the cabin door and immediately opened it. Breath left his lungs in a rush.

Miss Chase stood with her back to him, long hair twisted up in a towel, hands behind her as she strained to do up the row of tiny buttons at the back of a green muslin gown. Only one button at the bottom was closed, leaving the dress gaping, her back exposed save for a frayed-edge chemise so thin he could see the freckle beside her right shoulder blade.

She whirled to face him as he slid the door open, her face flushed. From exertion or embarrassment, he wasn't sure, but he liked it.

"Having some difficulty, Miss Chase?" He carefully schooled his expression, keeping any wolfish grin at bay.

"No, I, ah…" She dropped her hands as her shoulders slumped. "Yes, I…" She took a deep breath, no doubt steeling her resolve. "I would appreciate your assistance." He could practically hear her gulp from across the cabin, though her voice didn't waver. Nick barely restrained himself from rubbing his hands with glee.

As he stepped toward her, he did rub his hands together, but only because they were numb with cold. He blew on his fingers while she turned around again.

The row of tiny buttons mocked his cold, clumsy fingers. He had a button hook hidden away in his desk somewhere, useful for doing up m'lady's buttons. Usually he employed it only after having had the pleasure of *un*doing her buttons, with all sorts of fun in between undressing and dressing. Miss Chase was already prone to think the worst of him. He didn't want to prove her point quite so soon in their relationship by bringing out a tool so obviously used for licentious purposes.

And he wasn't about to consider the fact he'd just thought of them as having a relationship—he had encounters, not relationships—not when presented with so much creamy skin visible from her gaping neckline. It wasn't exactly smooth creamy skin at the moment, as it was covered with goose bumps. As he watched, a shiver racked her body.

He would really like to linger when presented with such a delightful opportunity—she was already half-undressed—but his icy fingers and her obvious discomfort were not conducive to seduction.

He did the buttons up as best he could, biting back a curse when they slipped back through the tiny holes more than once. A delicate silver chain caressed her nape. He was amazed she hadn't lost it in the sea. He wanted to follow the chain with his fingers as it curved around her neck to the hollow of her throat. Better to wait until his fingers would cause shivers of desire, not cold.

By the time the last button slipped into place he was feeling warmer in front from the close proximity of her body, though his backside was still freezing. He wouldn't have been surprised if the seawater dripping off him formed icicles rather than puddles at his feet.

He gave her shoulders a pat to signal he was done, just in case she missed the fact he was no longer breathing on her neck, and moved over to the wardrobe to rummage for a dry set of clothes for himself. From the skin out.

Hmm. Would she turn her back to give him privacy, without him having to ask? He was not normally shy—far from it—but he had just been immersed in freezing cold water, and cold water had less-than-complimentary effects on a man's, ah, manhood.

She bent over at the waist, drying her hair with the towel, giving him a lovely view of her derriere outlined in green muslin.

Ahem.

She straightened and began running a brush through her tangled hair, still facing away from him. Nick stripped and dropped his sopping wet clothes and boots on the deck as quickly as he could, noticing with some surprise his hands were shaking with cold. After a quick towel down, fumbling with the buttons on his breeches convinced him to forgo the formality of a shirt that also required a buttoned waistcoat and neatly tied cravat, and skip to one of the draw-string shirts he normally didn't wear until they'd been at sea for a week or more. He tightened the strings, leaving them untied. His poor boots would need work before they could be worn again, if Flynn could save them at all. He slipped into a pair of canvas shoes. Better than going barefoot.

As he reached for his caped greatcoat that usually hung on a hook by his desk, he glimpsed Miss Chase wrapping a threadbare shawl about her shoulders, her hands still trembling. Those were the warmest garments she had?

He looked at the empty hook and remembered his coat was abovedeck, tucked in the maphouse where he'd stashed it before leaping into the water. He could climb the ladder and fetch it easily enough, or call for someone to get it for him. But the burst of energy that zinged through his blood when he leaped to save the damsel in distress had not only completely disappeared, it had taken away his normal level of energy. It was getting difficult for him to remain upright, in fact. The wind and rain pounding on the small window seemed to be battering at him.

Miss Chase sat on the edge of the bunk and wrapped the blanket about herself.

Smart girl.

She shivered.

"The best way to ward off a chill after a dunking like ours," Nick announced, making his way back to the bunk, "is for two or more people to huddle together under shared blankets." He kicked off his shoes and plunged his feet into a pair of thick wool slippers. Ah, his toes felt better already. He dug a spare blanket from the trunk and climbed onto the bed beside Miss Chase, and scooted all the way backward until his back leaned against the bulkhead, his legs straight, feet hanging over the edge.

"Two ... or *more*?"

Without warning her, he clasped Miss Chase by the hips and hauled her back beside him. "We'll have to make do since it's just the two of us."

Ignoring her startled squeak and sputtered outrage at being manhandled so, Nick set about tucking the blankets around them, making sure she was secure under his arm. If he just put her on his lap and had done with it, would she hit him? Having her on his lap would get them both warm faster. Faster yet would be to lie on their sides curved together like spoons, but there was no sense risking a bloody nose over it. He sensed his little brown wren would pack a wallop if pushed too far.

Soon he had them in a warm wool cocoon, only his slipper-covered feet and their heads sticking out from the blankets. She might object to the situation on principle but her good sense won out, as she didn't fight off his arm around her shoulders. Or his thigh alongside her thigh. They sat hip to hip, her shoulder tucked under his arm, their backs against the bulkhead, still trembling from the chill. Their shared body heat should take care of that soon. He let out a tiny sigh of satisfaction.

"Madame Zavrina would be very upset," she mumbled, breaking the silence except for the storm outside, lessening but still battering the hull.

"Beg pardon?

"Madame Zavrina was the proprietress of the Ladies Academy where I taught for four years. She would not approve of our current ... position."

He had a schoolmistress tucked against him? Now that he thought about it, Nick had no difficulty picturing Miss Chase instructing a gaggle of girls on proper behavior.

"Why did you leave her employ?" Miss Chase's adventurous nature had undoubtedly got her in trouble before. He was now convinced her prim and proper façade was just that, a façade. A proper lady would not have jumped to help restrain a loose gun on deck, or have the gumption to hang on underwater, carriage dragging her down, for as long as Miss Chase had. He opened his eyes quickly, to dissipate the image that sprang to mind of her white-knuckled grip on the rope, the rest of her out of sight in the deep, dark sea. He shivered again.

"She died."

Crazy old ape-leader.

"She left no will so the school reverted to her brother."

Old bawd should have known better and had a will. No telling when the ol' ticker will give out.

"No one thinks they will die before thirty, but no one plans to get hit by a runaway carriage, do they?"

Thirty? "The brother didn't keep the school? Offer employment to you teachers?"

"He did offer employment. We all declined his ... proposition."

"Ah, no doubt a lower wage than paid before."

"No, actually a much higher salary. Nearly double."

"Yet *all* of you declined?"

"He turned the school into a brothel."

Nick laughed, then quickly sobered at the glare Miss Chase directed his way. No, not an appropriate source of amusement for someone who had lost their livelihood. He cleared his throat. "My sympathies."

"Thank you."

There was a moment of silence, grieving for the lost school and employment, before she spoke again.

"Those slippers are unexpected."

Nick wiggled his toes, encased in red and black striped wool. "My middle sister knits them. Gives me a pair every Christmas."

"You have three sisters?"

"Five. None of the others can knit worth a da— darn, though."

She was quiet a moment. "Where do you fall in the family order?"

"Youngest."

She tilted back to look at him, then tucked her head against him once more. "It must have been quite a relief for your mother, to finally bear an heir for your father after having five girls."

Nick wasn't going to respond to that. Ever. Fortunately, she didn't seem to need a reply. Her shivering had almost stopped.

Nick noted the swells were lower, the troughs not as deep. By morning they should have calm seas again. He itched to be up on deck, overseeing the repairs, checking on the broken jib boom, searching for a break in the clouds to get a sextant reading, checking their position on the charts. Instead he cradled Miss Chase a little bit closer, letting her head fall on his chest, her quiet breathing indicating she'd fallen asleep. Nearly drowning tended to take the wind out of one's sails.

He'd let her sleep for a bit and make sure she was all warmed up again before he went topside. His own warmth and comfort had no bearing on the decision, none whatsoever.

The cabin door slid open, startling Nick awake. His neck had a crick in it and his mouth was dry. He'd been snoring? At some point Miss Chase had wrapped her arms around his waist, her cheek flush against his chest. He couldn't see her eyes—couldn't see much of anything in the now-dim cabin for that matter—though her breathing was deep and even.

"Moon's poking through the clouds, Cap'n," Jonesy said softly, holding aloft a lantern. "Thought you might want to try for a fix."

At his voice, Miss Chase popped her head up, clipping Nick on the chin. "Oh!" She pushed back from him, her hands flat on his chest, until she slid off the bunk and jumped to her feet. By the flickering lantern light he saw the flush steal across her cheeks, the imprint on her left cheek of the lacing of his shirt, her damp hair mussed. Sleep-tousled was a good look on her. He already missed holding her warm little body in his arms.

For crying out loud, they'd only been out to sea a few days. He shouldn't be missing female companionship this much already.

Jonesy cleared his throat.

Fix on their position. Right. "Be there in a jiff."

Jonesy nodded, lit the lantern in the gimbal beside the desk, and slid the door shut on his way out. Nick threw off the blanket and slipped into his canvas shoes, and set about digging in the wardrobe for a heavy woolen waistcoat to put on over his cotton shirt until he got his greatcoat. Miss Chase sat at the table, examining her fingertips.

"Are you feeling quite the thing, Miss Chase?" Seemed silly to keep to the formalities after snuggling together, but she was a teacher from Madame Zavrina's Academy for Young Ladies.

"I am much recovered, Captain, thank you." She briefly looked into his eyes, then let her gaze drift down his chest. He halted in buttoning up his waistcoat to let her look her fill at where she'd recently rested her head, trying not to let his chest swell with pride. Her blush deepened and she quickly went back to examining her nails.

He stifled his snort of laughter as he left the cabin.

His snort turned to a grunt of pain as he stepped on something small at the base of the ladder, irregular and sharp-edged enough to feel through the soft leather sole of his shoe. He felt around in the inky darkness until his fingers brushed a cold piece of metal. He took it up to examine in the light of the lantern at the maphouse.

A broken carriage bolt.

The reason the gun fell off its carriage when it crashed over the side and plunged to the bottom of the Channel.

The reason Miss Chase was alive and mortified in his cabin instead of cold and dead in Davy Jones's locker.

Nick wrapped his fist around the jagged bit of metal until it warmed. His new good luck charm.

He tucked it into the pocket of his waistcoat, picked up the sextant, and searched for a break in the clouds.

Chapter 6

Harriet waited until her heart calmed a bit after Sheffield left, then began to tidy herself. Her hair was snarled, her gown wrinkled, and she'd stared at his chest after falling asleep on him. If Sheffield didn't think her fast before, surely he did now. Though, she allowed, these were quite unusual circumstances. Her heart raced again at the memory of her terrifying slide over the side of the ship, the wooden carriage pulling her down, the certainty she was about to drown in the cold, dark depths of the sea.

When Sheffield suddenly appeared before her in the water, she'd first thought him a hallucination. The edges of her vision had begun to darken as she ran out of air. He'd sliced off her gown with his knife before she had a chance to realize what he was about. So grateful to be rid of the weight and the chance at rescue, she hadn't spared a thought for her nakedness or brazen actions until after she'd come below deck.

Memories flooded back, faster and faster. After her rope broke, she'd wrapped her body around his and held on with all her might because her life depended on it. A tiny part of her, as though observing the proceedings from a distance, had registered his hard chest and flat abdomen, warm male body, and muscles that flexed with each powerful stroke as he swam to the surface.

Did Percy, her intended, have muscles like that? She'd never given much thought to his body before, only noted that Madame Zavrina would be pleased with his proper behavior and sartorial choices when he'd attended the village assemblies. He must have muscles, since his family owned an enormous farm and farming required a great deal of effort in order to be fruitful. Though she could never remember him being dirty, and certainly he'd never labored in the fields. He'd always been the epitome of a well-turned-out gentleman, even when riding his gelding on the road bordering his fields.

Percy had once kissed her. On her gloved hand. Harriet had just kissed Sheffield. On his cheek! She put her fingers to her lips and thought she could almost feel the imprint of his rough whisker stubble. What would his lips feel like? Smooth? Soft and welcoming? Hard and unyielding?

Harriet shook her head. Enough nonsense. She was going to marry Percy. It was beyond improper to even think about kissing Sheffield, which she had no intention of ever doing again. The peck on his cheek had just been a symptom of excessive exhilaration, a celebration of being alive. Kissing Sheffield was a once-in-a-lifetime event. Like almost drowning. Something never to be repeated.

The thought unexpectedly dampened her spirits. Before she could ponder why, the bell rang for the second dogwatch. She quickly rallied, tucked the last pin in her neatly coiled hair, and went to the galley in search of food and company.

As she entered the common area, the assembled men suddenly stood. Some whistled or tugged their forelock, some clapped their hands, and all were smiling at her. Harriet glanced behind her to see the cause for the commotion. No one else was there.

"Here, miss, take my seat," Jack said, vacating a place at the table for her. Luigi quickly set down a full bowl of stew for her and a steaming mug of tea.

Madame Zavrina had often taught that it was improper for a lady to sit in a chair which was still warm from a man having been sitting in it. Deprived of Sheffield's warm embrace under the blanket, Harriet was feeling a bit chilled again. She took the offered seat on the bench, still bewildered by the men's reaction to her presence. She sipped her tea—heavily laced with rum—and noted the other men were eating cold beans and hardtack, their tankards filled with ale. "Thank you," she belatedly remembered to say.

Jack nodded, took what would have been her less-comfortable perch on a cask, and the men resumed eating.

"That was a right brave thing you did this afternoon, miss," one sailor said after a bit.

"Crazy, if'n you ask me," said another.

"What was it like, under the water, 'olding on for yer life?"

Jack she recognized, but not the first two. The sailors began to lob questions and comments at her, faster than she could form answers.

"Pipe down!" The men immediately hushed at Jonesy's order. "How are your hands, Miss Chase?" he said. "The sawbones has some liniment we could fetch for you. Laudanum, too, if you need it."

"I, ah, thank you, no, that won't be necessary." She glanced at her hands. She hadn't noticed the redness on her palms and fingers earlier, or how tender they felt while holding her mug or spoon. Rope burn. Her shoulder ached too, where she'd heaved up on the cannon and from Jack pulling on her arm, trying to keep her from going over the edge. And she'd sat on the bench gingerly, thanks to her rump being sore from falling so hard on the slippery deck. "Considering the alternative, I'm feeling fit as a fiddle."

That generated a laugh, someone thumped her on the back, and the men got on with their meal, chatting and telling tall tales just as they had the night before. The main storyteller tonight was Tucker, the Scottish sailmaker, who recounted the results of a drinking contest between two rival captains that damaged both ships. Took him the rest of that voyage to repair the sails.

She did not attempt to join in the conversation though she listened raptly to every word.

"How does it feel," Sheffield said in her ear a short time later, "to know that your adventure this afternoon will be the subject of fo'c'sle chatter for years to come?"

"*Our* adventure," Harriet corrected, warm and self-assured from the rum-laced tea she'd imbibed, shivering in pleasure at his intimate tone. "I'm sure it will be suitably embellished in the retelling."

Sheffield grinned and saluted her with his tankard, freshly filled by Luigi, then he was gone again, up the hatchway ladder, as quickly as he'd come.

When the watch changed, Harriet returned to the cabin and prepared for bed as best she could while still trapped within a gown. The green muslin would show wrinkles much worse than the brown wool. She had no choice, since she couldn't undo the buttons by herself any better than she'd been able to do them up. It had taken Sheffield's assistance to make her decent this afternoon. She trembled at the memory, though she was no longer cold.

A swift knock on the door startled her. As though conjured by her thoughts, Sheffield stepped in and closed the door.

"I offer my services as lady's maid." His eyes twinkled though his expression seemed earnest. No wolfish grin in sight.

As she continued to stare at him, his expression became politely remote. "But if you'd prefer to sleep in your gown again, I understand—"

"Yes!" She'd already taken the pins from her hair, so she quickly gathered the long brown mass to one side with her hands, baring her nape, and turned slightly away from him. Her heart pounded anew as his footsteps drew near. She closed her eyes as his fingertips, warm this time, brushed her skin as he undid the buttons on her gown. His breath softly ruffled the fine hairs on the back of her neck, sending delicious frissons of pleasure down her spine until her toes tingled. She felt his large, capable body standing close behind her, radiating warmth. So attuned were her senses that she felt his callused knuckles on her spine, through her shift, as he unbuttoned lower and lower. She only needed the first twelve buttons undone in order to get in and out of this dress, but he was undoing every last little mother-of-pearl button and she couldn't for the life of her tell him to stop.

His fingers lingered when he reached the base of her spine, toying with the flimsy green muslin which gaped open, exposing her back to his gaze, only her thin chemise providing any hint of modesty. "Do you need help with anything else?"

The words were mundane but his voice was low and smoky, like honey being poured through gravel. The same tone that no doubt enticed women into his bed.

She was indeed going to sleep in his bed, or rather his bunk. Alone. "Thank you, no. That will be all." She used both hands to keep her gown from sliding off her shoulders and pointedly turned so her back was no longer in his view. For all her proper behavior and good intentions, however, she felt sure her face betrayed the pleasure she'd taken from the intimate service he'd just performed. Her cheeks grew hotter as she thought of other meanings for those words. "Good night, Captain."

He took her dismissal with good grace, though his eyes told her that was far from all. "Good night, Miss Chase."

Alone again, Harriet hurriedly changed into her warm flannel nightgown and huddled under the blanket, her flannel wrapper draped on top for extra warmth. Her body ached and her mind roiled, reliving the events of the day, good and bad. She tried to concentrate on listening to the sounds of the ship and waning storm, and staying awake to see if Sheffield would sleep in a hammock by the door again.

The exertions of the day took their toll, however, and the next thing she knew, bright sunlight was streaming through the window.

The hammock was neatly coiled on its hook so she had no indication if Sheffield had come in or not.

She quickly completed her morning ablutions and was reaching for a pin to put her hair up when she realized these were all the pins she had left. The others had been lost to the sea. She didn't even have Betsy to borrow from. If she lost any others, she wouldn't be able to properly dress her hair when they reached port. With a shrug, she braided her hair into one long plait down her back. Get some cotton or leather cording to wrap around it, and her braid would look like the queue Jonesy and a few of the other sailors wore.

Her good humor vanished as she eyed the green muslin gown with dismay. Her only other dress, a sprigged yellow print, was even more formfitting, requiring *all* of the buttons to be done or undone in order to get in or out of it.

If Sheffield had made any attempt at seduction last night, she doubted she would have resisted. Even in the bright light of day, she dare not subject herself to such temptation ... which is why she tugged on the green muslin, threw on her wrapper to hide the gaping open back, and left the cabin in search of Luigi and breakfast before Sheffield could come below and lead her into temptation.

She had just finished her porridge and was about to go back to the cabin when a sailor stopped in front of her. She'd seen him before, part of the larboard watch, and noticed he tended to stay quietly in the background.

"Ahoy, miss," he said. "The Old Man said you might wanna borrow somethin' from the slop chest. Wanna take a look at what we got?"

Harriet was so intrigued by the man's accent, it took a moment to register the meaning of his words. "Slop chest?" Isn't 'slop' what was fed to pigs? She'd seen dwarf goats brought on board, but no pigs.

"Yes, miss, it's just fore of the galley." He pointed the way. His sun-bleached blonde hair was long enough it hid his eyebrows and fringed his sea-green eyes. His skin was tanned with a smattering of freckles on his nose and cheeks. Just a handful of years older than Sheffield, he also was so tall he had to duck periodically to avoid the crossbeams overhead.

"Where are you from, Mr. ...?"

"Smitty, miss. Joshua Smith. Everyone just calls me Smitty." He fished a small ring of keys from a cord tied inside his shirt and unlocked a door on the far side of the galley. "I'm from Nawlins but haven't been home in a while." He slid the door open.

It took her a moment to translate. New Orleans. "American." She'd never met anyone from the Colonies before.

"Yes, miss." He reached in and hung up the lantern he'd carried. "See anythin' you like?"

Smitty was quite handsome in his own right. Since she was planning to marry Percy, though, she tore her gaze away from the intriguing American and glanced through the doorway, half expecting to see a pig's trough, or more likely a large sea chest or two.

She put a hand to her cheek. It was as though the entire contents of Miller's Dry Goods shop in Brixham had been crammed into a closet. Shoes, hats, shirts, oilskin, and other clothing items overflowed baskets and chests, stacked high on the wall and on shelves, held in place by ropes and brackets. Other crates held toiletries, sewing kits, tobacco and pipes, knives and marlinspikes. Everything a sailor might need to bring or replace on a long voyage. There were even skeins of yarn and knitting needles of various sizes. She tried to picture any of Sheffield's sailors knitting a shawl. Or perhaps his sister had taught him how to knit? Harriet almost chuckled. Scarves and stocking caps would be practical items for the men to knit, though, as well as warm slippers. She should keep an open mind.

Another basket held brightly colored skeins of delicate embroidery floss and folds of cloth ready to embroider. She'd heard of a naval officer's wife who was so bored on their long deployment she'd embroidered an entire set of chair covers for their formal dining room at home.

"I think you'll find this one of most interest." Smitty unearthed a chest in the far corner, lifted it to the top of a stack and unlocked the lid. Inside was a rainbow of shimmering silks and satins—some simply bolts of cloth, others already made into dresses, nightgowns, and other garments. How in the world did a ship run and staffed entirely by men come to have, or need, such feminine articles?

Oh, right. Privateer.

As she slid the shimmering silk between her fingers, she thought of the former owners of this abundance. Had they been treated well when their goods were confiscated?

A chill ran down her spine. Had they been killed?

Her question must have shown on her face. Smitty pointed to the chest of silk. "A lot of this came from a French merchant that tried to outrun us a couple years ago. We already sold most of that load."

"And the rest?"

Smitty grinned. "The captain does like the ladies. Some of the gals have left things on board."

Harriet dropped the scarlet silk wrapper as though burned. She thought Smitty laughed but he was apparently coughing into his elbow.

Her situation had not changed, so she reluctantly began looking through the chest's contents more seriously, searching for anything to replace her sensible woolen gown. Or at least anything she could get into and out of by herself without the assistance of a privateer who 'likes the ladies.' Was there such a garment already made up, or would she have to attempt sewing a gown from whole cloth?

She set aside a green satin dress and a few other potential items as she dug deeper in the chest, determined to look at everything. Nothing was very promising so far. It was all so fine, much more suited for a ball room or boudoir than a ship, and the gowns required assistance. From the corner of her eye, she saw Smitty retrieve a slim leather-bound book from a high shelf and begin writing in it with a pencil he'd had tucked above his ear. "What's that?"

"As ship's purser, it's my duty to record everything that's taken from the slop chest, and then the cost is deducted from the sailor's wages at the end of the voyage." He grinned. "Though in your case, I'm sure the Old Man will make an exception."

Sheffield would charge her? Deduct the cost from her share of the treasure?

But what if they didn't find the treasure? Or they did find it, but it wasn't worth what Papa thought it was?

She folded the silk and put it back in the chest. Wool was more practical anyway. Just how long would it take her to knit a dress? Once she learned to knit, that is. Both Mama and Madame Zavrina had tried at different times, with little success. Perhaps there was some muslin or cotton or other practical fabric. She just needed to keep looking.

Her fingers fell on rough wool spilling out of another chest. Men's breeches. "Just out of curiosity," she said, unfolding and holding them up, "what would these cost, compared to the red silk?"

Smitty showed her similar entries in the ledger book. A sailor could purchase multiple complete changes of clothing for a fraction of one silk gown. "Dungarees are even cheaper." He pointed to a different line in the ledger.

That seemed so unfair, when a man could wear the same clothes day after day while a woman needed several changes. Even at the Academy, they'd needed to change for dinner every evening.

Harriet fought the urge to sigh. Even if she found practical fabric, she doubted she could sew together a presentable garment before they reached Spain. She couldn't go about wearing her wrapper all the time.

She held up a pair of brown dungarees with brass buttons on the fall. They had wide legs designed to reach about mid-calf, and were cut generously through the hips, to reduce the likelihood of splitting a seam when spending so much time kneeling to holystone the deck or bending over a yardarm furling sails.

They weren't all that different from the drawers Amber Barrow-Smith had worn under her gown to an assembly, just made from heavier cloth. They also had laces at the back of the waist, to accommodate a wide range of sizes in wearers. It was unlikely the crew of a ship this small included a tailor, though the sailmaker could probably make do in an emergency. She held the dungarees to her waist.

Dare she?

Dungarees would not have got caught in the axle of the cannon carriage. She shivered at the memory of being pulled overboard and underwater, those awful moments when she thought she was about to die, and even worse, had failed Gabriel and Mama.

She fingered the silver H on its chain around her neck. Did she dare continue to let Sheffield button her in and out of her gowns?

"Mr. Smitty, can you help me find the smallest of these you have? And a shirt like that one." She pointed to an undyed drawstring shirt of homespun cotton.

"Pretty sure that ain't what the Old Man had in mind, but I'm game if you are." Smitty set aside his ledger. "Let's see if we can find the clothes Charlie wore. They should fit close enough."

"Did Charlie ... is Charlie dead?" Harriet pictured an unfortunate cabin boy.

Smitty let out a laugh, then shook his head. "Married one of the captain's best friends less than a fortnight ago."

Charlie, married ... Oh, he meant Charlotte! "What a small world. I didn't realize Charlotte had ever dressed like this." Harriet looked at the clothing with a fresh eye and fished out a waistcoat that looked small enough.

"Came in handy more than once to have her not look like a girl." Harriet wanted to ask more, but Smitty fished out a pair of blue-and-white striped dungarees. "Here ya go!"

They sorted through the clothing until she was kitted out with two changes, plus a knit wool cap and other items Smitty recommended for her new wardrobe. Which wasn't exactly new—the dungarees already had a patch on each knee and several stains from tar, and the shirt had been mended at the elbow. Madame Zavrina was surely rolling over in her grave. Harriet didn't care, because she'd be decently covered and most importantly could get dressed—and undressed—all by herself. And no one she knew would ever see her like this. Besides, Charlotte had once worn them, which was immensely more comforting than thinking some unknown cabin boy or sailor had last worn them.

She signed her name in the ledger, thanked Smitty, and hurried to the cabin with her bounty.

If only Gabriel could see her now, Harriet thought half an hour later, slipping on the canvas shoes. She gave her toes an experimental flex. Not so different from dancing slippers. If only *she* could see herself. From head to toe she was now dressed like a common sailor. Her looking glass and Sheffield's shaving mirror only let her see a few inches at a time so she had no idea of the total effect, and how badly was she exposed from the rear? What if she lined up her looking glass and his shaving mirror just so...?

Nick handed off the tiller to Bos'n and went below. Miss Chase was probably anxious to get dressed and leave the cabin by now. He'd meant to go down earlier but the sun had finally poked through the cloud cover, allowing him to get a fix on their position. They hadn't exactly been blown backwards by the storm but it would take several extra days to reach Spain.

He slid the cabin door open ... and froze.

Miss Chase froze, too, one hand raised over head, the other low and behind her. More puzzling than her position was her clothing. She didn't need his help buttoning her gown because she was now dressed like a deckhand. A drawstring shirt was tucked into striped dungarees that outlined her legs nicely, her décolletage hidden by the tightly laced shirt overlaid with a checked wool waistcoat in dark blue. Knowing she would never choose the red silk, he had hoped Smitty would steer her toward the green satin.

"The dungarees are unexpected."

Her cheeks flushed a lovely pink as she dropped both hands to her sides. "I, ah, didn't want to inconvenience you any further. I know you have much more important matters to attend to than, ah, acting as lady's maid."

Nick finally noticed his shaving mirror in one of her hands, her looking glass in her other. Now he understood her odd pose. "I'd be happy to hold a mirror if you'd like to continue inspecting yourself." And he wouldn't mind the chance to openly scrutinize her new mode of attire, especially how it differed in the way it concealed and revealed her figure.

Her blush deepened. "Thank you, no. I'm done. I'll just be putting this back." She stumbled as she went to his desk to put his mirror away. He stood, transfixed, as she bent over to put the mirror in the desk drawer.

This could be interesting. He hadn't realized he'd been looking forward so much to buttoning her in and out of her gown until the opportunity was taken away, but the way the dungarees hugged her derriere offered interesting consolation.

She straightened and held her hands stiffly at her sides. He quickly raised his gaze to her face.

"I'll just go back up, then." As the captain, surely he must have more important matters to attend to than a passenger's apparel. Even if he found that passenger oddly fascinating. When he'd first met Miss Chase in the ballroom, he'd have wagered she'd die before donning a pair of men's breeches. Certainly that must be true of a teacher from Madame Zavrina's Academy For Ladies.

His hand on the door handle, Nick paused.

Had the old Miss Chase died when she almost drowned?

* * *

Harriet paced the cabin. Even the captain's quarters, the most spacious on the ship, were too small to contain her energy. She barely had room for five strides, anyway. Five long strides, with the freedom of movement in the dungarees. It still felt odd to have fabric between her legs. It chafed the inside of her thighs a bit. She'd probably get used to it soon, since men didn't seem to be bothered by chafing and they wore breeches or trousers all the time. She paused in mid-stride. What would Sheffield's men think of her dressing this way? It was beyond the pale. Madame Zavrina would never approve. She could never show her face in public if word got out back home in Brixham.

Then she decided it didn't matter what the crew of a privateer thought. And her reputation would be in shreds simply by being here unchaperoned on the ship should anyone find out. Her wardrobe was irrelevant.

Wanting fresh air, she climbed the ladder to the weather deck, slid open the hatch cover ... and froze, her gaze riveted to the starboard gunwale, where the cannon used to be.

Where she'd almost died.

Boards had been nailed over the hole where the cannon had smashed through the side, where she'd plummeted into the sea. The whole catastrophe, from getting her skirt caught to Sheffield's rescue to being hauled back up on deck, had probably lasted only three or four minutes yet felt like a lifetime. The timid spinster who'd left the village of Brixham couldn't even bring herself to pull on breeches, and now look at her.

Well actually, no one but Sheffield had seen her dressed thus. With her chin up and shoulders back, Harriet stepped up on deck, prepared for any disdainful reaction.

"Beg pardon, miss."

Harriet stepped away from the hatch cover as Jack hurried up the ladder and past her toward the bow, a large bundle of canvas balanced on his shoulder. She quickly sat down on the hold cover and tucked her legs in under her, to be out of the way as others hustled past, coming up or heading below again. Most ignored her, though a couple tugged their forelock in deference. No one shouted, pointed, or gasped. As she looked around, her gaze fell on Jonesy at the tiller.

He briefly took in her attire and braided queue, then touched his own queue and gave her a grin and approving nod before going back to scanning the horizon.

Harriet folded her arms. How anticlimactic. Apparently she was the only person who cared what she wore. At home, her reputation could be torn to shreds in minutes if she showed too much ankle or wore the wrong color gown. Here on a ship full of men, they couldn't care less how she covered her body. Attire that was practical for the task at hand and weather conditions seemed to be the only rule.

How ... liberating.

She watched as two men worked together to adjust the angle of the rear-most sail, following Jonesy's command, and realized she knew very little about the operation of the ship. This was their fifth day at sea, but she'd spent the first three below hiding her maid's absence from Sheffield, and the fourth in a raging storm and nearly dying. Her innate curiosity demanded satisfaction.

The storm had cleared away, scrubbing the sky bright blue, gentling the seas. Canvas was unfurled on every mast. Harriet watched for a bit, the sun warm on her face, the wind with enough of a chill that she was glad she'd taken Smitty's advice and worn the wool waistcoat.

Everyone else had something to do. When not adjusting sails, the two other crewmen on deck were busy repairing rope. It looked like picking oakum, work performed in the poorhouse. Harriet shuddered. Tucker, the sailmaker, sat just aft of the foremast on the windlass with yards of canvas spread around him, busy plying needle and thread—possibly the largest needle she'd ever seen—undoubtedly repairing or replacing sails damaged in the storm. She couldn't sew together a dress from a bolt of cloth by herself, but Harriet would wager she could help sew the seam on a sail, and Tucker could answer some of her questions about the ship.

She headed over.

Chapter 7

Nick sat down at the desk in his cabin, a mug of coffee, wedge of cheese, and a ship's biscuit at his elbow, and tried to bring his logbook up to date. He kept losing his train of thought because he glanced at the door every time he heard footsteps in the passageway. He'd expected Miss Chase to be here since she wasn't eating in the fo'c'sle with the larboard watch. He'd seen her keeping them company several times now, avidly listening to their chatter. He only enforced the Swear Jar when there was a woman on board. Casually letting the men see him walk a shilling across the back of his fingers was all the reminder they needed to keep their tongues civil. So far no one had needed to contribute to the Jar.

Blast—he was overdue to check their position. He grabbed the logbook and headed topside.

There she was, seated on the windlass with Tucker. How did the addition of one woman, dressed like a deckhand no less, make a grizzled sailmaker with more than three decades at sea under his belt look like he was part of a ladies' sewing circle? Their heads were together in deep conversation, the wind carrying away their words, as they stitched on the same sail. What did she have in common with Tucker to discuss so intently? Needlework techniques? She hadn't even noticed Nick was on deck.

And why did he care that she hadn't noticed him? Nick blew out an annoyed huff and took the readings he needed. As soon as he'd recorded the results, he went back down to the hold, where he'd already spent much of his morning overseeing part of the starboard watch. Some of the load had shifted or broken free during the storm, and in addition to setting cargo to rights, his crew had livestock to soothe. Bessie's milk production always dropped off after a storm unless someone cuddled her like a lapdog.

As absurd as it was, he couldn't help comparing the cuddling he'd done with Miss Chase after their dunking yesterday. He couldn't explain why last night it had been so important to stand motionless, listening to her steady breathing, before he'd hung up his hammock. Why he'd done so rather noisily at the risk of waking her up, or why he'd felt a twinge of disappointment when he'd left the cabin this morning, with her having slept through his entire presence, even folding and putting away his blanket in the chest at the head of the bunk.

When he deemed Bessie suitably soothed—and the various casks, crates, and barrels safely stowed again, unlikely to shift or burst open—he went to the fo'c'sle to let Luigi know he was ready for a meal to be brought to his cabin. Miss Chase was stirring the common stewpot, deep in conversation with the cook. This was the second crewman he'd seen her spending time with, and no telling how long she'd chatted up Smitty in the slop chest this morning. Who was next—Jack?

Nick almost smacked his forehead as Jack sat down at the table and Miss Chase immediately joined him. Instead of leaving, as any sensible common tar would have done, Jack pulled out his scrimshaw knife and handed it to Miss Chase, who began asking him questions about the intricate carving on the bone handle. Nick really hoped it wasn't the knife with the two naked ladies. Oh wait, Big Jim had won that from Jack in a card game in Amsterdam last month.

"*Buona sera, capitano*," Luigi said, and Nick had to move out of the shadows.

"*Buona sera*." Nick tried to smile rather than just bare his teeth when he looked toward Jack with Miss Chase.

"Think I'm needed topside," Jack said upon hearing Nick. Jack retrieved his knife and got up from the bench so quickly he tangled his legs. He tugged his forelock toward Miss Chase and climbed the ladder, double time.

Smart man.

Miss Chase frowned.

"Your supper will be at your table *molto rapidimente, capitano.*"

"*Grazie*, Luigi." As Nick entered his cabin and stripped to the waist to wash, he wondered if Miss Chase would continue flirting with Luigi as soon as Nick had left the galley.

Hold on. If he didn't know better, he'd think his irritable mood stemmed from jealousy. Why should he be jealous? He was not interested in Miss Chase, other than her being the only female within hundreds of miles of ocean. Her presence on this voyage was merely the means to an end: getting the treasure his father didn't want him to have. And she had assured him she was betrothed, so she couldn't seriously be interested in stepping so far out of her social stratum as to socialize with any of the tars in his crew.

Then what in blazes was she doing chatting them up all day?

Nick flung his shirt into the corner and plunged his face into the basin of cold water. He'd have to remember to pick up the shirt before his cabin mate arrived—it wasn't like he had a maid on board, a valet, or even a cabin boy since the last one had decided to go home to his mama after only one voyage. Nick had left London so quickly he hadn't had time to hire a replacement.

Maid.

Miss Chase had no other females on board with whom to keep company. Not even her maid.

Of course she was chatting with the sailors. She was bored! Some of his other female passengers had done the same; Charlie had even learned how to cook from Luigi and Flynn. Not many ladies, though—most stayed within their level of society even if they were the only one on board within it, and had no interest in fraternizing with his lowly tars.

There had better not be any fraternizing. Chatting, yes. Fraternizing ... he'd flay anyone he caught fraternizing with her.

His face buried in the towel as he dried off, he heard the door open, then a soft gasp. When he lowered the towel, Miss Chase was frozen in the doorway, hand to her mouth in astonishment, her gaze fixed on his torso.

"Something wrong, Miss Chase?" Surely the chit had seen a man's naked chest before? Perhaps she'd never seen a tattoo before. The tribal design circling his left bicep had been acquired during a stop in Samoa and a night sampling stronger-than-expected local booze. He couldn't tell from this distance, in this light, if she was expressing good shock or bad shock.

"Does it hurt?" She advanced quickly into the cabin, then cautiously reached toward his side, fingers close but not quite touching him, though he felt the heat of her hands. "That looks dreadfully painful. I had no idea the rope did that to you. It surely couldn't have helped to be holding my weight as well."

Nick glanced down at the angry red and purple marks that circled his torso at the bottom of his ribcage, a souvenir from the safety rope during their underwater adventure yesterday. At Jonesy's insistence, Nick had let Norton poke and prod him this morning. After several minutes of torture, the surgeon had assured him there were impressive bruises but no broken ribs.

She tutted. "Oh, you poor man. Do you need me to rub some liniment on it?"

That could be fun. "Thank you—"

Flynn knocked on the door before sliding it open, a dinner tray balanced against his hip.

"—but that won't be necessary." He waved Flynn in, who set the tray on the table and quickly left, a knowing smirk plastered across his face as he shut the door.

"Are you sure? Those bruises look quite painful. Liniment would speed the healing process, make you more comfortable. They must be paining you."

Nick shook his head. "Hardly noticed them," he lied. He shrugged into a clean shirt, knowing she watched his every movement. He briefly debated, then decided against opening the fall of his trousers to tuck it in. If she had been in such shock just at the sight of his chest, no telling how she might react to inadvertent exposure to other parts of his anatomy. When he pulled out a chair at the table for her, she dutifully sat down and they ate in companionable silence.

"I must confess I'm a little surprised," she said after they'd taken the edge off their hunger.

Nick raised his brows in reply but kept chewing.

"I've counted nearly a dozen members of your crew so far, and not once have I seen anyone make the sign of the cross or otherwise convey a superstition about having a woman on board. They all seem to either like me or are indifferent, but none seem to resent my presence."

"Superstitious old dogs don't sail with me. They get used to women on board or they get off my ship." He ate another spoonful. "If any still harbor any superstitions, you're the lesser of two evils." Before she could sputter with indignity, he went on quickly. "Since we left London so quickly, I didn't have time to replace my cabin boy. You prevent us from having only thirteen souls on board."

She seemed somewhat mollified.

"You may have earned respect from some of them by helping with the gun carriage yesterday. And not letting go of the rope."

She sat a little straighter in her chair but showed remarkable restraint in not preening, as he would have done in her place. "How silly of me to have forgotten. You must have females on board often, what with having five sisters."

Nick choked. Miss Chase patted him on the back. "None of my sisters have even been to the docks, let alone on board *Wind Dancer*."

"Never? Then who ... er, never mind."

No doubt she thought he had lightskirts aboard at every port. Should he set her straight as to the nature of his usual female passengers? "Charlie, er, Charlotte, may have helped them get accustomed to females. The first time she and her brother sailed with me, she was in pigtails. My grandfather had let me take the ship out while I was on holiday from school, and she hid in the hold until we were well out to sea." Upon reflection, it was eerily similar to how he'd been duped by Miss Chase. Really, he should have learned his lesson the first time.

She had the grace not to mention it either, and they continued to eat in quiet, with the gentle rocking of the ship, the slap of water against the hull, and the soothing creak of wood and rope for accompaniment. They were steady on course, with no changes in helm due for a while. He could relax.

"Quite a Heliopolis you have on board," she said after a bit. "An Italian cook, American purser, Scottish sailmaker, Chinese gunner, German carpenter. And I think Jack said Winston is from Jamaica. I couldn't place his accent. I thought an all-British crew was typical."

"Boring." Nick took a sip of tea. Ah, the reward for suffering through a miserable rainstorm—once the waves settled, the rain barrels were set out, and the influx of fresh water made it possible to have a good cup of jasmine tea brewed from his special stash. If he ever had to abandon ship, he was taking his logbook and instruments and tea chest.

"Though I suppose an international crew often comes in handy for your pirate, er, *privateer* activities. During the war it did, I mean."

Nick smoothly set his cup back in its saucer and glanced at her from the corner of his eyes. "I'm a merchantman."

Miss Chase patted her mouth with her serviette, and her tone was excruciatingly polite when she spoke. "As you say."

"An honest merchantman." Since protesting further would only prove he was lying, he decided to give her a different truth. "My grandfather was a smuggler."

She leaned forward in her eagerness. "Do tell." The lantern light caught the sparkle of interest in her brown eyes, her rosy lips curved in a half-smile, and for a moment Nick forgot what he was going to say. She continued to look at him expectantly.

"With this very ship."

She glanced around, as though seeing the cabin anew. He could almost see her reviewing every inch of the ship she'd seen. "So there are secret compartments? A hidden hold?"

"Wouldn't be very secret if I told you."

She gave a conspiratorial grin. "Silk? Brandy?" She tapped her bottom lip in thought. "No, I'll bet it was tea he smuggled. Am I right?"

"We Langstons do appreciate our tea." He inhaled the flowery aroma before taking another sip, and savored the light floral taste with smoky undertones. "But Grandpapa smuggled whatever would pay well or would stock Grandmama's pantry."

"A practical man."

"A trait I inherited from him, along with this ship." Nick glanced at her sharply. Whatever had made him reveal that personal tidbit? Was he succumbing to the intimacy of dining with a female alone in a small space? Often, he was attracted to tall blondes with long legs—the better for wrapping around his waist—whose tops'ls threatened to spill from their bodice. Certainly not little brown wrens whose modest bust could be hidden by a masculine shirt and waistcoat.

"Oh. I would have thought you inherited it from your father first, like your title."

"The only ships that interested my father were His Majesty's men-of-war."

Something in his tone must have warned it was a sore subject. Though she looked like she wanted to press him further, she dug into her meal again with uncalled-for gusto. Luigi's stew wasn't *that* good.

She quickly regrouped. "Smuggling would explain why the *Wind Dancer* has a windlass for bringing up the anchor instead of a capstan. A windlass leaves more room in the hold—or holds—for more cargo on each voyage. But why is she rigged with a tiller instead of a wheel for steering? I thought all pirate ships would have a wheel." Before he could open his mouth to correct her, she added, "Privateer. I beg your pardon. You are a privateer, not a pirate. *Were*. Were a privateer."

He took another drink of tea. Too bad a splash of whisky would spoil the delicate jasmine flavor.

"Now, of course, you're an honest merchantman."

Given the smile lifting the corner of her mouth, he decided to ignore her condescending words. "It's a matter of gears and ratios. She responds faster to a tiller than a wheel, and sometimes it's handy to be more maneuverable."

She nodded slowly, undoubtedly trying to picture such instances. "But a tiller requires more effort to steer, especially in bad weather like the storm we just had. It wouldn't be practical on a larger ship such as a man-of-war."

He touched his finger to his nose.

She ate another bite of stew, then put her spoon down to stare at him. "Why are you smiling?"

He hadn't noticed he was grinning until she pointed it out. "I just realized you are the first female in a very long time to ask an intelligent question about my ship." He relaxed against the chairback. "When did you learn about tillers and wheels?"

"Tucker was most loquacious today when we were stitching the bolt rope around the new jib sail."

Nick raised his eyebrows. "He was?"

She shrugged one shoulder. "For an old salt."

And just how did she know to use the nickname for sailors? Oh yes, she had said she was from the coastal village of Brixham. He imagined the majority of its male residents went to sea at one point or another, even if just on a fishing smack.

"I think he misses his wife."

Tucker was married? How had Miss Chase managed to draw more personal information from the grizzled sailmaker in one day than Nick had learned from him in five years of sailing together? Though to be honest, Nick hadn't interviewed him for the position so much as inspected the man's seam rubber, fids, and other tools of his trade. The intricate carving and other details on the handles had told him all he needed to know about the man's skill and pride of craftsmanship.

"She died more than six years ago, but I think he still mourns her."

Nick had recognized at the time that Tucker desperately needed to sail away to far corners of the globe but hadn't known the man was escaping sad memories. Tucker was usually the most sober one, safely leading his soused watchmates back to the ship after carousing in port. Trust a woman to sniff out intimate details—like a dead wife—in a short time. "Learn anything else of interest today?"

She fingered the silver H pendant on its chain, almost hidden by her shirt, as she stared at him, evaluating the sincerity of his query. "Of interest to me, yes, but would bore you. You already know the things I learned."

"Such as?"

She ticked each item off on her fingers. "I didn't know before today that you stock a small dry goods shop on board with the misnomer of 'slop chest'. I didn't know the sails are stitched from bolts of canvas only two feet wide, woven from flax and hemp, and that there must be 108 to 116 stitches to the yard. I didn't know that if you ... how did Tucker say it ... 'crowd the canvas,' you have almost five thousand square feet of sail, and the ship has over six miles' worth of rope. I forgot, most of it is correctly called rigging or lines, not rope. I also didn't know—" She lowered her hands to her lap. "I beg your pardon." A delicate flush stole across her cheeks as she stared down at her bowl and spoon.

He couldn't take his eyes off her. "Why?"

"I didn't mean to carry on so. I'm just used to—"

"Sharing your knowledge with a room full of students?"

She gave him a sad smile. "I taught at the Academy for four years. Old habits die hard."

Nick could certainly relate to that. Since Napoleon's defeat, he'd been trying to figure out what to do with himself now that the Crown no longer had need of his services. There had been a few months of work that amounted to ferrying passengers and messages back and forth during the Congress of Vienna, with all the politicking going on as the Continent sorted itself out. But now, with Britain at peace, Nick was at loose ends. Most of his recent voyages had been for the sake of keeping his crew gainfully employed as much as for his own amusement, or running errands. He might even start carrying cargoes for pay, like an actual merchantman.

His friend Tony had been at loose ends this summer and ended up marrying a reformed smuggler and hiring her gang to start a cheese factory. One day he left London on a walking tour of England, a carefree bachelor, and a month later he had a wife and a business enterprise to run with her.

Just last month his other chum from school, Alistair, had fallen in love with and married Charlie—he should probably call her

Charlotte now—and if Nick's instincts were right, had joined her in being a spy for the Crown.

Both men, sworn bachelors, had fallen into the parson's mousetrap within months of each other.

Nick eyed the woman across the table from him. She had said she was betrothed, and she was dressed in sailor's togs, not a seductive gown, but she was still an unmarried miss, alone with him in the small, relatively dark, private space of his cabin. "I'm needed topside," he said abruptly, and bolted from the cabin.

Harriet stared, mortified, at his retreating back until the door slammed shut. Had she really been such poor dinner company?

She picked at the remains of her meal, Sheffield's abandoned dishes opposite her accusing her of... Wait. He had asked the question and she had warned him he'd find the answer boring. He'd pressed her for the answer anyway. It was his own fault he'd become bored to tears. And leaving so abruptly was simply boorish manners. She should feel insulted, not ashamed.

Satisfied she was not at fault, she gathered the dishes to return to Luigi and join the larboard watch mess. Four bells had just been rung, so they would be coming below for the last dogwatch. They'd be much better company.

"*Signorina*, you no have to bring Luigi dishes. Flynn will collect them." The cook took them from her, sweat dripping down his temples.

"I know." She would never again think of her cottage as small. Compared to the galley, her kitchen was a mansion unto itself. In the same compact space as the slop chest, the galley had racks and shelves from floor to ceiling, plus baskets hanging from hooks in the ceiling swaying with each roll of the ship, and the smallest of work surfaces. Standing in the cramped space, Luigi barely had enough room to change his mind. That he managed to prepare food for over a dozen people three times a day amazed her.

She hitched up to sit on a water barrel lashed to the starboard bulkhead, out of the way of those eating. Someone had already dropped the table and benches down, the mess captain had brought the cook pot, and she could practically hear the hum of delight as the crew dug into beans and sauerkraut in addition to the usual stew and ship's biscuits.

One of the men let out a loud belch.

Harriet studied her fingertips. She was not here to correct their manners. She was intruding in their world. She would not blink, even if someone broke wind.

She wouldn't, she wouldn't, she wouldn't.

She didn't, but only because she squeezed her eyes shut.

No one else noticed—neither her reaction, nor the fart.

This is what it's like to spend time in the company of men, she reminded herself. Coarse men who have no interest in protecting or even recognizing she *has* delicate sensibilities. She would just have to become less delicate if she wanted to spend time with them. Staying alone in the cabin would drive her stark raving mad. Tonight's bizarre meal had proven she couldn't rely on Sheffield for company.

"So you're the Maiden of the Sea," intoned a cultured voice beside her. Startled by the refined accent, Harriet glanced up to see a grey-templed gent settling on the water cask next to hers. His coat, trousers, and silver-buckled shoes bespoke money, but his hands were work-roughened.

"The Mai—what?"

"That's what the crew calls you." He nodded toward the men at the table. "I'm Norton, by the way. Ship's surgeon and idle hand." He grasped the fingers of her right hand and raised them for a kiss that landed in the air just above her knuckles. Instead of letting go, he turned her hand over, then exposed her left palm as well. "Mm, just as I thought. Nasty rope burn, but it seems to be healing nicely." He laid her hands on her lap and gave them a gentle pat, then withdrew a meerschaum pipe and small pouch of tobacco from his coat pocket and began filling the pipe bowl. "We're all quite impressed. Most misses only have that tenacity, that unwillingness to let go, when they're hunting matrimonial prey."

Well, she couldn't very well marry Percy and provide for Mama and Gabriel if she was fish food at the bottom of the Channel. "You're the one I saw brought aboard at Southampton. I thought you'd gone ashore again since I haven't seen you."

"All part of my master plan." He winked, his mouth curving up in a sly smile.

"Your hands are not those of an idle man." She touched one callused knuckle. Several scars dotted the landscape of his sinewy hands.

"Means I don't have to take a watch like them." He gestured at the men, now done with their meal, cleaning up. Two set up a checkers board drawn on canvas, another tuned his fiddle. "I can stay in my cabin and read to my heart's content, and surface only when the need for food and a good smoke drive me from my den." He tamped the tobacco down. "Or when someone is injured."

"You didn't come up on deck when Sheffield and I were fished from the sea."

"You weren't injured."

Fair enough. "You have books?"

He grinned, showing deep creases at the corner of his eyes. "Meet me at my cabin at the end of second dog watch, when you hear them ring the bell eight times."

"Where is your cabin?"

He rose, stuffing the tobacco pouch back in his pocket. "Two steps from yours, my dear." He clamped the pipe stem between his teeth, climbed the ladder, and quickly shut the hatch again.

Harriet itched to go up on deck and talk to the surgeon more, but he seemed to need time alone with his pipe. Besides, Sheffield was up there.

She nibbled on a ship's biscuit, tapped her toes in time to the fiddle music, and eagerly anticipated the end of the second dogwatch.

*   *   *

Nick noted their location and speed in his logbook and took a final glance around the deck. Winston had settled in for bow watch. Jack had the tiller. The seas were calm, and the wind from the north-northwest.

Jonesy strolled back and forth on the quarterdeck. "All's well, Cap'n," he said on his next pass.

Nick nodded. Time to go below. If it was any other passenger sharing his cabin, he might invite them to play a hand of cribbage before he took a catnap prior to his next reckoning at the start of the middle watch. Did Miss Chase play cards? Probably silver loo.

He remembered his cowardly retreat from the cabin at dinner and winced. With any luck she wasn't speaking to him, which would preclude any need to pretend politeness.

Just as he stepped off the ladder onto the lower deck, Miss Chase exited the aft cabin—the *portside* aft cabin. "What the devil were you doing in Norton's cabin?" His harsh voice reverberated around the passageway, unintentionally as loud as when he barked orders from the quarterdeck.

Startled, she dropped whatever was in her arms to the deck. She wiped her palms on her duck trousers. "There is no need to bellow, Captain. A polite inquiry would suffice." She bent to retrieve the objects at her feet.

Nick took one from her. "Books? You were in Norton's cabin for books?"

She looked at him askance. "Mr. Norton gave me to understand it's quite a regular thing to exchange books while at sea. Did he lead me astray?"

He felt a pounding in his temple. "Just so long as it's only *books* you're exchanging." He opened the door to his cabin and ushered her in, then shut it firmly behind them. "If I'd known you were a bluestocking, I would have offered you my chest." He turned from lighting the lamps just in time to see her jaw snap shut. "*Sea* chest." Next to the head of his bunk, he slid the top chest to the side, unlocked the bottom chest and flung open its lid.

Was there anything incriminating inside? Too late if there was; Miss Chase was immediately at his side, lantern held aloft, digging through the contents with her free hand.

"Byron? Coleridge? Shakespeare's comedies?"

"What did you expect? Religious tracts?"

She shook her head. "Manuals on navigation, seamanship, that sort of thing."

"Never let it be said I disappointed a lady." He rummaged toward the bottom of the trunk, then presented his prize on his forearm like a fine bottle of wine.

"*Practical Navigation and Seamanship*, by William Nichelsen," she read aloud.

"After my grandfather gave this to me, I must have carried it everywhere for months. Even slept with it under my pillow." He expected a tease about treating a book like a favorite stuffed toy.

Instead she tilted her head to one side. "You were much closer to your grandfather than your father. I wonder why?"

Nick slammed the trunk lid shut. "I'll show you where I keep the key. Help yourself to reading material any time." He made a production out of stuffing the key in his desk drawer. He didn't worry about her discovering anything in the desk; she'd likely already gone through it anyway. At least twice.

"Thank you. That's very generous." She hung the lantern above the table and sat down to read ... the book on navigation. The short stack of books from Norton was pushed to the center of the table, ignored.

"That's your choice for relaxing?"

She marked her place with a fingertip. "I have decided to pass the time on our voyage by learning everything I can about sailing and this ship. Mr. Tucker gave me a good start today and I intend to continue in the same vein."

"Why?"

"Why?"

"Yes."

Her tongue darted out to moisten her pink lower lip. "Because I don't intend to embroider chair covers." Her answer must have made perfect sense to her, for she bent her head to read again.

Still baffled, Nick pulled out a chair and turned it around. He sat beside her, his forearms resting on the chair back. "Because you lack embroidery floss and needles? We probably have some in the slop chest."

Like a teacher who's already given a student the same answer several times, Miss Chase marked her place again and looked him straight in the eye. "Soon after we return to England with the treasure, I'm going to be married. Sir Percival has a large estate with many fields and animals. One never knows what bits of knowledge may prove useful."

"You're marrying a farmer? And you think knowing how to reckon your position with a sextant might come in handy?"

She pursed her lips. Despite her obvious annoyance with him, or maybe because of it, he suddenly had the urge to kiss those pink lips.

How many times had Sir Percival kissed them? Had Norton kissed her? He'd wring Norton's neck and toss him overboard.

No. Couldn't do that. Nick would never hear the end of it from his sister.

Something less obvious.

"As I said, one never knows what knowledge will prove useful at a later date."

He couldn't help grinning. "That's your lecture voice."

Her spine stiffened. "My what?"

"I imagine that's the tone you used when conveying—what was it you taught again?"

She flushed. "Geography and deportment."

Nick leaned close enough to catch one of the strings tying her masculine shirt closed, and caressed the length of the string between his thumb and forefinger. "Mm, yes, a teacher of the correct behavior and mode of dress for proper young ladies." He let the string fall to her chest, which had stopped its normal rise and fall movement. He felt the puff of air when she released the breath she'd been holding. "You have one tone for normal speech, another when it sounds like you're standing before a roomful of disinterested students."

"You keep asking me questions. It is not my fault the answers bore you." She pointedly returned to her reading.

He startled as though she'd just poked him with a spar. Bored? In turns she was annoying, amazing, amusing ... but never boring.

They'd been together for five days now and not once had she bored him. When was the last time that had happened? Even Lady Slavin, with her lush, agile body, erotic mind, and total lack of inhibition, bored him after only hours in her company.

Was Miss Chase as agile as Lady Slavin? Was there a drop of eroticism in her schoolmistress body?

A schoolmistress who no longer had a school. Would she become a mistress?

She was willing to toss her reputation in order to reach her goal. Would she be willing to toss her skirts?

Even though she was no longer, technically, wearing skirts.

Nick concentrated on breathing very slowly, evenly, so as not to disturb her with his thought process.

She'd only allowed him to button and unbutton her gown two times before making the drastic decision to wear men's clothing. As proven by her reaction just moments ago, she hadn't been unaffected by his nearness, by his fingers brushing her soft, naked skin as they stood so close together while he helped her in and out of her gown. Her breathing had become soft gasps, her body perfectly still so as not to miss a single sensation. Had he seen her face, no doubt her cheeks would have been flushed, her eyes dilated with desire.

She said she was betrothed. To a farmer. A man surrounded by fertile fields and procreating animals. Surely he had already sampled her wares? Surely she had switched to attire that precluded Nick's assistance solely to avoid giving in to the temptation of his touch?

She turned the page, oblivious to the new course his thoughts had set. Her shirt shifted with her movement, allowing lamplight to glint on her delicate silver chain as it dipped into the hollow of her collarbone. He propped his chin on his crossed forearms to prevent himself from tracing the chain as it disappeared inside her shirt. He needed to gather more intelligence before he acted.

"Since your father has died, from whom did Sir Percival ask for your hand?"

She stilled for the space of a heartbeat before glancing up, though she did not speak.

"Have you an uncle or other male relative? Someone who came to take care of things after news was received of your father's passing?"

She shook her head. "There is just Gabriel, Mama and me. But we have many friends, and we all look out for each other." She held eye contact just a little too long before bending her head to her book again.

What was she hiding?

No male relatives. No one but a cub of a younger brother to call Nick to task should things turn out badly.

But what could go wrong? Miss Chase was already betrothed, had likely already sampled pleasures of the flesh. While at sea on long voyages, many people sought sexual pleasure in ways, and with whom, they never would on land.

They were both here. Alone in his cabin. His crew already thought he was tossing her skirts. Because of her trying to help with the loose gun, and her heroic recovery from the sea and subsequent lack of hysterics, the men thought well of her or were at least neutral. Her change to dressing like a sailor had barely merited a second glance—they'd seen too much while in his employ, done too many odd things, to be fazed by a woman's unusual attire. They would treat her no differently if she was warming his bed. Nick glanced from the bunk to his rope hammock, hung by the door. Was warming *him* in his bed.

How to get her there?

He made a deal of stretching and yawning. "Are you going to read for a while?" At her nod, he stood and leisurely stretched again. "Then I'm going to take a nap before I go topside again." He toed off his shoes, stretched out on the bunk, and covered up with the blanket, all without looking at her.

But he heard her. A muffled squeak. He kept his expression perfectly neutral. It was nothing for him to climb into the bed in which she'd been sleeping.

The plan was to get *her* thinking about him in bed. Instead he inhaled her scent, a barely-there blend of rosewater and soap on his pillow. What would her hair look like, unbound and splayed across the pillow?

"Shall I douse a lantern?"

To anyone else her tone might seem nonchalant, but Nick heard the slight strain. She was more affected than she wanted to admit. A good start. When she retired tonight, would she think about his hair unbound and splayed on the pillow? His face above hers?

He shook his head, still not opening his eyes. "A sailor can sleep anywhere, anytime, any condition. Please, by all means, keep reading."

To his consternation, she proceeded to do just that. She even got out one of the charts from his desk and spread it across the table, comparing the examples in the navigation book to the chart. She muttered under her breath as she struggled to understand the lessons, completely oblivious to him.

Perhaps his plan needed refinement.

Chapter 8

Harriet awoke with a start, disoriented. The last thing she remembered was trying to understand longitudinal shifts the farther one ventured from the equator, seated at the table. Now she was stretched out in an unfamiliar bed.

She squinted. Familiar cabin, though. Just the scent was unfamiliar.

On second thought, she knew this scent ... sandalwood soap, underlain with just a hint of salty hemp, masculine sweat, and something indefinable.

Sheffield.

She twisted to see behind her, but she was alone in the bunk. Alone in the cabin.

The hammock was hanging from a different hook, though.

He must have risen from his nap and gone topside for the midnight fix of their position, then come back down and slept in the hammock.

How did she get from sitting at the table to lying in the bunk? She racked her brain but only remembered putting her head down on her crossed forearms on the table, since Sheffield was softly snoring in the bunk when she grew too fatigued to prop her eyelids open. Or perhaps it was just that instruction on navigation was a fabulous cure for insomnia.

Sometime during the night, Sheffield must have lifted her, carried her to bed.

And she slept through it? She covered her face with her palms.

BOOM!

Harriet fell out of the bunk.

She jumped to her feet, then climbed up on the bunk to look out the window. Why was the ship's cannon firing? Were pirates attacking? She craned her neck this way and that but saw no ship, no sails on the horizon. Her field of vision was limited, even after she stuck her head through the small opening. The gentle breeze felt good with just a hint of autumn nip, brushing away any last vestiges of sleep, the sun warm on her cheeks—a summer-like day, a gift after the storm before the dreary winter settled in.

BOOM!

She cracked her head on the upper window frame. Rubbing the back of her sore head, she jumped down, headed for the door, and stubbed her toe on a chair leg.

Bare toe. Her feet were bare. Sheffield had taken her shoes from her feet when he put her to bed last night? Of course he had.

Like viewing a diorama through a filmy curtain, images from a barely remembered dream flooded her senses. Strong arms about her, a warm chest and steady heartbeat beneath her cheek. Callused hands stroking her ankles, one after the other, exposing her toes to the cool air as her shoes were slipped off. The soft, warm weight of a blanket settling over her like a caress. A ghost of a touch to her cheek.

Not a dream.

She fell onto the chair, her every heartbeat almost as loud as the cannon blasts.

She glanced down and assured herself with shaking hands that she was still fully clothed. Even the strings on her shirt were snugly tied.

Surely a man bent on seduction would have taken advantage of the situation? Taken some liberty? Sheffield had put her to bed like ... like ...

Like a brother putting a sibling to bed. He had five sisters, after all.

She felt relieved. And yet strangely disappointed.

But then, what about last night, when he had played with the string tie on her shirt? It was almost obscene the way his thumb and fingers had held the soft cotton, like a lover's caress, the back of his hand nearly brushing her breast. His words had seemed so innocent, yet he had stared at her with such intensity she could almost feel it as a touch, his eyes dark, the blue irises almost obscured by black pupils.

BOOM!

She shoved her feet into her shoes and bolted for the door, then up the ladder until she peeked out of the hatch.

No cannonballs were flying. Jonesy paced on the lee side of the quarterdeck. "Again! Faster! They'd have shot our mainmast to kindling by now!"

"Again, aye!"

"*Wieder, jawohl*!" came the reply from Winston and Dieter, who were standing by the port cannon, the only cannon remaining after the storm. Chang, the gunner beside them, brought his palms together and bowed, still holding aloft a short rod with a glowing slow match at the tip.

"Fire when ready!" Jonesy shouted.

Harriet climbed another step and stayed in the hatchway, trying to see around the mainmast yet stay out of everyone's way while she watched them practice loading and firing the cannon. They didn't actually load a cannon ball, just mimed the action of doing so. Chang held the slow match to the touchhole on the cannon and Harriet regretted not covering her ears soon enough.

BOOM!

The explosion vibrated deep in her bones. The noise ricocheted around her brain, muffling all other sound for several moments. When the huge cloud of smoke cleared, the three men were readying the cannon for another charge, their movements swift yet controlled, working in concert like dancers. This time she covered her ears as soon as the match touched the opening.

BOOM!

"That enough, or you want 'em to go again?" Jonesy's voice, much quieter this time, was directed behind him. "I think we can squeeze 'em closer together yet."

"Have him practice on a swivel gun."

Even craning her neck Harriet could not see Sheffield, though the wind carried his voice to her.

"Aye, Cap'n." Jonesy faced the port cannon again. "Dieter, aft!"

"*Jawohl!*" The carpenter pounded up the portside steps to the quarterdeck, a canvas bag slung around his neck and over one shoulder, in addition to his usual work apron tied at his waist.

"You'll be out of the way and able to see everything from back here, Miss Chase." Sheffield's voice held a touch of humor.

Harriet didn't care if he was mocking the way she was gawking. She climbed the rest of the way up to the deck, closed the hatch, and had a good look around.

Sheffield leaned at his ease against the quarterdeck's aft railing as though he leaned on a fence surrounding a bucolic pasture, not a twenty-foot drop to the ocean rushing by below. She doubted any farmer had ever worn a gold hoop in his ear. Sunlight glinted off Sheffield's earring, the breeze ruffled his long black hair though most was constrained in a queue much like hers, and stubble darkened his square jaw.

No eye patch, no cutlass. Though she did see the handle of a knife sticking out of one boot top. She shook her head, trying to reconcile this pirate on deck with the man who'd put her to bed so gently the night before.

Giving a wide berth to the opening in the deck where the tiller connected to the rudder stock, Harriet nodded to Jack at the tiller and joined Sheffield at the stern.

"Fire when ready!" Jonesy shouted. Dieter loaded the starboard swivel gun—with powder but no shot, though he mimed the action of doing so—and took aim at an innocent fluffy cloud floating a few degrees above the horizon. She covered her ears when he pulled the trigger, though the explosion wasn't much louder than a rifle. He worked quickly to reload and fire, though his movements lacked the smooth finesse of working with Chang and Winston at the cannon.

She tore her eyes from Dieter just long enough to glance at Sheffield. "Why are they not firing actual shots?"

"We carry more powder than balls." Sheffield leaned against the gunwale with one foot crossed over an ankle, arms folded over his chest, a tiny smile crinkling the corner of his eyes at his double entendre.

Harriet tried to mimic his posture ... and lost her balance as the ship rolled to port. To her embarrassment, Sheffield impersonally steadied her, then went back to his relaxed posture. "Again," he said, in the same smooth tone he'd use conversing in a drawing room.

"Again!" Jonesy repeated louder.

"*Wieder, jawohl!*" And Dieter went through the whole process again, firing smoke at the fluffy cloud.

"Are all the men on watch going through the same training?"

Sheffield shook his head. "Dieter's only been with us since this spring. Everyone else has been here since before Waterloo."

Harriet thought of the implications for a moment. "What happened to your previous carpenter?"

"He ... retired." Sheffield took his time choosing the final word.

Harriet folded her arms over her chest, deciding she probably didn't want to know any details. Since she couldn't replicate Sheffield's nonchalant stance, she spread her feet farther apart like Jonesy, and immediately felt more secure as the ship continued its slow side-to-side roll while climbing and descending gentle swells.

Dieter adjusted the gun to take aim at the same cloud several times. She watched every movement now that she was close enough to see the details, trying to understand why he did what he did in that particular order, and mentally translated Chang's broken English instructions into complete sentences with correct grammar and punctuation.

"That will do," Sheffield said after a dozen or so practice shots. Harriet had been counting how long it took to reload between shots and knew Dieter had increased his firing speed. Chang looked pleased, too. Jonesy passed on the praise and dismissed the carpenter to his other duties on deck. Chang began putting away the tools of his trade.

Harriet eyed the starboard swivel gun, and its mate on the port side.

"Want to try?"

Oh, she couldn't possibly ... could she? In what ways could harm come to her? Aside from misfiring and blowing off her hands, of course. Or worse. Undoubtedly Sheffield would consider the loss of the gun worse. They were already short one cannon.

"You think I should?" She'd watched Dieter enough times to feel confident she could repeat his actions. From a purely theoretical point of view.

"It's an important aspect of sailing."

Harriet glanced at Sheffield sharply, realizing he had just repeated her words of last night, with no hint of mockery.

"Every crew member needs to know how to defend the ship," he added.

She bit her bottom lip. "Well, if you insist." She stepped to the starboard side, her stomach trembling like a Christmas pudding. As she got close enough to see the detailed workmanship of the gun's stock, she barely maintained enough decorum to not run the last three steps. Sheffield spoke to Chang in Mandarin, and soon the gunner was handing his bag of charges to Harriet and showing her how to load the gun.

She dropped one of the charges and glanced back to see Sheffield's reaction. His expression was impassive. Chang tapped her knuckles, drawing her attention back to the gun. She had to focus on the gun, on what she was doing with her hands. Just below, the ocean swooshed past them, threatening to take her stomach with it.

Harriet smiled an apology. This time she got the charge in place, aimed at the same fluffy cloud Dieter had used for target practice, and fired.

Boom!

Gunners must soon go deaf, she decided, her ears ringing, though she couldn't help grinning. She restrained herself from jumping up and down on the deck. She'd fired the gun! And she still had all her fingers!

"You get powde' in teeth, you smi'e dat way." Chang flashed a grin. "Go boom is good, yes?"

Harriet's cheeks hurt from smiling so wide. "Yes, going boom is good. Can I do it again?"

"By all means, Miss Chase. One never knows when firing a weapon will come in handy, especially on a farm."

She didn't care that this time Sheffield sounded like he was indulging her. She was having too much fun.

She soon understood why Chang wore two gold earrings instead of one, slightly bigger hoops of a thinner gauge than the rest of the crew wore. When he wasn't firing, he took the protective wads of wax out of his ears and stowed them on his hoops. If she kept at this, perhaps she'd pierce her ears and do the same.

By the third shot, she didn't need Chang's guidance. And having good hearing was overrated. The only way her mood could be any better was if she'd been able to load an actual shot. What would that feel like?

Madame Zavrina would have had heart palpitations at the mere thought of handling such a weapon. Two weeks ago, so would

Harriet. Perhaps dressing like Chang and Dieter made it easier for her to act like them. Heaven knew she'd drilled it into her students often enough how important it was to dress properly in order to behave properly.

Not only was it easier for her to act like the sailors, it was getting easier to understand Chang's accent. All of the crew members' accents, actually. More than once she'd overheard a conversation in two or more languages. All the men seemed to understand one another though each spoke their native tongue. How long did it take one to understand Mandarin? She'd struggled with advanced French grammar, but then she hadn't been surrounded by native speakers.

"I'm going to update our position." Sheffield spoke briefly with Jonesy, then headed below.

Harriet took his statement as an invitation to follow. Shooting lesson over. On to navigation.

She had time to settle herself at the table in the cabin, expectantly waiting for Sheffield to gather the logbook and chart from his desk and explain some of the baffling things she'd read in the book on navigation last night, before there was a perfunctory knock at the door.

Sheffield barked "Come!" and Flynn let himself in and set a tea tray on the table just as Sheffield sat down.

"Thank you, that will be—" Sheffield glanced up. "There's no milk."

Like a man who had almost escaped the gallows, Flynn slowly turned back. "Big Jim's 'ands got 'urt moving some crates this morning, and you know 'ow Bessie is. Won't 'old still for no one else."

By the grave expression and tone from both men, Harriet would have thought they were discussing being out of food. Or worse, rum.

Sheffield's shoulders raised and lowered with a sigh. "Only one thing to do." He poured tea in his cup, stirred in his usual two sugars and left the cabin, cup in hand.

Harriet followed.

They climbed down the hatch to the hold. She'd never been in the bowels of the ship before. Lanterns in gimbals swayed with each roll of the vessel, poor at dispelling the darkness but excellent at creating shadows since little daylight filtered down this far. Crates and barrels were stacked to the ceiling, lashed in place with ropes, crowding the aisle. Though her lungs struggled to take in enough air in the cramped dark space, she refused to retreat, and stayed at Sheffield's heels.

He turned a corner and suddenly the hold became a barn, complete with straw bedding on the deck, nets full of hay or straw suspended from the ceiling, crates of grain stacked and strapped in place, a small milking stanchion, and three dwarf goats chewing their cud.

"Are you being naughty, miss?" Sheffield strode toward the largest of the goats, a black and white doe. "You know what happens to goats who don't give milk? They become *stew*!" On the last word, Sheffield gestured to the stanchion. To Harriet's amazement, the goat obediently jumped up onto the stanchion and poked her head through so Sheffield could lock the bar in place. He sat on the edge of the platform, reached under the goat, and squirted a stream of milk into his cup without spilling a drop.

He patted Bessie's haunch as he took a long drink, his eyes closed in apparent bliss.

Harriet froze, her hand covering her mouth to stifle a laugh. Who'd ever have thought she'd witness a pirate milking a goat?

"Right sorry I am, Cap'n," said a sailor coming out of the shadows of the aisle. He headed toward them, a large pewter mug held between his bandaged hands.

Sheffield set the mug on the platform and began milking Bessie into it with his left hand, drinking tea with his right. "Have you seen Norton?"

"Aye, Cap'n. Nothing broken, 'e says. Swelling should go down in a day or two."

Sheffield took another swallow of what must be ambrosia and soon emptied his cup, and tucked it in a coat pocket. With obvious practiced efficiency, Sheffield finished milking the goat and turned her loose. Big Jim strode forward to take the full mug and replace it with an empty one. "I'll just take this to Luigi," he said.

Sheffield pointed to the fawn-colored doe with a white blaze and stocking who'd been watching them from her perch on a stack of crates. "Your turn, Daisy." With a plaintive bleat, she climbed down her make-shift mountain and obediently took her place in the stanchion.

"How rude of me," Sheffield said after a few pulls. "This is exactly the sort of knowledge that would come in handy on—what's his name, your betrothed?"

Harriet shook herself. "Percy. Sir Percival."

"The kind of knowledge that will come in handy on Sir Percival's farm. Or do you already know how to milk a goat?"

She shook her head. "I milked a cow once."

"Entirely different technique. Come, I'll show you." He unfolded his long legs from the stanchion and gestured for her to take his place.

Harriet gingerly seated herself on the edge of the platform and patted the fawn-colored flank mere inches from her face. "Nice goat," she said softly, as much to reassure herself as the goat.

She thought she heard Sheffield chuckle, but his expression was serious when he leaned close. "Grab the teat close to the udder and squeeze your thumb and forefinger around it, then squeeze your other fingers down. See, like this." He bent even closer so there was hardly any space for her between the goat, who smelled of sweet straw, and Sheffield, who smelled of leather and fresh air and danger, and squirted milk into the mug. "Now you try."

Harriet reached under the goat's softly furred underbelly, grasped the teat, and squeezed. Milk splashed all over the wood platform and Harriet's dungarees. Some droplets bounced into her eyes. Daisy gave a nervous "*baa-aa*" and shifted her stance, knocking over the mug and bumping her hip against Harriet's forehead. Sheffield gave the goat a reassuring pat.

"That did not go well." Harriet swiped the milk from her eyes. Perhaps it would do her complexion good. Milk was supposed to be good for one's skin.

"You're giving up so soon?" He sounded disappointed.

"Of course not. Just regrouping."

"Or re-gripping." His teeth flashed in the dim light. Harriet couldn't help smiling in return.

She righted the mug, got a better grip on Daisy's teat, and tried again. This time half the stream went into the mug.

"Try to get all the milk in the mug, or we'll have—" Soft paws landed on Harriet's knee and suddenly an orange tabby stretched up and leaned in, lapping up the milk. "—Oscar licking it up."

Harriet petted the cat, who purred and didn't stop licking until all traces of spilled milk were gone. Oscar looked up at her expectantly, long pink tongue swiping his nose.

Sheffield reached in again. Instead of streaming milk into the mug, he squirted the cat. "Begone, ye lazy furball, and go catch yer dinner." With a saucy flip of his tail, Oscar leaped to the top of a crate, where he began to clean every drop of milk from his fur.

"Now where were we?" Sheffield hadn't moved back but Harriet didn't feel crowded.

"We were ... squeezing."

"Yes. Squeezing." She felt he was referring to something other than the goat but she didn't care. He was right there, so close she could lean into him. If she wanted.

She wasn't sure what she wanted. She wasn't worried, alone in the twilight-dark hold with him, a devilishly handsome man rumored to have bedded over a hundred women. She probably should be worried.

Daisy made an impatient noise and stamped a back hoof, breaking the moment. The third goat, light grey with a white blaze and white stockings, came over and nudged Sheffield's leg.

"Mustn't keep Daisy waiting." Sheffield moved back a few inches. He bent down to rub the grey goat's head while it kept its forehead butted against his calf. "Hullo, little one," he said so softly Harriet barely heard him. "How is Dusty this fine morning?" The grey goat gave a soft bleat in reply.

"You have pets!" Harriet said. "The goats, the cat—they're all your pets!"

"I'll deny that to my dying breath." His dangerous tone was belied by the twinkle in his eye. When he moved away, Harriet missed his warmth and immediately chided herself.

Sheffield unlocked a chest, scooped out a bowl full of feed, poured some into the bowl on the stanchion, and set the rest down for Bessie and Dusty. "That should occupy Daisy while you finish."

Harriet bent back to the task of learning how to milk. All spills and splashes were immediately cleaned up by Oscar. Daisy was starting to get restless again by the time Harriet finished, and her hands and arms were cramping from the unfamiliar work. At this rate, she'd have muscular forearms like Big Jim. Who surprisingly wasn't very big.

"All done." She released Daisy. "Is Dusty next?"

Sheffield shook his head. "She's Bessie's kid from this spring, too young to breed yet."

A bubble of warmth spread through her at this further evidence of his softer side. "You kept the family together."

He grunted. "Let's get this mug to Luigi before Oscar drinks it all." Just as they were leaving the barn area, Big Jim turned the corner. "Have they been topside yet today?"

"No, Cap'n. Was just comin' to get 'em."

Sheffield turned back to the goats and patted his thigh as though calling dogs. "Walkies!"

All three goats brushed past in a mad scramble, loudly bleating and nearly knocking Harriet over in their haste to get to the ladder. They climbed without assistance, without waiting for Big Jim to follow, which he did with more speed than she and Sheffield, and were quickly out of sight.

It was almost as though Sheffield was reluctant to leave the quiet, private space, as was Harriet. Fresh air and daylight were good, but there was something about being alone with him in the near darkness. Rather than suffocating, it now felt like an embrace.

"Big Jim doesn't seem to be especially big. Or tall."

"Oh, he's big. Ah, elsewhere."

They reached the bottom of the ladder. Sheffield stepped to the side, his hand warm and large at the small of her back. Her foot on the bottom rung, she looked up at Sheffield, trying to decipher his expression. Muted daylight spilled down the hatch from two decks above, highlighting his sculpted features, hiding his eyes in shadow. She couldn't see the playful man who kept pets at sea. Now he looked like the dangerous pirate again.

Bessie poked her head in the hatch opening above and bleated impatiently.

Harriet chuckled. "I believe you're being summoned."

"Coming, dear." Sheffield subtly increased the pressure at the small of Harriet's back, and they climbed the two ladders to the top deck.

Blinking in the bright sunlight, Harriet watched the sailors obligingly jump out of the way as Dusty and Daisy chased each other around the deck. After Sheffield gave Bessie the scratch behind her horn buds she was waiting for, she joined in the romp, too.

"I haven't seen them on deck before."

"You were below deck the first few days we were at sea. Since the storm, this is the first day it's been calm enough to let them up."

A large bush seemed to suddenly grow from the forward hatch and kept rising until Smitty appeared. Another bush popped up as he stepped aside, held by Norton, and then another, until the surgeon and two sailors had arranged three wooden barrels filled with bushes around the foremast.

Her eyes now adjusted to the bright light, Harriet squinted, still not believing her eyes. "Roses?"

"Yes." Sheffield's tone implied that every ship carried rose bushes.

"You are a man of many talents, Captain. Privateer, milk maid ... and a horticulturist, too?"

One side of his mouth quirked up. "While her husband was trying to conquer the Continent, Josephine collected roses from all parts of the world. Even at the height of hostilities, any ship carrying rose specimens to the Empress was to be confiscated, not destroyed, by decree of Bonaparte himself."

"And you never had occasion to deliver them to her?"

"Let's say we never had to go quite that far."

A wily pirate. Well, of course he'd have to be wily, to be successful. To survive. "Hostilities ended well over a year ago. Yet you still carry them on board."

Sheffield gave a shrug and a lop-sided grin.

Harriet made her way forward to examine the rose bushes up close. She had to climb onto the hatch to get past Bessie and Daisy, who were playfully butting heads and blocking the deck. This late in the year, two rose bushes had been pruned to just leaves and stems but the third still had several hardy blooms valiantly hanging on. "I've never seen a tri-color rose such as this."

"It's from Singhapura."

Harriet had only seen the exotic place on a map, but Sheffield had been there. How sheltered her life had been. She must have visited many parts of the world when she and her mother sailed with Father on his ninety-eight-gun triple decker. But Mother had gone ashore for good when Gabriel was old enough to start crawling, and the little family had hardly ventured from Brixham since.

This trip she was on could prove disastrous, in many ways. And yet she couldn't turn back. Even if it was possible, even if she could still attain her goals by doing so, she wouldn't turn back.

The woman she'd been just two weeks ago had been too timid to even try on a pair of breeches, yet here she was, kitted out like a common tar and lending a hand on a sailing vessel. Sailing, if not halfway around the world, at least to another continent. She'd summoned strength she didn't know she had to hold on to that rope when she'd been dragged into the stormy sea, her skirt caught on the cannon's carriage axle. Strength she wouldn't have believed possible two weeks ago. She wondered if Amber Barrow-Smith could have held on.

Harriet would still marry Percy. Still be the epitome of proper deportment for an English lady and be a jewel in her husband's crown. But she wanted this adventure first. Just as Sheffield had accused that day at Gunter's in London.

How had he seen through her, known her better than she knew herself?

Her hand stilled just above the top-most blossom. What else had he seen?

She tipped her head to the side, close to Sheffield who had bent to breathe in the sweet fragrance of the petals, a sparkle in his sky-blue eyes.

If she didn't know better, she'd think he'd been privy to her thoughts just then.

She straightened. How silly. Her wily pirate thought she yearned for adventure because *he* yearned for adventure. He had no great insight into her thoughts, her character.

"Back off, Bessie," Sheffield suddenly growled.

The goats had apparently completed their exercise and were now hungry for a snack. Smitty waved his kerchief, shooing away Daisy, and Sheffield pushed back Bessie. While both men were occupied—Norton laughing instead of helping—Dusty snuck in and nibbled a low trio of leaves.

Sheffield let go of Bessie to push Dusty away. "Norton, why didn't you leave the bushes in your cabin until the goats were below?"

"We're heading south." The surgeon folded his arms over his chest, his chin set at the same stubborn angle as Sheffield's.

In Norton's cabin? How had she not seen the roses when she'd borrowed books the other night? They must have been behind the partition, which she thought hid the infirmary portion of his cabin. Of course the roses would be next to the window, the only source of natural light below decks other than Sheffield's cabin, since the two cabins were side by side at the stern. And heading south, they would only get weak northern light, which even she knew was not sufficient to sustain healthy rose bushes for long.

Big Jim climbed out of the center hatch, setting a small manger stuffed with hay on top of the cover. "Din-din!" he called.

The goats knocked into each other in their hurry to leave the roses for the feast in the manger.

Norton and Big Jim soon went below, Sheffield went to consult with Jonesy at the tiller, and Harriet was left to her own devices to think over all she'd learned so far.

The afternoon proved just as educational as the morning, if not as exciting, since there was no more cannon practice. Luigi extolled the virtues of having dwarf goats at sea—their milk production was much higher per pound of animal than any other goat or cow—because the luxury of milk for their tea boosted the crew's morale. Tucker showed her more sail repair techniques. Chang showed how he kept gunpowder charges, matches, and other supplies separate in the pockets of his apron.

Harriet sat on the starboard step to the quarterdeck, observing the scene after Jonesy had allowed her to ring the watch bell. Bessie, Dusty, and Daisy were resting on the mid-deck hatch cover, basking in the late afternoon sun and chewing their cud. As the larboard watch came above deck, they each gave the goats an affectionate pat before going to their station. Oscar sunned himself on the coiled anchor rope near the rose bushes at the bow, lazily flipping his tail now and then.

How bucolic. She could get used to this.

She went below to eat with the larboard watch. Jack had promised to teach her how to play a new card game. Gambling was not allowed on board, so they played just for fun. So the men said.

The days melded one into another as the weather held fair and the ship made good progress. Harriet spent her days learning everything she could, even how to milk Bessie and Daisy into the pewter mug without spilling anything for Oscar to clean up. Jack and Flynn showed her how to properly belay the ropes after changing the set of the mains'l. She began to notice the subtle shifts in wind and anticipate the commands to adjust the sails accordingly.

One day, she spelled Dieter for an hour on bow watch, perched on the newly replaced jib boom out in front of the bow. Letting her bare feet dangle above the water whooshing past below, she was splashed by waves and quickly dried by the breeze that ruffled her hair. Dolphins swam alongside the ship for a while, their grey heads breaking the surface now and then. One jumped up, bumping her bare foot with its smooth, cool back. She was startled at first, and then laughed when the creature did it again. Holding on to the jib with both hands so she wouldn't lose her balance, she stretched her leg to stroke her toes along its sleek back.

Another day, they sailed past a pod of whales frolicking near the surface. She watched in awe as the majestic creatures, bodies almost as long as the *Wind Dancer,* surged half out of the water, turned, and splashed on re-entry. Others dove down and slapped the surface with their gigantic flukes. Jack, Chang, and Winston, high in the rigging, whooped and hollered, egging on the whales with big arm gestures. Harriet whooped and held on tight to the railing as the whales seemed to oblige, coming so close the ship rolled several degrees when they leaped out of the water and flopped on their backs, creating waves and drenching the deck with spray. One rolled to its side, so near she could almost touch it, its enormous fin flapping as though waving to them.

"Come watch 'em from up 'ere!" Jack called to her.

She tilted her head back to see where he perched, looking as at ease straddling the main tops'l yardarm as he did sitting at the table in the fo'c'sle. Her stomach lurched, and she could only give him a tight shake of her head.

Sometimes she sat on the windlass cover, drowsing in the sun, Oscar the orange tabby purring in her lap, one or more of the goats resting against her like lapdogs, a length of canvas nearby that she would work on when she was fully awake again. She and Tucker had nearly finished replacing the storm-damaged sail.

Jonesy let her throw out the log line and bring it back in, checking their speed and direction and noting it in the logbook. Chang taught her how to fire the three-pound port gun, incorporating her in his place in the intricate dance with Dieter and Winston.

Madame Zavrina would have fainted dead away. Harriet's chest puffed with pride.

And her nights ... Nights were spent in the cabin, with Sheffield only a few feet away. A solid presence, almost magnetic, drawing her toward him. Outwardly he maintained a decorous appearance, the perfect gentleman. But the inner pirate wrapped his arms around her while showing her how to view through the sextant rather than just handing her the instrument. His broad shoulder brushed hers as they marked their progress on the chart and logbook in his cabin, his warm breath ruffling the loose hairs at her nape.

Of course there was a great deal of physical contact between them. Completely innocuous. To be expected, really, in such close confines as the ship.

She chose not to contemplate the fact that the crew barely made even the most incidental contact with her, and apologized profusely if they accidentally bumped her in the companionway or galley. And none of them made goose bumps rise on her flesh, or her breath come faster.

Only Sheffield.

Fifteen days after they left Gravesend and headed into the Channel, Winston on bow watch yelled, "Land ho!"

Harriet froze. She was on the quarterdeck taking a turn at the tiller, Jack at her side since it was his duty this watch, and Sheffield and Bos'n just steps away at the maphouse. She'd known, intellectually, that they were getting close to Corunna by checking the chart several times each day with Sheffield after they'd taken a heading. But after so many days with nothing but endless sea and sky to view, it still came as a shock.

By this time tomorrow, she might have her treasure in hand.

Chapter 9

The coastline began to take shape. The rugged cliffs of Spain rose up from the ocean, a formidable wall that had repelled invaders for centuries. Rocky outcroppings gave way to sheltered coves here and there. Seagulls wheeled overhead in greater numbers with raucous cries. Structures became discernible on the shore and on the hills above the bay of Corunna, and masts of other vessels in port poked the sky, their canvas furled.

It seemed to take forever—tacking back and forth, their forward momentum slowing as more and more sails were furled—but at last the *Wind Dancer* neared her slip on the quay. Jack grabbed a line and nimbly swung down to the dock, caught the line Flynn tossed from the bow, and made it secure on the bollard. They hurried to the stern and repeated the exercise, and the *Wind Dancer* was docked.

Harriet was in Spain.

Well, almost. Her feet were still on the deck. Her bare feet. Her bare shins were visible below her dungarees.

Her heart pounded. How foolish of her not to have thought of how many people there would be at the docks, and changed into proper attire while the ship tacked. Already people were coming toward them. Vendors offering to revictual the ship, women in low-cut gowns to welcome the sailors who'd been at sea for who-knew-how-long, and an officious-looking gent in frothy neckcloth and lacy cuffs carrying a leather folder—probably a customs official. And she was dressed in dungarees and homespun cotton. She'd saved enough hairpins so she could properly dress her hair. Wouldn't take long to brush out the braid and pin it up in a style of which Madam Zavrina would approve.

Sheffield was too busy to button up her dress, even if she had the nerve to ask him. Not the nerve to request his assistance, but to handle her own reaction to him touching her bare skin.

She could stay aboard and let Sheffield go collect their treasure.

The very idea made her recoil.

She bit her bottom lip. She hated being indecisive.

Flynn and Jack were setting the gangboard in place. The rest of the crew hurried to and fro with their various tasks, men from both watches moving in organized chaos, and she tried to stay out of their way.

Jonesy stopped beside her and bent to speak in her ear. "You want to be Miss Chase, or Harry?"

Her mouth fell open in surprise. What?

"Our passenger, Miss Chase, or Harry, the cabin boy. Up to you. But you have to decide right quick."

Young, unchaperoned Miss Chase would be scandalous. Harry could go wherever the rest of the crew went. This must have been how Charlotte became Charlie. "Should Harry wear shoes, or go barefoot like the other tars?"

Jonesy pointed at the rutted, bumpy wreck of a cobblestone road leading away from the docks, up the hill into the city proper. "Doubt that would feel comfortable to walk on barefoot."

Harriet nodded and dashed below decks. Minutes later she was back up top, carefully placed smudges of ash from the brazier darkening her cheeks and chin to disguise her lack of beard and conceal her porcelain complexion, a length of cotton wrapped around her plait just like Jonesy, and wearing scuffed leather shoes with a bit of cotton wadding in the toes so they'd stay on. Her blue plaid waistcoat was buttoned all the way up, her shirt laced up to the collar and tied.

Jonesy gave her a quick, impersonal head-to-toe perusal, and a nod of approval. "The cabin boy would know the Cap'n is about to need the leather folder that's in the bottom left drawer of his desk."

She tugged her forelock and couldn't help a big grin as she said, "Aye," then hurried to collect the folder.

At the railing, Nick had been conversing in Spanish with the customs agent, who still stood on the dock. Both men glanced over as she approached with the folder.

Nick did a double take, then accepted the proffered folder. He stared at her, a raised eyebrow silently asking if she was sure about this. She raised her chin and met his gaze unflinching. He gave a slight shrug. "Go help Winston with the water casks."

Cognizant of the customs official watching, Harriet tugged her forelock and went off to find Winston.

Nick watched her as she walked away, and gave Jonesy a narrowed-eye stare. Jonesy paused on the quarterdeck bottom step, followed Nick's glance at Miss Chase's retreating form, and returned Nick's glare with an innocent, insouciant smile. The customs agent coughed, and Nick turned his attention once more to business.

Harriet waited until she'd reached Winston before allowing herself another big grin.

This could be fun.

Rolling empty water casks, it turned out, was challenging work. She could only imagine how much more difficult they'd be to handle once they were filled. She and Winston and Chang formed a line to pass the casks to the waiting hoist, and she joined in singing the "*heave away, haul away,*" chorus of their work song as they hauled on the line. They'd just lifted the third cask up and over to the dock when Nick tapped her on the shoulder and gestured for her to follow him down the gangboard.

"We're here. Do you know where to go?"

She paused at her second step onto the dock, standing on an immobile surface for the first time in weeks. She fought the need to sway.

Then it hit her. Her father had been here. Perhaps to this very dock. Perhaps he had stood in the very spot she now stood.

She swallowed the rising emotion before it could turn her into a watering pot and took a good look at the portion of town that was visible, comparing the reality before her to the memory of the map her father had drawn and mailed home. The map she had stared at for countless hours, memorizing every line, every stroke. The map that had been stolen.

Was the thief here? Had he reached Spain before them, perhaps already absconding with the treasure? She pointed up the city's main street, to the top of the hill. "Up there. That church was on the map, I'm sure of it. *Iglesia de Nuestra Señora del Dolor.*" Her pronunciation was likely off as she'd never heard it spoken, only seen it on the map. No matter. It was on the map, and the real building was in sight. She could be there within the hour.

Her heart pounded. She clenched her fists to control her trembling.

Sheffield shaded his eyes to view the spire of the church. "This is a nation of Catholics, Mi—Harry. Spain has more churches than my sisters have shoes. How can you be certain that's the same church as on your father's map?"

Harriet froze at hearing Sheffield speak the informal name, and immediately decided she liked it. She shielded her eyes from the bright sun, somehow so much hotter here on land than out at sea, and wished she'd asked Smitty for a straw hat from the slop chest as a bonnet was out of the question. "One way to find out."

"Fair enough." Nick gave the bos'n the signal he was leaving, got the acknowledgment hand signal in return, and he, Miss Chase—no, no, must think of her as Harry for now—and Jonesy headed for the church, pushing their way through the crowded dock area and uphill, where the crowds soon thinned out. There were newly constructed buildings along the street, mixed in with weather-beaten structures, crumbled ruins, and those heavily damaged but still in use that bore silent testimony to the war that had marched through just a few years ago.

Would the treasure have survived? If it existed in the first place. Would it have been stolen by looters once the bombardment stopped?

A soft gasp of dismay beside him brought Nick's thoughts back to the present, and the realization that they'd reached the top of the hill, and the church. Or what remained of it.

Most of the roof had caved in, as had three walls, leaving just enough of two corners of the roof to hold up the spire. Miss Chase—no, Harry—stood with one hand over her mouth, her eyes wide, as she surveyed the damage.

Jonesy let out a low whistle. "Hope the treasure wasn't hidden in the church."

Harry shook her head. "It was hidden with a person, not a place. Papa was worried the fighting would come this way. He and Viscount Sheffield hoped the padre would move it to safety if the need arose."

"They gave the treasure to a padre?" Trust his father to trust a man of the cloth more than his own son.

"Someone who had taken a vow of simplicity, yes."

"What if the padre was in there when, you know..." Jonesy gestured with his hands and made a sound mimicking a cannon ball blasting everything to smithereens.

"Let's find out." Harry turned determinedly toward the nearest structure that still seemed intact and occupied, a house with a sagging roof and shaded patio in front.

Nick put a hand on her shoulder. "Do you speak Spanish?"

"I'm fluent in French and know a smattering of Greek and Latin." Her shoulders drooped. "But hardly any Spanish."

Nick nodded. He walked over to the two elderly men seated outside the front door, playing chess in the shade. "*Hola, señores,*" he called.

"More Englishmen," said the one wearing a faded, dusty black *boina*, slouched low on his forehead.

"Oh, you speak English?" Harry looked like she was going to conduct the interview.

Nick rested his hand on her shoulder again, silently reminding her of appropriate behavior for a cabin boy. She took half a step back.

"*Si*, and we have had much practice today," said the other one, who had a big grey mustache.

"We were hoping you might know what happened to the padre from that church." Nick jerked his thumb over his shoulder. "Father..." Belatedly he realized he didn't even know the name.

"Miguel," Harry interjected. "Father Miguel was serving here in 1811."

The two Spaniards exchanged what Nick thought was an odd look.

"*Si*, he was here. He left when the shelling began. The Frogs came into the harbor and set off their cannons, day and night." The next statement from Boina slipped back into Spanish, a slur on each of the French sailors' parentage, and Nick was glad Harry didn't speak the language. Though given her wide eyes, perhaps she recognized the root words and had figured out the nature of the insult.

"Do you know where Father Miguel went?"

Mustache shook his head. "As soon as he saw the flags on the masts in the harbor, he finished carving the last headstone and left with what he could carry on his horse."

Nick wanted to ask if the priest had any paintings, statuary, or other treasure-like large objects strapped to the horse, but resisted. "He took the time to carve a headstone?"

"*Si*. In the graveyard, behind the church."

Jonesy and Nick started walking toward the graveyard. Harry hung back. "Why have you had much practice speaking English today?"

"You are not the first to ask about Father Miguel," Boina said, sliding his beret further back on his head.

"No one has asked about him for five years," Mustache added, "and today there are four."

Nick and Jonesy abruptly returned, flanking her.

"Three others have asked? Just today?" Nick said.

"*Si*."

Mustache stroked his upper lip. "May have been today. May have been yesterday."

"Or the day before." Boina squinted and tilted his head to one side. "Come to think on it, one of them looked a lot like you," he said to Nick. "But older. Maybe your father?"

Nick felt the words like a blow. Took him a moment before he could draw breath to speak. "My father is dead." He kept his voice flat.

Boina shrugged. "All you English look alike."

Harry stepped forward. "Do you know why these Englishmen asked about Father Miguel, or where they went?"

Boina pointed downhill, toward the marina. "Probably to the cantina. They were very thirsty."

"And dirty," Mustache added.

Jonesy looked toward the marina. "A drink sounds good."

"After we see what the padre carved," Nick said.

Harriet barely heard them, as she was already walking toward the graveyard. "*Gracias, señores*," she called over her shoulder.

Just past the bombed shell of the church, farther up the road, the graveyard stretched for several acres, row after row of headstones in varying degrees of succumbing to the elements and the occasional cannonball crater.

Jonesy looked out over the rolling field in dismay. "How are we going to figure out which headstone the padre carved last?"

"Someone already did." Harriet marched directly to a grave three rows up, four stones over from the edge, her heart pounding, her fists clenching and unclenching in a very unladylike show of anger. She could not have come this far, endured almost drowning in a storm at sea, only for someone else to have taken the treasure before her. No!

"No wonder they were thirsty," Sheffield said, eyeing the recently dug grave. The hole was empty, dirt haphazardly piled beside it.

"So that's it? The treasure is gone?" Jonesy rested a hand on Sheffield's shoulder. "Sorry, Cap'n."

Harriet refused to believe this was the end. Papa meant for *her* to have half the treasure, not some random Englishman. Even one who looked like Sheffield. Then she remembered what the Spaniards had said, or rather not said.

"The *señores* didn't say the Englishmen looked happy when they went to get a drink," Harriet said. "If they'd found the treasure, they'd have been crowing in triumph."

Sheffield dropped to one knee by the headstone, his fingers tracing the carving. "It's a damn clue!"

Harriet knelt next to him, practically shoving him out of the way in her excitement to read the stone.

Chase Langston

1811

May He Rest in Porto

The sun disappeared briefly, and Harriet realized Jonesy was blocking the light as he leaned over her to read the headstone.

Jonesy pushed his queue back over his shoulder when it swung forward. "Odd coincidence, some cove with your da's last name dying right before the padre left town."

Harriet shook her head. "No, no, that's the clue. My father's name, and the viscount's family name. The padre went to Porto and wanted them to follow him."

Sheffield stood and dusted off his knees. "I'm thirsty. Let's go have a drink. *Wind Dancer* will have enough water and stores on board again to leave when the tide turns, and we'll head for Porto." He reached a hand to pull Harriet to her feet. They waved to the two chess players as they walked past.

The cantina was easy to find, with music from two guitarists and a horn player wafting out the open doors and windows, and sailors and women milling around the shaded portico entrance. Sheffield spotted an empty table inside and they sat down, though Harriet gave the stained, scarred chair and tabletop a dubious glance. Conversation in at least half a dozen languages floated through the air along with the scent of several flavors of tobacco smoke. A serving wench greeted them.

"*Tres cervezas, por favor,*" Sheffield requested.

She nodded and left in a swish of skirts and flash of trim ankle.

Harriet coughed, and Sheffield dragged his gaze back to her, not hiding his grin.

She shook her head and tried not to inhale too deeply as she inspected the cantina, looking over every face, listening for English accents.

"Bloody hell," Sheffield growled, barely audible.

Harriet followed his gaze to two men sitting near the bar, their heads almost touching as they studied a document on the table. One had the browned, weather-lined face of someone who had spent decades at sea, dressed in a coat and neckcloth that had once been fine but were due to be handed off to the rag merchant. A captain, perhaps. Certainly not a common sailor.

His companion, a gent in his early thirties or so, clean shaven and hair mussed, would look at home in a London drawing room with his white cravat and lace cuffs peeking from his coat sleeves.

His dirt-smudged cravat, and dusty cuffs. Smudges of dirt marred his blue superfine coat, dusted his aquiline nose and one chiseled cheek.

Harriet sat up straighter. "They're dirty," she whispered, trying to contain her excitement.

Jonesy hit the table with the flat of both his hands. "Great greasy codswallop, that's—" He broke off as Sheffield touched his arm, shook his head. "What's he doing here?" He spat out the word, as though the *he* in question was something Jonesy would scrape off the bottom of his shoe.

Harriet looked between Sheffield and Jonesy. "You know them?"

"We're acquainted with the captain, yes." Sheffield grimaced, his nose wrinkling in disgust. "It's bad, but I didn't think you'd be able to smell him from this distance."

"Dirty. As in, they've been digging." Harriet glanced at the men again. "What are they studying so intently?"

"Your map?"

Harriet worried her bottom lip. "Can't tell from here." She scooted her chair back. "I'll just go have a peek over their shoulders."

Sheffield clasped her wrist, his grasp just firm enough to keep her from standing up. "*I'll* go look. You stay here."

"What if he recognizes you?" Jonesy kept his voice so low that even at this proximity she barely heard him. "Me, he might not remember, but I doubt he'll ever forget or forgive you."

Harriet scooted back to the table. "Why? What did you do that was so terrible?"

Sheffield looked out the front window, ignoring her question, but Jonesy leaned close to Harriet.

"Piloted Cap'n Ruford's ship after smugglers got aboard and commandeered it from him. Their leader didn't know how to sail, so she asked Cap'n here to sail it back to her home port."

Harriet had been listening intently while observing the other men, but one of the words made her whip her head back to stare at Jonesy. "*She*? The smugglers were led by a woman?"

"Oh, aye, indeed."

Harriet turned to Sheffield. "You, an honest merchantman, were consorting with smugglers."

"My friend Tony had expressed interest in purchasing *Wind Dancer* from me," Sheffield said. "As a gift."

"For the lady smuggler," Jonesy interjected.

Sheffield nodded. "Completely above-board transaction. I had no idea until we got there that Tony's lady love was tired of the nonsense from the smuggling captain they'd been dealing with—that cur over there—and had decided to cut him out and take his ship to transport their goods themselves. Tony wanted to give her my ship so she wouldn't steal one, but her gang had already taken over the *Polly Ann* by the time we arrived."

Harriet let that sink in. How ... romantic. "But you have your ship, and the other captain still has his, apparently."

"They reconsidered. Gave back the ship. Sylvia and her gang make cheese now. We had some of it with dinner the other night. Much safer business. And Tony doesn't have to worry about getting seasick."

"Just lovesick," Jonesy said. "Though that will probably ease off now they're shackled."

Harriet raised her brows in silent query.

"They got married in August," Sheffield explained.

The tavern wench set three tankards of beer on the table and left. Sheffield and Jonesy took a long drink each, while Harriet lifted her tankard and sniffed, then took a cautious sip.

Blech. Second sip didn't burn as much. Her throat was still dry so she took a deeper, longer drink.

Ruford and his companion briefly interrupted their heated discussion to signal for another round of drinks.

"We have to know what's on that paper." Harriet pushed back her chair. "As he might recognize either of you, it has to be me." Before either man could object, she made her way through the crowd. Another advantage of being dressed as a lad soon became apparent, because she didn't have to worry about any of the lecherous men she passed pinching her bottom, something the fathers and other male family members visiting the girls at Torquay Academy for Ladies had a troubling tendency to do.

She wended through the tables, ducked under a laden serving tray held aloft by a serving woman with bigger arm muscles than many men, and worked her way toward the bar. She casually walked behind Captain Ruford and his companion, slowing to peer over their shoulders. They were studying a navigational chart of the Iberian Peninsula, and beside that was a smaller, familiar-looking map. She wanted to freeze in shock but forced herself to keep walking, keep breathing, winding through the crowd back to her seat at the table.

"You've gone all white. What is it?" Sheffield reached toward her forearm but rested his hand on the table, just shy of her arm.

"The map. It looks like mine, or the one my father sent me, but it was clearly drawn by a different hand."

Jonesy swore. "There's another copy of the bloody map?"

"I'll hazard a guess that it's my father's version. The map he did not send to me." Harriet heard Sheffield's anger, though his face did not betray any strong emotion.

"The other paper is a navigational chart. I think it shows Spain and Portugal, down to the Strait of Gibraltar."

"They're going to head for Porto," Jonesy said.

"We'll just have to beat them to it." Sheffield drained his mug and slammed it on the table, then dug into his purse and fished out coins of the proper currency and value. He caught the serving wench as she passed, dropped the gold pieces into her hand and curled her fingers around them. "*Gracias, senorita*," he said.

She said something, too soft for Harriet to hear, but Sheffield shook his head, still smiling, and stepped toward the door. Harriet and Jonesy followed.

They were almost out when an angry shout halted them. "You!"

Sheffield looked back into the cantina, as did Harriet and Jonesy.

Ruford was marching toward them, shoving people out of his way. "You mangy cur! What the hell are you doing here?"

"And a good day to you too, sir." Sheffield spun on his heel and went out the door, Ruford still shouting insults at him as he struggled to pass through the crowd. The tables, patrons, and servers unwittingly acted as an obstacle course.

They hurried out to the street and down the hill toward the harbor, Harriet practically running to keep up with Sheffield and Jonesy's much longer strides, again thankful for the freedom of movement allowed by her dungarees.

They were still three hundred feet away from the ship when Sheffield put two fingers to his mouth and gave a loud three-note whistle to catch the attention of the bos'n, who was supervising the loading of crates and barrels. Sheffield raised both hands high and made a gesture that must have indicated they were leaving in a hurry, as the bos'n called out orders and there was an immediate change in the activity of the crew, both on the ship and on the dock, with a new air of urgency.

A now-familiar voice cut through the buzz of conversation among the throng on the docks, casting aspersions on Sheffield's parentage amid other insults. Ruford, with his companion beside him, was heading for a dock on the far side of the harbor.

"We going to race them all the way to Porto, Cap'n?"

Sheffield strode up the gangboard, oblivious to the slight bouncing of the wood that made Harriet dearly wish for handrails. "If need be."

All hands were on deck, working in controlled chaos that she didn't get to see when they had left London. Now she joined in where she could, hauling on a line, wishing she were brave enough to climb the ratline and help unfurl a sail. She listened to Smitty the purser engage in final negotiations with a dock merchant in American-accented Spanish, until the crew started another work song. "*Heave away, haul away*," she joined in the chorus. Tucker led the verse, singing about the charms of a merchant's daughter spilling over her tops'l.

Dieter had not had time to complete repairs on the hastily patched starboard gunwale where the cannon had crashed through, and there were still crates and barrels on the deck to be stowed below. But just moments after coming on board, Sheffield gave the signal to depart. Smitty and Flynn untied the lines on the bollards, and as soon as they were back on deck the gangboard was pulled up and stowed.

Harriet ducked when she heard a loud snap. Ruford obviously had no love for Sheffield, but he wouldn't actually shoot at him, would he?

But it was just canvas filling with wind.

The ship began moving faster, picking up speed as more canvas unfurled and filled. Another ship, a cutter, was moving toward the same narrow channel out of the bay.

"Aye, there be the *Polly Ann*," Jonesy said from his stance on the quarterdeck near the tiller, pointing his chin at the other ship. Ruford's crew was also scrambling aloft, unfurling more of their sails before they cleared the mouth of the bay, traveling at a speed the harbor master would no doubt frown upon. But so was Sheffield's crew. Clearly both had experience at making hasty departures.

Instead of making straight for the harbor mouth, the *Polly Ann* took a port tack, heading directly at *Wind Dancer*. Sheffield and Jonesy steered closer to the cliffs, close enough Harriet saw bird's nests snuggled in the crags. Surely Ruford wouldn't run them aground?

At a signal from Sheffield, Chang left the line he was helping to pull and climbed the quarterdeck steps to the starboard rail. With exaggerated movements, he loaded the swivel gun and aimed for the cutter's single mast.

"Ruford!" Sheffield shouted, his booming baritone voice echoing off the cliff. "Change course or we'll blast your mast into toothpicks!"

Just as Harriet feared they'd need to get the oars out of the longboats to push the *Wind Dancer* away from the cliffs, the *Polly Ann* veered north, toward the mouth of the harbor. As Ruford's ship gained speed, Sheffield gave chase, steering directly behind the cutter as both ships exited the harbor. By the time they were out in the Atlantic, Ruford's ship had slowed to almost nothing, its sails hanging slack.

Having stolen Ruford's wind, the *Wind Dancer* veered hard to port, the tip of the jib boom on the bow missing the *Polly Ann's* stern by mere inches, and *Wind Dancer* sped past, her sails all unfurled and filled.

Ruford shouted more invectives, which Harriet couldn't make out over the sound of *Wind Dancer's* crew singing another work song as they adjusted the sails.

Instead of heading farther out to sea, Sheffield continued to steer *Wind Dancer* hard to port, angling between the mainland and the archipelago sitting just offshore, the craggy islands much too close for Harriet's comfort. Maybe they'd need the oars after all to avoid being dashed on the rocks. She climbed to the quarterdeck where Sheffield was conferring with Jonesy at the tiller.

"Aren't you afraid of wrecking?" she said, gesturing at the narrow channel.

Sheffield shook his head. "We're shallower on the draft. *Polly Ann* can't get through here without tearing up her hull."

Before long they passed the end of the chain of islands and started moving away from the rocks and farther out to sea, southwest by west. They'd just cleared the western edge of the islands when Jonesy shouted, "Ship astern!"

Sure enough, there was the *Polly Ann* bearing down on them. After stealing the cutter's wind to slow it, Sheffield's gambit on the shortcut had gained them the lead by a quarter mile. *Polly Ann* veered to port, coming parallel with the brig's starboard side. Activity at *Polly Ann's* starboard cannon had Sheffield changing course again, heading southwest by south. The crew scrambled to adjust the sails. Harriet jumped in to help.

She heard the boom from the cannon, whistle of the cannon ball, and crack of a yardarm breaking almost as one sound. The yard of the main topgallant fell to the deck a few feet in front of her, its descent slowed by the various halyards, sheets, and tearing of the canvas. Crew members raced to cut it loose and stow it. The swivel guns on the *Wind Dancer* barked a reply.

While belaying a line, Harriet tipped her head back, back, back, to watch Jack and Flynn climb to the very top to secure the remaining bits of the t'gallant sail. Her stomach lurched and she felt lightheaded as she watched them climb higher. Good Lord, how could they bring themselves to climb so high?

Chang and Dieter kept firing the swivel guns. Their small guns couldn't cause nearly the damage that Ruford's three-pounder cannon could inflict, but the *Wind Dancer* was still too close to the cliffs to turn and bring her port cannon to bear.

Another boom, and this time grapeshot spattered the mainsail and topsail. Seconds later another barrage of grapeshot blew more holes in the canvas, then another. Clearly Ruford's crew had also practiced for speed and accuracy.

Chang and Dieter kept firing at the same spot on the single mast of the *Polly Ann*, until with a great groan and splintering sound the top half of the mast fell to the deck and dangled over the rail, the flag dipping into the sea, crew members darting out of the way of the wreckage.

Polly Ann's speed slowed dramatically, but the *Wind Dancer* was also slowing from so much damage to the sails. Holes from the grapeshot continued to widen, ripping the canvas until the big sails were almost useless.

Sheffield called out commands to adjust the remaining sails to take advantage of the wind and minimize the damage they were taking, his powerful voice conveying urgency but not panic. She heard the exhilaration in his tone, as though he was playing a game, with him as a cat and Ruford the mouse.

The crew had been stowing cargo below and bringing up small arms. Harriet began to notice men had stuck pistols through their belts along with pouches of powder and shot. Several now wore a short sword or cutlass or—she suppressed a shudder—a boarding axe. Open crates with grappling hooks and muskets were placed at strategic spots on the deck.

She glanced at Sheffield to gauge his response to the weaponry suddenly on display, and sucked in her breath at the sight of him. His long black hair was whipped by the wind and his greatcoat flapped about his legs, revealing a cutlass thrust through the belt at his waist.

He stood tall, feet shoulder-width apart, one booted foot slightly behind the other, one hand on the tiller. Sunlight glinted off his gold hoop earring.

All her pirate lacked now was an eye patch.

It would be a shame to hide one of his gorgeous blue eyes. A crime if one of them were to be damaged.

He caught her staring and winked at her. His cocky half-smile exuded confidence, and was no doubt the same expression that had enticed numerous women into his bed.

Astonished that he was directing such a blatantly flirtatious look at her, she stifled a laugh, worried that if she gave in to any one emotion, the mix of excitement and fear surging through her veins would turn to hysteria. With great effort, she tore her gaze from him and focused her attention once more on helping to adjust a sail.

A cannonball hit the foremast, shattering a yardarm. Splinters flew. Harriet ducked but felt stings just above her left eyebrow and a couple of spots on her neck. She ignored them and kept hold of the rope, helping to change the direction of the sail as Sheffield maneuvered the ship.

They swung around, parallel with the *Polly Ann*. Chang left the swivel gun that was now on the far side from their opponent, and jumped to the deck. Winston met him at the cannon and they quickly loaded and fired at the *Polly Ann*, aiming for her mainmast.

More grapeshot hit the *Wind Dancer's* mainmast and yardarm above them. Fragments of wood rained down. Winston fell to the deck, his hands covering his eyes, blood seeping between his fingers.

Jack, hauling on the line with Harriet, tilted his head toward his injured shipmate. "I got this," he barked. "Go 'elp 'im to the sawbones."

Harriet let go the rope, her hands feeling on fire, and guided Winston over to the hatch where Norton was waiting on the ladder, just below deck.

Should she go below and assist the surgeon? Or stay in the middle of the fray and help on deck?

With the crew busy controlling the damaged sails, no one was free to help Chang fire the cannon. They had to defend the ship. *She* had to help defend the ship, because if *Wind Dancer* sank, there would be no retrieving the treasure. If there was no treasure, then Mama and Gabriel would be sunk, too.

Two people could return fire much more quickly than one. Harriet had observed and practiced enough that she felt confident she would be more help than hindrance.

She grabbed the rod Winston had dropped and took his place at the cannon.

Chapter 10

Nick saw Winston go down, and watched Harriet guide him to Norton waiting at the aft hatch. She didn't flinch or even seem to notice when he grabbed her arm with his bloody hand.

Good. He had more important things to worry about, like heaving his weight against the tiller to turn the ship quickly. She'd be much safer belowdecks assisting Norton in surgery.

Wait. What in blazes was the chit doing at the port gun?

Nick scanned the deck and rigging and realized no one else was available to assist Chang return fire. Dieter was still inflicting damage with the swivel gun.

Chang loaded and fired. Harriet leaned over the side rail far enough—too far for Nick's comfort—to swab the barrel between shots.

Heaven help them if she missed any embers. Or the ship rolled and she fell overboard. Or...

He had to concentrate on dealing with Ruford. At least the smuggler seemed more intent on inflicting damage to Nick's rigging than to his crew. If Ruford's men aimed the grapeshot lower, Nick's men would be mown down like ninepins.

Chang had time for just a couple more shots before Nick would have to change course again, away from the rocky coast that was already getting too close for comfort. He knew his ship, how low she rode in the water with this much on board in crew and cargo, how tight he could turn her.

More grapeshot hit the foremast t'gallant and mains'l. At this rate, he'd soon have nothing left but the flying jib. "Hit her just below the water line," he shouted to Chang.

That should slow the *Polly Ann* enough that he could get out of range of her guns. His crew was good, but so was Ruford's, and *Polly Ann's* two three-pounders could do far more damage than his swivel guns and single three-pounder. He had no interest in capturing or sinking her; he just wanted to beat her to Porto, beat Ruford to the treasure.

Wind Dancer shuddered as a cannon ball struck amidship below the water line, just as Harriet leaned over to swab the barrel. Her torso was out over the water, past the tipping point, one leg in midair. She dropped the rod on the deck as she grabbed for the railing to keep from going over. Nick fought the need to jump to her rescue. He couldn't let go the tiller. Many more lives were at stake than one bold miss out where she didn't belong.

Chang lunged and grabbed Harriet by the ankle that was waving in the air. He wasn't much bigger than Harriet, but he was tenacious in his grip. The ship righted, balance shifted, and they both thumped to the deck on their arses. They jumped up and resumed preparing to fire as though nothing had happened. Harriet did wipe her face with her forearm after she swabbed. Well, sure, anyone would sweat a bit after that.

Nick exhaled a deep breath, puffing out his cheeks, now conscious of the sweat trickling down his own back. That he was more worried about her than he was any member of his crew was simply because she was inexperienced and untrained, thrusting herself into the action when she should be sheltering below deck. He refused to examine his feelings any further.

Both ships slowed from the damage they'd inflicted on each other, and gradually moved out of each other's firing range. Nick resumed course south for Portugal. He had every scrap of canvas unfurled on every yard that could still stand the strain, trying to put more distance between them and the *Polly Ann*.

"We'll need to put in for repairs soon, Cap'n," Jonesy said, eyeing their ragged sails and splintered yards. "Squall comes up, we'll be floundering with nothin' but kindling and rags."

Nick had already selected a chart from the maphouse and was comparing the rocky coast on their port side to the chart. "Here," he said, jabbing his finger at a spot on the map. "We should be able to reach this cove before dark. Nice sandy beach, forest comes up practically to the water's edge. Ought to be safe there while we work."

Jonesy peered at the chart. "Methinks we've been here before, aye? Just enough of a bend to go 'round getting into the cove, Ruford will sail right past without seeing us."

Nick scanned the horizon behind them. No sign of the *Polly Ann*. "If he hasn't already put in somewhere. Chang hit at least one below her water line. She was riding low last I got a good look." So was the *Wind Dancer*.

Jonesy stayed at the tiller while Nick jumped down to the deck to inspect the damage to his ship. He wanted to check Harriet, see how she fared after her first sea battle. After his first, his hands had been shaking so badly he'd nearly chipped a front tooth bringing a bottle of rum to his mouth for a bracing drink.

There she was, hauling on the line to set the bow sprits'l. Her contralto voice joined with the men's baritone and tenor in their work song, her face split in a big grin.

Well. Maybe she wouldn't want a sip of rum to calm her nerves after all.

Jonesy had things under control on deck, so Nick went below. Big Jim and Luigi were working the bilge pump. Dieter and Bos'n had hammered boards into place over the hole and were stuffing rags around the cracks to further slow the leak. Nick gave them a curt nod, then continued to Norton's cabin. Winston lay stretched out on the table, his long, beaded braids dangling over the edge, a swath of bandages wrapped around his head completely obscuring the upper left third of his face.

"He'll live," Norton said, tossing a handful of bloody cloths into a basin. "Too soon to know about his eye, though."

Nick walked around the table to Winston's right side, not surprised to see the crewman was still conscious. "You're a good man, Winston. Strong." He rested his hand on the sailor's shoulder. "And you've got the best surgeon in the Navy tending to you."

Norton sputtered in protest—his distaste for the Navy was as strong as Nick's—and Nick winked at him. Norton harrumphed and resumed cleaning up the surgery.

Winston lifted a hand, and Nick grabbed it. "Da miss, Cap'n." He swallowed hard, pushing down the pain. "Da Maiden o' Sea."

Nick squeezed Winston's hand. "She's fine. Miss Chase is helping with the sails and learning Tucker's least bawdy chants."

"Helped me. She's a good one, mon."

"Yes, she is," Nick replied, surprised by the sudden welling of an unfamiliar emotion in his chest. He didn't want to examine it. He rested Winston's hand on his belly and tugged the blanket higher on him. "Rest now. We're putting in for repairs and we'll need all hands tomorrow."

Winston nodded once, and his eye slid closed.

Norton looked at him closely, saw Winston's chest rising and falling steadily. "I'll be up top soon, see if anyone else needs tending."

Nick grunted in reply and went to tend his injured ship.

A couple of hours later they were tacking into the little bay Nick had picked out, one they'd used as a respite at least once before. There were fish in the bay, wild boar up the hill in the forest, fresh clean water from a waterfall, and timber aplenty. The sandy beach was ideal for carrying out repair work.

At nearly low tide when they arrived, Nick beached the *Wind Dancer*. High tide would float her out, and beaching her made it easier to work on patching the hole in her hull.

Luigi and Big Jim started hauling cookware and other galley items to the beach and building a fire, while Chang went up the hillside, hunting. Bos'n and Dieter were already sorting through the lumber in the hold for new yardarms and patch material for the hull, while Smitty and Jack took a turn working the pumps. Jonesy had the lads bringing down the splintered yards and the rest of the torn canvas. Tucker was inspecting and clucking over the damaged fabric. So many holes, Nick doubted any of it was salvageable.

Miss Chase was in the thick of it, hauling on a line beside Flynn. Her arms trembled as she reached up again. Nick drew her aside. It was the first chance he'd had to speak with her since they'd left the harbor at Corunna, and he couldn't wait a moment longer.

She was a mess. Frizzy hair had escaped her braid and clouded around her face, soot marred one cheek and the tip of her nose, sweat dripped down her temples, and ... and was that blood?

"Yes, Captain?" She looked at him expectantly.

"You're hurt," was all he could manage, his heart lodged in his throat. He fished a kerchief from his coat pocket and swiped at the drops of blood on her temple. He showed her the stained cloth.

"Oh." She took a few breaths. "I'm not even sure that's mine. I was near Winston when he, uh, was injured." She pointed at the bloody smears on her sleeve, vaguely finger-shaped, and gulped. "This is his blood. I haven't been below deck. Is he, uh, did he...?"

"He's asleep in Norton's surgery." Miss Chase had been shaking when Nick first took her arm, and somehow it must be contagious because now he detected a tremble in his own hand as he plucked a toothpick-sized splinter from just below her ear. A drop of blood welled at the spot. Nick pressed his kerchief to it with one hand and showed her the bloody splinter with his other. "You *are* hurt."

She reached her hand to touch her neck in surprise, connecting with his hand instead. She didn't immediately drop it. Nick dropped the kerchief and turned his hand so he could clasp her fingers, and drew her hand to his mouth for a courtly kiss to her knuckles. She smelled of gunpowder and hemp.

Her lips formed a silent "*Oh*."

Nick was trembling, and the only cure was to touch his mouth to hers in a kiss. Gentle, soft, barely more than a brush of lips and sharing breath. Still holding her left hand with his right, he reached with his left to caress her cheek, slide down to her neck, swipe his thumb over her pulse point. He returned to that spot over and over to feel the reassuring beat of her heart. Her fingers, so small and delicate, curled tight around his.

Dimly he registered that she flattened her free hand against his chest.

He'd overstepped the bounds. He was about to move back, relinquish her lips, when she fisted his shirt and tugged him closer.

What could a man do but comply?

She tasted of sunshine and jasmine tea. Delicate. Subtle. Shy, even. He wanted to teach her. Her talent was raw, unjaded, and gaining in enthusiasm.

Enthusiastic. Yes, he was all for eagerness. So nice. He was going to wrap her in his arms and never let go, hold her close, coax all her passion, all her attention, onto him.

Close.

His men were close.

Jonesy called to Flynn, just steps away, and Nick came to his senses.

He broke off the kiss. He was several inches away before Miss Chase opened her eyes, and they suddenly widened. Color suffused her cheeks, but she kept her gaze locked with his, a look of wonder on her face, her lips still slightly parted.

"I'm glad you're all right." Nick's voice was gravelly by the time it emerged past the emotion clogging his throat. "No serious injury."

"No," she said slowly, her voice barely audible. "Nothing serious."

Abruptly she stepped away and returned to helping Flynn.

Nick slapped himself on the forehead.

He walked aft, stopped just short of the quarterdeck steps, and leaned over the rail. The waves were small and uniform this close to shore, so calm compared to his racing thoughts and inconvenient raging desire.

Just the thing. He kicked off his shoes, shucked off his coat, unbuckled his cutlass, and jumped into the bay.

Submerging in cold water finished bringing Nick to his senses. He pushed off from the sandy bottom, came up for a breath, then dove under to swim along the *Wind Dancer*, inspecting her hull.

Damn Ruford for hurting his ship.

Damn Miss Chase for being such a delightful kisser.

* * *

The fire on the beach was roaring, built up again after burning down to coals to roast a wild boar earlier. Harriet sat on a log drawn up to the fire pit, between Jack and Flynn, finishing her plate of boar. The meat was delicious, a succulent cross between beef and pork, and she realized she was focusing on the mundane subject of a dish she'd never eaten before rather than the fact that just hours ago she'd brazenly kissed a man. On his mouth. For the first time, ever. Her first kiss.

And the man she'd kissed was not her intended husband.

Fortunately, the sun had set long ago. In the dodgy light from the lanterns and the fire, no one noticed the way color flooded her cheeks at random moments.

Moments like when she recalled Sheffield's caress to her cheek and neck, and how much she enjoyed it. Wanted him to do it again.

Or when she thought about his mouth, his lips. On hers. Unexpectedly soft lips for a man who spent so much time at sea out in the weather, not chapped at all. Inviting. That wonderfully mobile, expressive mouth, at turns aggravating and humorous, that could make her knees weak.

How the kiss felt even better than she had imagined it would. Her imagination was a poor substitute for reality.

And it could never happen again. She was going to marry Percy.

Kissing another man once was good. It gave her a reference point.

When Percy finally kissed her and took her in his arms, she'd have something to compare it to, to know she was making the right decision. She'd know what she was giving up and what she was getting.

And she was absolutely done blushing over the matter.

Plus, she was sure the kiss meant nothing to Sheffield. She'd seen the way he looked at the senorita who had flirted with him at the cantina earlier today. If they'd had more time, she was certain he'd have availed himself of more than a *cerveza.*

Like so many things on this journey, the kiss was a valuable experience to have had, knowledge gained.

And like the battle they'd fought this afternoon, no need to ever do it again.

Smitty persuaded her she wouldn't like the sand fleas if she slept on the beach near the fire, as some of the crew were doing, so she reluctantly headed to Sheffield's cabin. She'd caught only glimpses of him since their kiss, with him busy overseeing the repairs. He'd barely taken the time to grab a plate of food before climbing back aboard the tilted ship.

When they saw how much repair work there was to do, they'd set the anchor so the high tide wouldn't move them too soon. Harriet managed the climb down to the cabin without losing her balance, and stared at the bunk in dismay. Even if she switched which end she put her head, she'd still practically be standing up. Maybe even slide off the bunk during the night.

Perhaps the sand fleas wouldn't be so bad.

Then she spotted the hammock coiled on its hook.

Perfect.

* * *

Nick debated sleeping on the beach, decided he didn't want to end up scratching, and went to his cabin. His hammock would compensate for the tilt of the beached ship.

He stared at the hook for several heartbeats before he registered the fact that not only was the hammock uncoiled and the other end hooked up, the hammock was already occupied.

The ropes creaked as Miss Chase shifted in her sleep. She'd wrapped herself in a blanket, though one foot poked out, pale pink toes visible in the flickering light from the lantern she'd left lit over the table, the wick turned low. She'd folded his red and black plaid blanket neatly at the foot of the bed, which now angled up. Too steep an angle even for him to sleep in.

He stared down at her freshly scrubbed face, no trace of soot or blood left behind, and yearned to run the pad of his thumb over her lush bottom lip. Trace his fingers over her cheekbones, stroke her soft lashes.

What the hell had possessed him to kiss her this afternoon in the first place, and right in front of his men?

And why did he so desperately want to do it again?

He thought back to the pretty serving wench at the cantina today, and the invitation she'd offered. He'd been flattered yet completely uninterested, and not just because he was hot on the trail of the treasure his father didn't want him to have. Even if they had stayed in port longer to revictual, he wouldn't have gone upstairs with her.

His hand reached toward Miss Chase's cheek, seemingly of its own volition. He caught himself just in time and swerved to pull the blanket over her exposed foot instead.

It wasn't just lust. Certainly she was more attractive, physically, than he'd first thought when they'd been introduced at the Hartwell's ball. She was more like a fresh rosebud rather than a showy rose in full bloom like Lady Slavin. But it was more than physical.

He'd dived into the Channel to rescue her when she was still new to him. Back then he'd admired her gumption, her tenacity. Today she'd jumped in to help defend the ship after Winston was injured. She hadn't recoiled when the Jamaican put his bloody hands on her—had even helped him below—and when she came back and started helping Chang, she'd almost gone overboard again. Nick's heart had been in his throat until her arse hit the deck, safe.

And then he'd seen the blood on her temple, on her neck. A close call to a serious injury. Or worse. And he'd had to reassure himself that she was fine, mingling their breath, tasting her in a kiss. He wanted to cradle her in his arms and protect her. Kiss her until she moaned in pleasure.

What was wrong with him?

He loved women. Long Meg or Pocket Venus, so thin he could span their waist with his hands or plump as a Christmas pudding, skin pale as cream or dark as coffee, and everything in between. Their curves, their soft skin, soft voices. Their soft hands, all over him. Pleasuring him as he pleasured them. A satisfying interlude, nothing more, before he moved on to his next adventure, next task, next comely lass.

He loved women, plural.

Not one woman, singular.

They should reach Porto in less than a week. With any luck, they'd beat Ruford to the treasure and be on their way back to England with it within a fortnight, and he and Miss Chase would go their separate ways.

Why did that prospect not give him a feeling of satisfaction?

He left his cabin in search of another hammock, shaking his head.

It wasn't just his ship that tilted crazily.

Chapter 11

Harriet felt she was in the way of the men working on deck the next morning. She'd helped Big Jim milk the goats and stake them out on a patch of grass near the beach, and then looked for something useful to do. She eyed the men climbing the rigging, standing on the footropes, removing the shredded mainsail.

Jack waved for her to come up. With her gaze, she traced the path he'd taken to get to his precarious perch, across ropes that hung over the water. She'd have to swing over the railing to climb up. To work beside him, she would have to stand on a rope barely thicker than her thumb, suspended eighty feet above the tilted deck and shallow water below. The bottom of her stomach dropped out and her heart skipped three beats. Breakfast threatened to make a reappearance.

She shook her head.

Jack shrugged and went back to work.

She stared at the surf rolling ashore until the gentle rhythm and lulling sound steadied her pulse. What work *could* she do?

Winston came out to the beach and sat on the sand, his back braced against the log near the fire pit, with coils of rope and a pouch full of sewing supplies beside him. He tilted his head this way and that while he worked, adjusting to seeing with only one eye. A bandage still covered the upper left third of his face, the white linen a stark contrast to his ebony skin.

Harriet sat on the log to peer over his right shoulder. "You're sewing rope?"

"Whippin' da ends so dey don't fray, miss." He held up the rope in his hand so she could see the neat rows of thread wrapping around the ends of the strands. "Den we marry da short pieces to get a long one."

Standing on a rope eighty feet above the deck was impossible but sewing she could do. She found Smitty, explained what she wanted to do, and they went below to the slop chest.

"If you're working with rope, you'll need these, miss." Smitty held up a marlinspike in one hand and a leather pouch for it in the other. She'd noticed how the crewmen all had a similar pouch slotted through the belt around their waist—even if said belt was just a length of rope—and a thin rope tying the spike to the pouch. If the spike wasn't tied, Jack had explained, and you dropped it while working with it, it could injure someone on deck and or fall into the sea.

Supplies in hand and tied around her waist, she settled on the beach near Winston to learn how to splice rope.

* * *

"I'm sorry, Tucker. We don't have time to stay here while you mend all these." Sheffield stood at the bow of the brig, close to the beach, surveying the torn and shredded sheets spread across the deck.

"Ach, no, Captain," Tucker said, his hand to his heart. "You dinna mean..."

"I do." Sheffield raised his voice. "Bring up the spare set of sails! All of 'em!"

At the chorus of groans and curses from the crew, Harriet looked up from the rope she was splicing. Soon the crew was hoisting crates up from the hold. Her legs were going numb from sitting in the same spot so long, so she left the rope with Winston and climbed aboard to help Tucker, Chang, and Jack fold the damaged sails out of the way. The watches had kept working their regular shifts, engaged in repairs instead of setting sails. They had already removed and replaced all the damaged yardarms.

"And 'ere I was 'oping we'd never 'ave to use the spares," Jack lamented as he and Harriet grasped the edges of the remains of a sail and folded it like a bed sheet.

"Why?" Harriet asked. "What's wrong with the spare set?"

"Ach, lass, 'tis a crime." Tucker placed the folded sheet on the growing pile of canvas, gave it a gentle pat, and they started folding another.

"We was carrying a load of beetroot when the Frenchies got us with a lucky shot well below the water line," Jack said. "Ball busted open several crates, includin' the spare sails. Beets went everywhere, rolling around in the water what was pouring in the 'ole in the side."

"Last year I begged the Old Man to replace them, but he said it ain't in the budget, and this year is even worse." Tucker heaved a great sigh as Jonesy wrenched open the first crate.

When they'd stowed all the damaged canvas, Harriet went back to sitting cross-legged on the beach, splicing rope. She knew how to repair a sail but nothing about hanging one, so she stayed out of the crew's way, and watched the men install the spare sails.

Soon she understood the men's reluctance, the groans, the curses. She put her hand over her mouth to stifle her laughter.

Every sail was pink.

Speckles, spots, spatters. Stripes along what had been folded edges. Every sail was stained from the beets. Some places the pink was a pale rose, others it was a rich burgundy, with every shade in between. Some patches were clear, places that had been deep within the folds, while others were solid pink in varying intensity.

"Glad you find my crew's discomfort amusing," Sheffield said as he seated himself on the log, his knee close to her shoulder.

"I'm sorry, it's just..." She took a deep breath to stifle a giggle. Which made her inhale Sheffield's scent. She closed her eyes as he slipped down to sit on the sand beside her and opened them in time to see him reach across her lap for the rope she'd been working on.

He gave it a tug, testing the strength, checked how smoothly she'd woven in the first three ends of the long splice, the neatly whipped ends barely visible. Marry the rope wrong, lumpy and uneven, and it would get hung up in the block and tackle. Worse than useless. Winston had her take it apart and start over twice before declaring she'd got it right. She felt a swell of pride when Sheffield gave her an approving nod and gave it back.

"Just what?"

"Just the most inconsistent dye job I think I've ever seen." She waved a hand at the nearest blotchy pink sail. "No woman worth her bonnet ribbons would leave fabric looking like that."

Sheffield stroked his chin. "You think we ought to boil up a big trough of beets and finish the job? Do them up right and solid?"

Harriet laughed at the image his words conjured. "I think Tucker would keel over with an apoplexy if you made them solid pink."

Sheffield tipped his head to one side, watching his crew hoist the pink splattered mainsail into place, and glanced at the pained expression clearly visible on Tucker's face, even from this distance. "You're probably right." He patted her on the knee and went back up to the deck.

Harriet stayed immobile, feeling the warm imprint of his hand on her knee. What was that about? Had he interpreted her brash action yesterday in kissing him as giving him permission to touch her? Not that she was certain she minded.

She wasn't sure if he'd come to his cabin last night. The lantern had burned out this morning rather than being blown out. His blanket was still folded neatly on the bunk. Had he found another hammock elsewhere to sleep in? He didn't seem upset today that his usual hammock hadn't been available. Perhaps he'd slept on the beach. He didn't have the dark circles under his eyes of one who had not slept at all.

No matter. Once they finished repairs and the ship was afloat again, they'd be on their way to Porto and she and Sheffield would return to their usual sleeping arrangements. She would do everything she could to help out the crew and speed up the process. They had to beat Ruford and his companion to the treasure.

Sheffield emerged from the hatch carrying a plank tucked under his arm and headed for the quarterdeck. Jonesy noticed him and joined him at the railing. "We going incognito, Cap'n?"

Her curiosity piqued, Harriet climbed to the quarterdeck as well. The plank Sheffield carried had the name *Dawn Cinder* painted in fancy script in yellow letters outlined in black, on a blue board that had a metal loop at each end. With a start, she realized it would blend in with the blue hull of the ship, at least from a distance, and look like it was painted on.

"There's a good chance we're going to pass Ruford on our way to Porto," Sheffield said. "I'd like to make it more difficult for him to recognize us."

Harriet leaned over the stern railing far enough to see two hooks already in place, one at each end of the ship's name. She'd never noticed them before when throwing out or bringing back in the ship's log line to check their speed. "It looks like you've done this before."

Sheffield grabbed the waistband of her dungarees and hauled her back up. "A time or two."

"Why *Dawn Cinder*?" My, he was getting familiar with her person. But Harriet had indeed been in danger of overbalancing, and even though the bay was shallow and the weather mild, she had no desire to go swimming.

"Has to be the same number of letters and spaces, miss," Jonesy said.

Sheffield retrieved two gaff hooks from their spot under the railing. "Superstition—or tradition, however you want to view it—requires that you never give a ship a name that challenges the power of the sea, and you keep the same number of letters if you rename her. However temporarily." He held out one of the gaff hooks. "Want to help?"

Jonesy took the other hook, and Sheffield showed her how to hook the rings on the plank. In unison she and Jonesy lowered the board into position and slipped the plank onto the hooks below. She tried to concentrate on lining up the metal ring on her side to the waiting hook at just the right angle, and not on the heat of Sheffield's hand hovering at the small of her back. Just in case.

"What happens if it falls off while you're at sea?" Harriet straightened too quickly and saw stars for a moment. "If there's a storm or something?"

Jonesy took her gaff hook and stowed them both.

"We have others," Sheffield said.

"Should we do any painting, Cap'n?"

Sheffield gestured at the stained sails. "I think that's enough of a color change," he said over his shoulder, already stepping down to the main deck, off to the next task.

By the next watch change the tide was turning. Sheffield declared they could finish the rest of the repairs while they were underway. The crew hustled to get the goats and everything from the beach back on board, the fire doused and the ashes spread, all traces of their presence brushed away by a leafy tree branch.

Big Jim, Flynn, Jack, and Dieter waded into the surf, pushing the ship in time with the waves, until they had her turned and floating enough to maneuver. When the water became too deep for the men, Harriet joined in hauling on the line to bring them aboard. Within the hour they were out of the bay and on the open sea, following the cliffs of Spain south to Porto.

The next morning, Harriet sat on deck with Oscar on her lap, taking a break from splicing rope because the cat wanted to play with the strands. The goats rested on the hatch cover chewing their cud, and the rose bushes were soaking up sun near the foremast. Winston sat near the windlass, also repairing rope, as was Tucker. Sheffield had declared it more important to repair the lines before attempting to patch the sails.

"Ship ahoy, starboard bow," Flynn called from his perch on bow watch.

Harriet set Oscar on the hatch and hurried to lean over the starboard railing, shading her eyes from the sun. She could barely see the top of a mast in the distance, so she went up to the quarterdeck.

"She's limping along," Sheffield said, handing the spyglass to Jonesy. "He must not have a replacement for the mast Chang shot in half. Looks like they kept going last night."

"We going to pass her on our port side?" Jonesy handed the spyglass to Harriet.

Now she could see the *Polly Ann*. Ruford's ship had all the canvas they could get on what remained of the cutter's single mast. *Wind Dancer* had a full complement of sails unfurled on her mainmast and foremast, and was traveling faster.

If they passed her on the port side, *Wind Dancer* would have a cannon to bear. Though Dieter and Bos'n had repaired the gunwale where the starboard cannon crashed through, the only ordnance they had on that side was the swivel gun. To pass *Polly Ann* on their port side, they'd have to change their tack.

Sheffield shook his head. "That will raise suspicions. He should already be able to see us." He leaned over the quarterdeck railing and spoke quietly to Dieter. "Tell Winston and Chang to get below."

"*Jawohl, Kapitän.*"

Moments later, Winston, Chang, and the roses disappeared down the forward hatch.

Sheffield took back the spyglass and stared at the *Polly Ann* again, then cast a considering glance at the pink sails, then Harriet. "How would you like to be captain for an hour?"

Harriet's mouth fell open in shock.

Jonesy called Smitty over. "Take Miss Chase and get her kitted out fit for a female captain."

"And don't dawdle," Sheffield added. "You're her first mate."

Smitty's grin practically split his face. "Aye, sir!"

In a blur, Smitty escorted her to the slop chest, calling for Tucker to help them. The men rummaged through the crates of fabric while Harriet loosened her plait, finger-combed her hair, and put it up into a chignon with the hair pins she'd denied herself days ago. She took off her rope belt and put the marlinspike back in its chest. Tucker pinned a length of dark blue velvet around her waist in a makeshift skirt, hiding her dungarees and bare shins, and gave it a few basting stitches to keep it in place.

Smitty handed her a floral-embroidered handkerchief, a yard of frothy lace to tuck into her neckline, and a wide-brimmed chip straw bonnet. The bonnet's feather had seen better days. Tucker stuck a pin in it to keep it upright. She kicked off her canvas shoes and put on a pair of pearl-studded dancing slippers that were too small for her to actually dance in, and unearthed a generously sized shawl in light green wool to wrap around her shoulders and hide her still decidedly masculine shirt and waistcoat.

Smitty put on a jacket of blue superfine. The sleeves were a little too long and the jacket fit so loose he was able to shrug into it by himself. It was similar to Jonesy's attire—slightly better than the deckhands, not as fine as the captain's. Like her transformation, it would never pass muster in a drawing room but should be good for a spyglass viewing. Smitty locked up and they rushed toward the ladder.

Word had passed through the crew about the subterfuge. Luigi stepped out of the galley as they passed. "*In bocca al lupa, Signorina Capitano.*" He tugged his forelock, smiling.

It took Harriet a moment to translate his wish for good luck. "*Grazie*," she replied, and gathered her skirt up and out of the way to navigate the steps.

As she got her balance on the deck and twitched her skirt back into place, Jack swung by on his way up the ratline. He tugged his forelock and murmured "Cap'n," his eyes twinkling, before he began to climb.

Big Jim ushered the goats past her down into the hold. "Cap'n," he said, tugging his forelock, grinning.

Sheffield had climbed down from the quarterdeck and patted Smitty on the shoulder. "Let's hear some Cajun."

"Aye, sir."

Sheffield turned to Harriet and tugged his forelock as well before going below deck. "Take good care of her, Captain Harriet," he said quietly before he went down the ladder.

Later she'd reflect on how hearing him utter her given name for the first time had sounded like a caress. For now Harriet climbed the steps to the quarterdeck, where Bos'n was at the tiller, and took her place by the maphouse. Butterflies fluttered in her stomach, unaffected by the reassurance of having the second mate directly behind her.

"You'll do right fine," he said in his raspy whisper voice.

The stories told in the fo'c'sle said his windpipe had been crushed in a dockside tavern brawl, over a card game or a woman, depending on who told the tale. In charge of the larboard watch, he didn't seem handicapped by not being able to raise his voice. He used hand signals or specific whistles to communicate commands to the crew.

She knew Sheffield and Jonesy were not far. Bos'n could see what she saw and whisper guidance as needed.

She unclenched her fists to rub her palms on her smooth velvet skirt. "We're doing this," she whispered. "I can do this."

She took the spyglass from the maphouse and checked their position relative to the *Polly Ann*. They'd come much closer while she was getting dressed. She couldn't see people on deck unaided yet, though the short mast made it obvious the cutter had suffered damage.

She glanced around at the crew on *Wind Dancer's* deck and up in the rigging and noticed the smiles. Their anticipation, their excitement, was almost tangible. Flynn actually rubbed his hands together when he grinned at her.

With a shock, she realized they were enjoying this. They'd engaged in this kind of subterfuge, or something like it, before. Their glee was infectious. The butterflies in her stomach flew upward, making her giddy. She stifled a hysterical giggle.

The forward hatch cover slid open. Jonesy was just visible on the ladder.

Smitty took his spot by Harriet at the maphouse and shot her a big grin. "*Laissez les bon temps rouler*," he said loudly in a broad accent.

The sentence didn't follow French grammar rules so it took her a moment to understand the Cajun idiom. "Let the good times roll indeed," she replied.

By now she could see Ruford at *Polly Ann's* wheel. Which meant he could also see her.

"Do we need to make any changes?" she asked Smitty, gesturing at the pink spotted sails. "How close are we going to be when we pass them?"

He took a look through the spyglass. "About a hundred yards, Mi— uh, Captain. If we make any changes now, it will look suspicious."

In nautical terms, a hundred yards was like passing another pedestrian on the street.

"Steady on course," Sheffield said softly from the aft hatch. He was on the ladder, his head just below the deck.

Harriet took a deep breath and released it, then repeated the exercise. She fingered the good luck charm her father had sent her, the silver H pendant on its chain around her throat.

Should she greet the other captain? On long voyages it was common to stop and chat when meeting at sea, the captains to even share a meal together before going on their way. And if Norton was to be believed, exchange books to read. Obviously that was not going to happen today. She decided she'd choose her actions based on what Ruford did.

The laughter caught her by surprise. Shouldn't have, as that had been her own reaction upon seeing the pink-speckled sails. Ruford's crew pointed and laughed. Harriet stiffened her spine, surprised that it bothered her to have other people laughing at her ship.

She also realized the breeze had stiffened, and an offshore wind was pushing them closer to the *Polly Ann*.

"Now, Bos'n?" she said quietly.

"Aye, Cap'n." He spoke the commands to Smitty, who in turn instructed the crew to adjust the mainsail and other sheets in his broad American accent. Flynn, Big Jim, and Jack hustled to make the changes. Chang had gone below with Winston, as it was too distinctive to have Chinese and Jamaican crew on a ship flying the British flag. Ruford or his men may have noticed them during their previous encounter.

"I'm surprised Sheffield didn't run up an American flag and make you temporary captain," she said, keeping her voice low. "Or don't you have one aboard?"

Smitty gave her a sly grin.

Harriet couldn't help returning his grin. "We have a flag aboard for every nationality in the crew, don't we?"

"And every language spoken fluently, aye."

Harriet went back to watching their approach to the *Polly Ann*, wondering what other tricks she'd learn her wily pirate had up his sleeve.

By now, amidst the laughter she could hear *Polly Ann's* crew joking and shouting insults. Wondering if the lady captain's crew wore pink-spotted drawers. Insults that questioned her crew's masculinity and choice of bed companions. While her crew kept quiet, keeping their accents and native tongues a secret, they had no reticence in offering rude gestures to the sailors on the *Polly Ann*.

When they had pulled even, Ruford doffed his hat and bent over double with laughter.

"Are you in need of assistance, Captain?" she called, her voice dripping with sweetness and concern. "It appears your ship has taken a beating." The *Polly Ann's* mainmast ended as a jagged stump above the mains'l. A crude patch of boards on the port side was visible off and on as the *Polly Ann* rolled with the swells. Dieter and Bos'n had made a much neater patch on *Wind Dancer*, Harriet thought, even painted to match the hull.

Ruford abruptly straightened and put his tricorne hat back on with far more force than necessary, its tall feather quivering. "Thank you for your concern, madam," he replied, his voice stiff. "But I do not require help from the likes o' you."

"Suit yourself." She waved her handkerchief at him as the *Dawn Cinder* began to pull ahead.

"Take care, madam, that you not fall prey to the pirates that roam these seas," Ruford called. "Dangerous ruffians, they be."

"I shall take your warning to heart, good sir." Harriet faced her bow, unable to keep a straight face any longer. "Do warn me if you see any such ruffians," she said to Smitty.

"Aye, Cap'n."

Behind her, Bos'n snorted with laughter.

Chapter 12

Nick decided to let Miss Chase play at captain until they could no longer see any of the *Polly Ann's* mast. Confident Jonesy and Bos'n had everything in hand while he waited below deck for the ships to pass, Nick took the opportunity to eat a meal sitting down in the fo'c'sle, his back against the bulkhead, his legs stretched out on the bench. He stared at Chang and Winston in their hammocks, catching a nap while they couldn't be on deck, and practiced walking a coin across the back of his left hand.

It wasn't long, though, before Nick had to poke his head up through the hatch to scratch his itch to be in the middle of things. Miss Chase went through all the tasks he would have done—throwing out the log line to check their speed, using his sextant to take a fix on their position when the clouds parted, and entering the data in his logbook in her precise hand that put his penmanship to shame. She'd performed these tasks before, of course, at his side, when he'd thought she was peppering him with questions, the teacher studying a new subject, merely to stave off boredom.

But on their voyage she'd barely touched the books she'd borrowed from Norton, the fictional tales of romance and adventure. Instead, she pored over Nick's books on navigation, on seamanship.

Watching her at the helm beside Bos'n, her shoulders back and chin up, Nick's chest felt tight, a bit congested, and gradually he identified the odd sensation as pride in the way she was handling herself. Her voice had been steady when chatting with Ruford, and how brazen was *that* conversation? His *pequeño wren marrón*, little brown wren, was turning out to be a peacock. Peahen. Whatever.

Maybe she enjoyed partaking in amateur theatricals at home, or back at the academy where she'd taught? When they were younger, his sisters were forever staging one play or another, though Nick had thought they were mainly for the entertainment value of ordering around him and the neighboring boys.

Several times Miss Chase and Smitty compared notes between the chart and the coast visible off the port side. Offshore winds this close to land required frequent adjustment to stay on course. Each time he began to think it was time to correct, he'd hear the commands called to adjust the sheets, keeping them on course.

The bell rang to signal the change of watch, and Miss Chase appeared at the top of the hatch.

"It's getting dark," she called down. "We can no longer see any of Ruford's ship, just his lanterns."

Nick stepped aside as his men went up or down the ladder, depending on their watch. In a traditional show of respect, they tugged their forelock and said "Cap'n," as they passed him. With amusement, he noted they did the same when they passed Miss Chase on the deck. Within moments she stood beside him in the passageway, Smitty coming down the ladder behind her.

"Join me in my cabin for tea after you've changed?"

"With pleasure," she replied.

Nick saw Luigi gesture acknowledgment of Nick's request for tea, and headed for his cabin while Miss Chase and Smitty went to the slop chest to return their costumes.

Nick eyed the coiled-up hammock just inside his door. Would he finally get to sleep in it again tonight? Two nights in Norton's cabin was too long. The hammock in the surgery was just as comfortable, but too far from Miss Chase.

For her safety, he told himself, calling himself a liar in the next breath.

He didn't have long to stew as Miss Chase appeared within moments, dragging her fingers through her hair, undoing the haphazard chignon she'd put it in under the bonnet. He'd done a double take upon seeing her dressed like a lady, so used to her in dungarees and waistcoat, and now she was dressed like a deckhand again. Except her long, light brown hair flowed loose over her shoulders, still wavy from so much time spent in a braid.

The dichotomy was enough to make Nick's head swim.

Flynn knocked and then at Nick's bark to come in, set a tray on the table, laden with biscuits, fresh fruit, and jerked boar in addition to the tea things. "Luigi figured as how you might be a tad peckish, Cap'n," he said, clearly addressing Miss Chase.

"Thank you, Flynn," she replied, color flooding her cheeks. "And tell Luigi *grazie*."

Flynn tugged his forelock, turned to Nick and did it again, and closed the door as he left.

Miss Chase didn't sit down. Instead, she fished the leather cord out of her waistcoat pocket and grabbed her brush from her portmanteau, then moved over to Nick's desk, away from the food, and began brushing her wayward locks.

Nick bit into a piece of meat to distract himself from the act of intimate domesticity going on four steps away.

"How far in advance of Ruford do you think we'll reach Porto?"

He slowly tipped his head from one side to the other, indicating he was giving it great consideration, while he chewed and swallowed. "About a day, if we're lucky." He finally dared look at her. "Maybe less," is what he intended to say but it came out as a croak. She was working on a knot, her brow furrowed. What clenched his gut and sent blood singing through his veins was the tip of her pink tongue just poking out between her lips. Her luscious, berry-colored lips. Were they chapped? In his shaving kit, he kept a small tin of a beeswax and African shea butter concoction that he applied to protect his lips from chapping. Wonder what it would taste like on her lips?

He must have made some other sound because she suddenly looked up at him, the tip of her tongue still visible.

He cleared his throat. "May I?" Before his brain caught up with his body's intent, he'd crossed the few steps separating them and held his hand out for the brush.

She slowly raised her hand, as if not sure why she was doing so, and gave him the brush. She licked her lips, and her tongue disappeared.

He took a quick breath and stepped behind her, putting her tongue and mouth out of his mind.

Right. Tell yourself another one, boyo.

He gathered her wind-mussed hair in his hands, gently collecting the strands and pulling the length back over her shoulders, his fingers brushing the side of her neck. He wasn't sure her sharp intake of breath was related to him touching her so he causally did it again, just checking there were no loose strands left around her face, a slow stroke of his fingertips on her neck, from just below her jaw all the way around to her nape.

Her breath definitely hitched.

Nick filed the information away for later.

He started brushing at the bottom of her hair, below her shoulder blades, working in small sections, barely moving an inch or two higher at a time. Slow, steady strokes. When he encountered a knot, he held her hair so as not to pull on her scalp, and gently worked it free.

One small section finished, smooth all the way to her scalp, he pushed it in front of her right shoulder and started on the next section.

"Do you do this often?"

Nick paused in lifting the brush for another stroke.

"Have someone else pretend to be captain, that is."

Nick resumed brushing. "It's come in handy now and then. We saw French navy near Singhapura, so we had Captain Chang for a day. Luigi was captain when we were off Sicily once." He stroked from the crown of her head all the way down to the end of her hair. "Did you enjoy it?"

She hummed.

He gave another long, slow stroke, crown to tip.

She took a deep breath, which enabled Nick from his height and close proximity to notice that she'd missed tightening the strings on her shirt, where the lace had been tucked in. A patch of creamy skin was briefly visible in the gap, a hint of the top curve of her breast. "It was an experience I'm glad to have had," she said thoughtfully, "and happy to give Jonesy back the helm with the watch change."

It took Nick several heartbeats to remember what she was talking about. He dragged his attention away from her chest and back to her hair, which now softly reflected the lamplight, and resumed brushing.

He'd always paid close attention to women's hair. Not so much for the styles, but because its condition was an indicator of health and hygiene habits, and played a big part in deciding with whom he'd share a bed. Or a convenient wall. He was especially fond of long hair. Loved to see it splayed across his pillow or forming a curtain around his face when his partner was on top. He liked to unpin it, let it cascade over her naked shoulders, and spill through his fingers like silk.

He'd had many a pleasant interlude at an otherwise dull ball, and after their fun he'd help her dress again and pin her hair back up, avoiding the need for her maid, enabling them both to return to the event with no one the wiser except for the afterglow of pleasure.

When there was time, he could make the brushing slow, relaxing. Ease her stress from the day until she practically purred like a cat, her scalp tingling with pleasure, her body melting in his arms. And he knew how to stir her to arousal, interspersing the gentle brush strokes with touches and kisses until she was ready to tear his clothes off, eager to lift her skirts for him.

Miss Chase wore no skirts.

As he untangled another section of hair, her breathing gradually slowed and her shoulders dropped, proof that pretending to be captain and bantering with Ruford had been more stressful for her than he'd thought.

Another section smooth, Nick pushed it in front of her left shoulder. Purely coincidence that his fingertips brushed her neck again each direction.

He froze when he realized the dark spot below her ear wasn't a freckle. It was the healing mark where a large splinter had pierced her skin. His hand faltered.

She started to turn her head to look at him. He gently pushed her chin forward, and began brushing the last, middle section. He lifted the brush to smooth the underside, making sure his fingers dipped just inside her collar and grazed the skin of her nape all the way up to her hairline. With her hair gathered in his hand and lifted, the wound on her neck stood out like an accusation.

He'd been proud of her when she jumped in to help protect the ship, and terrified she'd be hurt. Delighted at how well she'd learned what to do in firing the guns, but seeing blood on her neck and temple had shaken him.

This seesawing of his emotions was bewildering. And exhausting.

He focused on the silver chain around her neck. He slid a finger under it, testing its heft, then let it drop, the delicate chain once more disappearing under her collar. "You haven't lost it."

"I never take it off." She pulled out the silver H pendant and reverently stroked it. "In the letter that accompanied it, Papa said it was the key to my future."

Nick thought it looked more like part of a horse's tack. With a mother and five sisters, though, he'd learned the hard way to never say anything derogatory about a woman's jewelry.

"'Let us walk honestly, as in the day,'" Nick quoted softly, "'not in rioting and drunkenness, not in chambering and wantonness, not in strife and envying.'"

At her murmur of confusion, he went on. "That's what Adam, my father, said was the key to my future. Romans thirteen, verse thirteen." He gave a snort of derision. "Made me recite it hundreds of times. Thousands. Hypocrite." As well as verse fourteen, 'But put ye on the Lord Jesus Christ, and make not provision for the flesh, to fulfill the lusts thereof.' Best not to think about lust right now. Certain parts of his anatomy were doing it just fine on their own.

"He phrased it in those words? The key to your future?"

Nick paused, the brush halfway down her hair, and thought back. Letters, lectures, conversations at dinner—how many times had his father delivered pious sermons to him, admonishing him to follow these two scriptures? "Yes." He resumed brushing.

Miss Chase hummed again, though he wasn't sure if it was in response to his verbal reply or pleasure in the hair brushing.

He ran his fingers through her now tangle-free hair. He had no excuse to keep brushing, but he didn't want to stop touching her. Without conscious thought, he separated her hair into three sections and began braiding.

He was past her collar when she realized what he was doing and again tried to look over her shoulder at him. Again he gently pushed her face forward, three fingers lingering on her jaw. He'd mixed up the sections when he let go with one hand, so he smoothed out the braid and started over.

"You weren't joking when you offered your services as lady's maid."

Nick chuckled.

"Did you learn on your sisters' hair?"

Nick snorted. "The closest I got to their plaits was in the schoolroom when I threatened to chop them off when the girls annoyed me." He didn't think Miss Chase would appreciate knowing he'd actually learned by braiding his horse's mane.

"Oh, of course! You learned to braid your own hair when you went to sea. Is having long hair in a queue a requirement for being a pirate? Excuse me—privateer."

"Honest merchantman," Nick corrected reflexively, grinning. He was just a few inches from finishing.

She continued as though he hadn't spoken. "Braiding is just another skill, like navigating around the globe or eluding capture. And of course you have to be able to do your own hair, as you don't always have a valet or cabin boy handy. You and Jonesy are clearly friends, not just captain and first mate, but I can't see you two sitting at the table, braiding each other's hair."

Laughing at the mental image her words conjured, Nick dropped his head, resting his hands on her shoulders, the end of the plait caught between one thumb and forefinger.

She held a hand up, the short leather cord dangling from her fingers, the side of her mouth that he could see curved in a smile.

He took it and tied off the plait. "It's just a way to keep it out of my eyes and not worry about it being tangled by the wind. Or needing to get it cut." He glanced around the cabin. "Don't move."

He withdrew a length of cotton cording from a drawer in his wardrobe, folded it in half to find the middle, and began crisscrossing it in a wrap around her braid, starting at the top, and tied it off at the end.

He was reluctant to move away but could think of no other excuses for staying in such close proximity if he wasn't actually going to try seducing her. "Tea's getting cold," he said, his voice harsher than intended, and he moved to the table.

She brought the braid over her shoulder to examine his handiwork as she sat, and stroked a finger over the cotton cord. "Oh, lovely," she said softly. "This will keep the braid neat longer and protect my hair from breakage. Thank you."

He grunted a reply as they filled their plates and cups and got down to the business of satisfying hunger.

Hunger for food, at least. Nick repressed a sigh.

Several minutes passed while they ate, and Nick was reaching his breaking point. A drop of peach juice at the corner of her mouth was nearly his undoing, as she caught it with the tip of her tongue to keep it from running down her chin.

He shifted in his chair, willing his anatomy to obey, to not embarrass him like a schoolboy in the throes of adolescence. "You've acquired another skill," he choked out, desperate for a distraction.

She had picked up her teacup but set it back down without drinking. "Pardon?"

"Marrying."

She blinked, her expression blank.

Yes, maybe he had indeed lost his mind. "Rope. When you join the ends of rope together, it's called marrying."

Her lips rounded in a silent *Oh*. She picked up a biscuit and began crumbling it. "I was looking for something to do, and Winston was kind enough to teach me. Smitty let me borrow a marlinspike from the slop chest so I could do a long splice as well as short splice."

"You should have your own."

She gave a little shrug. "I don't want to run up my bill too high."

"If you're doing ship's labor, you can borrow ship's tools. I'll tell Smitty."

"Thank you. I did enjoy our work session on the deck, before the *Polly Ann* was sighted. Tucker, Winston, and I, all plying needle and thread and rope." She sipped her tea. "Reminded me a bit of a sewing bee."

Nick laughed. He pictured his tars sitting around a parlor, drinking tea and sewing on a quilt, and laughed harder.

Though Miss Chase did not join in his laughter, her generous smile told him she was pleased at provoking such a reaction from him.

He drained his cup. "Please don't tell them that. Not sure they'd see the humor in it."

"Is sewing an insult to their masculinity? But isn't sail-making a specialized form of sewing? And what about tailors?"

"Sewing is inherently neither masculine nor feminine, and is a valuable skill. It's good to know how to put a button back on or sew up a rip in your draw- ah, shirt. But we both know how society at large views certain skills."

She tilted her head in acknowledgment and tried to hide a yawn behind her hand.

Nick glanced out the cabin window. Stars twinkled in the black backdrop of the night sky. "I'm going to check our position. Why don't you turn in early? I'll take the tray so you're not disturbed."

"Thank you. It has been an ... interesting day."

As Nick dropped off the tray in the galley and climbed to the quarterdeck, he reflected on the women who had made him laugh. A short list, indeed.

The women with whom he'd wanted to share physical pleasure. A considerably longer list, though not nearly as long as society rumors would suggest.

And how little those two lists overlapped.

Miss Chase was on both.

Chapter 13

Two days later, luck and the tide were with them, and they were able to maneuver from the Atlantic, past a treacherous sandspit, and into the Douro River. They followed the harbor master's instructions to a slip on the quay, steering clear of the *rabelos*, small flat-bottomed boats carrying crates and barrels from the wineries farther upriver.

They were docked in Porto.

Portugal.

Where a priest five years ago had travelled with his father's treasure.

Nick had kept an eye open for Ruford's cutter as they sailed up the river. It would be almost impossible for the cutter to have caught up, never mind pass them, but Nick had to look anyway. He scanned the harbor with his spyglass, then handed it to Jonesy and took another look without the glass, taking in all the ships, searching for the *Polly Ann*.

"Don't see 'er, Cap'n." Jonesy tucked the scope in the maphouse.

Jack and Flynn finished tying up on the bollards as Miss Chase—no, no, had to think of her as Harry again—bounded up to the quarterdeck and handed him the leather portfolio he'd need for dealing with the customs agent.

She was in full character as the cabin boy, with smudges on her cheek and chin to hide her porcelain complexion. A light dusting of freckles was showing up across her nose and cheeks from her time in the sun. Her neat braid was wrapped in cotton cording, the same way he'd done it the other night. Striped dungarees and the blue plaid waistcoat hid her charms. Cotton shoes protected her feet, and a straw hat, identical to the hats worn by half the crew on deck, protected her from the bright autumn sun.

"Thank you, Harry." Nick took the proffered folio.

She tugged her forelock, flashed him a cocky grin, and scampered off to help lower the gangboard.

"Besotted," he thought he heard Jonesy mutter.

Nick realized he was smiling, and quickly changed his expression to a suitable scowl. "What's that?"

"Nothing, Cap'n."

Nick greeted the customs agent in Portuguese, welcoming the chance to practice speaking the language other than swearing, and took care of business.

An interminable half hour later, he called Jonesy and Harry up to the maphouse.

"Well?" he asked them. "Short of visiting every church in Porto, any ideas how we're going to find Father Miguel?"

"We won't have to visit all of them if we get lucky early on," Harry said, far too chipper for such a daunting task. Instead of looking at Nick, she was scanning the ships in the harbor.

"I don't see him," Nick said quietly.

"We may have anywhere from a few hours to a couple of days before the *Polly Ann* limps in," Jonesy added.

Harry took a deep breath, which Nick tried not to pay close attention to. The waistcoat only hid so much, especially if one knew what was hidden beneath the homespun cotton shirt. "In our favor, how many priests arrived in town with a horse?" she said thoughtfully. "A donkey or mule, sure, but given their vow of simplicity, not many men of the cloth would have a horse."

"There's that," Jonesy conceded.

"Let's not waste any of our advantage," Nick said, and strode down the steps to the deck. He gave quick instructions to Bos'n regarding the amount of water and foodstuffs to take on. "Mind you save plenty of room for port," Nick added as he stepped down the gangboard, Jonesy and Harry right behind him. "The London townhouse is running low on a decent port wine."

"Aye, Cap'n," Bos'n rasped.

"We can probably ignore any churches close to the river," Harry said as they left the quay, struggling to stay close together in the crowded, narrow street. "Father Miguel would need room not only to stable his horse but to exercise it as well."

"Good point," Nick said. Why hadn't he thought of that? "Let's start on this side of the river today. We can go over the bridge tomorrow if need be." He scanned the hillside rising from the river. "There's the most obvious candidate." He pointed to the huge church atop the hill overlooking the city. "*Sé Catedral do Porto.*"

They followed the main road up the steep Penaventosa Hill from the riverbank north into the city proper, winding through the narrow streets and to the church.

Harry's mouth fell open at the sight of the baroque interior with gold everywhere. The ceiling soared overhead, and light filtered through the stained glass windows set in a row of Gothic arches. Nick grinned as he tipped a finger under her chin to shut her jaw. She gave him an embarrassed smile. His toes did not curl at the sparkle in her eyes, but it was a near thing.

They arrived between services. A dozen or so worshippers still sat in pews here and there. An elderly priest was replacing burned-down votive candles at the side altar in the transept, overseen by a statue of the Madonna holding baby Jesus. Nick wouldn't wager a farthing they would find the answer they sought here—nothing in his life was that easy—but they had to ask.

After a brief conversation with the priest, Nick shook his head for Jonesy and Harry. "This padre has served here for the last thirty years. No Father Miguel, no priest with a horse," he said. He lit a candle and dropped a coin in the donation box. "Can't hurt," he muttered with a shrug.

They headed back out to the sunshine, to the crowded streets. Away from the harbor odors of fish, salt, and wet wood, other scents wafted on the breeze. Olive oil, onion, garlic, and spicy meat. Feeling his stomach rumble, Nick led the way into the next cantina they saw. They ordered drinks and the special of the day and sat back, looking around and listening.

Similar to the cantina in Corunna, musicians played in one corner, and patrons were conversing in at least four languages Nick could identify, none of them English.

When the serving wench brought their food, Nick walked a coin across the back of his fingers and flashed a smile at her, the same smile that had melted female hearts around the globe. "*Um pouco de informação, por favor, senhorita.*"

She promptly sat on his lap and wound one arm around his neck. "What information you seek, *senhor*?" she replied in heavily accented English, trailing her fingers down his jaw to his chest.

Nick ignored Jonesy's grin and Harry valiantly trying not to roll her eyes. "We are seeking a priest," he said. "Father Miguel would have arrived in 1811, riding a horse."

Her fingers stilled. "A priest with a horse?"

Nick nodded. "Where might he have gone? Which church would have room for him and his horse?"

Her gaze became distant as she pondered the question. Nick set the coin on the table, reached into his coat pocket with the arm not wrapped around the woman's waist, retrieved a piece of paper and a stub of a pencil, and slid them across the table to Jonesy.

Jonesy smoothed the paper and held the pencil, ready to record whatever insight befell. Nick resumed walking the coin on his fingers, noting the wench's warm brown eyes following it closely.

"*Igreja de Nossa da Senhora da Lapa* has fields. Their parishioners grow wheat and other crops to feed themselves and to sell," she said, tapping her bottom lip, then Nick's. "They might have welcomed a horse to pull the plow."

Jonesy wrote it down as well as the directions to the church.

Nick gripped the coin between his first two fingers and dropped it between her breasts, which were in danger of falling out of her low-cut gown. She smiled and quickly rattled off the names of other churches and monasteries on the outskirts of town and nearby villages, which had farms or wineries.

"*Obrigado, senhorita*," he said, patting her hip.

She took the hint and stood up. "My pleasure, *senhor*. Tell me if you desire anything else." With a wink and a coy glance over her shoulder, she went back to the kitchen to pick up the next customer's order.

Nick dug into his rapidly cooling *caldo verde*, refusing to think about what Harry thought of his information-gathering technique. With her head bowed to eat, the hat brim hid most of her face so he couldn't read her expression. Jonesy had a big grin and shook his head in wonder, and ate a big spoonful of the flavorful potato, chorizo, and kale soup.

"We'll need to hire horses," Nick said several minutes later, using a hunk of bread to sop up the last of the soup in his bowl. One of the delights of sailing was sampling the cuisine of far-flung lands. "Got a lot of ground to cover." He glanced at Harry. "Or should it be a carriage? Can you ride? I'm guessing you'd part my hair with a chair if I suggest that you wait on the ship."

"I can," she said, glancing at the top of his head as though deciding where to place the blow, "and I would."

Jonesy laughed and held up his empty mug to a passing servant for a refill of ale.

It had been close to mid-day when they docked. By the time they finished eating and paid their shot, Nick estimated they only had four or five hours of daylight. He and Jonesy were fine on foot after dark in a strange town, but he wouldn't risk Harriet's safety. If Father Miguel wasn't at the first *igreja*, they'd head out early the next day, prepared to look for days.

At the stables up the street, Nick negotiated the hire of three horses, quietly asking for an especially gentle mount for young Harry. The proprietor gave Harry an appraising glance, and soon led out an older grey gelding, much bigger than Nick would have chosen. At Nick's look of apprehension, the hostler assured Nick he was a sweet goer, perfect for a lad still learning to ride.

Harriet watched the horse approach her, awed by the gelding's beautiful, showy tack compared to English horses, and gasped when she realized just how big the horse was. She could barely see over his shoulder. And the saddle! She'd blithely told Sheffield that of course she could ride, and she could ... sidesaddle.

Two other grooms led out geldings for Sheffield and Jonesy. They checked the stirrup length, and Harriet noted the hostler doing the same for her. He gave her another look, then shortened hers even farther.

In a flood of Portuguese, the hostler offered to help her mount, making himself clear by bending down and cupping his hands.

"Obrigado," she said, confusing the hostler by shaking her head, until she pointed to the mounting block over by the stable.

"*Sim, sim*," the hostler said, and led the horse to the block.

She climbed the steps. Gave the horse a stroke down his forehead and a pat on his shoulder, looking him in his big brown eyes. He snorted and nodded his head, jingling his bridle, indicating what she interpreted as an eagerness to get going. Trusting the horse was agreeable to keeping her on his back, Harriet swung her leg up and over in a decidedly unladylike maneuver, and settled in the saddle. Astride.

Memories flooded back, of riding the vicar's pony through the fields when she was a child, her long hair blowing free in the wind, laughing and urging her mount to go faster, *faster*. They'd never had sufficient funds to keep their own horse, not even to pull a carriage, so she'd poured her affections on that pony, until she grew old enough to be sent off to school and have it drilled into her that proper ladies do not ride astride, and certainly not bareback.

A mere few weeks ago, she couldn't bring herself to pull on breeches and have fabric between her legs. And now she sat astride a snorting beast who could stomp her flat, her shins and calves bare below her dungarees.

Madame Zavrina would have an apoplectic fit if she could see Harriet now. The academy made sure their students knew how to ride, of course ... sidesaddle and at a sedate pace, so they could go for a quiet turn about the park or through the village while being courted.

Harriet was about to ride cross-country with two men who were most definitely not courting her. She put her feet in the stirrups, adjusted her grip on the reins, and gave the beast a gentle nudge with her heels. He obediently walked over to where Sheffield and Jonesy sat atop their mounts near the gate.

"Ready?" Sheffield said.

Harriet looked at the street and nodded, not trusting her voice.

Blood rushed through her veins. Her heart pounded. Fear, excitement, and anticipation flooded her body in equal measures.

This was it. She was about to embark on her future. Within a few hours, she might find the treasure her father had intended to take care of his family. Take care of Harriet's future and that of her younger brother. See that Mama was comfortable in her declining years.

They headed out to the street, following the direction the serving woman had given. The narrow, twisting streets were crowded with pedestrians as well as sedan chairs, handcarts, and other horses, so they went at a stately walk, which gave Harriet the chance to get used to her mount's gait, stretching and using muscles she didn't ordinarily use. And what a fabulous view from this high up!

Traffic thinned as they turned several times, wending their way through town, and eventually they found themselves on a road between rolling fields that had probably grown wheat but now lay fallow for the coming winter. Sheffield led and Jonesy was just behind Harriet, occasionally exchanging comments with Sheffield as they navigated.

Harriet tried to pay attention to the lovely countryside, the rugged hills in the distance, groves of gnarled olive trees, and houses with white-washed walls and red-tiled roofs, so different from the thatched roofs back home in Brixham, but much of her concentration was still focused on staying in the saddle. She paid close attention to Sheffield's body on his horse, noting the subtle motions of his legs and shifting of his weight as he guided his mount, and how those movements differed from those she would have made riding on a sidesaddle.

As traffic thinned further, Sheffield stepped up the pace to a trot. Her horse snorted, clearly eager for a gallop. Harriet wasn't sure she could stay on for that. Maybe later, she silently said as she patted the gelding's shoulder. His gait was smooth enough she soon felt confident enough to start experimenting with mimicking the movement Sheffield made, rising slightly from the saddle in time with the horse's strides, and discovered riding that way took less effort than sitting still.

She was so busy, time passed quickly. A church loomed in the distance, a Gothic structure with a high bell tower. Fields gave way to outbuildings including a barn and byre, and modest houses. Soon they could see people tending to animals, hear chickens clucking. Three mules meandered in a paddock, along with a horse.

Harriet's heart raced. Could this be it? Could the man in long robes wielding a hammer repairing the fence by the gate be Father Miguel? Could their search really be over this easily?

"*Olá*," Sheffield called as he halted his horse and dismounted—not entirely gracefully, Harriet noted with a silent chuckle. Apparently the sailor took a while to get used to another mode of transportation.

"*Olá*," the priest replied, a wary question in his voice at the sight of three newcomers.

Jonesy rode up alongside Harriet. They exchanged glances, then turned their attention back to Sheffield.

His gait steadied as he walked a few paces. He spoke to the priest in Portuguese, and they went back and forth in rapid conversation.

Harriet's hopes began to fall as the priest shook his head, then pointed farther up the road.

Sheffield approached them, leading his horse. "The only Father Miguel he knows died a decade ago, at the age of ninety. And he never owned a horse."

It took all of Harriet's control not to slump.

"There is, however, another *igreja* farm a little farther along this road, one with a horse to pull their plow instead of a cranky mule who kicks the gate when he gets annoyed." Sheffield stuck a thumb over his shoulder, indicating the padre still working to repair the gate. "It's maybe a half hour's ride. I think we can get there and back to the ship before dark if we don't dawdle. We're welcome to water our horses and get a drink from the pump before we go."

"I wouldn't mind washing down some of this dust." Jonesy nudged his horse over to the trough.

Harriet followed, Sheffield leading his horse beside her. While the men were busy with their horses, Harriet swung her leg up and over the saddle and jumped down to the ground ... and kept going down as her rubbery legs refused to support her weight. She grabbed the stirrup with one hand, trying not to grunt as she prepared to get off her knees, and suddenly Sheffield was there catching her free hand, lifting her up.

She started to feel embarrassed, then recalled his less-than-graceful dismount just minutes ago, and they exchanged knowing smiles.

"*Obrigada*," she said, trying to imitate the native pronunciation.

"*De nada*," he replied, his eyes crinkling at the corners with a hint of a smile.

Their horses drank from the trough while the humans took turns getting a drink from the pump and walking around, stretching their legs. Once they finished, Jonesy pumped more water to refill the trough.

Holding the reins with one hand, Harriet looked around the yard for a mounting block or something similar so she could get back up on the giant horse. No way was she getting her foot in the stirrup without help; the metal loop was even higher than her stomach.

Sheffield was back at her side. His eyes twinkling, he cupped his hands and bent down.

After a moment's hesitation, Harriet rested one hand on his shoulder—his broad, muscular shoulder—lifted her foot into his hands, and he boosted her up. He didn't even grunt from the effort, though she might have done so while getting properly settled in the saddle.

"Thank you," she said, definitely not staring at his shoulder.

He patted her knee and climbed up on his own horse, and they were back on the road. Again with the patting of her knee. She wasn't sure if she should feel flattered or insulted.

Sheffield set a teeth-rattling pace, and they arrived at the next *igreja* during evening chores. They dismounted in the deserted yard, tied up their mounts at the fence, and followed the sound of singing—a solo tenor voice raised in a song of gratitude, if she guessed the tune correctly—into the barn, where the padre was milking a goat. More goats milled around, impatiently waiting their turn to be milked and fed, as Harriet had learned from Bessie and Daisy.

"*Olá*," Sheffield called.

The padre looked up and returned a greeting without pausing in his milking.

Sheffield questioned the padre. Harriet didn't know the words, though she recognized some of them from before. Heartening was the fact that the padre didn't shake his head. He released the goat from the stanchion and ushered another into its place, taking the opportunity to point at the little house behind the church before he poured the milk into a large earthen jug, and started milking the next goat.

Sheffield gestured for Harriet and Jonesy to follow him as he crossed the courtyard. "Father Enrique has only served this parish for a couple of years. He suggested we talk with the parsonage housekeeper, who's been here for decades."

They retrieved their horses, led them closer to the house and tied them up near a water trough, then followed the smell of cooking food around to the house's back entrance. A boy in his late teens opened the door, dressed to work in the field or barn. He and Sheffield briefly conversed, and the boy gestured for them to follow him inside.

The kitchen was presided over by a matron with gray at her temples, a large white apron about her waist, and a wooden spoon in her hand that she tapped on the side of the pot hanging over the cooking fire. Delicious scents of carrot, garlic, and onion wafted in the air.

She gestured for them to sit at the rustic worktable, and at her instruction the boy brought them pewter mugs and a pitcher of new wine. Harriet and Jonesy drank while Sheffield and the housekeeper exchanged greetings. Harriet listened closely, recognizing only a word here and there.

"You are from England, yes?" the housekeeper said.

Sheffield grinned, and Harriet and Jonesy exchanged startled looks.

"Yes, madam, we are."

"My English is rusty. Father Enrique is a nice young man who serves his parish well, but only speaks Portuguese, Spanish, and Latin."

"Then we are happy to help you practice." Sheffield took a sip of his grape juice. "We are searching for a padre who helped my family. And Harry's family." He tilted his head, indicating Harriett. "He would have come to the area about five years ago."

The housekeeper glanced between them. "Father Miguel?"

Harriet struggled to keep her mouth from falling open. She barely heard Sheffield's reply over the pounding of her heart.

Sheffield calmly maintained a mild interest. "Yes. You know him?"

She shook her head, and Harriet's heart sank. "You are not the first to ask about a priest named Miguel."

Sheffield leaned forward to rest his forearms on the table. "Who else has asked? And when?"

She gestured to the boy and spoke to him in rapid Portuguese, then he brought them bowls and spoons, and set the soup pot on a trivet in the middle of the table. She unwrapped a towel around a basket, revealing a rustic loaf of bread, and lifted the lid on a crock of butter. "Eat, please," she said. "There is plenty. I always make extra."

Harriet barely restrained herself from continuing the questioning, but obediently ladled soup into her bowl and buttered a hunk of bread. Hard to believe she was hungry again already. Olive oil made the potatoes, carrots, onion, garlic, and watercress taste distinctly different from vegetable soup she'd eaten at home. She savored several bites, fighting the urge to fidget, to press for answers.

"Three, maybe four days ago," the housekeeper said at last. "He was charming, like you," she said to Sheffield. "The same dark hair, blue eyes, and smile. Close to my age, though." She patted the hair at her temple. "A dusting of silver and grey. Your father or other relative, perhaps?"

Harriet held her breath.

Sheffield didn't recoil as he had in Spain, but he went absolutely still. Then he calmly swallowed another spoonful of soup. "And what did you tell him?"

The housekeeper eyed him as she ate a bite of bread, then washed it down with a sip of new wine. "That I do not know of a priest with a horse who came from Spain five years ago."

They all took another bite, Harriet fighting not to show her disappointment.

"There must be an interesting story behind this search." The housekeeper refilled her mug.

"Just unfinished business." Sheffield scraped the bottom of his bowl. "What else did the Englishman say? And what did you tell him?"

Harriet was ready to scream at the polite back and forth interspersed with eating and drinking. *Get on with it!* she wanted to shout. Instead she drank the new wine and finished her soup, wondering if she and Mama could replicate its complex flavor with ingredients available back home.

The housekeeper smiled, her eyes crinkling at the corners. "He would not say why he sought the priest with a horse, either. I told him that my sister remembers priests being among the refugees coming from Spain to escape the French cannon fire. She may know the one you seek."

At a nod from Sheffield, Jonesy pulled the paper and pencil out of his pocket and prepared to write.

"She is housekeeper for the priest at *Igreja Paroquial do Nosso Senhor do Bonfim*, a few miles southeast of here. Parochial Church of Our Lord of Bonfim." She gave directions and Jonesy scribbled furiously to get it all down.

Sheffield rose, and Jonesy and Harriet followed his lead. "Thank you for your hospitality, and the information." Sheffield set coins on the table by his dirty dishes. "To help stock your larder, so you can feed more hungry travelers," he added when the housekeeper looked like she would refuse.

After a thoughtful pause, she gave a pragmatic nod and swept the coins into her apron pocket.

Jonesy tugged his forelock as he turned to leave, so Harriet did the same.

The boy followed them out, carrying a large jug. Harriet realized he'd delayed finishing chores and stayed in the kitchen to protect the housekeeper, probably his mother, from three strangers.

Out in the yard, Sheffield tossed her up in her saddle again but didn't pat her knee. She was pretty sure he stroked his hand down her calf instead. He walked to his horse without a word or look, so maybe she imagined it.

"*Ide com Deus*," the padre called, exchanging the full jug of milk for the empty jug the boy carried.

"Obrigado," Sheffield replied with a wave.

With darkness falling, they didn't stop again until they returned to the stables where they'd rented the horses, Sheffield leading them with the same unerring sense of direction on land that he used to navigate at sea. On the walk back to the ship, he and Jonesy kept Harriet between them as much as possible. The cobblestone streets narrowed and became noisy and crowded with carousers as they neared the riverfront. Some other time she'd appreciate exploring the city with two large bodyguards at her side, perhaps, but she was exhausted from the emotional and physical tolls of the day. Back on the ship, she barely had the energy to fall onto the bunk, kick off her shoes, and cover up with a blanket before she succumbed to sleep.

***

Morning light streamed through the window above the bunk. Harriet sat up and threw back the blanket, eager to go to Bonfim and resume the search. As she went about her morning ablutions, she stifled some decidedly unladylike groans as muscles in her back, legs, and buttocks protested yesterday's horse ride. Her body ached in places she didn't know she had muscles. She stretched to work out the kinks, and headed topside.

Bos'n was directing the crew loading crates and barrels up from the dock. Jonesy was absent, as was Sheffield. Surely they wouldn't leave without her? Perhaps he was in the hold with Bessie for morning cuddles and milking.

Her foot on the first step to go back down the hatch, she heard the distinctive whistle from Bos'n calling for attention. When she glanced at him, he waved for her to join him near the gangboard.

"Mr. Jones went to get the 'orses you rode yesterday," he rasped. "Cap'n said he wants 'arry ready to travel when he gets back, to be gone two or three days maybe. Find Smitty and get a cap and coat from the slop chest, something to keep you warm and dry if it comes on t' raining."

Harriet's mind raced, considering what to pack and what to pack it in. She paused at the hatch, one hand on the rail. "Where did the captain go?"

Bos'n grinned. "Drinking."

Chapter 14

Half an hour later, Harriet was back on deck with a packed saddlebag. She debated whether to put on the wool peacoat Smitty had helped her choose, despite the mild temperature and warm sunshine, or see if there was still room to tuck it in one of the pouches without horribly wrinkling it. She wiggled her toes, getting used to the half boots Smitty had also suggested she wear. Unlike the flat soles of the canvas shoes, boot heels would keep her feet from sliding through the stirrups. She'd also swapped her dungarees for full-length duck trousers and stockings, though she kept the plaid wool waistcoat and shirt. She knew how to layer chemise, fichu, pelisse, and shawls for warmth. Fortunately, Smitty had been a fount of advice about how to layer her sailor's garb to keep comfortable in the changeable late-autumn weather. She even had a wool cap tucked in a coat pocket.

A wagon approached on the quay, distinguishable from the usual cacophony of workers and carts and gulls' cries because the driver and passenger were singing. Loudly.

An English drinking song.

The driver brought the wagon to a halt just as they finished the chorus, and Sheffield climbed down, nearly falling to his knees before he staggered up to pat one of the horses. He waved up at the ship and had to grab the harness to keep from losing his balance.

The rest of the crew on deck joined Harriet and Bos'n at the gunwale.

"G'mornin'!" Sheffield loudly called, another expansive wave encompassing everyone on board. Only his grip on the horse's mane kept him upright.

Harriet glanced at the crew. No one seemed surprised or upset the captain appeared soused so early in the day. What the devil was Sheffield doing, getting intoxicated when they had such urgent, important business to attend?

Sheffield gestured at the casks in the wagon. "Load 'em!" He exchanged grins with the driver. "Load 'em all!"

Chang and Jack ran down the gangboard and began unloading the casks from the wagon, while Nick and the driver conversed—the driver in Portuguese, Nick in English-accented broken Spanish, his words slurred. Then Nick staggered up the gangboard, his caped greatcoat flaring out now and then around his boots. Harriet was certain more than once he was going to fall into the river below before he joined her and Bos'n at the rail.

He winked at her before he turned and rested a heavy hand on her shoulder and one on Bos'n, as though he needed their help to stay upright.

What was her wily pirate up to?

Within moments Chang and Jack had the wagon unloaded. The driver and Nick exchanged jaunty waves and exuberant goodbyes, then the driver turned his horses and began to work his way back up to town.

"You ready to go?" Nick asked her quietly.

Harriet stared at him with narrowed eyes. His breath had a hint of alcohol, but he enunciated clearly.

Smitty joined them. "Get a good bargain on the port wine, Cap'n?"

Nick retrieved a folded piece of paper from an inner pocket of his coat. "Here's the bill of sale."

Smitty scanned the paper and let out a low whistle. "You're good, Cap'n. This cost even less than the last load you bought in Gaia. This will fetch a nice profit back home."

Nick patted him on the shoulder. "I live to bargain." He glanced at Harriet and scanned the quay. "We can leave as soon as Jonesy gets back with the ... Ah, there he is."

Jonesy approached the dock, riding one horse and leading two others, one of which was the giant grey gelding Harriet rode yesterday.

"You ready?" Nick repeated.

"Been waiting on you," she said, feeling cheeky after witnessing his performance.

Flynn appeared at the railing holding two packed saddlebags, one for Jonesy and one for Nick. Close up, Harriet finally noticed Nick had changed while she slept. Gone were his casual at-sea clothes. Instead of a London gentleman, though, he looked like a moderately prosperous sea captain, with a simply tied neckcloth, checked wool waistcoat and navy coat beneath his caped greatcoat. The gold braid trim on his cocked hat of black felt highlighted his gold hoop earring. He didn't have a cutlass strapped to his side, though she did see the butt of a dagger handle at the top of his right boot.

Nick helped her tie on her saddlebag and coat behind the saddle, tossed her up, and within minutes they were riding toward the church in Bonfim, just to the east of Porto.

Two hours later, Harriet was struggling to keep her spirits up. The housekeeper's sister at the parsonage in Bonfim had indeed helped to welcome many refugees from Spain a few years ago ... and they had all long since moved on. There were at least a dozen different parsonages, monasteries, and other places the housekeeper could think of where Father Miguel might have gone, seeking refuge for his horse and a congregation for the priest to serve.

Nick called for a rest at a coaching inn, to water the horses and plan their search.

They sat at a table in the back near the kitchen door, Nick with his back to the wall and a clear view of the entrance. While they waited for their food and drink, Jonesy smoothed out the paper with the list of possible addresses, and Nick unfolded a map he'd had tucked in an inner coat pocket. They marked the map with locations the housekeeper had suggested as likely.

Harriet stared at the number and range of possibilities. Her heart sank. They couldn't spend endless days and weeks searching the Portuguese countryside for the treasure. Nick would likely cover his share of expenses for this trip with the profit he'd earn from selling Portuguese wine in England, but she was further in debt. Not only did she owe Nick for her share of the costs for the trip—good heavens, what if he charged her for half the cost of replacing the cannon?—but the mortgage was due soon. Mama and Gabriel would have nowhere to go. Winter was coming. Aunt Elizabeth might be able to take them in, at least briefly, but would they even have the means to travel from Brixham all the way to Elizabeth's home in Manchester?

"Like looking for a needle in a haystack," Jonesy gloomily pronounced, slumping in his chair.

"A needle at least looks different from the hay," Nick groused. "We're looking for a Catholic priest in a nation of Catholics."

Further conversation halted when the serving woman brought their food—*Cozido à Portuguesa*, a beef and sausage stew with root vegetables; a basket of maize bread; and mugs of ale.

After several bites of delicious food and downing most of her ale, Harriet began to feel more optimistic. "In our favor, though, is that unlike a needle, Father Miguel wanted our fathers to find him."

Both men stared at her.

"You're assuming he didn't decide to keep the treasure for himself," Jonesy said after a moment. "A man can only stand so much temptation."

Nick gave him a sidelong glance, which Jonesy returned. Something was silently communicated between them, but Harriet couldn't interpret it.

"Let me see that list again," Nick said after taking a long drink of ale.

Jonesy slid the paper across the table.

Nick studied it again, and Harriet leaned against his shoulder to look at it too, eating the last of her cornbread.

"Harry, you're brilliant," he said.

Harriet straightened, already missing the warm strength of Nick's shoulder. "Yes, of course I am. Why?"

With his finger, he stabbed a name on the sheet. "That's it. *Casa de Perseguição*. It's a winery run by priests."

Jonesy chuckled. Harriet still didn't understand.

"*Perseguição* means chase," Nick added.

"Guess there wasn't a House of Langston for him to bolt to," Jonesy said, "so he went to the House of Chase."

Harriet shared Jonesy's grin. Dare she hope? The weight on her shoulders felt a tiny bit lighter.

Nick located the winery on the map, then looked out the window at the sky and checked his pocket watch. "It's near the Rio Ferreira, east of here. Even if we ride hard we won't be able to reach it before dark today, but we should be able to get there before noon tomorrow."

They finished their meal, collected their horses, and were back on the road within the hour.

Mid-afternoon, with clouds obscuring the sun, they made another quick stop to rest the horses and refresh themselves. Much as Harriet enjoyed the warmth of the fire blazing in the taproom's hearth and a bowl of the delicious *caldo verde* that was quickly becoming her favorite soup, she was eager to get going despite the distinct drop in temperature.

Fully intending to get herself into the saddle without Nick's help, she led her horse to the inn yard's mounting block. She rubbed a chilled arm with her free hand. Was that her breath she could see in the air? She maneuvered her horse so she could reach her coat tied behind the saddle. Her horse was so tall, she couldn't quite reach the knot on the far side from this angle. She stretched but still couldn't see what she was doing. Probably making a mess of the knot. *You idiot*, she thought, and took the first step up onto the block so she could see better.

A soft whicker let her know Nick had walked his horse over to her. "Allow me," he said quietly. With the advantage afforded by his height, he made short work of the knot, shook out her coat, and held it open for her to slip into.

She put her arms through the sleeves, instantly feeling warmer, both from the coat and Nick's nearness. With her standing on the first step of the block, they were almost at eye level, so close she could see the indigo rings surrounding his summer sky-blue irises.

He brought the lapels of her coat together, close under her chin. The action reminded her of when he'd rescued her from the sea and draped a blanket around her shoulders. Exuberant from their scrape with death she'd brazenly kissed him then, on the cheek. He'd been as cold and wet as she at the time. She felt an urge to kiss him again now. On his mouth. After their kiss while moored in the bay in Spain, she knew what it would feel like, how warm and welcoming his lips would be. His crew wasn't standing around them now.

"Make sure you do up the top button," he said, his voice a barely audible rumble. "Don't want you to get chilled."

She nodded. He didn't move away or let go. She felt herself swaying toward him and put a hand on his chest, inside his greatcoat, above his waistcoat, below his neckcloth. Only a single layer of muslin separated her bare palm from his bare chest. His queue of jet-black hair had fallen forward over his shoulder. Silken strands brushed the back of her hand.

He was so close, his mouth right *there*. A sparkle in his eyes indicated he knew what she was thinking. He leaned forward, tilted his head a little to the left.

The jingle of a harness and Jonesy's murmuring to his horse reminded her they were not alone. She straightened and quickly buttoned her coat. After a flash of irritation, she couldn't help a fleeting grin when she saw Nick roll his eyes at the interruption.

Nick stepped back, looking on with approval as she got herself settled in her saddle. She retrieved her wool cap from her pocket, settled it low over her ears, and moments later the three of them were off.

Traffic thinned as they got farther from the heart of Porto and surrounding settlements. They passed elegant traveling coaches, mean freight wagons, curricles, fellow travelers on horseback, and numerous pedestrians. No one seemed to notice or care that Harriet was not what she appeared. None of the serving wenches had attempted to flirt with her as they did Nick, though none of them had paid attention to Jonesy, either.

The first mate was a handsome man in his own right but seemed a pale version of Nick, with medium-brown hair, long and tied back in a queue, brown eyes, and tanned skin set off by his small gold hoop earring. Away from Nick, she was sure he'd get his share of flirtatious advances. Just not from Harriet.

When traffic allowed, Nick rode beside her instead of in front, with Jonesy just behind. Nick pointed out some of the interesting landmarks they passed — centuries' old cathedrals, cork oaks with bright orange bark, craggy hills rising in the distance. Around one bend came an ox, his handler walking beside, pulling a cart laden with a towering stack of hay.

She and Nick looked at each other. "Wonder if it's got a needle," they said in unison, and grinned.

Twilight was fading into darkness when they reached *A Estalagem da Uva e da Videira,* an inn with a sign painted with vines and clusters of grapes above a bed. Nick pointed out the shadowy hulk of the winery in the distance, barely visible high on a bluff, still a couple of hours' ride away.

According to the hostler at the last inn they'd stopped at, the sprawling collection of buildings that made up *Casa de Perseguição* had been around since the twelfth century, and over the years had been everything from a monastery to a military fortress. Even if they were certain of a welcome, the twisting road up the terraced hillside to the bluff would be treacherous in the dark. Tendrils of mist had settled into the terraces like clouds tucking in for a night's sleep.

Harriet was starving, her fingers almost senseless with cold, and her bottom numb from so many hours in the saddle. Her muscles groaned in protest when she dismounted, and she gladly handed the reins over to the hostlers who came to take their horses. She blew on her fingers to get sensation back as she tried to unobtrusively flex and stretch.

She gazed at the faraway building on the bluff obscured by the fading light. Tomorrow she could be in possession of the treasure. Her stomach fluttered in anticipation.

Nick spoke with the groom to make arrangements for the horses, and soon he, Harriet, and Jonesy stepped into the blessed warmth and lamplight of the inn.

The innkeeper greeted them, tossing a towel over his shoulder and wiping his hands on a stained apron that indicated he was also the cook. While Nick discussed their needs with their host—the only word Harriet recognized in the spate of exchanged Portuguese was *inglês*—she eyed the fire blazing in the hearth across the room. Blocking her path to warming herself were several tables, occupied with diners alone or in small groups. One table had a pair of grizzled old men playing chess, and another had four men playing cards.

The innkeeper disappeared into the kitchen, and Nick turned back to her and Jonesy. "They've been unusually busy this evening. He's not sure how many rooms he has left for the night. Says we might need to double up. They'll feed us while the staff sorts it out."

"I could eat," Jonesy said with a grin. "And a bed of straw in the stall with my horse would be warm. I've slept in worse places."

Harriet raised her brows. She certainly didn't want to double up with any other travelers. She'd had to do that enough at coaching inns in England and could happily go the rest of her life without doing it again, though she wasn't sure a bed of straw in the stables would be all that warm or comfortable, either. But, well, she was on an adventure, in search of treasure that would affect the course of her life. She would just ignore the outraged sputtering Madam Zavrina would have made at the idea of sleeping in the stables. Nick and Jonesy hung their coats and hats on hooks by the door. Harriet was still chilled and kept hers on.

The card game broke up. Two of the players strode out the door, letting in a gust of cold air, and the third moved to the other table to chat with the chess players. She shivered and followed Nick into the dining room, not caring where they sat to eat so long as it was near the fire. Cross-legged on the stone hearth would be fine at this point.

Nick stopped so abruptly she bumped into him and bounced off his rigid back.

She would have fallen but Jonesy caught her under her arms and lifted her upright. Nick was frozen. Not a muscle twitched, his face a mask of granite.

She took a step to one side, Jonesy to the other, and peered around Nick.

A lone man sat at the table before them, shuffling a deck of cards with practiced ease as he smiled broadly at the newcomers. "Nicky!"

He fanned the cards out on the table and swept them up again. "Took you long enough to get here."

Chapter 15

Harriet's breath caught.

Nick still hadn't moved.

She exhaled and studied the stranger. Silver highlighted the fashionably short black hair at his temples, and deep lines around his eyes and mouth indicated he'd smiled often over the decades. His eyes were the same blue as Nick's as he flicked his gaze from her to Jonesy and back to Nick.

"Brought part of your crew this far inland, did you?"

Nick let out a deep breath. Really, he shouldn't have been surprised. He'd begun to suspect his relative might be in the area when the housekeeper at the second *igreja* had mentioned his older look-alike. "Uncle Zach." Nick pulled out a chair at the table and sat down. "Penrith was wondering why you hadn't been around London for him to win his money back from you." He jerked a thumb over his shoulder toward the door, where the other players had recently left. "You needed to travel all the way to Portugal to find more gulls to fleece?"

Zach set his cards on the table and studiously neatened the deck's edges. "I am here because of a card game, actually. It's a lengthy tale. Best told over a bottle of vino."

A serving wench arrived bearing a tray. She set down three bowls of stew, a basket of maize bread, and three tankards of cider. In Portuguese, she inquired if Zach desired anything.

He winked at her. In Spanish, he replied he'd have the same, gesturing at Nick's bowl and mug. There was already a mostly empty wine bottle and a glass with an inch of red wine in it on the table beside Zach.

Harry sat down to Nick's left, Jonesy to his right, and they both dug into the food.

Nick knew they had to be dying of curiosity. He was brimming with questions himself but knew Zach would only talk when he was ready. And well lubricated with alcohol. Nick began to eat.

The server came back with Zach's food and cider, and for several minutes they were all busy eating. Nick noted Zach watching Jonesy and Harry, undoubtedly sizing them up as potential marks. Nick's first mate rarely indulged in games of chance, but he didn't know if Harry played. Silver loo and piquet, probably. Did she know how to play whist? Unlikely, though it was entirely possible his rascally crew had taught her card and dice games just as they'd taught her to fire a cannon, splice rope, and sing bawdy chants.

Zach seemed fascinated by Harry, specifically her hands. She was buttering a hunk of cornbread. Nick knew she was developing calluses on her palms and fingers from hauling on lines and other work on the ship, but the backs of her hands were still smooth and mostly pale, marred only by a couple of scratches and a ragged nail or two.

The hands of a lady.

One side of Zach's mouth quirked up in a grin. Nick met Zach's knowing stare and uplifted brow with the same blank expression he wore when holding four aces. Or a junk hand.

"Jonesy and Harry know why we're here," Nick said. "Why are *you* here? And why were you expecting me?"

Zach gestured to get the serving woman's attention. He started to order another bottle of vintage port, but then with a smile at Harry asked for a bottle of *vinho verde* instead. She was, hopefully, too busy eating to notice the switch from a stout alcohol to a bubbly light white wine that Zach could drink like water and probably wouldn't get even a young lady tipsy.

"A few weeks ago in London the cards were against me," Zach began after a glass had been poured for everyone and the wine bubbles fizzed to the surface. "I was certain I could turn things around even though I had already lost all the blunt I had on me. You know I don't believe in vowels. I did have a piece of paper with me, however. One I've carried for five years. A map."

Nick was close enough to hear Harry's slight gasp. She quickly took a sip of wine and said nothing. "A treasure map?" Nick prompted.

"That's what Adam called it in his letter when he sent the drawing." Zach tossed back his glassful and refilled it. "I didn't put much store in it. Certainly didn't think it would be worth the bother to go looking for it on the Continent. The next morning I reconsidered. Thought perhaps I should buy it back and give it to you instead of letting Hornsby have it."

"And Hornsby is..." Nick prompted when Zach became absorbed in his meal.

Zach pushed aside his now-empty bowl. "The cove who was having a much better night with the cards than I was. By the time I was feeling up to snuff to pay him a call, he'd decamped. Soon learned he'd hired a ship and gone. If he put enough stock in it to set sail with a smuggler captain, I figured I ought to go after it, too. I'd looked at the map enough over the years to remember what was on it."

"Would the smuggler happen to be named Ruford?"

Zach didn't look the least surprised. "You know him."

"We've ... met."

Zach grinned and shook a finger at Nick. "Oh, there's a tale to that, isn't there?"

"Some other time."

"You're no fun, Nicky." Zach heaved a great sigh and emptied his glass in one long swallow. "I caught a packet in Dover, bought a horse in Calais, and rode to Corunna. But the treasure wasn't there anymore. It had been moved to Oporto."

The innkeeper approached their table then. With apologies, he explained they were unexpectedly busy, especially for this time of year, and had only one room left for the night. Did they mind sharing?

Jonesy understood enough Portuguese to follow the conversation, though Harry did not. Jonesy had finished his food while Zach talked. He swallowed the last of his drink and set the tankard on the table. "Stables it is. See you in the morning, Cap'n." He grabbed his coat and went out the door.

Harry looked torn between wanting to hear the rest of Zach's story and going out to the stables. Nick rested his hand on her knee to keep her from rising. If there was a room available indoors, she wasn't sleeping with the horses.

"Got yourself a new cabin boy, Nicky?"

"I'm confused," Nick said, deliberately ignoring the question. "If you gambled away your map to Hornsby, and he and Ruford sailed to Spain to look for the treasure," he turned to Harry, "who broke into your cottage and stole your copy of the map?"

She froze with her glass halfway to her mouth, which was open in a silent "*Oh*."

"Half the treasure rightfully belongs to Harry here." Nick swallowed a mouthful of wine, his mind racing.

Zach leaned forward, elbows on the table, resting his chin on interlaced fingers. "Do tell."

"Adam and his chum Giles were partners on the bet. Giles was Harry's father."

"The gunner's mate who saved Adam's sorry arse." Zach looked at Harry with renewed interest. "I never met your father but heard many things about him from my brother. A man of good character."

Harry nodded her thanks. She still hadn't spoken a word, helping to hide her gender. Nick had been careful about pronouns so as not to give Zach any improper ideas about his traveling companion. She hid a yawn behind one hand.

"And you're here at this particular inn because you think you figured out where the priest went?"

"Same as you, Nicky."

Nick folded his hands on the table. "What made you even think I was looking for the priest?"

Zach shrugged. "A couple of places I stopped to make inquiries, someone had already been there asking the same questions. Someone who looked like a younger version of me." He flipped over the deck of cards and shuffled them again. "Did Adam send a copy of the map to you?"

"No." Nick tried to keep the anger out of his voice. "I knew nothing about the treasure until Harry asked me for a ride to Spain to fetch it."

The serving girl came over to clear their dishes and offered to show Nick and Harry to their room. Their saddlebags had already been sent up.

"Come back for a nightcap, Nicky."

Nick followed Harry up the staircase, to a door at the end of the hall. As expected, the room was hardly bigger than his cabin on the *Wind Dancer*, dominated by a bed in the center that was much larger than his bunk. A dressing table and chair were against the wall near the window, next to a clothes press and a nightstand with washbasin and chamber pot. Two armchairs flanked the river rock fireplace, which had a freshly built crackling fire trying to dispel the chill. It could be a room at any inn anywhere in England or on the Continent, if not for the brightly colored, woven cotton blanket on the bed in the style popular in Spain and Portugal.

He gave the woman a coin and requested an extra blanket before she left.

Harry was standing at the foot of the bed, staring at it.

"Too bad there are no hooks for a hammock," he said.

"Ha," she replied without a trace of humor, still eyeing the bed and not him.

"I'm going to sleep by the fire," he said to put her at ease. "That's why I asked for the extra blanket."

She finally looked at him, tension leaving her body, and she hung her coat and cap on the hook by the door. "Fancy meeting your uncle here," she said, crossing to the fire. She put her hands toward the flames. "I couldn't help noticing you refer to your father by his given name."

A soft knock at the door precluded his need to reply. He accepted the blanket and tossed it onto the nearest armchair but didn't shut the door. "I'm going to see what else Zach knows."

She nodded and added another stick to the fire.

* * *

"Harry settling in all right?" Zach said as Nick sat down, in the chair next to him instead of across the table, so they could converse with more privacy. The dining room held fewer patrons now, but there was still a low hum of conversation and the clatter of utensils on dishes.

Nick nodded. "Going to turn in, I expect. We had a long ride yesterday and again today." He refilled his glass with more *vinho verde*. He anticipated needing a clear head to deal with his relative.

Zach stared at him in disbelief. "Good lord, lad, you really *are* inept if they're not throwing themselves at you."

Nick stared back blankly.

"How long has Harry been making do with cold water in a washbasin on the ship and while you've been traipsing about the countryside? Have a hot bath sent up for the girl, you nodcock."

Nick buried his face in his hands.

Just for a moment. Then he raised one hand to get the attention of the serving woman, and requested a bath be sent up to his room.

"Sim, senhor," she replied. She smiled at Nick but suggestively trailed her hand along Zach's jaw as she left.

"Are you waiting to toss her skirts until after you find the treasure?" Zach said as he lifted his glass. "Not that she's actually wearing skirts." He took a drink. "If you marry her, you won't have to split the money."

Nick didn't know whether to laugh or plant Zach a facer. His statement was too close to the truth. "What makes you think—"

"Because it's obvious you haven't touched her. I saw how she reacted when you put your hand on her knee. Girl's as untried as a six-month-old filly."

Nick choked on his wine.

Zach thumped him between his shoulders. "There, there, lad. We can't all be a dab hand with the ladies." He refilled his glass and Nick's with port. "Speaking of ladies, how is the *Wind Dancer*?"

Nick coughed and took a fortifying swallow of port. Then another. Oh, this was good. He sniffed it, swirled it, and watched the legs slide down the glass. He really must get some of this to take home. Half a hold's worth, at least. He studied the bottle's label and filed the vintage information away for later. "We took some damage leaving Corunna after we had a run-in with Ruford. He shot the sails full of holes with grape shot. Had to get out the spare set to make it to Porto."

"Oh no, not the speckled pink sails!" Zach laughed. "I wish I'd witnessed your arrival. Must have caused quite a stir."

Nick watched Zach, thinking about how thoroughly Zach kept track of the ship. "I've often wondered why Grandfather gave her to me instead of you."

Zach shrugged one shoulder. "Because the old fart knew I'd sink her in a storm or get lost and wreck her on rocky shoals. Or worse, gamble her away while deep in my cups." He briefly rested a hand on Nick's shoulder, then patted his cheek. "Even as a beardless youth with your voice cracking when you called out orders to the crew, you showed an aptitude for navigation and seamanship far greater than I ever did. It was obvious to us both that the sea would be your mistress, lad." He sipped his wine. "Me, I prefer something warmer. With lovely curves."

The serving woman walked by them just then, her hands full with a tray of dishes and glasses. Zach patted her bottom as she passed. She smiled at him over her shoulder and put a little extra sway in her hips.

"Mother told me, you know," Nick said softly. "About the masquerade ball." With one finger, he traced a droplet of wine sliding down the outside of his glass. He needed to finally say the words but couldn't bring himself to look at Zach.

Zach set his glass down with extreme care. "When?"

"Shortly before she died."

"You were, what, eighteen when she died?" Zach let out a deep sigh. "That's a heavy load for one so young to carry."

"It changed everything I thought I knew about my life." Nick tried not to sound bitter. "But it was also not surprising. Explained why Adam was such a harsh taskmaster. Mother wanted me to understand he meant well, that he was just trying to be certain I did not grow up to be like you."

"A profligate. Wastrel. Drunkard." Zach recited the words without emotion. They'd both heard them countless times before.

"When do you think she told him?"

"Never."

Nick's jaw dropped. He stared at Zach. "He had to have known, else why would he be so harsh with me? He was never that..." *brutal, insensitive* "...unyielding with my sisters."

Zach drank deeply. "Oh, he knew. First time he saw your little bare bum."

Nick fell back in his chair as though struck. "What?" *Adam knew, Nick's whole life?*

"I'm afraid you have the same heart-shaped birthmark on your right cheek that I do." Zach pointed to his hip, making clear which 'cheek' he referenced. "Which Adam did *not* have."

Nick resisted the impulse to glance toward his backside, or Zach's. Bullies in school had teased him about the mark when he was younger, and Nick had ended up in the headmaster's office more than once for his flying-fists response. As an adult, several lovers had traced the mark with their finger. Or tongue.

Nick tried to rearrange the mental pictures he had of his childhood, what they meant. "But he did not act toward her as though he knew she had betrayed him." He had often seen his parents kiss and embrace one another, especially the first few days each time Adam came home on leave.

Zach shrugged. "Apparently he forgave her. Understood her reason for doing it."

Nick's brows shot up. "Which was?"

"She was desperate." Zach took a fortifying swig of wine. "After Audrey was followed by Bettina and then Caroline and Diana and Evelyn, she was desperate. Each baby took more out of her, and it took longer to recover her strength. Carrying and birthing Evelyn almost did her in. She believed she wouldn't survive a seventh pregnancy, so the sixth child had to be the heir for Adam. I didn't know it was her until after I was already—well, until it was too late."

The couple who'd been eating at the next table finished and headed up the staircase. Nick watched them go, desperately wanting to hear what Zach was going to say. And also wanting to go up the stairs and not hear it. Ever.

The serving woman came back and set down a plate with two puff pastries filled with egg custard, dusted with sugar. The kitchen was shutting down for the night, she explained with a smile for Zach, and she didn't want these to go to waste.

"Obrigado, senhora." Zach gallantly kissed her hand as she gave him two clean forks, then he watched her walk away, her hips swaying suggestively.

Nick viewed the exchange, glad for the distraction, his amusement turning to mild annoyance when he had to tap Zach on the arm to get his fork.

Zach ate a bite of the *pasteis de nata* and closed his eyes in gastronomic bliss. He looked at Nick again, his shoulders rising and lowering with a sigh. "Where was I? Oh, yes. Your mother knew that I have three by-blows, all boys, with three different mothers. I like to think she would have chosen me over Adam if I'd had more than two thousand a year. But her parents wanted her to marry the heir, not the spare. Nothing less than a viscount for their girl." He ate another bite of pastry, then tipped back his glass and swallowed.

Nick's paternal grandmother had died giving birth to what would have been his aunt, and his grandfather had lived well into his seventies before succumbing to lung fever one winter. But Nick had only fuzzy recollections of his maternal grandparents. Both had died before he was out of the nursery. "You should have the title, not me," he said quietly, staring into the dark depths of his glass, his pastry untouched.

"Ah, Nicky. You make a much better viscount than I would. Even though Adam gave away most of the estate's money—"

"Pious hypocrite."

"—and you drive your steward mad with lack of attention, your tenants don't go hungry and they don't have leaky roofs. Even if you've had to smuggle loads of brandy and such along with the spies to earn enough blunt to take care of them."

"I am an honest merchantman," Nick argued reflexively. He met Zach's gaze, and they both chuckled.

"Family tradition," Zach said. He raised his glass. "To the third Viscount Sheffield. Crafty old devil." Nick clinked his glass to Zach's in a toast to his grandfather, and they both drank.

The two chess players finished their game. They put the pieces and board away on a shelf beside the fire, where there were decks of cards and a checkers set, and left the dining room with their friend, calling good night to the innkeeper and serving women.

Only one other guest remained in the dining room, a lone gent near the fireplace. He sat slouched down in his chair, feet close to the fire, black knit wool cap tugged low over his ears, chin on his chest, eyes closed. Could be asleep, or, from the empty bottle on the table, possibly passed out.

Zach ate another bite of the pastry and gave a tiny moan of delight. "Now that the Home Office no longer needs your services, and with the abysmal harvest this year, you're going to need to do something to keep everyone afloat. So in the morning we'll ride up to the bluff together and see what Adam and Giles left for you and Harry, eh?"

The serving woman walked to the door, now wearing a cloak and tying a scarf over her head.

"Yes, that sounds—"

Zach rose abruptly, nearly tipping his chair back in his haste. He cupped Nick's cheek and stared into his eyes. "I've always been proud of you, son." He lingered for a heartbeat or two, then strode to the door. He bent to whisper in the young woman's ear, one hand resting on her waist, then sliding around to caress her bottom. She giggled and nodded, and they went up the stairs hand in hand.

Nick raised his glass in a silent toast to them, then ate a bite of Zach's dessert.

While he enjoyed the privileges of being the viscount, he'd never wanted the role. Never wanted to take Adam's place, follow his example. Nick's sense of honor demanded that he take care of the Langston tenants, despite the estate's lack of funds, but he delegated the day-to-day running to the steward.

Adam's duty had been to God, country, and family, in that order. He stayed in the Navy during the war in service to the first two ideals. Nick felt a duty to England as well, but instead of taking orders from officers who too often had attained their rank because of influence rather than ability, he served the Crown as a privateer. He didn't follow any orders he didn't like.

But the war was over. Nick was a private citizen. And he was a member of the aristocracy, whether he wanted the title or not.

The gent by the fire rose and climbed the stairs. Nick was alone in the dining room.

He thought about what awaited him upstairs; the long uncomfortable night ahead sleeping on the hearth or sitting slouched in a chair so he wouldn't be tempted to break Harry's trust.

He sighed and polished off Zach's pastry, then drained his glass and went upstairs, carrying the plate and clean fork.

His key didn't open the door. He checked the hall to make sure he had the correct room. The knob turned freely but the door wouldn't open. He scratched on the door. "Harry?" he called softly.

After a moment he heard wood scraping, then the door opened a fraction and Harry peered around the edge. As soon as Nick was inside, she closed the door and wedged the chair from the dressing table under the knob.

"You don't trust the lock?"

She was wearing just a linen shirt, untucked, and striped dungarees. A towel was draped around shoulders, her damp hair loose and wild. "I don't know who else has a key."

"Good point. Here." He thrust the plate and fork at her, trying not to be distracted by her bare feet. And bare ankles. And where water droplets had turned her shirt translucent.

Her eyes lit up with the first bite. "Ooh! This is delicious! Thank you." She moved to the fire, where she had apparently been drying her hair. Damp spots on the floor indicated where the tub had recently sat.

No, he was not going to imagine how she might have looked, naked and wet in the bathtub. Or how she would have looked stepping out of it, water sluicing down her bare skin, firelight glinting off the droplets, making her skin glow. How he'd like to hold the soft woven towel and dry her off, caressing every inch of her body.

He cast his gaze about the room, desperate to change the course of his thoughts. "How did you learn that trick?" He gestured at the chair, with its back wedged under the doorknob.

She swallowed a bite of the pastry. He wished he'd brought a bottle of wine up with him. Just to help her wash it down. "Some of the men visiting their daughters or sisters at the Academy were not as gentlemanly as one would wish." She gave a one-shouldered shrug. "The teachers may not have all been best of friends, but we made sure to share useful information. Especially where our safety was concerned."

Nick was suddenly glad he hadn't brought up a bottle. Or drunk more than he had. He was not inept, as Zach suggested, and he had never forced his attentions on a woman. They'd all been happy. Welcoming. Eager, even.

He joined Harry by the fire and spotted her brush on the mantel, just as Harry gathered up the last of the custard and licked it off the fork, her pink tongue briefly visible.

Nick stifled a groan. He grabbed the brush and pushed her shoulders so she stood with her back to him. Much safer.

She giggled.

No, that wasn't Harry's giggle. Actually, he didn't know what her giggle sounded like. And the sound had been muffled.

Harry looked at him over her shoulder, eyebrows raised in silent query, and the sound came again.

From the room next door.

They both shrugged. The price of staying at an inn often included thin walls and loud neighbors.

She set the plate and fork on the mantel and lowered her chin as Nick got to work brushing her wild, wet hair. The hint of lemon-scented soap wafted up, mixing with leather from her clothes that had traveled in the saddlebags all day.

He was not inept when it came to women. Curse Zach for even suggesting such nonsense. Nick had had more than his share of women over the years who offered themselves up to him. From society ladies like Lady Slavin in London, to serving wenches at seaside towns, to the upstairs maid when he was sixteen, and all the others in between.

Wait a moment.

They'd all offered themselves to him.

He hadn't pursued any of them.

There wasn't a single woman he could think of who he'd had to pursue, persuade, or court. No one he'd wanted to expend the time or effort to entice into his bed or charm his way into theirs. He'd certainly given and received pleasure, been careful not to sire any by-blows, and left them without a backward glance, eager to get back to his ship. But they'd all come to him. Smiling, flirting, subtle or bold, all of them had ... thrown themselves at him.

He had never seduced a woman. Not a one.

When he wasn't distracted by women, he spent most of his time on his ship. Went sailing. As unpredictable and changeable as the sea could be, there was beauty and strength in the waves. A challenge. Puzzles to solve in the currents and wind patterns. Besting a storm, outsmarting enemies. Distant countries to explore, cultures and cuisine to sample.

After his mother's funeral, reeling with the still-fresh knowledge that in at least one respect he was a bastard, he'd spun the globe in Adam's study, closed his eyes, and taken more than a year off from Oxford to sail to Singhapura because that's where his finger landed on the globe.

Zach was right. Nick's mistress was the sea.

Nick groaned. The sound blended in with a groan from the next room. A male groan. To go along with another feminine giggle.

So why was he brushing Harriet's hair? Again? He brought the towel up to squeeze more water out of her tresses and stroked the brush through. When a small section was smooth, he pushed it over her shoulder, stirring the faint scent of lemon soap. The ends were already drying.

Harriet was the first woman he could recall who had ever expressed genuine interest in his ship. The first woman he wanted to take to bed who did not crook her finger at him first.

Sure, she'd kissed him—once on the cheek, once on the mouth, and almost kissed him at the other inn this afternoon.

But she was betrothed.

Wasn't she?

She hadn't mentioned what's-his-name in quite a while.

Perhaps he could persuade her to discover the delights of the marriage bed beforehand.

Did he have the right to do that? Assuming she had not already tasted the delights of intimacy. Her intended was a farmer, after all. A man of the earth and, one would suppose, earthly delights.

Zach had claimed her reaction to being touched was that of a virgin. Nick had a reputation among the *ton* as being a rake, but Zach was the one who had been in so many beds he was lucky not to have syphilis.

Nick groaned again. Damn it, Zach was right about him being inept.

He knew how to pleasure a woman, of course, but if she wasn't asking for his attention, he was uncertain.

He hated being uncertain.

Harriet was certainly enjoying what he was doing with her hair, though. Her eyes were closed and she swayed slightly with his movements. All the knots were out now. He was holding sections of her hair up, brushing it dry, letting the silky strands fall into place. He could see the tender skin of her neck, the silver chain caressing her nape. It would be so easy to lean forward, press his lips to that skin. More than once he'd made a woman shatter in pleasure by kissing and gently biting just below her ear if his hand beneath her skirt wasn't quite enough to push her over the edge.

Oh hell. Harriet wasn't in bliss. She was asleep on her feet.

Nick groaned. So did the gent next door.

He set the brush on the mantel and patted her shoulders, wanting to run his hands down her arms, to caress her. "All done."

She brought her head up and blinked at him as she turned. She looked disoriented for a moment, then gave him a slow smile as she touched her hair. "Thank you."

He grunted an acknowledgment and made a show of taking off his boots and neckcloth, settled the blanket over himself, and tried to get comfortable slouching in one armchair, his feet propped on the seat cushion of the other.

She draped the damp towel over the chair blocking the door, blew out the lamp, and climbed into bed.

As many nights as she'd slept in his bunk, he'd never actually seen her get into bed. There was the time he'd carried her there, after she fell asleep at the table perusing navigation charts. He'd wanted to climb in beside her and hold her all night. He'd settled for touching his lips to her forehead in a chaste kiss. His duties as captain and navigator had called him away.

Now, however, there were no distractions. He threw another piece of wood on the fire and tugged the blanket up to his chin.

Within moments he heard the soft sounds of Harriet's deep breathing. Fast asleep.

The couple next door, however, were still having fun. Whatever the gent was doing had her exclaiming her pleasure.

Nick groaned.

* * *

He woke suddenly, aware of movement in the room.

The fire had burned down a little and the sky outside was still black.

He strained his eyes, trying to see in the dark. A muffled "*Ow!*" and he was able to pick out Harriet standing beside the bed. He threw more fuel on the fire.

"Sorry, didn't mean to wake you," she whispered.

"Anything amiss?"

"Stubbed my toe on the bed post is all."

"But why were you out of bed?" If she'd used the chamber pot, it was directly across from the bed, clear of any furniture.

"Cold. There's a draft from the window. Just adding my coat to the blanket."

But her coat was short. Either her legs and feet or her chest and shoulders would still be cold.

Oh, he couldn't. What he was thinking went far beyond the pale to be thinking about doing with an unmarried miss. He wouldn't.

He did. "It's a big bed. What if I added my blanket on top of yours and we shared?" The chair was lumpy. And the side of him next to the fire was toasty but the other side was chilled.

Was that muffled squeak from her? Or the couple he could still hear moving around next door?

"Um. Neither of us is wet."

She was thinking of the time they'd shared a blanket to warm up after their dunking in the Channel. "True. But you are chilled."

"Actually, my hair is still damp. I shouldn't have washed it this late in the day, but I couldn't pass up the chance. That's probably why I'm cold." He heard her sigh. "Very well."

Not exactly throwing herself at him. Nick would take what he could get.

He stirred the fire and added more fuel. She hung up her coat, and together they spread his blanket over the bed. For good measure he also draped his greatcoat on top on her side.

In the brighter light from the fire, he watched her gingerly settle in the bed, on her back near the far edge of the mattress, and tuck the blankets under her chin.

Nick climbed in on the other side, glad to stretch out fully horizontal, even more grateful that the blankets were long enough to cover his feet and his shoulders at the same time.

It was a start. Yes, he may be inept, but he and Harriet were finally in the same bed at the same time, by his engineering. Who knew what might happen next in such close, intimate quarters?

The couple next door got louder. "Oh, Zach!" the female cried out.

Nick wanted to slap his forehead. Of course it was Zach and the serving wench in the next room. Could it get any worse?

Heavy footsteps. Creaking.

Rhythmic creaking. That went on and on. And on.

Good lord, how much stamina did Zach have? He was well into his fifties.

Another sound. Feminine. Nearby.

Oh, that's what Harriet's giggle sounded like.

Nick turned his head on the pillow to look at his bedmate. She was close enough he could touch her if he reached for her. Her eyes were sparkling in the firelight, a flash of white teeth visible from her smile. As the rhythmic creaking continued next door, her giggle turned to full-throated laughter.

He gave in and they laughed together.

Chapter 16

Nick awoke again just as the sky was beginning to lighten. He was accustomed to sleeping in four-hour shifts, so he wasn't surprised or alarmed. He did a quick inventory of his surroundings, also out of habit. The fire had died down to coals and a chill wind whistled through gaps in the window frame, but he was still warm, lying on his side ... with his arms around Harriet.

She was also on her side, snuggled up against him, her head tucked under his chin. She clutched his shirt with one fist, her other palm flattened against his chest. Push, pull. Perhaps he wasn't the only one who was conflicted.

He felt her warm breath against his neck, her cold nose brushing his Adam's apple when he swallowed. The faint scent of lemon wafted up from her.

In just a few hours, he could have his hands on the treasure his father—or rather, the man who'd raised him—had not wanted him to have. Nick could have his revenge against the wealthy man who'd left Nick nothing in his will except what the laws of primogeniture required.

Nick would have the means to keep the Sheffield tenants fed and sheltered this winter despite the horrifically poor harvest. It was as if summer had never fully appeared this year. Profit from the port wine he was importing on this trip should give him a cushion against further expenses, perhaps even cover the cost of replacing the starboard gun.

Yet he found himself more interested in this armful of woman.

He stroked her silky soft hair, now dry and fanning loose behind her on the pillow.

She murmured in her sleep and burrowed closer to him, tangling her legs with his.

Perhaps he should be grateful to Adam for hiding the treasure, and for the stranger who'd broken into Harriet's cottage to steal her copy, for they all played a part in bringing her to him, to this place, this bed with her body tucked against his.

He couldn't dredge up gratitude, however, for the man who wanted her to have a dowry before he'd marry her, though the need for said dowry was what had made Harriet seek out Nick in the first place.

In her sleepy state, he could touch her. Stroke her bottom, the delectable curve he'd seen revealed by her male attire. Cup her breast and thumb her nipple to an aroused peak, unencumbered by corset or other restraint. Caress her intimately. Putting his hand down a woman's dungarees would be a first for him. Nuzzle her below her ear to the gentle curve where her neck met her shoulder. By the time he kissed her awake, his lips to hers, she'd be in a sensual daze, eager for lovemaking.

It would be so easy to seduce her.

Which was why she had to be completely awake before he did any of those things.

Nick tamped down his desire. He indulged in stroking her hair once more, pressed a kiss to the top of her head, wrapped his arm around her again, and closed his eyes to drift off to sleep.

The sun was struggling to break through heavy clouds when he felt Harriet stir. He kept his arm loosely draped over her waist—making sure his hand was nowhere inappropriate—and pretended to still be asleep, even as she gave a quiet gasp and rolled back to her side of the bed.

He missed her already, and not just the warmth she took with her. What would it be like to wake with her in his bed every morning? To rouse her in a sensual haze and leisurely make love before facing the day? To make her moan with pleasure at night, enjoying each other with wild abandon?

He lay still, giving her privacy to get ready. He heard the rustling of fabric as she set her clothing to rights and added the daytime layers and her boots.

"You can open your eyes now," she said quietly, setting her saddlebags on the bed. Nick stretched and yawned. She retrieved her brush from the mantel and began brushing her hair. As their eyes met, a light blush stole across her cheeks.

"Zach intends to travel up to the winery with us this morning," Nick said, sitting up and swinging his legs over the side.

She cocked her head to one side and went still for a moment. "I don't hear any sounds from next door."

Nick shrugged and pulled on his boots.

She fished a length of cord from her waistcoat pocket and began braiding her hair at the dressing table, while he stood just behind her, looking at his own reflection above her as he tied his neckcloth.

Their eyes met in the mirror. A smile played about her mouth, and he felt an answering grin spread across his face.

Who would have thought when they met in the ballroom a few weeks ago that they'd be here, engaged in such mundane but intimate personal tasks after spending the night together, and her still as innocent as when they left London?

Harriet ducked her head in an unexpected spurt of maidenly modesty—had his thoughts been so obvious?—and quickly repacked her few belongings. She gave a last look around the room, then slid the chair out from under the doorknob. "I'll go see if I can order breakfast for us."

Nick waved her on.

Minutes later he entered the dining room ... and stopped short at the sight of Harry eating breakfast with Jonesy and Zach.

Zach saluted him with his coffee cup before taking a sip.

Nick shook his head and sat at the last place at their table, where a plate of eggs, chorizo, and *migas* already awaited him. There was a carafe of coffee and a teapot in the center of the table, and cups for everyone.

"Mornin', Cap'n," Jonesy said. He scooped up a forkful of egg. "Sleep well?"

Harry kept her head down, totally absorbed in the task of stirring milk and sugar into her tea.

"Yes," Nick said, unwilling to give anything away, even to his first mate. "You?"

Jonesy chewed and swallowed. "Stables were snug and warm. And the neighbors didn't snore."

Harriet let out a startled giggle but quickly schooled her expression to one of polite neutrality and dug into her meal.

"I also slept well," Zach announced.

Harriet choked.

Zach thumped her on her back.

She waved her hand, indicating she was fine, and reached for her teacup for a deep drink. Her shoulders shook with silent laughter when she set the cup down.

Company in the dining room was sparse. Locals came in to socialize mostly in the evenings, and fellow travelers came and went at various times depending on their agenda. They spent several minutes enjoying the food in relative quiet, the cheery fire crackling in the hearth dispelling the early morning chill.

"Zach is going to accompany us up to the winery," Nick said after he polished off his food, addressing Jonesy. "I'd like you to return to the *Wind Dancer*. Keep an eye on repairs, make sure everything is restocked."

Jonesy nodded. "And maybe look for a replacement for the starboard gun? Per'aps the Frogs left behind some ordnance that the British didn't find."

Before Nick could voice agreement, Zach slammed his cup down with a loud clink. "What happened to her starboard gun?"

"I'll tell you when we're on our way," Nick said. He waved the innkeeper's wife over and let her know they were ready to depart. The innkeeper came out and Nick settled the account for himself, Jonesy and Harry, his eyebrows climbing in shock when he saw the fee charged for the hot bath. After a glance at Harry, he shrugged and paid the bill without haggling. Harry looked well-rested and was accepting a small cloth-wrapped bundle from the serving girl that she put in her coat pocket. And she smelled good. Not that she had ever *not* smelled good, even when her scent was predominately gunpowder and wet hemp.

Their party trooped out to the inn yard, and soon Harry and Jonesy's horses were brought out. Jonesy swung up and waved goodbye and quickly rode out of sight. The rainstorm of last night had moved through, tapering off to a drizzle this morning, the droplets so fine it was more like a thick fog.

Zach gave a low whistle when he saw the grey gelding. He walked over to Harry, who was fishing a carrot out of her coat pocket.

"He's at least sixteen hands high," Zach said, stroking the gelding's nose. "That's quite a mount for a Pocket Venus such as you."

Harry held up a carrot on her upturned palm, fingers flat. Her horse snuffled it up and crunched. "That's what I thought when the hostler brought him out for me." She gave Zach a sidelong glance. "Except for the Venus part." She patted her horse's neck. "But he's been very patient and forgiving with me."

The horse finished his carrot and nuzzled Harry for another. Zach held the bridle and did a cursory check of the horse's teeth and bit, then the rest of the tack and girth on the saddle. Zach gave him another pat on the neck. "Older gents like this fellow tend to get either cantankerous or placid. Fortunately for you, he seems to be the latter."

"You are an expert on horseflesh?" Harry snatched her cap back from the horse, who was still looking for another treat.

Zach shook his head. "The expected path for a younger son is either the military or clergy. I have always liked women and cards too much to get up early on Sundays and give a sermon, so Father bought colors for me. The 15th King's Hussars. I learned to choose my mount carefully."

She tilted her head to study him. "I imagine you looked quite dashing in your cavalry uniform."

Zach preened. "For a few years, yes. Parading about and impressing the ladies was one thing, but it turns out I didn't have the stomach for battle. And the military insists we greet the morning absurdly early."

Harry chuckled.

Nick tamped down a spark of impatience. Fortunately, a groom brought out his own chestnut gelding just then and he swung up into the saddle, making the leather creak as much as possible.

Startled, Harry glanced at Nick, a pink flush stealing across her cheeks. She took the reins back from Zach and made to move to the mounting block, but Zach stood in her way.

He leaned over and cupped his hands. "Allow me, m'dear."

After a moment's hesitation, Harry rested a hand on Zach's shoulder and let him boost her up into the saddle. As she settled and adjusted the reins, a groom brought out Zach's black stallion.

Zach gave Harry a pat on the leg and then strode past Nick to his horse, a satisfied smirk tilting his mouth.

Nick tamped down another spurt of impatience. Yes, that's what he felt, impatience. "We're losing daylight."

"Keep your britches on, boy," Zach said. He mounted and wheeled his horse toward the road. "Shall we go?"

Nick swore softly in Mandarin, a handy phrase he'd learned from Chang, and led the way out of the yard.

As soon as they were on the road, Zach tossed out, "What happened to the starboard gun?"

Nick glanced over his shoulder at Zach. "Went overboard in a storm."

Zach urged his horse forward to catch up with Nick. "Come again?"

"Two days out in the Channel a squall blew through. The line was frayed, the carriage rolled, and it punched through the starboard gunwale."

Harriet couldn't help shuddering at the memory.

Zach slowed down until he was even with Harriet's horse. "What is it, m'dear?"

"My skirt was tangled in the carriage axle when it went overboard." She swallowed hard. "I nearly drowned."

"But the weight of the cannon—"

"The gun fell off the carriage when it tipped over the side," Nick said. "I jumped in to grab her, and the crew hauled on my safety line to fish us out."

Zach glanced between the two of them, his expression thoughtful. A lone rider trotted past, going the other direction. "And your dress?"

"At the bottom of the Channel, still tangled with the carriage. Unless fish have a taste for wool."

She felt Zach peruse her person, taking in her masculine attire with renewed interest. She kept her gaze on the road ahead.

A carriage drawn by a pair of bays approached, and Zach fell back, third in line. Harriet forced herself to relax, to enjoy the sun on her face as the fog dissipated. Clouds were clearing, and large patches of blue sky were becoming visible. Breathtaking views of autumn foliage in orange and brilliant yellow, mostly from rows of grape vines, covered the hillside they were climbing.

When they made the first hairpin turn she was glad they were on horseback. The hillside fell away so steeply it made her stomach flip if she looked over the edge. What if a driver lost control of their carriage coming down?

She focused her attention on Zach and Nick instead, how similar they were in the way they sat their horse. Jonesy had never seemed truly at ease in the saddle. Nick was a little awkward their first day on land, but since then it seemed like memories of a well-honed but long-unused skill had resurfaced. He had the same upright posture, head and hips in alignment, and relaxed hands as Zach. Both directed their horses without fuss or effort, whereas she wasn't sure sometimes if her mount was following her instruction or just tagging along with the other horses.

The turn completed and riding on a straight section of road again, she felt her equilibrium return, and tried to draw Zach out.

Zach ignored her attempts to learn about him or his journey to Portugal. "You were desperate enough to throw your lot in with this rapscallion, eh?"

"I'm right here," Nick gritted out, one horse length ahead of them. The road clear of traffic for a while, Zach caught up and rode beside Harriet.

Harriet stifled a chuckle. "It seemed my only option. And I *was* desperate." Zach coaxed and prodded and was so charming about it, she ended up telling him about her intended, Sir Percival, and needing her share of the treasure for her dowry as well as to secure the future for her brother Gabriel and pay the quarterly mortgage that was coming due in a fortnight.

"This Percival fellow," Zach said thoughtfully, "what color are his eyes?"

The eyes that came to mind first were azure blue with indigo rings around the irises. But those were Nick's eyes. She tried to picture Percy the last time she'd seen him, at an assembly in the village. Looking so fine in his bottle green coat and tan breeches, shiny Hessian boots, and impeccably tied cravat. She tried to look higher, to recall his face, his eyes. His smile. Did he have a chipped tooth like Nick? He was everything that Madame Zavrina would consider desirable in a suitor. He had never taken any liberties with Harriet. Always wore gloves and used the lightest of touches when they held hands to dance. Was always properly attired, comported himself with dignity as befitting his station as a landowner in their tiny village society.

He was deadly dull compared to Nick.

But then, who wouldn't be?

"Um, brown. No, green." Harriet craned her neck to look at the winery now visible high on the hill in the distance, trying to dredge up a clear mental image of the face of the man she intended to marry, would see on the pillow beside her in bed as she had Nick's last night. "No, they're hazel." She nodded firmly, trying to convince herself. "Yes, they're definitely hazel."

"And what color are his?" Zach pointed at Nick.

"Same blue as yours, you rogue," she said with a laugh.

They must have slowed down while they chatted. Nick had ridden farther ahead of them and was out of sight as the road made another sharp turn.

They turned the corner and came to a shocked halt. Nick lay facedown beside the road, blood running down his forehead. A few feet away from where Nick's horse was cropping the sparse grass growing beneath enormous trees, two men were bound and gagged, tied to a tree that had orange bark, just off the road in a shady copse at the base of the hillside.

"Nick!" Harriet jumped down and ran to him even as she heard Zach shout, "Wait!"

"That will do," came a stern voice from the trees.

Chapter 17

The speaker stepped out into the sunlight, his features obscured by a black kerchief covering his face below his eyes. A black wool cap worn low on his forehead hid his hair, and he wore a shapeless, oversized oilskin coat. But the bulk of his large form was unmistakable, and it wasn't from fat.

The pistol he pointed at Nick, however, was quite clear. And steady. He pointed at Zach with his free hand. "You. Dismount." He then pointed at Harriet, who was kneeling beside Nick's still form. "You. Don't move."

Zach dismounted and walked closer to Nick, holding his hands up beside his ears. He looked no more concerned than if someone had just revealed themselves to have a winning hand of cards. "If you want my purse, you have only to ask."

"Shut up," the highwayman growled. From the depths of a coat pocket, he withdrew a small coil of rope and tossed it to Harriet. "You. Tie his hands together behind his back." He gestured at Zach.

Harriet gave another glance at Nick to confirm he was still breathing, then moved to do as instructed. She tied the rope around Zach's wrists using a knot Jack and Winston had taught her, proud her hands barely shook, then looked expectantly at the stranger.

He pointed for Zach to sit with his back to the tree's thick orange trunk, near the other two men. He tossed another piece of rope at Harriet. "Now tie his ankles together."

Harriet did as ordered, again using the knot Nick's crew had taught her.

The stranger inspected her work, then grunted in approval. He tucked his pistol away and made quick work of tying Harriet's hands and ankles, though he didn't tie her to the tree. Then he dragged Nick away from the road and into the shadows of the copse, and tied his hands and ankles.

"I say," Zach said slowly. "Shouldn't you be bringing me another brandy, Marlow?"

She heard a startled, muffled oath from the well-dressed man tied to the tree beside Zach.

Harriet had been so focused on Nick and doing what the stranger told her that she had barely glanced at the men sitting at the base of the tree. Now she recognized Captain Ruford. The well-dressed gent in the middle must be Hornsby. She hadn't realized it was him without the dirt dusting his face and clothes, and with the gag distorting part of his face.

Marlow yanked the kerchief from his face, revealing coarse features, including a nose that had been broken more than once. "I won't be bringing you, or anyone else, a brandy ever again. Not after I get my hands on the treasure." He patted his waistcoat pocket, and Harriet heard the crinkle of paper. He patted another pocket, and she heard the jingle of keys.

"You're the one who broke into my cottage!" This pistol-wielding man who had injured Nick had been inside her home, pawing through her father's effects. Harriet's skin crawled.

"Oh, shut it," he said, and gagged her with the kerchief that had been around his face. "I have all I need to claim the treasure. I shall be well on my way before you lot manage to free yourselves or attract a rescuer passing by." He gagged Zach with another kerchief, tipped his cap with exaggerated courtesy, and disappeared between the trees. Moments later he emerged from the shadows on a horse and galloped away, up the road toward the winery.

No! Harriet fumed. She would not be cheated of her inheritance so close to achieving her goals. She tried to get Zach's attention and let him know that he should be able to free himself by pulling on the end of the slip knot. He was distracted, engaging in a muffled argument with Ruford and Hornsby.

She was closer to Nick anyway, and knew he kept a knife in his right boot. She just needed to reach it. With her ankles bound, walking or crawling was out of the question. She could roll, so she did that. The enormous cork oak trees in the copse did not shed their leaves to cushion the ground, but did drop copious amounts of acorns, which dug into her flesh. Nick gave a quiet grunt as she rolled over the lower half of his body but he didn't move. A little scrabbling and scooting and she almost had her hands to the top of his right boot.

"Not there," Nick said quietly as she was feeling his leg, blindly trying to find his boot top with her hands bound behind her back.

She froze.

"Blackguard took my knife," he said, his words a little more distinct but still barely audible.

She slumped. All right, she'd just have to roll over to Zach and try to untie him. Without being able to see what she was doing, odds were fifty-fifty that she'd pull the knot loose instead of tightening it.

Before she could roll over Nick again, he began to struggle from side to side, and gradually sat up. His eyes were scrunched closed and blood trickled down his forehead into his right eye from a gash near his hairline. "Waistcoat pocket," he said, breathing hard from the exertion and pain.

His dagger was gone. Maybe he carried a penknife? Good. A little trickier to open, but she could work with that. With a small blade they were less likely to cause serious damage to each other. She scooted and slithered, acorns poking into her hip and knees, her wool coat offering scant protection for her elbows, and worked her way to Nick until she was sitting up, so close she was practically in his lap. She groped.

"Little higher," he gasped, his voice strangled.

Her cheeks flaming, she bent forward so she could reach her hands higher, and found her way inside the folds of his greatcoat and coat, to the soft wool of his waistcoat and the edge of its pocket. She dipped her fingers in and found something metallic about two inches long with a hard, sharp point. "Got it," she tried to say around her gag.

"Hand it to me." They both shifted until they were back-to-back. She leaned against his long strong back, resting and trying to catch her breath. She felt Nick's shoulders rise and fall as he did the same, some of his weight a comforting pressure against her as they supported each other.

After a few more deep breaths, he groaned and reached for her. They fumbled until their fingers found each other, and she carefully transferred the item to his callused palm and felt his fingers close over it.

"Stay still," he said. She felt his hands move at her lower back, and the rope on her wrists shifted back and forth. Her shoulders were cramping and she desperately wanted to stretch, but she held as still as she could. Nick's fingers brushed over hers. The sharp item scraped across the bare skin of her wrist, and she hissed.

"Sorry," Nick muttered, and shifted his grip.

The argument had ended, as Zach, Ruford, and Hornsby were now avidly watching her and Nick. She mentally dismissed them, focusing on what Nick was doing.

The rope tightened again, the coarse hemp rubbing her wrists raw as it moved back and forth, and then suddenly it gave way.

She swung her arms in front of her and stretched, groaning with relief, then leaned down and untied her ankles. As soon as she was free, she yanked loose her gag and knelt behind Nick to untie his hands. He held his fist closed over the tool he'd used to free her.

"Zach," she called. "I used a slip knot. If you catch the correct end, you can free yourself."

Zach nodded and closed his eyes in concentration as he tried to pull the slip knot on his wrists.

She got Nick's wrists free. He sighed in relief and brought his hands in front, stretching, and then slowly listed to port until he was lying on his side, eyes closed.

"Nick?"

"'m here," he murmured.

She crawled on her knees to reach his ankles and quickly untied them, then folded the kerchief used as her gag and began to wipe blood from his face.

"Mmm, nice," he mumbled.

Impatient movements caught the corner of her vision. With another worried look at Nick, who was still lying on his side, eyes closed, she went over to the men tied to the tree. She yanked the end of the rope to free Zach's ankles, then had him lean forward so she could undo the tangle he'd made of the rope on his wrists. As soon as he was loose, she went back to kneel beside Nick.

"Can you sit up?" she asked.

"Soon as the ground stops spinning." He took a deep breath, then another.

Zach stood up, and with a muttered curse flung the rope away. The sound of his boots crunching on the acorns as he walked toward Harriet was quickly drowned out by muffled shouting from Ruford and Hornsby. Zach reared back when he got a whiff of Ruford, so he untied Hornsby instead.

Harriet stretched her hand out to wipe more blood trickling from the gash on Nick's brow. Her wrists had abrasions from the rope and a couple of bright pink scratches, instead of the lacerations she'd expected. He hadn't cut her, hadn't spilled a drop of her blood. "What did you use to loosen the knot?"

Nick barely moved his lips, and still didn't open his eyes. "Good luck charm."

He didn't resist when she uncurled his fingers so she could pick up the tool he'd used that she had removed from his pocket. It looked like a large bolt of some kind but it had sheared off, tapering to a narrow, sharp point.

Zach peered over her shoulder. "Your good luck charm is a broken carriage pin, lad?"

With a groan, Nick pushed himself up so he was sitting, pressing the heels of his hands to his temples, his eyes narrow slits against the pain. "It's why the gun fell off the carriage when it went overboard."

Harriet gasped, her hand covering her heart. She owed her life in large part to this broken piece of metal. Had the cannon stayed on its carriage, it would have dragged her straight to the bottom of the Channel with no chance of rescue. And Nick considered it *his* good luck charm?

Her throat grew tight. Blinking back a sudden tear, she carefully tucked the precious pin back into his waistcoat pocket. Blood continued to ooze from the gash on his forehead. She folded the kerchief into a long strip and tied it around his head.

"Seems more like it should be Harry's good luck charm," Zach said. He stood and scanned the area. He gave a whistle, and there was an answering neigh and the sound of horse's hoofs moving toward them.

Harriet cleared her throat, forcing herself to think of practical matters. "We need to catch up to—what did you call him?" she asked Zach.

"Marlow," Hornsby growled. "He was a footman at the club where we were playing when Langston offered the map. Fetched our drinks and food and stayed in the room to make sure everyone abided by the rules. Must have heard you blathering on about the treasure your brother and friend hid."

Harriet stood, holding one of Nick's large hands in both of hers. "Up you go." She heaved, he groaned, and he slowly climbed to his feet. He rested his hands on her shoulders until he stopped swaying.

"He was sitting by the fire in the inn's dining room last night," Zach said. "Didn't recognize him until I heard him speak."

More footsteps behind her indicated Ruford and Hornsby had collected their horses that had been grazing beneath the cork oaks. She couldn't tear her gaze from Nick.

"I didn't see him, but then I dined in my room and retired early," Hornsby said.

"We need to *go*," Ruford said, shaking the dust from his plumed tricorne hat and jamming it back on his head. "Be damned if that … that *footman* is going to cheat me out of my treasure."

"Your share of my treasure, you mean," Hornsby said.

At last Nick opened his eyes. "I'd have left them tied up," he said to Zach, jerking his thumb to indicate Ruford and Hornsby.

Zach lifted one shoulder. "A moment of weakness. Uncomfortable, sitting with tree roots up your ar— uh, backside."

Nick raked Harriet with his gaze, taking in the dirt and mud on her clothes from rolling around on the ground. "Are you all right?"

She must look a fright, but she was uninjured. She nodded because her throat was suddenly too choked up to get words out. She clenched her hands into fists to conceal their shaking.

"You acquitted yourself well," he said quietly, his deep voice a caress.

Tears welled up and she was mightily annoyed that she had been fine—angry, but fine—when a stranger pointed a pistol at Nick's motionless body and tied them all up, and now that the threat was gone and they were safe, she was in serious danger of turning into a watering pot.

"Come here." He tugged on her shoulders and she went, straight into his arms. She burrowed under his coat to wrap her arms around his waist and press her cheek to his chest, listening to the reassuring beat of his heart.

He ran a soothing hand up and down her back. "*Mi pequeño wren marrón*," he murmured, so quietly she felt the rumble in his chest as much as heard the words.

She relaxed against him, feeling safe and secure in his embrace. As at peace as when she'd awoken in bed with him this morning, until she'd realized it wasn't a dream and she had indeed boldly snuggled up against his big, muscular body. She didn't know the meaning of the words he'd just spoken so tenderly but recognized the first word as being possessive. His ... something.

She tried on the idea of being his ... something ... and found she didn't mind. Rather liked it. Probably. She'd need to know the meaning to be sure.

He was unharmed, relatively. She didn't want to examine why she'd panicked when she thought he'd been killed. A flash of desolation had slammed into her like a rogue wave. Even now, knowing he was safe, she still felt the aftereffect as though she'd been pummeled on a rocky shore before the surge rushed back out to sea.

They needed to get going. Marlow was getting away, farther ahead of them with every second that passed. But the drive to pursue the treasure was, at least for the moment, subsumed by Harriet's even more urgent need to hold Nick. She'd almost lost him, and she was beginning to suspect he might be more important to her than any treasure.

Her trembling eased. His scent—leather, horse, sandalwood soap, and essential Nick—washed over her. She wanted to stay here forever. Keep holding him.

Holding *Nick*. She wasn't sure when she'd stopped thinking of him as Sheffield or the Captain, but this was the first time she'd spoken it aloud. After the intimacy of sharing a bed, using his given name hardly seemed the breach of etiquette it would have in a

London ballroom. Besides, she'd left "proper" behind long before she abandoned gowns in favor of sailor's garb.

Gradually she became aware she had her arms around a man in an intimate embrace. A horse pawed the ground and another neighed, and harnesses jingled. There were five horses nearby and three other men. Witnesses to her shockingly improper behavior.

And she didn't care.

Nick angled back, just a little, and reluctantly she separated her body from his. He cupped her face with his big, strong hands, worry creasing his brow beneath his makeshift bandage. "He didn't hurt you when he tied you up?"

She watched his mouth as he spoke, those full, expressive lips, and she lifted up on her toes because she had to touch them.

Nick groaned and pulled her in for a kiss, one hand cupping her cheek, the other arm wrapping around her waist, holding her close. His thumb caressed her cheek. She poured everything into the kiss—the joy at waking up with him that morning, the fear that froze her blood when she thought he'd died, the relief he was fine other than a headache and dizziness. He was still Nick.

In the tenderness of his touch she felt his answering relief that she was unharmed. The first time he'd kissed her had been after the battle at sea, shaken when he saw her blood and minor injury. As if he actually cared about her well-being. That she mattered to him.

"Damned molly boy," Ruford muttered. "We're ashore, not at sea, Sheffield," he called impatiently. "Get yourself a wench!"

Zach chuckled and walked closer to Harriet, leading her horse as well as his own.

They did need to get going after the treasure. Harriet reluctantly broke the kiss, this intimate connection with Nick. There was another emotion evident in Nick's expression as she pulled away, an unfamiliar look in his eyes she'd never seen before. Took her a moment to recognize it.

Hunger.

For her.

Her breath hitched.

Nick leaned back in to steal a quick kiss before he relinquished his hold on her and stepped beside the stirrup of the huge grey gelding, his intent clear.

"Not this time, lad," Zach said. "Harry got you off the ground once. We're not going to pick you up again." He gently pushed Nick aside and cupped his hands. "Up you go, m'dear."

With a lingering glance at Nick, she let Zach boost her into the saddle.

Hornsby approached Nick, carrying a broken tree branch that was a little longer than Harriet's arm and twice as thick. Blood glistened on the side near one end. "Want your souvenir?"

Nick leaned away, his face a grimace of distaste. "Thank you, no."

Hornsby tossed the stick and the men mounted. By the time Nick had collected his proffered hat from Zach, settled in the saddle and opened his eyes again, Hornsby was galloping up the road, Ruford close behind.

Zach moved out at a much slower pace, as Nick seemed dizzy again now that he was in motion. Harriet rode beside him, not sure what she could actually do to help him but needing to be near.

Zach soon let Nick take the lead again to set the pace.

"Now we know why the innkeeper was surprised at having so many English guests last night," Nick said after a while. "There were seven of us." He was steady again, squinting only when the sun was directly in their eyes.

"Marlow must have left at first light to get ahead and waylay Hornsby and Ruford," Harriet said. "And then he waited for us." She shuddered.

"When Marlow set upon them, he took Hornsby's copy of the map," Zach said. "It hasn't been of help since Corunna, but he thinks having both maps will convince the priest to give the treasure to him."

Nick heaved a sigh. "You think Father Miguel would hand it over to someone other than Adam and Giles, or their heirs?"

Zach shrugged. "He's been responsible for it for over five years. That's a long time to wait for someone to come back for something they asked you to hold."

Now that Harriet wasn't worried Nick was going to fall out of the saddle, anxiety of a different sort set in, preventing her from enjoying the view of the grapevine-covered hillside, the valley spread below, and the Rio Ferreira sparkling in the distance as it meandered down to flow into the Sousa River before joining the Douro River and going out to sea. Marlow would surely reach Father Miguel first. And that was assuming their guess was correct and the priest had indeed gone to *Casa de Perseguição*, House of Chase, and they weren't on another wild goose hunt.

What would she do if Marlow got the treasure? Or if there was no treasure at all?

The road made another sharp bend as it climbed the hillside. She nudged her horse to go faster.

* * *

The sun was high in the sky when they finally entered the courtyard of *Casa de Perseguição*. A half-dozen buildings were set in a semicircle, from ivy-covered housing and offices to fragrant grape-processing areas, to barns and stables that emitted an entirely different earthy scent. In summertime the courtyard would be a colorful oasis, but in late autumn the vines climbing the red brick walls were naked branches.

They scanned the buildings, trying to decide which to approach first, when they heard raised voices coming from behind one of the outbuildings. Of one accord they headed for the sound.

Nick, Zach, and Harriet rounded the corner and stopped at the sight that greeted them.

Marlow was loudly arguing in English with a tall, thin man who wore the black cassock of a priest and replied in soft tones, while Hornsby repeatedly interjected in Spanish. Ruford looked like he was ready to throttle them all.

"*Olá*," Nick called.

The four men stopped and looked at the newcomers. Marlow scowled, Ruford rolled his eyes, and Hornsby pointedly turned his back on them, facing the priest.

"*Olá*," the priest replied with a broad smile, happy to interrupt the contentious exchange.

"Father Miguel?" Harriet dared ask, her chest tight.

"*Si*," he answered. "I am Father Miguel."

"The same Father Miguel who used to serve at the *Iglesia de Nuestra Señora del Dolor* in Corunna?" Nick added as he dismounted.

Harriet's heart was pounding so hard she could barely hear the priest's reply.

The priest tilted his head, letting the sunlight glance off his balding head. "*Si*, though it has been a while since I had to move on from there."

"*Mi nombre es Langston*," Zach said. "I believe you were entrusted with something left by my brother Adam, Viscount Sheffield?" He gracefully swung down from the saddle.

"And my father, Giles Chase," Harriet added, and jumped to the ground. Her horse nearly knocked her over, snuffling her for a treat. She quickly fed him a carrot from her pocket.

Hornsby and Marlow gave her a sharp glance. Ruford squinted at her, looking confused.

"It don't matter none," Marlow insisted. "I have the maps and the keys. The treasure belongs to me!"

They were drawing attention from workers at the winery, who slowed down to gawk as they crossed the compound, carrying out their duties. A cooper came out of the enormous building beside their group, holding a large hammer and a metal hoop. Despite the chill in the air, he'd stripped to his trousers and boots, his muscular torso covered in sweat and smudges of soot. He spoke to the priest in Portuguese and gave a menacing scowl at the assorted newcomers.

The priest apparently reassured him, and he went back inside, where they could see stacks of barrels, wood staves, and a forge.

"*Si*, I was entrusted with property by Señor Chase and Viscount Sheffield. They were not able to make the journey with you?"

"Their ship went down with all hands," Zach said.

"I am the current Viscount Sheffield," Nick added.

Father Miguel made the sign of the cross, closed his eyes, and his lips moved in a silent, brief prayer. "My condolences on your loss," he said with sincerity. Then he stepped closer to get a better look at Nick and Zach. "I can see the family resemblance," he said.

Harriet nudged her horse's nose out of her face and stroked his long, sleek neck. "As their heirs, we've come to claim the ... property ... they left with you. The hidden treasure Father mentioned in his letter."

Father Miguel walked over to Harriet and offered her horse a pat. "I see your father in you as well, and not just your face."

Harriet exchanged a puzzled glance with Nick, who shrugged.

The priest smiled. "You have come to claim *Tesoro Escondido*?"

Harriet looked at Nick and silently mouthed, "What?"

"Hidden treasure," he mouthed back.

"I claim the treasure," Marlow insisted. "I have both maps and the keys."

"I claim it," Hornsby said. He pointed at Zach. "He gambled with his map and lost. It's mine."

"Come, come," the priest said, beckoning. He led them to a rail where they could tie up their horses. Once all six were secured, Father Miguel led them through the stable and to the pasture beyond. Two mules were placidly grazing, as well as one large horse that towered over them, an old stallion with a grey muzzle and dull coat.

Father Miguel whistled and made kissing noises, and all three animals trotted over to the fence. He fished small apples out of pockets in his robe and gave one to each of the mules, then shooed them away. He stretched up to scratch the horse behind his ears and fed him an apple. "This is Tesoro Escondido," he proudly announced. "That is his name. Tesoro."

"What?" Hornsby shouted, his face and ears flushing red.

Nick let out a bark of laughter. "The hidden treasure Adam didn't want me to have is an elderly horse named Hidden Treasure?" He turned in a circle, taking in the winery, the stables, then back to the horse and priest, and laughed harder, longer, his voice getting louder as he tipped his head back, laughing at the most amusing joke he'd ever heard.

"This?" Marlow demanded, practically spitting in fury. "*This* is the hidden treasure I traveled across three countries, an ocean, and twelve hundred miles to find? This broken-down old *nag*?"

Nick whooped and slapped his leg with his hat, laughing so hard Harriet became concerned his head injury was worse than she'd originally thought. He stepped back from the fence and sat down on the grass, then lay back with his hat over his face. His shoulders shook with laughter, now muted.

Harriet stared at the horse, her heart sinking. She barely had the strength to remain standing. So much for her dowry. Gabriel's future. Paying the quarterly mortgage. After she paid Nick back her half of the expenses to get here and back to England, her share of the horse's value likely wouldn't even buy her coach fare home. Might not even cover her half of the expenses.

Tears sprang to her eyes. She refused to let them fall, forced herself to stand upright.

"Nice fella," Zach said. He stroked the horse's neck and watched him munch the apple.

Now silent, Nick slowly climbed to his feet and put his hat back on, watching Zach intently.

Tesoro was as tall or even taller than Harriet's huge rented grey gelding. His dark coat, possibly glossy black in his youth, was dull with age or illness. The hair around his mouth had turned grey, like the muzzle of Max, the black dog Harriet had had as a child. Father had given them the mongrel just before he went to sea for the first time without them. Max had accompanied Harriet on errands into the village, romped with Gabriel, and protected them from monsters under the bed until, his muzzle entirely grey by then, he had died of old age during the night while curled up in his usual spot at the foot of Harriet's bed.

She swallowed a lump in her throat. The horse's head collar had cracked leather and dull pewter instead of shiny silver hardware and was even missing a piece of metal. The poor horse probably wouldn't survive the strain of the journey back to England.

Nick wrapped an arm around her shoulders and squeezed. She leaned against him, grateful for his strength, trying to remember that he must be disappointed as well.

"Well, I suppose I could sell him to the knackers," Marlow said slowly. "Get back my travel expenses at least."

"You misunderstand, *Señor*," Father Miguel said. "As I was trying to tell you outside the pressing room, the maps only served for his owners to find me and Tesoro. In order to claim him, you must have the keys."

"I *have* the bloody keys!" Marlow dug in his pockets and held up a ring of keys Harriet recognized as her housekeeper's ring, followed by loose keys—to the pantry, the desk drawers in her father's study, her music box, even the spare front door key they kept in a pot of chives growing just outside the kitchen door. "It's got to be one of these!"

"You stole those from my house!" Harriet tried to snatch them back, but Marlow jerked his hand out of her reach.

Father Miguel shook his head and waved Marlow's hand away. "Not those kinds of keys."

"Then what the hell— Beg your pardon, Father," Hornsby said. "Then what kind of keys?"

"Viscount Sheffield and Señor Chase would know, as they set the keys."

"Well, that doesn't help us a whole he— heck of a lot then, does it, seeing as how they're dead!" Ruford fumed.

Harriet felt Nick's sudden intake of breath.

"Keys to their future?" Nick said.

Father Miguel gave him a gentle smile, as to a child who had just answered a question correctly in Sunday school. "*Sí.*"

Nick nudged her. "Your pendant," he said quietly.

Harriet reached inside her shirt and pulled out the silver H on its chain. "My father said this was the key to my future. He sent it in the same letter as the map." She pointed an accusing finger at Marlow. "The map he stole."

"May I?"

Harriet opened the chain and dropped the pendant into the priest's outstretched hand before putting the chain back around her neck.

Father Miguel offered Tesoro another apple, and while the horse was busy munching, the priest clipped the H into place on the head collar.

Harriet felt her mouth fall open in surprise. She snapped her jaw shut.

"Well done, m'dear," Zach said, beaming.

Father Miguel turned expectantly to Nick. "And you, my son? Do you have a key as well?"

Nick started to shake his head, but Harriet remembered a conversation they'd had in his cabin on the ship, when he'd been brushing her hair. She elbowed him in the ribs. "Romans thirteen."

He glanced at her, understanding dawning in his blue eyes, then addressed the priest. "'Let us walk honestly, as in the day,'" Nick quoted, "'not in rioting and drunkenness, not in chambering and wantonness, not in strife and envying.'"

"That rot," Zach muttered, shaking his head in disgust.

Father Miguel beamed. "Those are indeed the keys as set by Viscount Sheffield and Señor Chase." He looked at Nick and Harriet. "Tesoro belongs to you two."

Chapter 18

Chaos erupted as Marlow, Hornsby, and Ruford simultaneously shouted their objections. Hornsby was also furious with Zach and accused him of cheating.

"My dear Lord Hornsby, do take care in tossing about that accusation," Zach said. His words were polite, but there was steel in his voice. "When I offered the map in our game, I was clear that it purported to lead to a treasure. The map itself was the wager, not what it may or may not lead the bearer to find."

With a blistering set of oaths, Hornsby stalked off toward the stable. Ruford followed behind, demanding to know how Hornsby was going to reimburse him, as fifty percent of nothing wasn't going to pay his expenses, let alone turn a profit.

"Captain Ruford!" Nick called.

Ruford spun on his heel, the tall feather in his tricorne hat trembling with the force of his fury, in case the murderous expression on his face wasn't clear enough.

"You're docked in Oporto," Nick continued in a soothing tone, as though speaking to a growling dog. "Some of the best wineries in Portugal are right there by the River Douro in Vila Nova da Gaia. You'll have to sail past additional wineries and distilleries in Spain and France on your way home. Surely a businessman as enterprising as yourself can find a way to make this journey profitable."

Ruford's expression cleared as Nick spoke, and eventually his smile was broad enough to reveal his stained, uneven teeth. "Aye, laddie, I think you have the right of it." He gave a nod and strolled to the stable whistling, his plume dancing.

"But what about—"

Nick cut Marlow off. "You need to leave before I send for the *gendarme* and charge you with assault." He pointed at the bandage on his temple, visible under the brim of his hat.

Zach scratched his chin. "I heard tell of a boxing tournament being planned in Braga to begin day after next," he said. "Top purse is more than what you made in a year at the club, including vails." He assumed a boxing stance and mock-punched Marlow. "I may have placed a wager or two on my way south through the town."

"What makes you think I've ever stepped in a boxing ring?"

Harriet couldn't help chuckling.

Zach tapped the side of his nose, indicating Marlow's crooked nose.

"I'll have my dagger back before you go, if you please." Nick held his hand out.

Marlow retrieved it from his left boot and grudgingly handed it over.

"And my keys." Harriet held her hand out.

Marlow rolled his eyes but handed them over. She looked through them before she pocketed them.

"I'm losing my patience," Nick said when Marlow still made no move to leave.

Marlow gave a last sad look at Tesoro, shook his head slowly, and tugged his forelock. "Good day, my lords. Father." He glanced at Harriet. "Lad." He jogged to the stable.

Ruford and Hornsby mounted and cantered out of the courtyard, quickly followed by Marlow.

Zach clapped his hands together. "Right, then, now the riffraff have gone, let's have a good look at this fellow, see what's under all this dust and ash." He turned to Father Miguel. "I expect you have a saddle for him, not just a harness for pulling the plow?"

"I expect I do," the priest replied, with a surprisingly sly grin for a man of the cloth. He tucked his robe and climbed through the rails of the fence into the pasture, then made kissing noises and patted his thigh, and headed for the stable. Tesoro followed at his shoulder.

Nick and Harriet exchanged puzzled looks, then climbed through the fence and trailed after Zach.

In the stable, Zach grabbed the currycomb and began brushing Tesoro, while Father Miguel cleaned tack. A worker from the winery walked in with a pronounced limp, wearing a wine-stained apron. He spoke softly with the priest, gesturing at Nick and Harriet, and joined in cleaning the tack.

"He's asking if the owners have finally come to claim him," Nick translated for her. "He is sad to see him go but happy if Tesoro is going to a good home where he won't have to hide anymore."

"Hide?" Harriet asked.

The horse's coat changed with each stroke, and by the time Zach pronounced himself satisfied, the horse's coat was a glossy solid black, including his muzzle. Zach accepted the colorful woven blanket and saddle from the priest and made quick work of getting the horse ready to ride.

Not only did the horse gleam in the sunshine when led out to the pasture, the leather of his tack shone and the hardware, though still needing some polish as evidenced by the brighter shine of Harriet's H, had been restored to a bright silver.

"He's stunning," Harriet said, staring in awe.

"The teeth!" Nick said, slapping his leg as he figured it out. "You knew because of his teeth."

Zach grinned from ear to ear, then bent to check the saddle girth and length of the stirrup once more, and swung up into the saddle. "It's an old trick." He nudged the horse and they began to walk around the pasture.

"*Sí*," said Father Miguel. "It was the only way to save him when the armies marched through."

"The army would have confiscated a splendid animal like this," Harriet said, understanding dawning. "So you made him look old and feeble by keeping him coated in dust and ash."

Father Miguel nodded, then focused his attention on Zach riding Tesoro.

Zach sped the horse up to a trot. The mules voiced their consternation at the motion and hurried into the quiet safety of the stable.

The worker limped out of the stable and joined them at the fence. Father Miguel introduced Senhor Perez, who had served as an officer in the Portuguese army before being invalided out. They all climbed to sit on the top rail of the fence to watch, out of the way.

Zach urged Tesoro to a canter and then a gallop, turning tight circles and figures in the pasture.

Senhor Perez took his cap off and clutched it to his chest. He called something in Portuguese to the horse, who neighed in reply without breaking stride.

Zach whipped his head back to stare at Perez. "Truly? *Verdaderamente?*"

"*Sim,*" Senhor Perez said, smiling proudly.

"I'll be damned," Zach said, so softly they barely heard him. His face breaking into a grin of utter delight, he patted the horse's shoulder. "Show me what you can do, old boy!"

Nick spoke with Senhor Perez, then translated for Harriet. "He has been exercising Tesoro in secret, at night. They didn't dare let anyone know that he's not old, even though the war has been over for a while."

Zach had the horse walk to the center of the pasture and trot in place, facing his audience, lifting his hooves high.

"*Piaffe,*" Senhor Perez said, naming each maneuver as the horse performed it.

Still facing their audience, Zach had Tesoro trot sideways at an angle until they almost reached the fence, then turn and canter a lap around the pasture. They trotted back to the center and the horse reared up on his hind legs, forelegs neatly tucked ... and held the position until Zach gave him a quiet command in Spanish. "*Pesade*," Senhor Perez said.

The horse jumped straight up in the air, like a startled cat. "*Croupade*."

Zach had him trot around in a wide circle and back to the center. Tesoro jumped straight up again, but this time kicked out his back legs before landing on all four feet at the same time. Zach shouted in triumph while Senhor Perez proudly said, "*Capriole*."

Still smiling in delight, Zach spoke to Perez in Spanish. Perez ducked his head, his cheeks suddenly flushed.

"I do not know how to train a horse with these uncommon skills," Father Miguel said. "When I discovered that Senhor Perez used to train horses for Prince Dom Joao, I confided in him. He has been helping Tesoro."

Zach trotted the horse for a couple more laps, then slowed to a walk to let the horse cool down. He jumped down and led the horse in another lap.

"It appears not only do we own a healthy Andalusian stallion still in his prime," Nick told Harriet, "we have one trained in airs above the ground."

"That makes him more valuable?" Perhaps she could attain some of her financial goals after all.

"To the right person, very much so," Zach cheerfully answered as he walked past, Tesoro at his shoulder. "The airs above ground were originally designed to protect the rider in battle, but they're based on behaviors observed in wild horses. The trick is to get a glorious beast like him to want to do the maneuver when *you* want him to do it. This lad has just been waiting for someone to appreciate his talent." As if in agreement, Tesoro nodded his head and whickered. Zach stroked the stallion's neck while gazing at him. "He truly is a treasure."

Nick checked the position of the sun and the length of the shadows. "We won't be able to make it back to the ship tonight before dark."

"You must stay here, as my guests," Father Miguel said. "There are plenty of rooms. I wish to know more about the people who are taking Tesoro, and I am sure you have questions for me." He hopped off the fence and headed for the courtyard. "Come, Senhor Langston. It is time for lunch and siesta. Senhor Perez will send someone to tend to your horses—all of them—and then join us."

"If you're sure it won't be an imposition," Harriet said. She hopped off the fence, stepped around a pile of droppings, and followed the priest.

"It wasn't so long ago that an army garrisoned a unit here with more than fifty troops," Father Miguel said. "Three guests won't even require us to change how much food to prepare."

Household staff escorted them to guestrooms. Zach's room was between hers and Nick's, Harriet noted with a grin. They took a few moments to freshen up before joining more than a dozen people seated around a long table in an enormous, sunny dining room with a view of a garden terrace and the valley beyond. Introductions were made—a dizzying collection of unfamiliar names in a language with unfamiliar sounds—but the winery managers, top staff like cellar master and public dining room manager, and three other priests were welcoming to the English visitors, especially when Nick greeted them in their own language. Senhor Perez arrived and took the last open seat. He assured them grooms were tending to their four horses.

Platters and bowls of food were already set about the table. Everyone served themselves and passed each dish to the right. Father Miguel had seated Harriet and Nick to either side of himself with

Zach directly across the table and endeavored to translate as needed. She heard Portuguese, English, and Spanish, and noted the priest steered the conversation to general topics related to England and the rebuilding of Portugal, which had been ravaged in war by the French and English. She also noticed he avoided using any pronouns or titles for her, introducing her only as the child of Giles Chase, one of the owners of Tesoro.

It did not escape her attention that everyone else seated at the table was male. The only women she saw were the maids in bright red skirts, white blouses, and black aprons who quickly and quietly replenished the food and drink.

Harriet put her attention on enjoying the meal. She was determined to try at least a bite of each, no matter how unfamiliar the appearance. Like fried octopus. The meat was moist and light but she found the suckers off-putting, so she mostly ate the rice and black-eyed beans beneath it. Several dishes were new to her, like *bacalhau*, the salted cod that was so popular in Portugal. Eel stew was tasty. Strong cheeses were paired with walnuts and dried pears, and there were at least four kinds of olives.

The beer served with the meal was cleared away when the maids brought out port to go with the custard-filled pastries. Harriet dared not take more than a sip or two of each drink. She had become used to grog on the ship, and the beer she could probably handle, but the port was likely to make her silly. In present company, that would just not do.

She'd been so focused on escaping others' notice that she didn't realize Nick had hardly said a word since greeting their hosts until Father Miguel accepted a steaming teacup from one of the maids and urged Nick to drink the contents.

"A tisane of my own recipe," Father Miguel explained. "It will ease your headache, *meu senhor*."

Nick accepted the cup, not bothering to deny having a headache. The light coming through the floor-to-ceiling windows was making his head pound. He'd tried to ignore the throbbing since regaining consciousness on the side of the road, but it was reaching the point where he was in danger of losing what little lunch he'd managed to choke down. The tisane was spicy and warming, with ginger and other notes he couldn't identify.

The meal ended and people returned to work or went upstairs to rest. Footmen escorted Nick and his party back up to their rooms, where their saddlebags and Zach's small portmanteau had been brought. Nick kept his cup, sipping the pungent brew as they walked.

"I'm Jasper, milord," said the footman who followed Nick into his room. "Father Miguel asked me to check yer bandage and see yer comf'table." He set his armload of supplies on the dressing table and insisted on helping Nick out of his coat and boots, even though there was a bootjack by the door.

"Ooh, lawdy, that's a nasty one," Jasper said after he untied Harriet's makeshift bandage and got a good look at the gash on Nick's brow.

Nick grunted. He hadn't seen it yet and wasn't eager to do so. It would just make him angry at Marlow all over again. His headache was already sapping enough of his energy.

He sat on the edge of the bed and sipped the tisane while Jasper worked. The servant's accent seemed familiar but the throbbing in Nick's head made it difficult to concentrate.

Jasper cleaned the wound with a cloth soaked in gin, talking under his breath as he worked, describing each step. Norton would approve of the gin, Nick thought, wincing at the sting. "New Orleans!" he suddenly blurted.

Jasper smiled, his teeth bright white against his ebony skin. "Yessuh, I'm from Nawlins."

"My ship's purser is from New Orleans. Thought the accent was familiar."

"Hope I can go back someday for a visit. Jambalaya here just ain't the same." He wound a clean bandage around Nick's head and tied it off.

Nick peered into the bottom of his now-empty cup. Miraculously, the pounding in his head was gone. In fact, he felt light, as though gravity was doing a poor job of keeping him from floating off the bed. "Just what did the priest give me?"

"Ooh, lotsa good stuff in that particular tisane. There's ginger root and lemon, cinnamon, willow bark, chamomile, and valerian." He silently ran through the list of ingredients again, counting them on his fingers, and nodded. "Should help whatever ails you and make you sleep right tight."

"I don't need to sleep," Nick said, even as he felt himself slowly falling backward on the bed. "I feel fi—"

* * *

Nick opened his eyes and sat up. The blanket covering him fell to his waist. He didn't remember falling asleep, Jasper lifting his legs onto the bed, or covering him up. He had a wispy memory of a gentle touch to his forehead and cheek, but it was tied to the scent of lemon and leather. Had Harriet come to check on him? It was his job to check on *her*.

Shadows indicated almost three hours had passed, but it was still light out. His boots were beside the door, freshly polished. His coat, hat, greatcoat, and change of linen had been hung in the clothespress. He felt barely a hint of headache, and not the least hungover from the potent brew.

He made himself presentable, approved the rakish tilt of the bandage Jasper had applied, and went in search of Harriet and Zach.

He found them at the pasture. As he approached, Harriet brought Tesoro to a halt in the center, jumped down and handed the reins to Zach, who then swung up into the saddle and began putting the horse through more training maneuvers. Harriet climbed to sit on the top rail of the fence next to Senhor Perez. She was so intent on watching Zach, she didn't even notice Nick's approach until he climbed the fence to sit beside her. He was feeling a tad grumpy that she had been smiling as she chatted with Zach. Then she turned that smile on him, and it was like the sun coming out after a rainstorm. He felt his breath hitch.

Odd.

She stretched a hand toward him but dropped it to keep her balance on the fence rail. "How is your head? We stopped to check on you before we came downstairs."

Ah, so it hadn't been his imagination. "Much better, thank you. Father Miguel has the cure for insomnia in that tisane."

Senhor Perez pulled a pennywhistle from his inner coat pocket and began to play a lively tune. Harriet clapped in time, and with Zach still astride, Tesoro began to ... dance?

The stallion stepped to his left, then his right, then turned a tight circle to the right. Made a quarter turn, stepped to the right, to the left, then turned a tight circle to the left. He shook his head as he moved, rattling his bridle as a counterpoint to the clapping from Harriet. He repeated the moves until he'd made a full circle, back to facing his audience on the fence, and as the song ended, stretched one front leg out and bent the other in a bow.

Harriet and Zach applauded enthusiastically. Nick shrugged and applauded, too.

Perez put away his pennywhistle, and Harriet tapped Nick's knee. "Watch this," she said. She cupped her hands to her mouth, and in a tone deeper than her usual speaking voice, called out, "The army is coming!"

Tesoro let out what Nick could only describe as a groan and dropped to his knees. Zach swore and kicked out of the stirrups and jumped clear just before the horse dramatically groaned again and fell all the way to the ground and rolled to his side, his legs and neck stretched out, and went still.

Father Miguel stepped from the shadows of the stable. "He likes to nap in the sun this way." He gestured at the horse, who reminded Nick of a dog playing dead. "More than once a parishioner has come to tell me the sad news that he has passed away in the pasture."

"All clear," Harriet called.

Tesoro climbed to his feet, shook himself, and pranced—really, there was no other way to describe his gait but prancing—over to nuzzle Harriet. She laughed and fed him a carrot from her pocket. While the stallion munched, she petted and praised him and Nick refused to feel jealous of a horse. "He's showing off!" Nick exclaimed.

"He does appreciate having an audience," Senhor Perez said with a chuckle.

Father Miguel pointed over his shoulder at the stable. "Would now be a suitable time to discuss business matters?"

He had been addressing Nick and Harriet, but Zach handed Tesoro's reins to Perez and followed them into a small office off the tack room. Father Miguel withdrew a ledger book from a locked bottom drawer and opened it on the desk. Nick, Zach, and Harriet crowded around the desk to peer over his shoulder, trying not to bump into a bookshelf behind filled with ledgers, the labels on the spines written in Portuguese.

Nick braced himself to find out how much they owed for five years of the horse's upkeep. Given the profit he stood to make on the wine he was taking back to England, he was fairly confident he could absorb his half of the expense, though it would mean putting off buying new sails again and probably a delay in replacing the starboard gun. But the cost would be devastating for Harriet's finances.

Father Miguel flipped to the first page. "Before they returned to their ship after the game, your fathers gave me the money they had with them to pay for feeding and boarding Tesoro," he said. "A few weeks later they sent a bank draft after they'd received their share of prize money."

As he turned the pages of the ledger, two folded pieces of parchment fell out and fluttered to the floor. Zach picked them up, unfolded one, and went perfectly still as he stared at it.

Nick tugged the paper out of his unresisting grip and read the agreement that stipulated Father Miguel would hold the treasure and how it would be claimed. Nick's heart faltered a beat at the familiar no-nonsense handwriting of the man who'd raised him. Giles Chase had signed it, in addition to Adam and the priest.

Nick met Zach's gaze and held it as he rested one hand on Zach's shoulder, exchanging silent words of comfort. Nick still felt ambivalent about Adam's death, but Zach had lost his big brother. Now Zach's only living relatives, other than his by-blows, were Adam's progeny.

"What is it?"

Nick handed the document to Harriet, and stood shoulder to shoulder with Zach to read the second letter. Fighting was going in Wellesley's favor on the Continent, Giles wrote. The Navy was conquering the French at sea, and they were confident they would soon be able to return to claim their property. Until then, the enclosed bank draft should cover the cost of caring for their property. How fortuitous they'd finally been paid prize money owed them for over a year. They'd sent half to their families, and here was half for Tesoro.

The letter was dated just weeks before their ship sank in battle with all hands, the victim of an explosion in the powder room.

"I recognize this figure Adam contributed," Zach said. "He added exactly that amount to Evelyn's dowry so she could snag that pompous earl of hers."

Nick thought his youngest brother-in-law was a bit pretentious, too, but said, "Just because he disapproves of you doesn't make him pompous." Nick handed the letter to Harriet as Zach gave him a little shove with his elbow.

Harriet covered her mouth with her hand while she read one of the last documents penned by her father's hand. She blinked back tears as she folded the two letters and gently set them on the desk, trying not to shake. "Father didn't send any more money home after this. We spent the final bit of it to help pay last quarter's mortgage."

Zach blinked in surprise. "You made the funds last a long time."

She gave a negligent shrug. "Since losing my position when the Academy closed, Gabriel and I have been tending fishing nets, and Mama gives music lessons." She glanced down at the ledger. "Surely the prize money wasn't enough to take care of Tesoro all this time?"

Father Miguel shook his head. "Like you, I made the funds stretch as far as I could." He ran his fingers down the column of figures with entries for the cost of feed, farrier services, and other upkeep. The money had almost run out but then there were more entries in the credit column.

Nick had been silently translating the Spanish notations. "You rented him out?"

"*Sí*. In the spring many farmers welcome a horse to plow their fields. The armies confiscated or commandeered most of the horses when they marched through, in Spain as well as here in Portugal."

Zach snorted in disgust. "He's not a damned plow horse."

"True, but no more money came from the senhors. I had not heard from them in so long, I feared the worst. I have made a promise of simplicity for myself, and it is expensive to feed a horse. But I honored my oath to protect their property and keep Tesoro safe."

Harriet perched on the edge of the desk. "How did you come to hold Tesoro for them? And why did they have him in the first place? Seems an odd thing for two sailors in His Majesty's Navy stationed aboard a ship of the line to acquire."

Nick had been wondering the same.

Father Miguel folded his hands on top of the ledger book. "Your father took exception to the way Tesoro was being treated by his owner." He turned to Nick. "Your father tried to buy him outright but was refused."

"The old whip scars on his hindquarters," Zach said softly.

"Yes, he was mistreated." Father Miguel gave a sad nod. "When the owner would not sell him, Senhor Chase engaged the owner in a card game. Sheffield put up the coins to guarantee the wagering. The game lasted until almost dawn before they were able to achieve their goal."

"And that's how we became partners," Nick said.

Harriet smiled back at him, and his stomach did the same delightful little lift and roll as when his ship crossed from a river into the open sea.

She wasn't satisfied yet. The teacher needed to know more. "But you, Father. How did you become involved?"

"Lord Sheffield attended services in my humble *iglesia* when he could come ashore. We are not of the same faith but we worship the same God, he said. We had a small farm for our parishioners, and I was able to stable Tesoro there, away from the fighting and his former owner. Until the shelling started. I left the clue in the graveyard hoping they could follow me."

"And you evacuated to this winery. But how did you know to come here?"

"The bishop who presides here at Perseguição was one of my teachers when I was in seminary. I did not know that until I arrived in Porto, but I knew that several of the brothers in my class had been assigned in the area. After the French retreated and the winery opened again, I came here, praying your fathers would recognize the similarity in name and find me."

Father Miguel turned to the last page with entries in the ledger book. "The bishop does not charge me a livery fee here. Barring large fluctuations in the price of grain, I estimate there is enough money left to feed Tesoro through the winter, until plowing begins again in the spring, and to replace his shoes every six weeks. The farrier was here last month."

Harriet's mouth briefly fell open. "We don't owe you for his upkeep after all this time?"

"On the contrary, my child." He reached deep into the same drawer that had held the ledger and set a purse on top of the desk with a heavy *thunk* of coins. "Now the funds to care for him through the winter are yours."

"Or at least cover the expenses to transport him back to England." Nick straightened with a sigh of relief. He glanced at Harriet. "We're going to need more hay," they said in unison.

Zach glanced between the two of them, probably wondering what they found so amusing. Nick considered letting him in on the joke, but they heard a bell clanging from the main building.

"It is time for supper," Father Miguel said. He tucked the letters in the ledger and put it and the purse back in the drawer and locked it. "Tomorrow you will take these with you. Tonight, you will dine in the tasting room and enjoy *fado*."

"Is fado a local delicacy?" Harriet asked as they emerged into the waning daylight of the courtyard.

Father Miguel laughed.

Chapter 19

Farm workers, merchants, and other locals filled the tasting room, seated at tables clustered around the fireplace, the bar, and in neat rows before a small stage. Servants brought out platters of delicious-smelling food, and everyone had at least three wineglasses attended by the three servants going around with wine bottles, a different vintage served with each course. Olive oil, *piri-piri* sauce, garlic, and other spices and seasonings livened up even peasant fare like potatoes, *bacalhau*, and boiled cabbage.

Zach ate a particularly spicy bite, then quickly downed a gulp of wine and fanned his mouth, drawing a smile from Harriet. Once his mouth sufficiently recovered, he forked another bite of chorizo and held it closer to the candles in the center of the table. "Note the flecks of pepper, clove and other spices," he said to Harriet. "You won't see this back home." She leaned near to get a better look. "England conquered half the world in search of spices," he confided, staring at her intently, "and decided they didn't like any of them." He popped the bite into his mouth.

She sat back in her seat and burst out laughing, a musical sound.

Nick did not grind his teeth in annoyance at Zach flirting with Harriet, or her lapping it up with such obvious delight. Though he did chew his bite of chorizo with greater intensity than the hapless hunk of spicy sausage warranted.

The mood in the room was joyous, tongues loosened by the free-flowing wine and excellent food. Father Miguel checked on them often but did not stay with them. Instead he went from table to table, checking with all the guests, helping to make sure everything went smoothly in the kitchen and bar.

They had reached the dessert course when performers came out on the stage—two musicians in somber black, and a female vocalist. She wore a tall tortoiseshell comb in her upswept gleaming black hair, yellow lace mantilla flowing from the comb down to her brilliant yellow gown and dyed-to-match silk slippers. The musicians tuned their instruments—one playing a twelve-string round guitar, the *guitarra Portuguesa*, the other on a ten-string baroque guitar—and began to play.

The crowd instantly hushed, avidly listening to the melancholy tune and heart-rending voice of the singer. They applauded wildly at the end of the song, and after briefly basking in their adoration, she launched into another equally mournful yet beautiful tune, accompanied by the guitarists.

"Fado," Father Miguel told them quietly. "It has become our most popular form of entertainment. Senhora Gomez and her brothers play for us tonight. She sings for her lost love, for the war that ravaged her village, for the hope of a good harvest to see us through the winter."

Nick watched Harriet watching the performance, how her face lit up at the fantastical guitar solos, how she empathized with the anguish and yearning in the songs, understanding the emotions even if she couldn't understand the words.

Senhora Gomez finished her last song and curtsied deeply, then one of her brothers escorted her to a reserved seat and waiting glass of wine.

Two trumpet players and more guitarists came out onto the stage. Diners pushed their tables and chairs to the sides of the room, opening up a wide area in the center, near the stage. As the musicians struck up a lively tune, couples formed a circle and began to dance. Nick and Zach had scooted their table farther back and watched, alongside Harriet.

"*Ranchos Folclóricos*," Father Miguel said, pausing on another pass around the room. "This folk dance is *vira*. Turn dance."

The quick three-step pattern of the dance made Nick think back to the waltz he'd shared with Harriet when they first met in London. They'd danced only the one time. What had she been wearing? He remembered mostly that she had blended in, looking demure and unremarkable. Drab, even, especially compared to Lady Slavin.

He would never make that mistake again.

There were more men than women, which did not deter the dancers. Having a partner of the opposite gender was superfluous for most of the dances. The participants stood in a circle, arms raised above their shoulders, snapping their fingers, as they each turned in a tight circle before the circle as a whole moved to the right and they turned again. The music was lively, as joyous as the fado had been mournful and full of longing. And infectious. Nick noticed Harriet's knee bouncing as her heel kept time with the music, her eyes sparkling with joy in the candlelight as she watched the dancing.

The song ended. Some dancers sat down while others got up, and the circle was forming again. Nick was about to ask Harriet if she wanted to dance when Zach stood, pulling Harriet's hand with him, and tugged her out to the circle. Not about to be outmaneuvered or left out, Nick joined the circle on Harriet's other side.

The music started. She looked from Zach to him, a broad grin on her face, raised her hands, and began to dance the *vira*.

Given her masculine attire, he couldn't hold her in his arms for a waltz or for the later dances that were for couples. But he could share the pleasure of this moment with her.

Laughter bubbled up from her as they moved to the music. Nick felt buoyed up by her high spirits, his feet barely touching the ground, lighter in spirit than before he'd inherited the title, before his mother's confession.

The three of them sat out the *fandango* and other dances for couples. Some of the patrons put on their coats and left, and Nick noted how much time had passed. "We're getting up early to ride back to the ship tomorrow," he said to Zach, loud enough to make himself heard over the music. "Are you spending the winter on the Continent, or do you want to come back to England with us?"

Zach drained his glass and slammed it on the table. "I'm in love, lad! Of course I want a lift home!"

Nick felt his mouth fall open, and before he could ask for clarification, Zach grabbed Harriet's hand again and led her, both of them laughing, to open spots on the dance floor.

Nick sat there, stunned. What the devil was Zach talking about? He loved cards and drink and beautiful mistresses, in that order. He'd never married. He'd been known to abruptly cast aside a mistress when the whim struck him to travel, to attend a horse race or boxing tournament. He'd often said he liked the freedom to go where he wanted, when he wanted, without having to consider other people. He couldn't possibly have designs on Harriet, after barely a day's acquaintance.

Several songs later the crowd dwindled further, long before a London or even country assembly would break up, but many of these were farmers who had to tend animals and fields in the morning. And Nick and his party had a long ride back to the ship in Porto tomorrow. They needed an early start, too. The longer he stayed in the dining room, the more tempted he was to sample more of the vintages. And the more he wanted to dance with Harriet in his arms. And he wanted Zach to *not* be able to dance and laugh with her.

Father Miguel refused to allow them to pay for their meal. Jasper was waiting at the bottom of the stairs in the house to escort them up to their rooms and see to any last-minute needs for the night.

Nick stood in the doorway of his room, looking at the bed he'd sleep in alone, then glanced down the hall. Harriet had paused in her doorway as well. Even in the flickering shadows of the hall sconces, he saw her cheeks flush when she glanced toward him. Was she also remembering how it felt to hold each other last night, to sleep in each other's arms? Wondering what it would feel like to caress bare skin, to pleasure one another?

Zach came back into the hall to light a candle from the wall sconce, saw them both, and made a great show of stretching and loudly yawning as he went back into his room and firmly shut the door.

Harriet ducked her head and gave Nick a little wave before she went into her room and shut the door.

Ah, well. At least this room had a warm fire going and no wind whistling through a draft around the window.

He had grown accustomed to having Harriet sleeping nearby and found it strangely difficult to fall asleep without her presence. He could tiptoe down to her room, of course. He was not certain she'd let him in, however, and she likely had a chair lodged under the doorknob to prevent any intruders. And he would not risk Zach catching him outside of a woman's door, giving Zach something more to tease him about. Nick was not a pious hypocrite like Adam, but neither did he tarry with every woman who caught his fancy like Zach, no matter the tales the *ton* tabbies spread about him.

He punched his pillow and began naming the lines of rigging on each mast from bow to stern.

He awoke early, dressed quickly, and went downstairs. As he turned at the bottom step, the room suddenly spun, and kept spinning madly. He clutched the newel post to keep from falling to his knees, holding on as though the hall floor had suddenly become a ship diving deep into a trough, waves swamping the bow, threatening to wash him overboard. He couldn't tell which way was up. Bile rose in his throat and he fought to not cast up his accounts. *What the hell?*

After what seemed an eternity, he dared open his eyes. The earth was settling back on its proper axis. He eased his death grip on the post to wave away a concerned footman who was heading toward him. Soon the vertigo passed, and Nick continued down the hall and out the door.

He found Father Miguel just coming out of the chapel after conducting dawn mass. "I have a business proposition for you," Nick said. "Is a winery manager available?"

A short while later he sat in the winery office with Father Miguel and two other officers of the winery, and expressed his desire to buy quantities of the port wine they'd had last night and take it back to England. If it sold as well as he expected, he'd come back for more on a regular basis.

Father Miguel clasped his hands together in an attitude of prayer. "This is a most excellent plan. I will be blessed to see you again."

Nick swallowed down an unexpected lump. Perhaps he was more sentimental than he'd thought, wanting to keep this tenuous connection to Adam through the priest. "Just so."

They quickly worked out the details. As with most of the wineries in the Douro valley, they had a cellar and tasting room in Vila Nova de Gaia stocked with quantities Nick wanted, so he didn't have to delay his return to England while they transported the wine downriver.

Nick tucked the signed sales agreement in his pocket, then bounded up the stairs to the guest quarters and knocked on Harriet's door. After her muffled, "I'm up, I'm up," he rapped on Zach's door. No answer, so he knocked again, louder. Something hit the other side of the door with a dull thud. Probably a boot. "Don't dawdle," Nick called.

"Confound you early risers," Zach groused. He mumbled other imprecations as Nick walked away, to pack his belongings before going back downstairs.

Harriet and Zach arrived in the dining room together. Nick scowled and Zach grinned, while Harriet was oblivious to the undercurrents and sniffed appreciatively at the food on the sideboard before loading her plate.

After eating a hearty breakfast, Harriet requested fresh carrots and wrapped them in a cloth in her coat pocket. Nick arranged for his own little cloth-wrapped bundles of bread and cheese and tucked them into various pockets of his greatcoat. Great invention, pockets.

Father Miguel arrived, along with a footman bearing a picnic lunch in a knapsack as well as skins of wine and water. "So you will not have to stop as often or as long," he explained. He folded his hands. "I confess, after so many years, I am sad to see Tesoro go," the priest said. "But I am greatly relieved to know he will be safe, appreciated, and treated with the care he deserves."

"Oh, he will be, Father," Zach said. "He will be."

"You're sounding rather possessive about something that does not belong to you," Nick observed.

"That can be remedied," Zach said, with a wink at Harriet.

She was adjusting the bundle of carrots in her pocket and missed it.

Nick narrowed his eyes but followed Father Miguel out to the stable without pursuing the comment.

Grooms had already saddled Tesoro when they arrived, as well as their rented horses. Senhor Perez was speaking softly to Tesoro, stroking his neck. To let him have a private farewell with the horse he'd spent so much time training, Nick and the others went to the office. They made quick business of retrieving the ledger and purse and tucking them into Nick's saddlebags.

More words of goodbye and thanks, and they headed out, with Zach riding Tesoro and leading his stallion. Nick decided not to argue the point, as Zach did have more experience with horses, and there was no telling how Tesoro would respond to a long ride.

They made good time riding downhill, the fog lifting and allowing them to enjoy the view of the valley and terraced hillside covered in grapevines, occasionally broken up by clusters of olive or cork oak trees.

They rounded one of the hairpin turns and Nick inhaled sharply. This was where Marlow had tried to bash in his skull yesterday. Nick had seen two gagged men sitting with their backs to the tree and dismounted to investigate. He'd heard the crunch of a footstep on dirt and acorns behind him, and before he could even turn his head the world had gone black. Marlow was tying Nick's hands behind his back when his senses returned, his head throbbing. He had pretended to still be unconscious in the hope that Marlow wouldn't feel the need to tie his feet or gag him, like Ruford and Hornsby.

A soft gasp beside him alerted him that Harriet had recognized the spot, too. She gave him an anxious glance. He shook his head and flashed her a smile. The bright spot of the incident had been having Harriet's hands all over him. She'd come close to finding out just how much his body appreciated her touch when blindly reaching behind her. Her tender ministration of the gash on his brow, her hands gentle on his face, had been a balm.

At some point in the near future he was going to contrive to have her touching him again. Without other people nearby.

They rode to the bottom of the hill, to the estalagem they'd stayed at two nights ago. Another bout of vertigo slammed into Nick when he dismounted. He closed his eyes and clutched the saddle with one hand and his horse's mane with the other until the dizzy spell passed. When he turned, Zach and Harriet were walking the horses across the inn yard. He quickly caught up with them. They watered the horses, and the humans had a light meal of bread, cheese, and wine.

Nick went in to have a discussion with the innkeeper about the port wine he'd drank the other night. No, he didn't want a bottle or two; he wanted two dozen cases. The innkeeper was delighted. His cousin owned the winery and was already loading a shipment headed to their shop in Vila Nova de Gaia. He could have Nick's order delivered on a rabelo alongside the *Wind Dancer* by noon tomorrow.

Business concluded, Nick went back out to the yard.

"You want to try it again, don't you?" Zach said to Harriet when they were ready to leave.

She briefly ducked her head, then proudly lifted her chin and looked him in the eye. "Yes," she declared.

Zach handed her Tesoro's reins and took the reins of her grey gelding as he mounted his black stallion. Nick moved closer, planning to boost her into the saddle. Zach subtly shooed him away.

Puzzled, Nick watched as Harriet patted Tesoro on the neck and fed him a bite of carrot. She gripped a large clump of his mane near the wither with her left hand while standing with her back to his shoulder, took a deep breath, then turned and hopped up at the same time she swung her right leg up. It took her a moment to settle into the right spot on the saddle but then she was steady, reins soft in her hands, ready to go, big smile breaking across her face. Apparently Tesoro hadn't been the only one practicing in the pasture yesterday while Nick had napped.

She was so pleased with herself, Nick couldn't help sharing her joy.

"The vicar's pony was just as big to me as Tesoro is now when I first started riding her," Harriet said as she urged Tesoro out to the road.

"Bareback," Nick said.

"Of course."

"With the vicar's permission?"

She gave him an impish grin. "He was awfully busy with the people in his parish."

Zach laughed.

"I begin to suspect that Harriet the schoolmistress—the teacher of deportment, the shy miss with the maid—that I met in London was a façade," Nick said slowly as they traveled down the road, "and adventurous Harry is your true personality."

Harriet tilted her head, considering his words, but didn't reply.

They traded off horses every time they made a stop, so everyone had a chance to ride Tesoro and give their horse a rest or give Tesoro a rest. Nick finally got his first chance to ride the Andalusian, and quickly realized the difference between his docile, rented chestnut gelding, and the fierce intelligence and spirit in the black stallion. As a rider Nick was in charge of the chestnut gelding, whereas the stallion nearly unseated him before Nick recognized and acknowledged the degree of cooperation required between Tesoro and rider. He'd have to learn the signals Zach used, so he didn't inadvertently ask the horse to do one of his dramatic airs above ground maneuvers.

Harriet continued to use the ground mount technique, asserting her independence from needing a boost or mounting block, and preventing Nick and Zach from silently arguing over who got to give her a boost.

The first time she tried the maneuver on her rented horse, the grey gelding stepped to the side just as she was swinging up and she fell to the ground, flat on her back. She was still for a moment and Nick was about to dismount to come to her aid, certain she was injured. Then she sat up.

Laughing.

Instead of mortified at being shown to disadvantage, she let out full-throated laughter as she got up and dusted herself off. She offered a bit of carrot to the gelding and tried again. And they were off.

They made it to the stable at the edge of Porto as dusk was falling.

Nick had another bout of vertigo when he dismounted. This time he was expecting it, and disguised it by patting his horse. Once the yard stopped spinning, Nick took care of the rental fee for the horses, including the one Jonesy had returned the day before, and arranged for the hostler to stable Zach's stallion and Tesoro overnight. After confirming Zach intended to take his stallion back to England, Nick also negotiated for the quantities of straw, hay, and grain they'd need for the voyage, and arranged for it to be delivered to the ship tomorrow. He nudged Zach to pay for his horse's share.

They ate a hot meal at the same cantina as on the first day in town. Nick fought the urge to hurry everyone, especially when Zach requested another refill of his tankard. His impatience must have shown on his face.

"Keep your shirt on, lad," Zach said. "She'll still be there in an hour."

Harriet at least finished without dawdling. To Nick's surprise, Zach paid for the meal, and they were on their way to the dock.

Riding about the beautiful countryside was nice, finding and claiming the treasure was good, and spending time with Harriet was even better. But Nick didn't fully relax until the masts of the *Wind Dancer* came into view, and he was across the gangboard. He patted the railing as he stepped onto the deck. Home.

"Welcome back, Cap'n," Jonesy greeted him. He looked him up and down, as well as Harriet right behind him. "I don't see no masterpiece painting. No treasure chest."

Zach had dallied on the quay, checking the ship from bow to stern in the growing twilight, and finally stepped on deck. "Don't I count?"

"Mister Langston, sir!" Smiling broadly, Jonesy reached out and they shook hands. "I didn't expect to see you again so soon." A puzzled frown marred his brow.

"Alas, I am not the treasure," Zach said, hand to his heart.

Nick snorted.

"But it was fortuitous meeting up with you," Harriet said.

"A lass after my own heart," Zach said, giving her a fond smile.

Nick did not growl. Some sound must have emerged from his throat, however, given the sharp glance from Jonesy. No one else seemed to notice.

More of the crew came over, greeting them and exclaiming over Zach, who had not sailed with them since Nick had given him a ride to Aberdeen last autumn, to attend a Scottish friend's house party.

"Have the center hold cleared in the morning and set up the braced stalls," Nick told Jonesy. "We're bringing two horses back with us. Supplies should be delivered before noon."

"Aye, Cap'n," he said, not batting an eye.

While Zach and Harriet went below to stow their gear and settle, Nick satisfied himself that all was as it should be with the *Wind Dancer*. Dieter and Bos'n had finally had time to properly repair and paint the starboard gunwale. All the damage to the masts had been repaired, at least as well as Nick could see in the darkness. Now they just needed a gun.

With a final pat to the tiller, he went below, greeting crew as he went.

Harriet had tossed her saddlebag and coat on the bunk, and someone had brought his down and draped it over a chair back, but his cabin was empty.

Just as he stepped into the passageway to go looking for her or Zach, he heard a burst of laughter from next door. He slid open the door to Norton's cabin. The three of them sat at the long rectangular table that was also used for surgery, with pewter mugs and a half-empty wine bottle.

"Nicky, what took you so long?" Zach hooked the last chair with his ankle and dragged it up to the table, and patted the seat.

Luigi came up in the passageway behind him, a tea tray in hand. "Good to see you back, *Capitano*," he said.

"Good to be back," Nick murmured, and sat at the table.

Harriet poured tea for herself but did not pour for anyone else. In her sailor's togs, she didn't feel the need to play hostess. It was Norton's cabin, and Nick's ship, and she just wanted to drink something that wasn't going to muddle her brain. If they wanted tea, they could pour their own.

"Update me on the crew's health, if you please," Nick said.

Harriet realized she had stopped thinking of him by his title long before he'd been knocked unconscious. Before they shared a bed for the night. How far back? She wasn't sure.

"Winston is healing well," Norton said, "but there's been a development." He poured a cup of tea and added milk and sugar and pushed it toward Nick. "On shore leave with his watchmates, they ran into friends of Winston's, and a cousin. They're in Oporto on holiday and plan to stay in Portugal for the winter."

Nick took a long drink of tea. "I'm losing a crew member, aren't I?"

Norton waggled his head from side to side. "We won't know for weeks yet how well his vision will recover. He's still adjusting to seeing with only one eye while he has to wear a bandage. It will be some time before I clear him for duty aloft. How long are we planning to stay in port?"

Harriet fought a swell of panic. She liked Winston and wanted him to be safe, but she needed to get home. The mortgage was due in a fortnight, and she still didn't know how she was going to pay it. Being half-owner of a stallion trained in the high school airs might eventually make money come her way, but what could she do in the next two weeks?

"Miss Chase has obligations in England. We're sailing as soon as we have supplies and our cargo onboard." Nick drained his cup. "Possibly as soon as tomorrow afternoon. I need to review the tide tables."

"Good thing I already did my shopping, then." Norton refilled Nick's teacup as well as his own, and topped off Harriet's.

"Oh! What did you buy?" Harriet had to ask. After riding cross-country in an exotic land for the better part of three days, all she'd purchased was food. Delicious food, but still...

Norton gestured at his supply cabinet against the wall. "Usual, boring medical supplies to restock." He got up to retrieve a box from one of the cupboards. "And a gift for Caroline." He untied the string on the box and removed the lid with a flourish.

Inside was a tall tortoiseshell comb set with glittering jewels, nestled atop a delicate lace mantilla like the one Senhora Gomez wore last night, this one in a beautiful deep green.

Harriet couldn't resist an appreciative "Ooh." She glanced at the smiling surgeon as he showed it to Nick and Zach. "Who is the lucky Caroline?"

"My wife," Norton said at the same moment Nick said, "My sister."

Harriet's brows rose.

Zach leaned close for a conspiratorial stage whisper in her ear. "Makes for interesting conversation at family dinners."

Harriet fiddled with her teacup, trying not to giggle. "The sister who knits?"

Norton touched his nose. "You've heard about her."

"I saw Nick's slippers after our, uh, excursion overboard." Her mind raced at the implications of Norton being Nick's brother-in-law. She hadn't really thought about Norton's age before.

He must be about halfway between Nick and Zach's age. "But you're at sea, gone from home so much of the time."

Norton tied the lid back on and stored the box in the cupboard. "The secret to our wedded bliss. After I've been home for a while, she can't wait to see the back of me."

Harriet took a sip. "She trusts her husband and brother to look after each other."

Nick and Norton exchanged a glance and shrugged.

Just then Flynn tapped on the door and poked his head in. "Usual arrangements, sir?" He held up a hammock in his hand.

Zach turned a questioning look to Norton and, at his nod, said, "Thank you, Flynn."

Flynn hung the hammock on a hook and closed the door behind him.

As if triggered by the sight of his bed, Zach let out an exaggerated yawn and stretched.

Harriet felt an answering yawn overwhelm her. It had been a long, physically demanding day. "I bid you good night, gentlemen." She may be dressed like a man, but she noted with a tiny thrill of feminine pride that they all rose as she left.

In Nick's cabin she unpacked her saddle bag and hung up her clothes. Nick didn't need to take a fix on their position. Apparently he was still chatting with his uncle and brother-in-law, or checking on his ship. Or perhaps just giving her privacy to wash and change clothes. She meant to stay awake until he came in, but the exertions of the day took their toll.

When she awoke in the morning, the hammock hung on its hook by the door. She had no idea if she'd had company during the night.

She returned her saddlebags to the slop chest, but Smitty talked her into keeping the hat and pea coat.

"It'll get colder the closer we get to England, miss," he said.

She ate breakfast with the larboard watch and went below to pet the goats, only to learn they'd been "hired out as landscape contractors," as Bos'n put it. They were happily grazing in one of the terraced gardens near the river, accompanied by Big Jim. He and the goats would be retrieved just before the ship set sail.

Jonesy had gone to oversee delivery of the horses and their supplies. Bos'n was overseeing the preparations in the center hold and ensuring the crates of wine that had been delivered when they'd first arrived were securely stowed elsewhere. Of Nick there was no sign. Even Oscar the cat was gone. He'd seen a rat climbing up the mooring rope and gone hunting. The rose bushes were on deck, getting sun by the windlass.

Harriet was at the rail admiring the hillside that rose up beyond the river, committing every detail of Portugal to memory and wondering what to do with herself, when Zach climbed up from the hatch.

"Good morning, m'dear," he said, joining her at the rail. "I was thinking of going to the market." He pointed to a spot up the hill. "I hear there are more shops here per square mile than on Bond Street. Care to join me to investigate that claim?"

She grinned in delight. "I'd love to!" She quickly retrieved her leather purse, tucking it securely inside her shirt on its long strap around her neck, and followed Zach ashore. He aborted his instinctual gesture to offer his arm, and instead patted her shoulder.

The open-air market was a cacophony of sound, color, and scent. Vendors under canvas shelters and open tables offered everything from hot pies, fruit, and other grocery items to small tools, clothes, blankets, and other textiles.

"If Caroline is going to receive a lace mantilla, I think I'll get something similar for her sisters," Zach said. He examined the tortoiseshell combs and other hair accessories, asking Harriet's advice, and eventually picked out a brush and mirror set, a colorful shawl, and two distinctly different combs. He tucked his purchases into a linen sack that he pulled from a coat pocket.

At another merchant, he bought a currycomb and other tools he'd need to care for his stallion and Tesoro on the voyage home and tucked those in the linen bag, too. The ship already had a pitchfork and other big tools on board for cleaning up after the goats.

Harriet was loath to spend any money but couldn't resist bringing home souvenirs from her adventure. She bought a simple tall comb and lace mantilla set for Mama, in a lovely shade of lavender given that she still wore half mourning. At the next booth was a display of knives and small leather goods. She perused the knives, thinking of Gabriel. She liked one with a large bone handle that was long enough to wear in a scabbard. "This looks like the knife Jack showed me that he'd carved," she told Zach, pointing to it.

Zach looked shocked. "He showed you his knife with the naked women?"

She frowned, trying to recall the details. "The carving was of a mermaid. I think her breasts were covered by seashells."

"Never mind. I must be thinking of a different knife." In Spanish, he inquired the price from the shopkeeper, a woman about the age of Harriet's mother, with graying hair peeking out from her colorful headscarf.

Oh. It was much higher than she'd thought. With the modest budget she'd set, she'd have almost nothing left to buy anything for herself. She picked out a small folding knife instead that was half the price.

As she pulled her purse out, a large hand reached in front of her, grabbed her purse, and the thief took off running.

Chapter 20

The thief had gone only gone a couple of steps when Harriet's brain caught up with what had happened, and she instinctively gave chase. The crowd of shoppers in the market slowed his escape and she was able to catch up before he'd gone far.

He was tall and broad, much bigger than her younger brother, so she decided her only chance was to take him out at the knees.

She dove, wrapping her arms around his legs, and he went down hard on the cobblestone street. He rolled over and she scrambled to straddle his thighs, making sure to hook the tops of her feet over his shins so he couldn't buck her off. His neck was too thick to wrap her hand around, so she rested the heel of her hand just below his Adam's apple as she reached between his legs with her other hand until she felt soft flesh, and squeezed.

In the act of swinging his fist at her, he yelped and froze.

"Thief," she ground out. "Give me back my purse!"

He had the dark hair, brown eyes, and olive complexion of the local men, and not much older than herself. He easily outweighed her by double. She focused on the anger in his eyes and tried to ignore the long scar that sliced one side of his face from cheekbone to mouth that bespoke a dangerous life, or the fresh abrasion on his chin she'd just caused.

Through the coarse wool of his trousers, she got a tighter grip on his family jewels. "Give!"

His eyes widened. "*Desculpa!*" he said, his voice strained. "*Peço desculpa!*"

She didn't break eye contact with him, but from the edges of her vision saw people gathering around them.

"He says he's sorry," came Zach's amused voice from behind her left shoulder.

"Tell him to give back what he stole."

Zach briefly addressed the thief.

The thief's hands had been out to his side, but he slowly moved one toward his coat pocket. She tightened her fingers another fraction.

"*Aqui!*" His voice rose an octave. He reached into his coat pocket and retrieved three purses, one in floral silk brocade, one in ivory muslin embroidered with grapes and vines, and Harriet's plain leather drawstring pouch, and dropped them on the ground. "*Está aqui o que roubei!*"

"Here's what he took," Zach quietly translated.

"*Ladrão!*" shrieked a woman. Harriet recognized her from the booth with the leather goods. The lady merchant plucked the brocade pouch from the ground, tucked it into her apron pocket, and let out a torrent of angry Portuguese at the man, with plenty of finger poking. The seller of hair accessories picked up the embroidered muslin purse and joined in chastising him as she checked the contents before putting it in her apron pocket.

"They're calling him a thief and telling him his despicable actions have brought shame to his family," Zach said.

Harriet grabbed her purse with the hand that had been at the thief's throat, but didn't let go of his crotch until she was on her feet. He immediately rolled to his feet and darted away through the crowd.

The merchant ladies continued to speak, now in happy tones. "Obrigada, obrigada," they both repeated, practically fighting each other for the privilege of shaking Harriet's hand.

Harriet put her purse away. "De nada," she replied, only now noticing Zach tucking a small pistol back into his coat pocket.

The crowd began to disperse but the ladies kept Harriet's hand and towed her back to their booths, their torrent of happy words washing over her the whole way.

"They wish to show their gratitude," Zach said. He interrupted the flow of words to ask a question of the knife seller, then turned to Harriet. "The thief would have made off with two days' worth of her sales. She wishes to reward you. Pick any item."

"Sim, sim," the merchant said, smiling broadly and emphatically gesturing at the table laden with knives, belts, and leather purses.

Harriet eyed the modest folding knife she had planned to buy, then picked up the knife and scabbard she had originally wanted for Gabriel.

The merchant clapped her hands together in delight and rushed around the table to Harriet, a leather belt in hand. Before Harriet knew what was happening, the woman fed the scabbard through the belt, reached under Harriet's coat to wrap the belt around her waist, and buckled it. She stood back to admire her handiwork, her hands clasped under her chin and a beatific smile on her face.

Harriet adjusted her coat, getting used to the feel of the belt and scabbard against her body. "Obrigada," she said.

The seller of hair accessories impatiently tugged Harriet the few steps over to her table. She held out the box with the comb and mantilla that Harriet had paid for, dropped and forgotten in her quest to retrieve her purse, and gestured at the stock on her table, animatedly speaking to Harriet.

"She's saying you bought one of her least expensive combs, but wants you to choose a nicer set for your sweetheart. Or add something else. Whatever you like."

Harriet felt a blush heat her face as she glanced at Zach, then addressed the seller. "Not for a sweetheart," she said. "It's a gift for my mother. She still wears the half mourning of a widow."

Zach translated.

The seller reached across the table to cup Harriet's cheeks in her callused hands before she spoke again, a tear in one eye.

"'Such a dutiful child,' she says."

Harriet cleared her throat. "This is fine, really," she said, pointing to the comb set. "Mama would not be comfortable wearing anything fancier than this one."

The seller held up a finger, indicating they should wait. She selected a beautiful painted silk drawstring pouch, filled it with hairpins, then tucked it into the box with the comb and mantilla before tying the lid back on and handing it to Harriet.

Ah. This was something Mama could definitely use. Harriet smiled. "A woman can never have too many hair pins."

After Zach translated, the seller laughed and kissed Harriet on each cheek before letting her go.

They were finally able to move on. Harriet steered them toward the booth selling blankets and other textiles. They had only gone a dozen steps, however, when she realized her hands were shaking and her legs felt like *blancmange*. Luckily, they were near the outer row of market booths. She stumbled toward a staircase to an upstairs office and sat down heavily on the third riser.

What on earth had she been thinking, taking on a thief so much bigger than herself? Money was important but certainly not worth her life.

She didn't notice she had been alone until a steaming cup appeared in front of her face. "Drink up," Zach said, pushing the cup toward her mouth.

She wrapped her hands around the warm mug, gratefully soaking up the heat, and took a cautious sip of what turned out to be mulled wine, then took a deeper swallow. She swirled the warm wine on her tongue, tasting the orange and cinnamon, trying to identify the other flavor. Clove? After another swallow, she looked up from the depths of the deep red drink and saw that everyone in the market, shoppers and sellers alike, were going about their business as usual. As though nothing had just happened. Zach sat beside her on the step, elbows resting on his thighs, hands dangling between his knees, the epitome of a man at his leisure, as if he hadn't just seen her almost faint.

"Thank you," she managed, not sure if she was more grateful for the wine to settle her nerves or him ignoring her ignominious behavior.

"De nada," he replied with a grin that looked so much like Nick's. "I confess I'm a tad relieved."

She stared. "Relieved?"

"If you were able to threaten a man in such a way without the slightest reaction, I might fear for my safety."

She let out a shaky laugh and took another sip.

"You appeared quite confident in your actions. Have you considered a career with the Bow Street Runners?"

The warmth of the wine spread through her, and she let out a full-throated laugh. "I have a younger brother. Sometimes I was in charge of watching him and his friends, who were not always well-behaved, especially when they started to grow big." She tilted the cup to her mouth, disappointed there was only a drop left. "And sometimes the men visiting their daughters and sisters at the Academy did not behave themselves as one would wish."

Zach squeezed his knees together and folded his arms over his lap. Harriet laughed again.

She stood and dusted off her bum. "I have a gift for my mother and brother, but I still want to get something for myself."

Zach also rose and dusted off his backside. "What has caught your fancy?"

With the hand holding the empty cup, she gestured at the textile booth.

Zach again aborted the move to offer his arm and instead patted her on the shoulder, and they set off, returning the cup to the booth with mulled spirits on the way.

There were shawls, scarves, and colorful capes woven in wool and cotton. They'd be practical for staying warm, but distinctly not an English fashion. When she got home, she wasn't sure she wanted to stand out as having been abroad.

Brightly colored woven-cotton blankets drew her gaze. She ran her hand over a stack of them, feeling the thick strands of soft cotton, remembering the night at the estalagem covered with two of them. Remembered snuggling with Nick under blankets like these.

This was absurd. She was going back to England. And if she could figure out how to get enough money from her share of Tesoro for a dowry, she was going to marry Percy.

He was the epitome of a proper English gentleman. Would he appreciate a foreign blanket such as this on their marriage bed?

Was that still in her future?

Did she really still want to marry Percy?

She thought back to her quiet life in Brixham and considered what she could expect her life to be like married to such a man as Percy. She reflected on what her life had been the past few weeks—almost drowning, acting as powder monkey in a battle at sea, pretending to be a ship's captain. Riding a horse astride, across a foreign countryside. Trying new foods. Getting tied up and freeing Nick. Dancing the *vira* with abandon after dinner at a winery. Riding Tesoro and remembering how to get up on a tall horse without help.

"I'll take this one," she said to the seller, patting a blanket with a similar color scheme as the one at the estalagem. She carefully looked in all directions before she took out her purse again. Transaction complete, she rolled the blanket into a comfortable shape to carry over her shoulder.

"Excellent choice," Zach said. He glanced at the sky. "We should head back to the ship. It's getting close to noon and the tide will turn soon."

When they got aboard the *Wind Dancer*, a rabelo was tied up alongside, and the crew was hauling crates of wine from the little flat-bottomed boat into the aft hold.

Nick was still nowhere to be found.

When she came back on deck after stowing her purchases, a wagon rolled onto the quay loaded with hay, straw, and bags of grain, with Tesoro and Zach's stallion tied behind. Jonesy walked the horses around the riverfront while the goods in the wagon were lifted into the center hold. Zach went below to help Big Jim and Jack spread a thick layer of straw underfoot in each stall that had been erected, and otherwise finish turning the hold into a stable.

Once the wagon from the stables was empty, the driver headed back uphill, passing another wagon coming onto the quay. This wagon was loaded with crates of wine, and Nick riding with the driver. He seemed entirely sober when he walked up the gangboard.

Flynn and Chang loaded the cargo net down on the quay, and Harriet helped Smitty and Tucker haul it up and into the forward hold, where Dieter and Luigi waited to unload. As the first full net lowered past her, Harriet almost lost her grip on the line when she recognized the crest stamped on the containers.

Casa de Perseguição.

Nick met her gaze from the quarterdeck and gave her a slow nod.

They were bringing back to England another connection to her father, however tenuous. Tears suddenly blurring her vision, she smiled at Nick and returned to work.

The second wagon emptied and sent on its way, they set about the delicate work of loading the horses into the center hold. Zach oversaw getting the slings under Tesoro's belly and around his chest and rump just right and connected to the line above, and applied a blindfold so the horse would be less likely to panic. Harriet joined Nick in the hold, to help release and calm the stallion. She was prepared with a pocketful of carrots.

Zach joined them in the hold as soon as his black stallion had been prepped and hoisted up.

The narrow stalls were just wide enough for a horse to stand in, each with a sling on a hook on one side, ready to fasten under the horse's belly to offer support as soon as the ship put out to sea.

The crew had made a tack room of sorts, separating the horses in the main space from their feed and other supplies with a wall of planks. Nets full of hay and straw were hung as high as possible. Dieter had built a rack on which to store the saddles, and Tucker had sewn canvas dust covers for them.

Nick stood off to one side with his arms folded, hand stroking his chin, as he watched Zach at the head of the stalls, petting both horses and speaking softly to calm them. "Do you need a room?"

Without breaking off his litany of soothing sounds and still petting one of the horses, Zach lobbed a carrot at Nick. It bounced off his chest.

"Come along, Harry," Nick said. "I think they need to be alone."

Harriet glanced back in time to see Zach make a rude hand gesture at Nick. Trying not to giggle, she followed him up the steps to the main deck.

"Jack and Tucker are securing the cargo in the forward hold, Cap'n," Bos'n reported.

Nick acknowledged him and watched Winston emerge from the aft hatch, an enormous knapsack slung over one shoulder. He still had a bandage wrapped around his head, covering his left eye.

"Smitty paid my final wages, Cap'n, but I think he miscalc'lated." Winston dropped his knapsack to the deck, holding to the drawstring tie.

"No miscalculation," Nick replied. "Compensation in case you end up losing the eye or the use of it."

"But—"

Nick clapped him on the shoulder. "When you're done healing and if it turns out it's fine, you can pay me back next time we meet."

A slow smile spread across Winston's face, showing his gleaming white teeth. "Aye, sir." He gave a look around the ship. "I sure do hate to leave you shorthanded." He spotted Harriet, who'd been hanging back, out of the way. "But da Maiden o' Sea will prob'ly help out, least 'til you get back to London."

Harriet couldn't hear or see Nick's reply, as crew started coming up to say goodbye to Winston. They shook hands, hugged, and clapped each other on the back. When he reached her near the gangboard, she stuck her hand out for him to shake. Madame Zavrina would never approve, but while Harriet dressed like a member of the crew, she fully intended to enjoy the freedom of acting like one. She certainly wasn't going to curtsy wearing duck trousers.

After a slight hesitation, Winston clasped her hand in a firm shake, her pale hand swallowed up in his large, work-roughened hand the color of coffee.

"Thank you for what you taught me," she said.

He grinned. "You's a good student."

She stepped back, and he hoisted his knapsack over his shoulder and left the ship. He didn't get far before he stopped on the quay to say goodbye to Big Jim and the goats, who had just returned. With a final wave at the ship, Winston joined a trio of men waiting for him and the four of them disappeared into the crowd.

Harriet helped get the goats into the lower hold. After gorging on fresh vegetation for two days, they just wanted to lie about on the straw bedding and chew their cud.

She wandered the ship to witness the departure preparations she'd slept through in London and that had been so rushed in Corunna. Nick was in the galley, reviewing the amount of water and foodstuffs Luigi had arranged to bring on board. Smitty sat at the drop-down table next to the galley, consulting bills of sale and updating the account ledgers. Bos'n and Jonesy were overseeing the rest of the crew, making sure that everything that was supposed to be tied down was secure.

When she went up on deck, Oscar was sitting on the windlass cover, vigorously washing his face and front paws. "Have a nice snack, did you?" She sat beside the orange tabby, absently stroking his long, silky back to the tip of his fluffy tail.

She looked up when Nick rang the ship's bell in a pattern she'd never heard before. The crew quickly appeared on deck, and Jonesy joined Nick on the quarterdeck. Chang walked down the gangboard, then pushed the board up while Flynn and Tucker pulled, and soon they had the board stowed. After Chang untied the mooring ropes from the fore and aft bollards and tossed them aboard, Harriet helped haul on the line to bring him back up on deck.

Dieter quickly coiled the mooring lines, while Chang and Flynn swung over the port side gunwale and began climbing the ratlines.

Jack paused beside Harriet. "Winston used to climb up the starboard side wi' me to loose the main t'gallant."

Before she could reply, he'd swung over the side and started climbing.

Biting her bottom lip, Harriet stared up at the footropes, where Chang, Flynn, and Jack would soon be, and how high above the deck those lines were.

The water was calm. The ship was still beside the quay, though beginning to drift out into the river channel. Nick needed the sails unfurled quickly so he could maneuver the ship. She took a fortifying deep breath, kicked off her canvas shoes to be barefoot like the rest of the crew, careful they were out of the way up against the gunwale, grabbed the line, and started to climb.

*****

Nick stood at the tiller, simultaneously keeping an eye on the river and watching his crew getting the ship underway. As usual when leaving port, Big Jim, Smitty, Tucker, and Dieter climbed aloft to unfurl the fore mainsail, while Chang, Flynn, Jack, and Winston were unfurling the mainmast topgallant.

Zach joined him at the maphouse. "Horses calm?" Nick asked, scanning the ship and river, then did a double take at the mainmast. He tipped his head way back to get a clear look, certain his eyes deceived him.

No, not Winston. Winston had gone ashore, probably permanently.

"Yes," Zach said. "They're— What in holy hell is Harry doing up there?"

Nick couldn't speak past his heart lodged in his throat. Harriet was on the outer edge of the starboard footrope, bent over the yardarm to untie the strips holding the t'gallant.

He shouldn't be surprised she'd finally gone aloft. She'd done almost every other sailor's task. Did it need to be on the starboard side, though? He glanced at the open gun port. She hadn't exactly had good luck on the starboard side.

Not that Nick was superstitious.

"Winston's job," he said softly. "She's doing Winston's work." He struggled to not shout for her to get the hell down from there.

The fore mains'l unfurled and filled with a loud snap, and with increasing speed the ship moved out into the river's main channel.

He heard laughter from the quay. People pointed at the pink-speckled sail.

Nick adjusted the tiller to get the ship brought about in the river and headed back out to sea, dividing his attention between watching for signals from Bos'n, who had climbed out on bow watch to help navigate the congested river, and looking up at Harriet's shapely backside bent over the t'gallant yardarm.

Zach gave a low whistle of appreciation.

Ignoring the fact that he had also been staring, Nick jabbed Zach in the ribs. "Eyes elsewhere, you lecherous old man."

Zach gave him an unrepentant grin. "And here I thought you or I would end up needing to go aloft." He gestured at Nick's forehead and grew more serious. "Though you're not going up until the dizzy spells pass."

Nick self-consciously adjusted the bandage wrapped around his head. He thought he'd been clever at hiding when the ground seemed to shimmy and roll beneath him. Norton had checked him over early this morning and declared Nick should expect the headaches and dizzy spells to plague him for a fortnight or more, gradually reducing in frequency and intensity. Nick tilted his head to one side, still trying to watch both Bos'n and Harry but not be obvious about it. "Not like I haven't done every task needed on this ship, at one time or another."

"Been a while since you did some of them though, eh?"

The crew on the foremast climbed higher to loose the t'gallant, just as the main t'gallant filled with a snap. Moments later, the mainmast crew began climbing down to unfurl the mains'l.

There was an urgent whistle and arm gesture from Bos'n, and Nick steered hard to avoid a cluster of rabelos that hadn't seen the bigger ship bearing down on them. The brig rolled to starboard just as Harriet was making the transition from the footrope to the ratline. Her foot slipped off, and for a few of Nick's thundering heartbeats she hung by her hands while her body swung out, suspended high above the water. Nick barely had time to gulp before she swung back in as the ship righted, got a foot planted on the rope ladder, and resumed her climb down to the mains'l footrope.

Now she was on the inside, close to the mast. Nick's heart still pounded. If she fell from there, instead of dropping into the water she'd land on the deck with all its hard surfaces and sharp edges fifty feet below, not to mention the open hatch of the center hold. It was irresponsible of him to let her take such risks. She may be dressing like a crewman, but she was still a lady.

He didn't want to have to bear sad news to her mother and brother, that was all.

The wind snatched the words away, but he could see Flynn and Jack encouraging and instructing her. Her face was split in a broad grin when she turned her head to reply to Flynn.

Nick forced his breathing to slow. From this angle, he finally noticed the scabbard hanging down from a belt around Harriet's waist. "The knife is new," he murmured.

Zach clapped him on the shoulder. "You have a hellion on your hands, m'boy," he said, and enthusiastically related the tale of their shopping excursion and how Harriet had acquired the knife and scabbard.

At one point in the story Nick reflexively moved his hand that was not on the tiller down in front of his groin. "She did *what*?"

* * *

They soon made it past the sandspit at the river's mouth and out into the Atlantic proper. Nick's blood raced and his stomach did a little flip, as always happened when he got out on the open sea. He kept them going west-northwest for a while, moving farther away from the coastline.

"You're grinning like a fool," Zach said. "As usual."

Nick didn't bother to reply. The breeze was drying the teeth exposed by his grin.

Turning his face into the wind, Zach took a deep breath and exhaled loudly. "This never gets old, does it?"

Jonesy had been standing at the forward rail of the quarterdeck, directing the unfurling and adjusting of the sails. He looked over his shoulder. "Orders, Cap'n?"

Nick glanced up at Harriet, who was nimbly following Jack across a footrope, the sound of her laughter drifting down. "Crowd the canvas," Nick said.

Jonesy followed his upward gaze and grinned. "Aye, Cap'n."

They soon had every scrap of canvas unfurled and catching the light breeze. Tucker had managed to salvage enough material for a clean white flying jib and inner jib. All the other sails were from the spare set.

Speckled pink.

Nick hated beets. Had hated them ever since crates of them had broken open in the hold during a battle and stained his canvas.

Getting ready to make notes in his logbook, he looked for Harriet to see if she wanted to join him, as she had on the previous leg of their journey. Near the port bow, Bos'n was correcting her on the way she'd belayed a line and making her re-do it—something his grumpy second mate would never have done with her on the journey out from London. Then again, the Miss Chase who had boarded the ship in London would never have dreamt of becoming Harry barely three weeks later, dressing and acting the part of a sailor.

Would she?

Chapter 21

Nick was looking forward to dinner with Harriet in the privacy of his cabin, as they had done so often before. He was a little disgruntled that he had to tell Flynn to ask her to join him after she sat down to table with the larboard watch in the fo'c'sle. His mood did not improve when Norton and Zach invited themselves to dine at the captain's table.

Nick couldn't help noticing that Harriet moved a little stiffly after she'd been sitting for a while and had trouble grasping her utensils.

"Luigi prepared bacalhau and caldo verde?" Norton said in disbelief just before he ate a spoonful of the spicy soup.

"He consulted with Flynn," Zach said, cutting his cod into bite-size pieces.

Harriet nodded when Nick silently offered to ladle more soup into her bowl as he served himself. "Why would Luigi consult with Flynn about dinner?"

"Luigi has never cooked Portuguese cuisine before," Nick said. "Flynn was still our cook the last time we stopped in Portugal."

"They just ... swapped jobs?" She tried to hide a wince when she cut into her fish.

Nick resisted the impulse to reach over and cut it for her. "Luigi hurt his shoulder last summer. Still can't climb very well. Flynn wanted to spend less time below deck. So they taught each other and traded duties." She was staring at him in awe. "What?"

"You accommodated an injured crew member so he wouldn't lose his job. Two of them, actually, if you count when Bos'n's voice was damaged." Oblivious to the other men at the table, her smile spread across her face, brightening parts of him that he hadn't realized had been dark.

He cleared his throat, though his voice still came out gruffer than he intended. "Skills can be taught. They're good men. Didn't want to lose them."

Whatever it was that she liked about what he'd said or done, he determined he had to do it again to get her to look at him that way, bordering on adoration. Often.

While they ate, Zach regaled them with tales of his mad dash on horseback across France and Spain to beat Hornsby. Nick tamped down irritation at the laughter Zach's skill as a raconteur drew from Harriet. After all, this was part of how Zach got himself invited to so many dinners and house parties, allowing him to live at a loftier level than his modest annuity would fund. Gambling and charisma were his main sources of income.

"And then there was Bordeaux," Zach was saying. "Oh, the wine! I could have stayed there for weeks and still not tried all the varieties. I did stay two nights, but only because Button threw a shoe and the farriers were busy."

Flynn entered then with a tray laden with cheese, nuts, and a bottle of port wine, and removed the empty soup tureen and other dishes.

Harriet wasn't leaving, and the men weren't lighting up cigars, so Nick poured her a couple of inches of port.

"Button?" Harriet giggled. She'd barely had a sip.

"The previous owner had named the horse *Beauté Noire*," Zach explained. "I find the French language pretentious. He seems to like being called Button." He tossed back the wine in his cup and poured himself more.

Harriet laughed again, though she covered her mouth with her hand to muffle it. Nick began to suspect she was exhausted rather than tipsy, confirmed when she kept her hand up to hide a yawn.

She'd spent all afternoon working as hard as any of the crew, after the morning adventure she'd had in the market.

"Before we go back to London," Norton said, "are you going to put in to Lulworth Cove to get more of this cheese?" He cut off another hunk for himself and offered a piece to Harriet.

"Oh, yes, yes," Zach said excitedly. "We must see how your friend Tony and his smuggler bride are doing."

Nick ate a bite, not looking at Harriet who had paused mid-chew to stare at him. "She's not a smuggler anymore. She and her gang make cheese now." He held up a sample of their product before he ate it. "Though they can probably still get you a bargain price on excellent brandy."

Dinner broke up soon after that, with Zach taking a cup full of wine and a chunk of cheese with him. As Norton rose to leave, he discreetly dropped a packet of headache powder in Nick's lap, and set a tin of salve on the table with a significant tilt of his head toward Harriet. Nick tucked the packet in his coat pocket.

Flynn came and took the tray and finally, *finally*, Nick was alone with Harriet for the first time all day. Since their night at the estalagem, actually. Last night didn't count, as she had been sound asleep the entire time he was in the cabin. After taking care of updating his logbook, he'd given in to the pounding in his head and mixed a packet of the headache powder with a generous shot of rum, settled in his hammock, and hadn't awakened until dawn.

"Let me see your hands," he said.

She set them palm-down on the table. "Why? They're fine."

He tilted his chin down to look at her through his lashes. When his friend Alistair did that, women fluttered and melted at his feet. When Nick did it, green sailors had been known to freeze. Or at least stammer.

Harriet just looked at him like butter wouldn't melt in her mouth.

So much for fluttering or freezing.

He moved his hand next to hers on the tabletop, close enough to feel the warmth radiating from her skin, and resisted the urge to flip her hand over. "Because you've been hauling on lines and climbing ropes all day. I saw how it hurt to use the knife to cut your food."

She grimaced, still reluctant to admit any weakness. That was a trait he understood. He opened the lid on the tin of salve.

"Oh, that smells delightful!" She leaned closer to get another sniff. "Is that lavender?"

He narrowed his eyes. "You were expecting it to smell nasty? Harsh?"

"I, ah..."

Nick grinned. "The stuff Norton used to make did smell nasty. This was made by Sylvia, the former smuggler, who also developed the recipe for the cheese we just ate. They have an abundance of lavender in Lulworth Cove, and her salve recipe works just as well or better than Norton's. Though he'll never admit it. Now give me your hand, if you please."

He cradled her slowly proffered hand in one of his and began to gently massage the salve into her reddened palm. He used both hands to rub the salve into all the creases and curves, between each finger and out to the fingertips, working the melting beeswax with its healing herbs and essential oils into every bit of skin up to her wrist.

Her initial reluctance quickly disappeared, her hiss at first contact giving way to a sigh for the pain-relieving effects of the salve, and, he hoped, the pleasure of his touch.

If he'd called her down from the foretop, her hands wouldn't be this sore. He also wouldn't have the excuse to hold and caress her hand, which was surprisingly erotic for such a tame activity. They were both still fully dressed.

As he stroked the pad of his thumb in slow circles on her palm, he tried to gauge her response, to see if she was deriving as much pleasure from this as he was. Her gaze followed the movements of his fingers as though mesmerized.

"Other hand," he said softly.

She gave him her other hand, leaving the first resting palm-up on the table.

He took his time, thoroughly working the salve into every bit of her flesh, the beeswax quickly melting from the heat of their skin and the extended contact.

He had mixed feelings about the thicker skin she was developing on her palms and finger pads from the work she'd been doing on this journey. Miss Chase would never develop such calluses. Harry seemed to welcome them.

Though starting to tan, the backs of her hands were still soft and smooth. Perfect for kissing. He could drop a gallant kiss on her knuckles. He wanted more.

"All right, lie back on the bunk."

Her eyes, which had been half-closed, now popped open. "I beg your pardon?"

"So I can do your feet." He vaguely gestured at her limbs in question, tucked under the table. "I saw how you limped. It takes a while for one's feet to develop the muscles and calluses to not hurt when working the footropes." He scooted his chair so it was sideways beside the bunk, and gestured at the mattress.

She valiantly tried to muffle her groan when she got up from the table, but her grimace gave her away. He could make her feel better by rubbing the sore muscles in her neck and shoulders. All the way down her strong back, to her gently curved hips. Even better if he got her clothes out of the way...

He had a bottle of lavender-scented liniment in his desk. He'd start by rubbing the salve into her feet, then get the liniment and work his way under her trouser legs to massage her shapely calves. He'd smooth the oil into her muscles higher and higher up her slick skin. Loosen the laces at the back of her trousers and slide her shirt up so he could have access to all that lovely, soft skin. He'd have her moaning in ecstasy in no time.

She gingerly perched on the edge of the bunk.

"Lie back and give me your feet." He patted his lap, looking as innocent as he could. Really, he just wanted to help her feel better. The fact that she'd make him feel really good in the process was just a bonus.

Tell yourself another one, boyo.

She kicked off her canvas shoes, lay back, and lifted her feet. He settled her lower legs across his lap, the tin of salve in easy reach on the table. He scooped a generous amount of the salve, rubbed it between his hands to warm it, and began massaging it into her right foot.

She flinched and giggled when he touched her instep. "Sorry," she said. "That tickles."

He filed the information away for later, and used a firmer touch as he resumed working in the salve. He felt the tension leave her, not just the muscles in her foot but in the way the weight of her legs on his lap increased as she relaxed and gave in to his ministrations. He rubbed his knuckles deep into her arch, stretched and wiggled each of her toes in turn, and stroked his fingers in long sweeps from heel to toe. He glanced at her from time to time as he worked, monitoring her response. Her eyes were closed, her hands loosely folded over her stomach.

He checked her again as he scooped more salve, ready to take care of her left foot. This time she was looking at him through eyes at half-mast, a subtle smile playing about her lips.

He knew what those lips felt like against his.

Every kiss they'd shared so far, someone else was nearby. Too close.

They were alone now, though. No one to interrupt them. Sound carried and the bulkhead separating the two cabins was thin so they'd need to be quiet, but he and Harriet were finally, blessedly, alone. He had plans for those lips. Not to mention the rest of her body.

He massaged her left foot just as he had the other, his touch firm enough not to tickle, pressing his knuckles or thumb to loosen knotted muscles, giving long sweeping strokes to relax, thoroughly working in the healing salve.

He wrapped one hand around her ankle, gently rotated her foot to work the joint loose, and began to stroke up her calf. He looked to confirm she was on board with what he was doing, the liberty he was taking.

She was sound asleep.

Her hands had fallen to the mattress, limp at her sides. Her chest rose and fell with steady, deep breaths.

His hands on her shins, Nick slumped in his chair.

He stared at her. At her slightly parted lips.

He could wake her with a kiss on that delectable mouth.

Then he considered the day she'd had. The hard physical labor she'd performed.

He'd given a foot massage to an exhausted woman, and rather than falling into his arms, she'd fallen asleep. Should he be surprised?

When it came to seduction, he truly was inept.

With a groan of frustration, he gently gathered her legs in his arms and maneuvered her until she was fully stretched out on the bunk. He leaned over to grab the blanket to cover her, and froze with his arms braced on either side of her as the ship suddenly seemed to pitch and roll wildly. He closed his eyes against the dizzy spell.

The world kept spinning and wobbling. As he tried to rise, a wave of nausea slammed into him. His arms trembling, he lowered himself to the bunk beside her to avoid crushing her if he collapsed.

Just a minute. Or two. He'd get off the bunk as soon as his cabin stopped spinning.

* * *

The next morning, Harriet was belaying a line after adjusting the fore mains'l when Nick first appeared on deck to check their position. As he retrieved the sextant from the maphouse, he gave her a sweet, small smile that was almost bashful. He had fallen asleep in the bunk beside her, after she had fallen asleep with her legs on his lap. Part and parcel for their unusual relationship, she thought. They'd been sharing a cabin for weeks and twice now they'd shared a bed without sharing their bodies. Other than for warmth. If he'd been trying to seduce her, he would have taken off his coat and shoes before getting into bed with her, right? Perhaps he'd been overcome by one of the dizzy spells he tried to conceal. As a sop to his ego, she'd avoided mentioning them. Her pirate undoubtedly saw them as a sign of weakness.

While Nick checked their position, she felt her cheeks heat anew at the memory of falling asleep last night and waking up in his arms—again. She'd had to leave before she gave in to the temptation to kiss his mouth so close to hers. He'd briefly tightened his grip on her when she slid out from beneath his arm, then rolled over onto his stomach, to the warm spot she'd just vacated, and sighed when she slipped off his shoes and covered him with her Portuguese blanket because he was lying on top of his red and black plaid blanket.

The rest of the crew on deck had now entered the stay-busy phase of their watch, cleaning and finding odd chores to do until a sail needed adjusting or they were called to some other task. The goats were sunning themselves on the forward hatch cover.

Jonesy waved her up to the quarterdeck while Nick was using the spyglass to check the horizon.

The breeze cooled her flaming cheeks as she moved past Nick to the tiller.

"Take a turn," Jonesy said. "Me arm needs a rest."

She took the tiller, knowing that his arm was fine but happy for the excuse. She hadn't had a turn as helmsman since before they'd arrived in Porto. It didn't take long to notice the difference in the way the ship handled, how more effort was required to keep the ship on its heading.

"We're heavier now," she exclaimed, thinking aloud.

Jonesy tapped the tip of his nose.

Nick lowered the spyglass and patted his flat stomach. "Speak for yourself."

Harriet chuckled. "I knew we were riding a little lower in the water, but I didn't think about how that would affect steering." She stared up at Nick. "Just how much wine did you buy?"

He grinned and resumed his scan through the spyglass.

While Nick was scanning off the stern, she saw Zach poke his head out of the aft hatch and wave her over, one finger held to his lips. Jonesy silently took back the tiller and gestured with a tilt of his head for her to go.

Harriet followed Zach below. He didn't stop until they were in the center hold. With no mares to fight over, Button and Tesoro had become roommates with little fuss. They stood quietly in their stalls, shifting a bit with each roll of the ship, watching every movement of the newcomers, alert for any hint of a threat or treat.

Zach gave each horse a pat before he turned to her. "Yesterday, you demonstrated that you know how to fight like a woman defending her virtue. So I've been thinking—yes, Nick would say that's a dangerous thing—as you're dressing like a man, perhaps you'd like to learn how to fight like a man defending his honor?" He cocked his head, as though maybe he shouldn't have made the offer.

Harriet felt her mouth fall open in surprise. She quickly closed it and impetuously hugged him. "Yes, please! I picked up a few tricks watching my brother and his friends wrestling and engaging in horseplay, but I never had much of a chance to practice them."

Zach grinned. "Then by all means, let us continue your education." He gestured at the net full of straw he'd lowered, with a length of canvas pinned to it. He'd drawn a crude outline of a man in charcoal on the ragged canvas. "It's not Gentleman Jackson's Salon, but here's a target. Now, show me how you make a fist."

* * *

When the bell rang for the larboard watch to come below, Harriet joined them in the fo'c'sle for their meal. With Winston gone, she no longer needed to perch on a water cask as there was space to join them at the table.

"No disrespect to Mr. Langston—'e's great guns—but 'e's teaching you to fight like a gen'leman," Jack said.

Tucker nodded. "Aye. S'pose you're in a pub near the docks, just mindin' yer own business, wettin' yer whistle, when a fight breaks out? You need to know 'ow to fight like a sailor."

Chang enthusiastically jumped into the conversation. Harriet had been practicing with him to learn phrases in Mandarin but so far didn't know much more than yes, no, thank you, and please. She looked to the other men to interpret for her.

Jack gestured at Chang. "Since you're small, 'e says you need to know 'ow to fight against a bigger opponent."

Chang nodded vigorously.

"Good points," Harriet said. "If not Mr. Langston, who is going to teach me?"

All three men wore broad grins.

They quickly finished their meal and the four of them adjourned to the center cargo hold for her first lesson in how to fight like a sailor.

Of course she knew about the vulnerability of a man's groin—especially his "dangly bits," as another teacher at the Academy had called them—knowledge she had put into practice in the Porto market.

But now Tucker, Chang, and Jack showed her new things, or at least new to her. How to kick out a man's knee, and how to break a chokehold if someone was standing in front of her or if they seized her from behind. Previously, another teacher at the Academy had told her to just go limp if someone grabbed her, and when the attacker was caught by surprise by her unexpected weight, to then stomp on his instep and run away.

She had never thought of using her head as a weapon. Her wits, of course, but to actually shove her head backwards into the face of an attacker had not occurred to her until Jack pretended to attack Chang. Elbows also had uses she'd not thought of before, with forearms blocking blows and shoving the point of her elbow into someone's throat or stomach.

"If you 'it 'im this aways," Jack said as he slowly pretended to hit Tucker on the side of his nose with a closed fist, "you'll make 'im bleed. Might be messy but you can get away, or cause 'im more pain."

"If you hit him this way," Tucker stopped with his fist just shy of touching the tip of Jack's nose, "you'll stop him. Maybe permanently." He flattened his hand as though he was trying to shove Jack's nose back into his head. "Dinna do this 'less you're willing for him to end up dead. If it comes down to you or him, I say kill him."

Harriet let that sink in. "This is all very, uh, helpful, not to mention a little bloodthirsty." She took a deep breath. "But what if I just want to discourage someone from fighting me? Something to distract them while I extricate myself from the pub fight?"

Jack and Chang exchanged words, then Jack charged at Chang. The gunner grabbed Jack, flipped him over his hip, and suddenly Jack was flat on his back on the straw-strewn deck. Tucker cheered. Chang reached a hand down to help Jack up. Jack pulled at the same moment he put his foot in Chang's stomach, and the smaller man went flying over onto his back, and Jack jumped up.

Harriet watched in awe. "I definitely need to know how to do that. Both of those moves."

Up until this point, they had just been practicing by kicking or punching the charcoal man on the canvas against the net full of straw, or mock hitting each other to demonstrate moves, but not actually hurting each other. Now they spread even more straw on the deck for padding and began teaching Harriet how to flip someone over her shoulder or her hip.

The third time she went flying over Chang's shoulder and landed on her back with an "*Oof!*" he reached a hand to assist her up ... and she managed to send him flying, then used his momentum to help herself jump up, just as Jack had done earlier.

She was practically quivering with excitement. In the back of her mind she could hear Madame Zavrina sputtering in outrage not only from engaging in such unladylike pursuits but also her physical contact with men. Harriet mentally flipped the woman over her shoulder. Chang dusted himself off and all three men critiqued her move, offering suggestions to make it more efficient and safer for her. Didn't want to injure her back while throwing an opponent.

The next few days settled into a routine. Gentlemanly fighting lessons with Zach in the hold if the larboard watch didn't need her on deck to help change the sails, lessons on how to fight dirty with her watchmates after they ate, and dinner in Nick's cabin with Norton and Zach. As soon as the guests exited the cabin, she fell asleep in the bunk, exhausted.

One time Chang took her aside for a private lesson, for something he said he had not taught his crewmates. He showed her how to use the edge of her hand to strike an attacker on the side of his neck, below his ear.

"Hit ha'd," he said. "Hit ha'd and fast."

Once she was getting the hang of that, he taught her to quickly follow up with the same kind of blow on the other side of the neck, followed by sharply shoving her attacker's chin back with the heel of her hand. He moved so fast his hands were a blur. He did it slowly several times until she got the hang of it.

When she finally did it to his satisfaction, he put his palms together and gave her a small bow from the waist. Harriet mirrored his gesture.

She still spent a great deal of time with Nick, who let her practice her nascent navigation skills. He didn't say anything about falling asleep in the bunk with her, and she didn't bring it up. He left the tin of salve on the table for her but did not offer to apply it.

On the fifth day out of Porto, Big Jim was still mucking out the hold, so the larboard watch stayed at table after they'd eaten.

"You going to leave your handle nekkid?" Jack said, setting out his scribing tools and an ivory comb on which he was working.

It took Harriet a moment to realize he meant her knife handle. She'd used the knife numerous times already, and like the other crew, had tied a cord around the handle to the scabbard in case she dropped it. "I hadn't decided one way or the other." She tugged the knife out of its scabbard to look at it.

"Something to consider," Tucker said. "No one can mistake it for theirs if you've put your stamp on it." He and Chang set up the checkers cloth and began to play.

Harriet had planned to give the knife to Gabriel. How much more personal, though, would it be with a scrimshaw carving on the handle? "What would you recommend for a design? I'm fair at painting with watercolors and can sketch with charcoal, but I've never had the chance to carve or etch before."

Jack produced a slate and chalk from his kit bag, and they drew one design after another. None seemed worth the effort or within her ability until she thought of the sleek dolphins that swam alongside the ship periodically and bumped her bare feet when she was on bow watch. She sketched one leaping out of the water.

"Simple is good," Jack said. He showed her how to prepare the bone handle with beeswax and let her use his supplies. She spent time making sure it was properly buffed and sealed to get it ready.

Jonesy came down for a mug of grog and briefly stood beside the table, watching the checkers game and chatting with Jack about his latest scrimshaw project. Norton sat on a water cask while he fussed with his pipe and tobacco before going up for a smoke.

While Jack was scribing, he let her use his pencil to sketch the pattern on her handle. It didn't take long to get the simple design to her satisfaction. She couldn't borrow Jack's scribing tool while he was using it, so she set aside her knife to watch the checkers game and observe Jack transform the plain comb into a work of art.

"I'm surprised you want flowers on your comb," she couldn't help saying when she saw enough of the design to recognize the image on it.

"T'ain't going to be mine for long," he replied with a wide grin. "I always 'ave things to sell when we get into port."

Smitty came through and set a small, rolled pouch on the table in front of her. "For Harry, with Mr. Jones's compliments," he said, and was gone down the passageway before she could respond.

She untied the cord and unrolled the dark leather pouch, revealing all the tools and supplies needed to complete a scrimshaw project, except for the object to be decorated.

Jack poked through the kit. "That's from the slop chest," he said. "Good kit."

Harriet frowned. How much would it cost her? She already owed Nick for so many expenses.

Jack must have recognized the direction of her thoughts. "Smitty ain't going to charge you for it."

"No?"

Jack shook his head. "It's from the first mate; 'e said so."

"Oh. Well in that case, I should get to work." She slipped the cork off the scribing tool's sharp point and started etching the design of the dolphin into her knife handle.

Chang jumped a checker over two of Tucker's, reaching the far side. "King me," he said.

"Blast you," Tucker said. He kinged the checker and took his turn.

There was quiet while Chang considered his next move, and Jack and Harriet worked on their projects.

"Mrs. Brown," Tucker said out of nowhere.

They all stared at him.

"William Brown, of the HMS *Queen Charlotte*," Tucker added.

"Oh, aye," Jack said. He looked up from his comb to grin at Harriet. "You could be another Mrs. Brown."

"Who?"

"'Twas all over the Navy news last year," Tucker said. "William Brown signed on as able seaman with the *Queen Charlotte* and served for 'bout eleven years. When prize money was owed, her husband got wind and sued to get his share of her prize money. Went to court."

"William Brown is a woman?" Harriet said in disbelief. She was familiar with many of the larger ships in the King's fleet. "She served for years on a hundred-gun ship with over six hundred crew, and they didn't know William was a woman until her husband took her to court?"

"Aye." Tucker impatiently gestured for Chang to make his move already.

Chang moved a checker. "Did he get money?"

Tucker jumped three checkers. "King me. I dinna know, but when all was done, she went back into service on the *Queen Charlotte*."

Harriet felt her mouth fall open. She closed it.

Tucker shrugged. "Captain said he saw naught amiss with her work. Kept her as the captain of the foretop."

Harriet had only been in the foretop once, when the ship was floating down a calm river. She wasn't sure she could go up there if the ship was rolling in heavy seas, and certainly not in a storm. The starboard watch had furled some of the canvas on their watch when the wind picked up, so since then she'd only needed to help adjust the sails.

Chang jumped another of Tucker's checkers and used it to point at her. "Ching Shih."

"She who?"

"Pi'ate queen. Ching Shih."

"Oh, I heard o' her," Jack said. "You could be like 'er. Had more than two thousand ships and seventy thousand men under 'er command a'fore she retired. Most feared pirate in the South China Sea."

Harriet shuddered. "Didn't she nail to the deck the feet of anyone who displeased her so she could beat them?"

Chang dismissively shrugged one shoulder.

"Ann Bonney," Tucker said.

"Mary Read," Jack added.

Harriet shook her head. "I don't want to become a pirate, queen or otherwise, and I'm not interested in any Calico Jack. Or associating with any pirates, for that matter."

All three men froze, staring at her.

She grinned. "I have grown fond of privateers, though. And honest merchantmen."

They laughed, and Tucker clapped her on the back.

"My father was a Navy man," she continued. "A gunner's mate on the HMS *Peregrine*."

Chang spoke, all of it in Mandarin.

"'E says you come by it naturally then," Jack said. "Being a powder monkey or gunner's mate, that is."

"I was just helping out after Winston got hurt." She thought back to her early childhood, searching her memories. "My mother and I used to carry powder from the magazine to the guns. We went ashore for good soon after my little brother learned to crawl."

Tucker furrowed his brow. "*Peregrine* is the ship the Old Man's da served on, innit?"

She nodded. "That's how we became joint owners of Tesoro. He belonged to our fathers."

* * *

Nick swung out of his hammock and held tight to the rope while the cabin spun. Countless times he'd gotten by on a half-hour nap every few hours for days at a time, during a storm or sneaking around a blockade. But sleeping during the day just because his head pounded and he was tired made him feel feeble. Norton said it was to be expected, and given the impressive bruising on his brow around the healing gash, was surprised Nick didn't need to sleep even more. Judging by the dreary light coming through the window, he'd been out for a lot longer than a half hour.

Finally the cabin stopped spinning though the deck was still pitching. Cautiously he took the few steps to the bunk and looked out the window. The light had changed not just because of the passage of time. A storm was brewing. He grabbed his greatcoat from the hook on his way out the door. He'd check on the horses, make sure they were set up in the slings correctly, and then go up and check the weather.

He rounded the corner into the center cargo hold in time to see Harriet flip Zach over her hip. He fell flat on his back in the straw with an *"Oof!"* Behind them, the horses watched, placidly munching on hay.

Nick's jaw went slack.

"Good one!" Zach said. He held out a hand for Harriet to help him up. Instead of rising with her aid, though, he yanked and twisted until she was on her back, and pinned her with his body.

"What the *hell* is going on here?" Nick roared, blood pounding in his ears at seeing Zach and Harriet in such an intimate position. Both had their coats off, down to shirtsleeves and waistcoat.

They turned startled gazes on Nick, then glanced back at each other. Zach quickly rose and reached a hand, and with his help Harriet jumped to her feet. She dusted off her clothing, setting it to rights.

"Probably not what you're thinking," Zach said as he plucked a piece of straw from her braid, grinning.

"We, ah…" she began.

They all looked up through the open hatch cover at the sound of Bos'n's whistle.

"I'm needed on deck," she said in a rush. She grabbed her coat off a hook by the hay net and shrugged into it as she rushed from the hold.

Zach watched her go with a fond smile. "She's magnificent, isn't she?" He dusted himself off and shrugged into his coat. "Quick student."

"Student?" Nick's hands clenched and unclenched at his sides, furious at the idea some other man had his hands on Harriet. Even if—or *especially* if—that man was Zach.

Zach went over to the horses and checked the level of water in each stallion's barrel. Satisfied, he began stroking Tesoro, and offered pats to Button when he nudged Zach's shoulder. "If she's going to dress like a man, I thought she should be able to defend herself like one. You should see her punch and kick." He proudly pointed at a canvas sheet with a rough outline of a man drawn on it. "Glad it's him on the receiving end, and not me."

Nick's jaw worked but he couldn't get any words out.

Zach went into each stall to check that the slings were in the correct place and had the right tension—low enough they didn't apply any pressure, yet high enough the horse could lean down into it for added stability when the seas were rough—murmuring to them about keeping them safe in the coming storm.

While still petting Tesoro, he turned to address Nick. "I'm in love, lad, like never before." He rested his forehead against the Andalusian's neck. "I'm going to make Harry an offer she can't refuse."

Chapter 22

Before Nick could process Zach's declaration and respond, Bos'n whistled again, and the ship's bell rang in the pattern calling all hands to the deck. Fat raindrops began falling through the open hatch, pattering on the straw.

Nick pointed a finger at Zach. "We'll discuss this later." He spun on his heel, had to grab the canvas-covered net full of straw for a moment while the hold tilted crazily, then hurried up top.

The wind almost knocked Nick back below deck when he tried to emerge from the hatch. He buttoned his coat all the way and tossed his hat down the ladder, then closed the hatch cover behind him. Jonesy and Bos'n each had a safety rope tied around their waist and were working the tiller together to keep the ship on course. Dense, dark clouds swiftly headed their way off the port bow, their passage accompanied by a wall of rain and twenty-foot swells. The rain already pelting the deck was just a prelude.

"Batten down the hatches," Nick called unnecessarily, as Flynn and Luigi were already moving to do just that, starting with the center hold.

Nick made his way up to the tiller, hand over hand on the rail, bent almost double against the punishing wind. As he expected of his experienced crew, they had already furled the gaff sail and secured the boom. "Strike everything but the mains'l and forecourse," he shouted over the roar of the wind as he accepted the safety rope from Bos'n and tied it around his waist.

Jonesy saluted in acknowledgment, saving his voice to call to the crew. Bos'n went down to the deck.

Soon Flynn and Dieter were aloft reefing the fore t'gallant, and Smitty and Big Jim were reefing the tops'l. Bos'n directed Jack and Harriet to slack the mains'l weather braces while Tucker and Zach hauled the lee, easing pressure on the mast, and then went to help Chang and Luigi strike the main t'gallant.

As the crew trimmed the sails, Nick and Jonesy were able to steer west-northwest, keeping the bow angled at the oncoming storm. As long as Nick and the crew did their parts, he was confident *Wind Dancer* would live up to her name and dance atop the crashing waves. The cargo of wine in the holds, assuming it was all properly stowed, would help balance the ship, keep her rudder in the water, and let him steer instead of the ship being at the mercy of the tempest.

He had never lost a crew member in a storm—he was skilled enough as a mariner to know luck played a big part in that—though there had certainly been injuries over the years. Luigi had lost his grip in a summer squall earlier this year and fallen sixty feet to the deck. His bones had knitted but his shoulder had not been the same since.

They needed to stow canvas faster, before the freshening wind snapped a yardarm, or they were dismasted. Hauled-up sails flapped and snapped on the fore in the strengthening wind. They were going to tear if they weren't furled quickly. Wind buffeted the white-capped waves, making them look like jagged snow-topped mountain ranges, constantly in motion. Nick and Jonesy kept steering into the storm so the ship wouldn't roll and capsize. Waves now crashed over the bow at the bottom of each trough and washed across the stern as they climbed.

Only the safety line and his grip on the tiller kept Nick on his feet. Bile rose up and he desperately wished he could close his eyes against the conflicting information between what he saw and what his currently unreliable sense of balance said was happening. He steered another point to port, keeping the ship in a safe place in the still-strengthening wind while the topmen were aloft.

Chang and Tucker scrambled up the mainmast port rigging to furl the t'gallant, and Jack went up the starboard shrouds. Harriet finished belaying a line and saw Luigi grab the ratline and start to follow Jack. He only got a couple rungs up before he fell to the deck. He clutched his left shoulder as he staggered to his feet, his face twisted in pain.

Harriet helped him to the aft hatch.

Good. *Go below*, Nick silently commanded her. *Go below!* Already the wind was strong enough he and Jonesy had to shout to hear each other, even as close as they stood, the gale whipping Nick's greatcoat around his legs. Salt spray stung his eyes.

The mainmast shuddered, under pressure from too much sail in this wind. They had only minutes, if they were lucky, before they were dismasted. And God help anyone who was aloft when it fell.

Luigi closed the hatch after himself. Harriet was still on the deck, her head tilted back, looking at Jack alone high up on the starboard t'gallant footrope, at the canvas getting beat in the wind. She looked at how far the top of the mast swayed, how close it dipped toward the white-capped swells with each pitch, each roll of the ship.

No, Nick silently screamed at her. *Go below!*

Zach had been hauling on a line with Bos'n and let go with one hand, his intent to climb in Luigi's place clear. But Bos'n glanced at Harriet and stayed Zach with a hand on Zach's shoulder and a shake of his head.

Harriet climbed.

Eyes squinted nearly closed against the pelting rain, Nick aged ten years watching her climb the rigging, step off to the footrope, slide along several steps, and bend over the yardarm to reef the sail.

Her feet slipped out from under her.

Nick thought his heart actually stopped, watching in helpless horror as she hung eighty feet above the pitching deck, suspended only by the crook of her right arm hooked over the yardarm. She struggled to get a grip with her left hand, but her fingers slipped off the rain-slicked wood. The ship was climbing a swell, swinging her legs and torso well aft of the footrope.

After an endless moment, the ship topped the crest of the wave, rode it for an eternity, then began its dive toward the trough. With gravity now swinging her body toward the bow, Harriet managed to hook her legs on the footrope and haul herself up. She shook the rain out of her eyes, her shoulders rose and fell as she took deep breaths, and she got back to work.

Nick exhaled. His heart began beating again, so erratically it made his hands shake even with his stranglehold on the tiller. That had taken far too long for his sanity.

Shortly after, the crew had furled enough canvas that the mainmast stopped shuddering. Nick's heart was still thundering in his chest.

Bos'n and Zach worked frantically to keep up with repeated changes to the main and forecourse necessitated by the changing wind, while the topmen secured canvas. Eventually all the crew was back on the deck, everything but the forecourse and mains'l tightly furled. It was all the canvas Nick dared carry in this blow.

The storm continued to roar, impossibly high waves threatening to flip the ship aft over fore on one side of the swell, and swamp the stern on the other. Everyone held fast, safety ropes tied around their waists to keep from being washed overboard.

Nick soon had them shorten the forecourse, and then the mains'l as well, then returned to the regular watch schedule, releasing the larboard watch to go below and rest. There were sufficient hands on the starboard watch to handle the canvas in play now.

Once Harriet went below with the lads and closed the hatch, she hurried to Nick's cabin, ignoring the *splat* of wet clothing hitting the deck and refusing to look as her watchmates changed out of their sopping clothes. With the cabin door closed, she helped herself to a towel from Nick's wardrobe and began drying off and changing her own clothing. It was surprisingly difficult to unbutton and unlace. Slowly, she realized her hands were shaking.

Of course they were shaking. She was cold and soaked to the skin.

What had she just done?

Good heavens, what had she just done?

Climbed to the topmost footrope on the tallest mast and secured a sail.

In a raging storm.

Her knees buckled and she sat on a chair, her descent to the seat more of a barely controlled fall. She stared at her trembling hands, but what she saw was the roiling ocean viewed from high above, in the brief moments she *could* see it through the lashing rain that sometimes blinded her. She saw the crazy tilted angle of the deck when her foot slipped. She would have plunged to her death had she not been able to hook her arm over the yardarm.

She let out a chuckle at her rhyme. Ignored the hysterical edge to her voice.

The ship had eventually pitched the other way and she had been able to climb back up. Get on with the job at hand, just like Jack beside her and the other crewmen, though through the heavy rain she hadn't been able to make out more than their vague, blurry outlines.

She'd done it.

She had not only overcome her fear of climbing the tall mast, she'd climbed it in a storm.

She had helped defend the ship.

Defended it in a battle with the elements rather than an opponent like Ruford, but more sailors died because of storms than gun battles or committing acts of piracy. Going aloft in foul weather was the last sailor's task that she hadn't yet attempted, and now she'd done it.

She'd done it!

Her palms burned. Icy needles coursed through her veins as feeling and warmth returned now that she was out of the weather. She blew on her cupped fingers, then reached for the towel.

Soon she was able to get the rest of her wet clothes off and hanging up to dry, toweled her body off briskly to restore sensation, and dressed in her spare set of clothes.

Just weeks ago she couldn't bring herself to put on a pair of men's breeches, and now she could do the work of a man, while wearing masculine attire. Well, the work of a new sailor. A landsman. She had no delusions about her fledgling sailing skills being anywhere near on par with the lads in the crew, who all had years—if not decades—of experience. But now she was confident she could practice each skill required of a member of the crew and increase her proficiency.

The salve eased the burning in her hands. She considered checking on Luigi and getting a bite to eat from the galley—triumphing over one's fears and cheating death certainly stirred one's appetite—but the bunk and blanket beckoned. The surfeit of energy that had helped her work the sails and carried her aloft had utterly deserted her, and now her eyelids were too heavy to keep open.

* * *

Hours later, the storm was dying out. Gradually Nick was able to get the ship heading once more north-northeast. As soon as there was a break in the clouds, he'd get a more accurate fix on their position.

Nick handed off to Jonesy and went below, intending to have sharp words with Harriet for how she had risked her life and scared ten years off his.

He found her sprawled flat on her back in the bunk in his cabin, sound asleep. One bare foot peeked out from under her Portuguese blanket, one arm flung out, her damp braid off to the side on the pillow. Her wet clothes were hung up to dry, a towel on the deck beneath them to absorb the dripping water, and she'd left the tin of salve on the table. The cabin smelled faintly of seawater, damp wool, and lavender.

He toweled off, changed, and hung up his own wet clothes, then stood motionless beside the bunk, watching her chest reassuringly rise and fall with each soft breath. At last he cradled her ankle and tucked her foot under the blanket. As he lifted her wrist to tuck her arm in, he stroked his fingers over her reddened palm, and felt the silky residue of the salve coating her calluses.

So different from the hands of Miss Chase who had boarded the ship in London. So many things had changed. He couldn't let her marry Zach, no matter how charming the rapscallion could be. She deserved someone steady, who would treasure her, and not desert her on a whim for a boxing match or a months-long jaunt to the Continent.

The thought of her on Zach's arm at a London ball or in Zach's bed disturbed him in a way he didn't yet want to examine.

Her fingers curled over his where he was still stroking her palm.

He looked at her face, to find sleepy brown eyes gazing back at him.

He cleared his throat and set her hand on the bed. "Just checking to see if you used the salve."

She sat up and swung her legs over the side, her bare shins and feet visible because her long duck trousers were hanging up, still damp, and she was wearing the shorter, striped dungarees.

She opened her mouth to speak but shut it without uttering a sound when there was a tap on the door and Flynn entered with a tray.

"Thought you might need summat warm," he said, addressing neither of them directly, and set the tray on the table. He tugged his forelock and shut the door behind him.

Whatever she was going to say was abandoned as her stomach loudly growled. She smiled self-consciously, quickly sat at the table, piled food on her plate, and dug in with an unladylike zeal that would have gratified Luigi to see.

Nick moved more sedately as he filled his plate and tucked in, enjoying watching her enjoy the meal of simple foods prepared during the storm. "Worked up an appetite, I see," he said. While she continued to eat, he poured two steaming mugs of tea, added a splash of rum, a squeeze of lemon, and stirred in a spoonful of honey to one, and silently offered it to her. Luigi would have offered the lemon and honey to the crew, to go with their allotment of grog.

She enthusiastically nodded approval and wrapped her hands around the warm mug before taking a deep drink. "Between working on deck, taking care of the horses, and training with the lads, sometimes I forget to eat."

The lads? Nick froze, his mug halfway to his mouth. Some of the 'lads' in his crew were old enough to be her father. Flynn had served with Nick's grandfather. "Training?" he finally managed, proud his voice betrayed none of his turmoil. He swallowed a sip of tea and ate a bite of bacalhau, chewing carefully, the picture of nonchalance.

She washed a bite down with more of the tea. "The lads in the larboard watch are short one hand, so I've been helping them out. They said Zach is teaching me to fight like a gentleman but they think I should know how to fight like a sailor. They've been filling in gaps in my education." She flashed him an artless smile before going back to her meal, slowing slightly now that she'd taken the edge off her hunger, her deeply ingrained manners returning to the fore.

Nick pictured Jack or one of his other tars flipping Harriet over his hip and straddling her, as he'd seen with Zach.

He'd gut them stem to stern and use their guts for garters. The galley had fillet knives. Nick would toss the remains overboard and let the fish dispose of any evidence. "They took it upon themselves to become your teachers." Nick was confident there was no hint of homicidal plans in his voice.

"I wish I'd known some of their skills a year ago. I could have helped Sabrina more."

He set aside mental images of a bloody deck. "Sabrina?"

"Miss Chetwynn. She taught sewing and embroidery arts at the Academy. She caught the fancy of one of the fathers who came to fetch his daughter at the end of Michaelmas term."

Nick's gut churned, now for another reason. "She did not appreciate his attention?"

"I heard them struggling in the salon. He'd snuffed out all the lamps so there was just the glow from the fireplace. Her dress was torn, her hair a mess. I stomped on his foot and shoved him to the floor while he was off-balance, grabbed Sabrina by the hand, and we ran."

She took another sip and her expression grew more thoughtful. "Actually, I wish I'd known these skills so I could share them with the other teachers. Maybe then Sabrina would not have been dismissed and had to suffer a black eye and split lip."

Nick, sadly, was not surprised. "Madame Zavrina turned her out?"

At the expression of fury that flitted across Harriet's face, Nick considered it a good thing she hadn't had access to Luigi's fillet knives back then. "He insisted. Said *she* had accosted *him*." She shook her head in disgust. "Best Madame Zavrina could do was pay Sabrina the next term's wages as severance and write her a glowing reference." She let loose a phrase in Mandarin.

Nick let his fork fall to his plate with a clatter. "It took me a fortnight to learn that one."

Harriet grinned. "It's strangely satisfying. Took me a while to get the pronunciation right." She glanced up and to the left, and then, looking directly at Nick, expressed the same sentiment in German. She took a dainty sip of tea, pinky extended, and set the mug down. "I much prefer swearing in German. The language is more guttural. Visceral. Almost as satisfying as slamming a door. In someone's face." She picked up a biscuit. "Or other body parts."

Nick chuckled. He couldn't imagine the Miss Chase who boarded his ship in London slamming doors in a fit of temper, but he could certainly picture Harry doing so. Or flipping someone over her shoulder.

Which reminded him. "About you and Zach—"

"Do you know he keeps track of you and the ship so closely that he knows what Jack carved on the knife that he lost to Big Jim in a wager last month?"

The ship's bell rang, signaling the end of the first dog watch.

"My turn to walk the horses." She slipped on her shoes and grabbed her coat and wool cap from the hook by the door. "Zach couldn't be more proud of you than if he could publicly acknowledge you as his son."

Nick felt his mouth fall open.

Her eyes sparkling with mischief, Harriet bent down and kissed him on the cheek.

Still leaning close, she pushed her mug toward his hand, her warm breath brushing his ear like a barely felt caress. "Be sure to finish this off. Might help your headache. Are the dizzy spells getting better yet?"

For the second time that day, Nick worked his jaw, but no words came out.

She spoke to him over her shoulder at the door. "Don't worry, Norton hasn't shared any information about your condition. Those symptoms are to be expected after a nasty blow to the head like you suffered. Though he's not very good at slipping you the twists of paper without being noticed. Headache powders?"

She smiled again, pleased with herself like a cat in the cream pot for flummoxing him, and slipped out the door.

Nick sat as though carved from ice, the absolute stillness of his body in stark contrast to the stormy maelstrom of his thoughts.

She knew.

Harriet knew his deepest, darkest, most closely guarded secret.

That he was actually a bastard.

A fraud. An imposter.

Not fit to hold the title of viscount.

Nick had the title only because Adam had decided to acknowledge Zach's by-blow as his heir.

The secret that had disrupted his whole life, set on its ear everything he thought he knew about himself and his parents and his uncle, had sent him running away to the far side of the world for over a year before he could bear to look at his home again, to look in the eye anyone who knew his mother, Adam, and Zach.

And Harriet didn't seem to care. It mattered not a whit to her.

Surely Zach would not have told her. How had she found out?

Nick jumped up and ran out of the cabin.

Up on deck, he took a glance at the still-overcast sky, checked that everything seemed in order and trimmed correctly for the still-stiff breeze, and got the all-good sign from Bos'n at the tiller. On his way to the aft hatch, he glanced down into the center hold, where the cover had been opened for the horses to enjoy the last bit of daylight, and froze.

Zach was there, speaking with Harriet. The waning daylight shone down on them, the black horses milling around them and melting into the shadows. Suddenly Harriet shouted "Yes!" loud enough that Nick heard her, and threw herself into Zach's embrace.

Zach wrapped his arms around her and lifted her off her feet, swinging her in a circle before setting her down.

The red haze that suddenly blocked much of Nick's vision made it difficult to see, but Zach bent his head and appeared to kiss Harriet.

Nick bolted down the hatch, shoved a crewman out of his way as he thundered down the passageway, and plunged into the center cargo hold.

Zach wasn't there.

Harriet was alone with the horses.

She was astride Tesoro bareback, leaning low over his neck to avoid hitting the ceiling, leading Button, and had started walking them in circles around the perimeter of the hold, exercising them as much as possible in the small space. A broad grin lit up her face.

Nick paused to collect himself. Forced his breathing to slow. "You're half-owner of only one of these beasts," he said, leaning against the bulkhead with one foot crossed over the other ankle, arms folded, the epitome of nonchalance. He could do nonchalant. "Why are you taking on so much of the care of both?"

Tesoro paused as they came abreast of Nick to snuffle at his hands, then snorted in disgust when there was no treat forthcoming and moved on. Button nudged at Nick's coat pocket, and when Nick pushed him away without a treat, tossed his head in Gallic derision and caught up with Tesoro.

Harriet was in shadow on the far side of the hold by the time she replied. "There is work that needs to be done. We're shorthanded and have extra animals to care for. I don't mind helping. And it makes time pass more quickly."

Damn, he could hear the joy in her voice.

His stomach knotted. His chest was so tight he could barely draw breath.

"You're also half-owner. We don't expect you to help with the horse, though, because you're busy doing things that no one else on board can do. Like safely navigate our way home. Keep us from being dismasted in a storm." Her circle with the horses brought her abreast of him again. She looked at him from atop the stallion's back. "So I stepped in where I could." Her smile was breathtaking.

Or perhaps he was just having trouble breathing, knowing that someone else was responsible for the degree of happiness she was clearly experiencing. A level of joy that hadn't been there even a half hour before. And he had not been the one to make her happy.

Wasn't that a kick in the gut? Since the upstairs maid who had seduced him when he was sixteen, he'd tried to make sure his bed partners were satisfied, but he hadn't given much thought to their happiness. Any of them.

He wanted to be the one to make Harriet happy.

"You look much more comfortable on horseback now than the first time you mounted the grey gelding. At the time I thought you had misled me about being able to ride."

"Simply took some getting used to that type of saddle." She gracefully swung one leg up and over the horse's rump and jumped down. "Grab a scoop of oats for each of them, would you?" She went to add more hay to the rack, then secured the horses in their stalls.

Nick couldn't help but grin. She dressed and acted like a member of his crew, but none of his tars would dare order him around so blithely.

He fetched the requested feed and earned an approving nicker as he gave each horse its feed bucket. "You aren't afraid of falling off?"

She gestured at the straw-strewn deck. "Zach made sure we put down an extra thick layer so the horses are comfortable. It's fairly well padded. I've been falling on it a lot." Her grin was decidedly mischievous. "Just not from a horse's back."

"And have ... the lads ... been falling on it, too?"

"They have been kind enough to let me practice both throwing and being thrown. It's important to know how to duck or take a punch as well as to give one."

Nick snorted. 'Kind' was not the word he would use. "Show me." He took off his greatcoat and tossed it into one of the nets.

She cocked her head to the side, staring at him, her hands on her hips.

He took up a stance on the far side of the hold away from the horses, and gestured with his hands for her to come at him.

She slowly shook her head as she sauntered toward him. "Don't want to make your head hurt."

"You won't." It was not his head that would hurt if she followed through on Zach's offer.

She stopped just within arm's reach. The distance they'd stood when he'd reluctantly asked her to waltz at the Hartwells' ball when they first met.

While he was mentally picturing the glittering ballroom and trying to recall the undoubtedly simple and demure gown she'd worn, Harriet grabbed his arm, yanked, and twisted her body in one fluid motion, and suddenly he was on his back seeing stars. Breath left his lungs in a rush as he hit the deck.

The sly minx had fooled him.

She bent at the waist leaning over him, fists on her hips, blocking part of the stars. Oh, hey, some of the clouds had cleared off.

"You're not going to cast up your accounts, are you? Big Jim just mucked the straw an hour ago."

Nick reached a hand up and she took it, her body braced to take his weight the way she'd helped him up when they were under the cork oaks. When he yanked to jerk her off her feet, she shifted to the side and twisted his arm. With a little more pressure, she could dislocate his elbow or shoulder.

He grimaced. "The lads have taught you well."

She let go and stepped back. "Not the same as experiencing an actual fight in a dockside tavern. And they pull their punches. They said you'd hurt them if they hurt me, however unintentionally."

Damn right.

"But I think I could protect myself if the need arose. At least long enough to get away."

He climbed to his feet, pleased the deck rolled only the expected amount, and dusted himself off. "Best two out of three falls."

Her grin was decidedly feral. She tossed her braid over her shoulder, and they circled each other.

The horses snuffled in their buckets, looking for more grain.

Without warning the hatch cover came down with a clang. No lanterns were lit in the hold. Other than the faint glow from a lantern down the passageway, they were in complete darkness.

Harriet took advantage of Nick's moment of distraction to grab him again, but this time he anticipated her maneuver. He broke her hold, twisted and spun, and suddenly she was against him, her back to his front, his right arm across her throat in a loose chokehold, his left arm tightly wrapped around her ribs.

"Got you," he whispered, deliberately brushing his lips against her soft skin.

Her body fit neatly against his, like spoons in a drawer, so snug he felt her shiver, heard her soft gasp.

He was going to loosen one arm so he could caress her cheek, but she dug her chin into the crook of his elbow, grabbed his arm, hooked her leg behind his as she swung her body to the side, and suddenly he was flying over her back to hit the deck again. This time she dropped to straddle him, the heel of one hand poised just below his Adam's apple, the other pressing his right shoulder to the deck. She hooked her lower legs over him, the tops of her feet pressing down on his knees.

He gulped.

Someone lit another lantern in the passageway. Enough light now filtered into the hold that he could see her warm brown eyes glittering in glee, her teeth bared in a triumphant grin, her breath coming in soft pants from her exertion.

She bent low to whisper in his ear. "That's two."

He shuddered. As she began to lift away, he grasped her head with both hands and surged up for a kiss. She met his hunger with a fierceness of her own, her enthusiasm making up for any lack of experience.

"You're magnificent," he breathed, and pulled her in for another kiss.

She slowly straightened her legs, covering him with her body as she met his kiss with equal fervor, twining her fingers in his hair.

One of them moaned. He cupped her face with his hand, stroking her cheek with his thumb.

"Not so bad yourself," she murmured when they separated for a breath, before diving in for another kiss. She made herself more comfortable lying on top of his body, making parts of him rise to attention.

He groaned. He lifted her head away from his, cupping her cheeks, holding her still so he could look in her eyes. "Marry me," he said, surprising them both.

Chapter 23

Harriet's eyes opened wide, her mouth open in a perfect *"Oh."*

He kissed her again. "You should marry me, not Zach or Sir What's-It, your farmer." He hadn't planned to propose, but now that he'd said the words, he realized he meant them.

She reared back, and he rolled so they were both on their sides, facing each other. He cradled her head in one curved arm, stroking along her jawline with his free hand. Now he could see her brow furrowed in confusion.

"Whyever do you think I'd be interested in marrying Zach?"

He stroked the pad of his thumb over her lush, kiss-swollen bottom lip. "He said he was going to make you an offer."

"He did." She kissed his thumb. "An offer to buy my share of Tesoro."

The horse? What he'd seen had been about the damn *horse*?

Nick let his head fall to the straw in relief. "From the deck I saw you two embrace, and I thought..." He shrugged with one shoulder.

"When we get back to England we'll research how much his full offer should be, but as a show of good faith, he's giving me a down payment that's enough to cover the mortgage next week. It's a huge relief."

When Zach had said he was in love as never before, he'd meant the horse? Not Harriet? Nick groaned. How very like Zach. "And your farmer? Will you jilt him to accept me?" He leaned forward for another kiss, sliding his hand under her coat to rest in the curve between her hip and ribs.

"No."

Nick's eyes flew open. "No?"

She shook her head. "No jilting. He hasn't proposed yet. Not exactly. Percival said his parents wouldn't approve the match if I had no dowry. I had hoped Father's treasure would be valuable enough to provide it."

In relief, Nick leaned forward to claim another kiss, his hand pulling her body close to his, roaming along her back. "So you fibbed to me when you told me you were betrothed to him."

She lifted her head from the deck, resting it on her palm, her arm bent. "I said I *intended* to marry him. And when I said that, I meant it."

Nick mirrored her position, making sure he wasn't putting any pressure on the healing wound on his forehead. "And now?"

She trailed fingers down through his hair and traced his ear, touching his earring and stroking his earlobe. The ensuing jolt of pleasure made it difficult to concentrate on her words. "I've since realized we won't suit."

He surged forward, pressing her back into the straw with his body, claiming her mouth in a kiss while his free hand continued to caress her, searching for access to bare skin.

She pushed on his chest, breaking the kiss. "I clearly recall you saying *we* would not be marrying. You accused me of trying to spring the parson's mousetrap on you."

Deprived of her mouth, Nick kissed along her jaw and found the sensitive spot on her neck just below her ear. He wanted to rasp his beard stubble against her, mark her as his. He gently bit and suckled on the flesh just beneath her ear. "I said a lot of stupid things."

She gasped and tilted her head back, giving him better access to her neck. "No— Oh! No argument from me."

Nick chuckled, his lips brushing her skin. She shivered when he gently puffed warm breath against her neck. He picked up her silver chain in his teeth, exposing the skin beneath, and she let out a moan.

Dimly he realized she was burrowing her hands under his coat. Clutching at his shirt, pushing on his back, pulling them closer together.

Damn, they were both wearing too many clothes. Or the wrong kind. If she was wearing a gown he could slide his hand under her skirt, stroke her bare thigh, pull her bodice down to expose her breasts and lavish attention on them. They'd be a perfect handful each.

"*Mi pequeño wren marrón*," he whispered at the base of her throat, her chin tilted back. She hummed as he kissed his way to her other ear.

He wanted to release her braid and run his fingers through the silky strands. Soon. Right now he could finally kiss her neck the way he'd wanted to when he'd brushed her hair. When they were in the privacy of his cabin, or the room at the estalagem. Where there was a real bed. Anywhere but on a bed of straw in the cargo hold. He'd fix that. Soon. But right now, he nuzzled his way under her shirt collar, kissing and nibbling toward her shoulder.

"What—Oh! Do that again!" She shuddered. "What changed your mind?"

Damned if I know. "You." He traced the shell of her ear with his lips. Oh, he did know. He just didn't want her to know what a jealous monster he'd discovered himself to be.

She pushed on his shoulders, and he leaned back, and they were both on one elbow again, on even footing as it were.

"Why?'

She wanted him to explain his feelings? Emotions he'd only just recognized? He was floundering on shoals. "You're magnificent." He stretched forward to kiss her again, but she stayed him with a hand on his shoulder.

"I have no dowry. Even with Zach buying my share of Tesoro, there probably still won't be funds for one. You're a viscount." She was searching his face in the twilight, anxiety and disbelief in her voice as well as her expression.

The teacher was not done quizzing her student. No matter. "You know my secret. I'm a bastard." To his surprise, saying those words aloud wasn't as painful as he expected. It was more like the memory of an ache rather than the acute throbbing agony he'd felt for years. "If Adam had not decided to acknowledge me as his son, I'd no more be the viscount than Zach's other by-blows. You're actually above my station. I have the audacity to ask you to marry beneath yourself." He tried to kiss her again but she moved just out of his reach. "And you like my ship."

He'd worked his hand beneath her waistcoat at the small of her back, and his palm was just one layer of homespun cotton away from her bare skin. He stroked her with his fingertips.

"Regardless of the circumstances of your conception, you're still a Langston."

He froze at the shock of hearing it stated so baldly, so matter-of-factly. "How did you find out?"

She pushed him, unresisting, onto his back. "For a skilled navigator and wily pirate, you can be incredibly daft." She climbed atop him, straddling his ribcage, planted her hands in the straw on either side of his head, and leaned down to kiss his mouth. She exhaled in his ear and stayed there so her lips brushed his earlobe when she spoke. "Anyone who's paying attention could tell."

He had difficulty following her words, what with his blood roaring through his veins like a storm surge.

She sat up and stroked her hands up and down his forearms. "You speak of Adam so coldly, I think you loved him but didn't like him much. And Zach keeps such close track of you. He looks at you and speaks of you with paternal love." Though she rested most of her weight on her knees, he still felt the heat from her body on his stomach.

How many others had noticed what she had? The lady who dressed like a sailor, who hoped people on land wouldn't notice her deception. Did other people know his secret, too?

"I am not a pirate," he said, slowly sliding his palms from her knees up her thighs. "I have a Letter of Marque signed by the Regent himself."

She shook her head, her braid swaying. "A privateer is just a pirate with a license."

He couldn't resist a sly grin. He reached the tops of her thighs and turned his hands sideways, fingers and thumbs massaging her inner and outer thighs. "The war is over. I'm an honest merchantman." He wished he'd taken off his coat in addition to his greatcoat, as she was still rubbing her hands up and down his forearms.

"So you keep insisting."

She hissed in a breath as he slid his hands higher. He had the point of her hip bones in his palms now, his fingers up under her waistcoat, massaging the soft skin he could reach. His control was about to snap. He'd carry her off to his cabin where they could lock the door and properly ravish each other. But she hadn't yet said that one word he needed to hear.

"Didn't you see the cargo I'm bringing back to England? Going to pay import duties on all of it, even." He let go of one hip to draw lazy circles on her stomach, circling higher with each stroke of his palm. "I'm embarking on the boring life of an importer."

"You, boring?" She leaned down, her lips brushing his ear. "I don't think so." She gently bit his earlobe, tugged on his earring, and sucked it into her mouth. He shuddered and his eyes rolled back in his head. While her lips held his lobe hostage, with her tongue she toyed with the ring and traced the edge of his ear.

A jolt of desire sparked down his spine to the soles of his feet, his toes curling, his body aching for release. Too bad he was the captain and couldn't preside over his own nuptials. He'd have them married within the hour.

She released his ear to gently nip on his neck and suck on the flesh in the most erotic kiss he could recall, though perhaps that was because his brain was turning to mush as most of his blood had surged south. His breath came in shallow pants.

He slid his hands around to cup and knead her backside. "Yes, boring. We can put in at Brixham and move your mother so she can stay with you, keep you company at Langston Hall. She can live in the manor until we get the Dower House up to snuff."

"You mean stay with *us*." She lifted herself a few inches.

He wanted to pull her back down, spend more time exploring her lush mouth. "I thought you'd want her there to keep you company while I'm gone."

She moved back a little farther. "Where are you going?" The sultry teasing tone was gone from her voice, replaced by uncertainty.

"Fetching cargo, of course. Merchantman, remember?" He curled up a little, trying to reach her mouth.

She sat up fully and let her weight rest on his midriff. "You're going off sailing, and you expect me to stay at home?" There was an unfamiliar edge in her voice.

Nick suddenly had a vision of an antique navigation chart his grandfather had had, with areas marked *Here Be Dragons*. He plunged ahead anyway. "Well, yes. My mother stayed at home while Adam went to sea. Caroline stays at home while Norton goes to sea."

"I'm not your mother or sister," she said softly.

"Of course you're not." He tried to rest his palms on her thighs again, but she grabbed his wrists and held them stretched out to the side. "Caroline stays at home, overseeing the running of their estate. You already have the skills to be a brilliant household manager. And she's there like a beacon, welcoming Norton when he comes home. So that he looks forward to going ashore. Mother did the same for

Adam. As I'm guessing your mother did for your father." He couldn't make out her expression from this angle in the semidarkness.

She let go of his wrists to fold her arms across her chest. "While you and Norton go off adventuring at sea, you want me to stay home."

Her words seemed like a question, but her flat tone made it a statement. He realized he was floundering but couldn't identify the hidden hazard. How could he steer around something he couldn't see? "Yes. Where I know you're safe." How could he tell her how the injury she'd suffered after the battle with Ruford, however minor it actually was, had haunted his dreams for a week? How he had to keep touching her, reassuring himself she was still with him and fine. How seeing her slip and lose her footing in the foretop during the storm had scared a decade off his life?

He'd just realized how precious she was to him. Not merely someone to lust after or laugh with, but whose company he enjoyed as no one else. No one had ever stirred these strong emotions in his breast, and he couldn't bear the thought of her being hurt in battle, or her broken body falling to the deck or being lost overboard. He shied away from those images.

She climbed to her feet. "That day in Gunter's, you claimed I wanted an adventure before I settled down as a respectable matron. Well, it turns out you were right. This trip has indeed been an adventure."

Missing her closeness already, Nick jumped up and dusted himself off. He reached to do the same for Harriet, but she took a step back. Out of his reach.

"The problem for us, it seems, is that I'm still not ready to be that respectable matron you desire for a wife." She dusted her backside and smoothed her hair, plucked bits of straw from her braid, and let them flutter to the deck. "If this trip has been a taste, it seems I've developed quite an appetite. I'm not done adventuring. You and your crew and this ship have opened my eyes to so many possibilities. I don't have to go back to that tiny, quiet life in Brixham. And I won't." She shrugged into her coat. "And as much as I've come to love you, Nick, I won't wait at home for you, wondering when or even if you're going to come home to me from the sea. I don't want my mother's life."

She walked toward the passageway. When she turned back to him, her body was outlined by the light from a lantern in the passageway, her face in shadow. "If that's the kind of wife you need, then it seems we won't suit, either."

Again, she'd flummoxed him. He couldn't move, couldn't speak, could barely draw breath. His feet felt lashed to the deck, his breath frozen in his chest. He squeezed his eyes shut, trying to regain his equilibrium.

When he opened them again, she was gone.

Chapter 24

The next morning, Norton insisted on a wound check and escorted Nick into the surgeon's cabin. Nick sat at the table and allowed Norton to unwind the bandage from his forehead and turn his head this way and that to examine it in the lantern light. The overcast day sent only dingy grey light through the window.

Norton leaned in for a close look, smelling faintly of pipe tobacco. "Shouldn't leave much of a scar," he pronounced. "I'll clean it again and put some salve on it, and let you go without a bandage from now on." He poured gin on a cloth. "As you're my employer and the grandson of my previous employer, I would never question your judgment." He dabbed a little at the edges of the healing gash. "Being your brother-in-law, however, I feel entitled to a little liberty. I was looking forward to having Harry at family dinners. What did you do to foul things up?"

Careful not to move his head, Nick glanced up. "What makes you think that I— Ow!" Norton used far more force than Nick thought necessary to clean the gash.

"I wanted to give another tin of salve to Harry and had to deliver it to her in the foc's'le, where she was sleeping in Winston's berth. With the larboard watch."

Nick's gut clenched anew, remembering the pain of seeing her things gone from his cabin when he'd come below for a nap before midnight, and the sight of her huddled in a hammock in the crew quarters, wrapped in her colorful blanket, only the top of her head visible.

"Clearly she no longer feels welcome in your bed." Norton tossed the cloth into a basin and applied salve to the gash.

Nick felt his cheeks heat under his brother-in-law's stare. "For the record, we never..." He cleared his throat. "I never joined her in my bed." Well, there was that one time, but it had not led to what Norton assumed.

Norton sat down, his brows raised. "Seriously? Comely little lass like that in your cabin all these nights, and you never..."

Nick forced himself to not look away.

Norton whistled. "All right, I believe you. But clearly something changed. What did you do wrong?"

Nick let out a huff of annoyance. "All I did was ask her to marry me. And talk about her staying home at Langston Hall while I'm gone, where she'd be safe. Like Caroline. Like her own mother."

Norton stared at him in disbelief, then buried his face in his hands and shook his head.

Nick felt like his wits were being weighed and found wanting.

Norton rested his hands on Nick's shoulders and stared into his eyes. "Can you picture Caroline dressed like a sailor and hauling on a line?"

Nick snorted. "She's never even come down to the docks to see the *Wind Dancer*."

Norton capped the gin bottle. "Precisely. She has no interest. She's content to run the house and estate in my absence. And do you know why I'm so often absent?"

Because you're off sailing with me didn't seem likely to be the correct answer, so Nick gingerly shook his head.

"Caroline and I get along well precisely *because* I'm gone so much. Don't get me wrong, we love each other. When we're naked together, we—"

Nick winced and held up a hand.

Norton cleared his throat. "Suffice to say, we have no problems in the bedroom. But she doesn't like that I smoke, even if I only indulge my pipe in my study or in the garden. I enjoy her book club meetings on the second Tuesday of each month, but she wants me to attend her bible study group every Wednesday and go to church with her on Sunday mornings, whereas I'd rather stay abed and worship at the altar of her darling little—"

"That's more than I need to know," Nick interrupted him.

Norton shrugged. "Harry is not conventional like Caroline. If you wanted a conventional wife, you could have your pick of the society misses in London. But they've never interested you."

Nick wanted to argue and prove he was in the right, but a ray of sunshine broke through the clouds and shone through the glass, gilding the rose bushes. He pointed at the windows. "I have to go check our position."

"Yes, you certainly do," Norton muttered.

* * *

Their position was that they were just passing Ushant, an island off the coast of France, which Bos'n communicated to the larboard watch on deck. Nick gave the orders to trim the sails as they steered two more points east-northeast. As expected, Jack set off singing the first verse of *"Spanish Ladies."* The crew sang it every time they sailed past Ushant or Scilly, unless they were running silent.

"Farewell and adieu to you Spanish ladies,
Farewell and adieu to you, to you ladies of Spain;
For we've received orders for to sail for old England
But we hope very soon we shall see you again."

His watchmates chimed in on the chorus as they hauled on the lines to trim the sheets.

"We'll rant and we'll roar like true British sailors,
We'll rant and we'll roar all on the salt seas,
Until we strike soundings in the Channel of old England,
From Ushant to Scilly 'tis thirty-five leagues."

It had always amused him that Chang, Luigi, Dieter, and Winston sang it with enthusiasm equal to their English mates. Jack was the only one who had actually taken the King's shilling for a few years. Nick's other crew were merchantmen or former pirates. Sometimes their skills and unconventional sense of honor came in handy.

But Winston was gone, and Harriet was singing in his place, her contralto blending in harmony with Jack and Chang's tenor and Tucker's baritone brogue.

Tucker sang the second verse, then without hesitation Harriet sang the third, then back to Jack. Though the wind carried parts of it away, Nick clearly heard Harriet on the final verse:

"So let every man toss off a full bumper,
And let every man drink up a full glass;
We'll drink and be merry and drown melancholy
Singing here's a good health to each true-hearted lass!"

Nick listened but couldn't look. Once again she was up in the foretop with Jack, Tucker and Chang. His gut clenched and he found it hard to breathe.

"I could call her down, Cap'n," Bos'n said, standing near the bell.

Nick was sorely tempted but he shook his head. "I trust you to manage your watch as you see fit."

"There's three types o' sailors, as I see it," Bos'n rasped quietly. "Them like Jack what loves the foretop, agile on the ropes like a monkey. Them like Big Jim, who don't want to climb above the mains'l but likes the sea enough to go up there anyway. And them who go aloft on one voyage and then go ashore for good as soon as they can."

Nick stared at Bos'n. It was the longest speech Nick could remember his second mate uttering that didn't include directions for trimming sail or dressing down a crew member.

"Harry is like Jack. She may not be strong enough to move a full water cask by herself, but she's nimble. Being small works to her advantage in the foretop. Got over her fear right fast once she got up there."

Nick heard the admiration in the other man's voice.

Just his luck that Harriet overcame her fear of heights right when Nick discovered his fear ... on her behalf.

The song ended and they started another, Tucker singing the call and the crew giving the answer.

"Could hold forth in a musicale, eh?" Zach said from beside Nick, joining him at the maphouse. "She wouldn't even need a pianoforte to carry a tune."

Nick grunted. "I'd wager no miss ever sang that in a London drawing room."

Zach chuckled. "How about you put us ashore at Torquay," he continued, sobering. "Offload the horses there." He dropped his voice. "I'll see that she gets home safely to Brixham. No tongues a'wagging."

Nick finally looked at him. He saw only sincerity in Zach's eyes. No recrimination. "You haven't told me lately how inept I am."

Zach clapped him on the shoulder. "No need to be redundant, lad."

* * *

When they entered the harbor at Torquay, Jack called Harriet to the bow and handed her a line. "One task ye ain't done yet, Harry," he said. "Tie up the bow, and I'll do the stern." With a grin he set off to the stern, grabbed the correct line, and gracefully swung down to the dock.

Harriet took a deep breath and stepped up on the rail. She could do this. Her muscles had become stronger from all the work she'd been doing—which made it easier to not think about her breaking heart.

From the dock Jack waved for her to get on with it.

She grabbed the line and swung out and down and didn't even jar her teeth when she landed. She let go and gestured for Chang to toss her the line to tie up the bow. After she made fast the line on the bollard, she met Jack to catch the gangboard Tucker and Dieter pushed out. She couldn't suppress a grin when Jonesy caught her eye and gave her an approving nod.

They finished the docking procedures. Soon Zach was in the hold to help fasten the slings and blindfolds on Tesoro and Button, sending them up one at a time, loudly whinnying in protest. Harriet stayed on the dock to help free them from the slings and walk them so they could get their land legs back, rewarding them with carrots and pats.

While Zach took care of getting them saddled, it was time for her to go below, gather her packed portmanteau, and take a look around to make sure she hadn't left anything behind. Since she'd given Betsy her trunk when the maid went ashore at Gravesend, Harriet was tight on packing space. She'd almost decided to chuck her wrinkled green muslin gown overboard—or sell it to Smitty for the slop chest—to make room for her Portuguese blanket. In the end she wrapped the colorful blanket around the outside of her bag and tied it on.

She checked her knife in the belt strapped around her waist. Last night she'd finished the scrimshaw design of dolphin and waves on the handle. Jack had pronounced it fair to middling, which she took as high praise. She committed the foc's'le to memory, where she'd spent so much time with the crew. The table and benches where they'd eaten, played checkers, and told yarns, were hauled up and fastened against the bulkhead. Hammocks were neatly rolled and stowed on hooks, including the one she'd slept in the last few nights.

Tucker snored, it turned out. One of the lads always broke wind in his sleep after eating oatmeal and peas. She tried not to figure out who.

This morning she'd said goodbye to the goats and Oscar when she'd done the milking. Nick was up on deck talking with the harbormaster, so she took a fortifying breath and headed for his cabin. She couldn't leave without one last look. She hadn't been in the cabin since that disastrous night.

She'd spent an hour in hysterics after she'd left Nick in the cargo hold, wildly swinging between calling herself a fool for turning him down, and crying into the pillow, assuring herself she'd done the right thing.

The woman who couldn't bring herself to put on breeches in her cottage bedroom two months ago would have been content with the married life Nick described. Happy, even. It was the predictable life of safety and security that marriage to Percival had promised, that she had once thought she wanted—albeit with long absences and the chance Nick would die at sea in a storm or battle.

The navigation book still lay on the table, open to the last page she'd been reading, inviting her to continue her study. She closed it and put it away in the chest at the head of the bunk, caressing the embossed leather cover before firmly shutting the chest lid.

Nick filled the doorway when she stood up.

She gulped. "I- I thought you were busy on deck."

He tilted his head to one side, his expression inscrutable. "Letting Jonesy have a go at it."

She took a deep breath, willing her racing heart to slow. Her cheeks heated from guilt at being caught in his cabin, a feeling as annoying as it was unwarranted. "Just checking I hadn't forgotten anything." She glanced around one more time, making sure she had collected all her things when she'd vacated the cabin. Tears had blurred her vision while she packed.

"Should we find anything you missed, I'll forward it. Zach has your direction."

How formal and polite they were being. Harriet wanted to scream.

He stepped fully into the cabin, his presence taking up all the space so that she had trouble finding enough air to inhale. Sunlight coming through the window burnished his black hair, glinted on his gold earring. Her cheeks heated anew, recalling what she'd done with that earring and her mouth. She quickly switched her gaze to his face, aiming for his blue eyes and not his lips. Memories assailed her anyway of how she had brazenly explored the jagged edges of his chipped tooth with the tip of her tongue, not to mention other parts of his mouth. And allowed him to explore hers as well. She knew what his lips felt like on her neck, her ear, his big hands stroking her thighs, caressing her bottom, and dear lord how she wanted to do it all again, and more.

"The horses will be getting impatient. I should go." She meant to step around him, never touch him again, but he lifted his hand palm-up, and out of ingrained habit, she held up hers, palm-down.

He gently grasped her fingers and bowed at the waist, and dropped a soft kiss on the back of her hand, his lips lingering on her skin. Unlike the courtly, impersonal gesture he'd performed when they first met in a crowded ballroom, he held onto her hand and leaned in to tenderly kiss her cheek.

"Farewell, Harriet."

Hearing his low, quiet voice speak her given name felt like a caress to her auditory senses as much as his hand on her skin. She closed her eyes against the overwhelming sensation, swallowing hard. If she allowed even one tear to fall, she feared she'd crumple to the deck in a puddle.

He straightened and their hands fell to their sides.

"Goodbye, Nick." With a last look at his beautiful blue eyes, the most somber she'd ever seen them, she hurried past him and out into the passageway, not trusting herself to look back.

Smitty met her at the steps to the aft hatch and handed her a folded slip of paper. "Your accounting, miss."

Harriet took the paper, trying to hide her trembling from her encounter with Nick, and wanting to not panic in front of the purser. How deeply was she in Nick's debt? She unfolded the first part and gasped when she saw the figures. "This can't be right." The only charges were for clothing and accessories from the slop chest, rental of one horse in Porto, and several meals ashore.

Frowning, Smitty opened his mouth to protest.

She waved her hand to erase any insult. "I thought it would be much higher, that's all." He wasn't even charging her for half the cost of the cannon that went overboard.

Smitty's expression cleared. "The Old Man said to charge you what it cost for you to come along to fetch the horse, instead of if he'd gone on his own." He handed her a small leather purse that clinked.

She peeked inside, startled to see it full of coins. "I don't understand."

"Your wages." He gestured for her to finish unfolding the paper and read.

The accounting continued, with debits for expenses, credits for wages, and the final tally at the bottom. Wages?

"We rated you as landsman on the trip to Portugal and upgraded you to ordinary seaman for the trip back." He gave her a grin. "Normally it takes a lot longer for a green sailor to get bumped up, but Bos'n said as how you was a quick study."

Still shocked at being paid wages—she had just been helping out to pass the time and defend the ship to ensure her own survival—the indirect compliment from the taciturn Bos'n banished some of the chill in her bones. "Bos'n bumped me up?"

Smitty nodded. "With the Old Man's approval, of course."

Nick approved. Harriet tucked the purse in her waistcoat pocket so her trembling wouldn't make the coins clink. "Of course." She hefted her portmanteau.

Smitty extended his hand. "It's been a pleasure sailing with you, Harry."

"With you as well, Smitty." She shook his hand, gave him the best smile she could muster, then hurried up the ladder.

There was a crowd around the hatch. Every crew member was on deck it seemed, in a line leading to the gangboard. Jack stuck his hand out, and she shook his callused hand. She dropped her portmanteau to the deck when he drew her in for a gruff hug. "Fair winds and following seas," he said when he released her.

"To you as well," was all she could get past the lump in her throat. She barely registered that her bag had been picked up and was being passed along from man to man to the rail and down the gangboard as she said goodbye to the crew. She and Chang exchanged bows. She got *"Arrivederci,"* and a kiss to her fingers from Luigi. *"Auf wiedersehen,"* and a bow from the waist from Dieter. "Ach, lass," and a hug from Tucker. A handshake and clap on the back or a tug on the forelock from the others. Jonesy interrupted his conversation with the harbormaster on the quarterdeck to give her a jaunty salute.

A month ago, she and these sailors would have barely acknowledged each other had they passed on a street, and now it felt like she was saying goodbye to dear friends. Holding her head high to keep the tears from falling, she walked down the gangboard for the last time and joined Zach on the dock. He was conversing with Norton while tying her portmanteau on behind Tesoro's fancy Spanish saddle.

Norton took her hand in both of his. "It's been a pleasure knowing you," he said. He slipped her a small tin of salve when he let go.

She managed a tremulous smile as she tucked it in her coat pocket. "You as well."

Norton let out an audible sigh as she led Tesoro to the bollard to use as a mounting block. "Family dinners are going to be so dull," he muttered as he headed back up the gangboard.

Harriet settled in the saddle and adjusted the reins in her hands, valiantly trying not to think about Langston family dinners that would never include her.

Zach mounted and nudged Button to walk over to her. "Are you sure about this? He's considered quite a catch."

Harriet had given the matter nothing but deep thought—agonizing, soul-searching contemplation—since walking away from Nick in the hold that night. "He calls me a little brown bird. I'm sure."

"Lad's an idiot," Zach grumbled. He turned his horse toward town. "Shall we, m'dear?"

Harriet cast one last look at the *Wind Dancer*, at the crew lining the rail waving goodbye to her and Zach and calling wishes for a safe journey.

She raised her hand in farewell and faltered when she saw Nick standing at the aft rail. His chin dipped in a nod. She gave him a salute, then wheeled Tesoro toward town.

Toward home.

* * *

Nick buried himself in work. His steward was frantic that Nick attend to matters at Langston Hall in Keyhaven after being absent again. There were a thousand details involved in legally importing wine into England and then selling it. The London man of business who'd managed such matters for Grandfather had retired long ago, but Nick was relieved to discover the man's son was still in business and delighted to handle these matters once more for Langston Shipping.

Alfred, the Langstons' ever-efficient and long-neglected London butler, had failed abysmally at hiding his delight that Nick was finally staying overnight in the townhouse, even if Nick seemed to perpetually be in a foul mood. Nick blamed his moodiness on headaches, gesturing at the almost-healed gash on his forehead. Alfred had ordered the maids to prepare Nick's childhood room, as Nick still couldn't bring himself to sleep in Adam's room.

The first thing Nick did upon taking up temporary residence was order the footmen to remove the straight-backed chairs that for years had been left in perpetual readiness for his father's prayer circle meetings, and relegate them to the attic.

Nick couldn't stand to be on the *Wind Dancer*. Couldn't bring himself to sit on his bunk in his cabin, never mind lie on it. The bunk where Harriet had slept.

Alfred had personally been checking on the fire built in the study to dispel the early winter gloom, practically hovering, awaiting Nick's slightest whim, and finally left him alone. Nick spent the long afternoon at the big oak desk, reviewing account books, signing bank drafts, and replying to correspondence. He was contemplating crawling inside a bottle of brandy when Zach strolled in unannounced and held his hands before the fire.

"And greetings to you, too," Nick drawled.

"Don't blame Alfred. I wanted to surprise you."

Nick hadn't seen or heard from Zach since he'd left the dock in Torquay a week ago, riding Button and taking Harriet home on Tesoro. He wouldn't ask about her. She'd made her choice clear.

Zach rubbed his hands together in front of the flames, then poured a snifter of brandy and set it on the desk before Nick.

Nick eyed the glass and Zach suspiciously.

"She's fine, by the way." Zach poured a snifter for himself and settled in the armchair by the fire, stretching his booted feet out towards the hearth. "We met a friend of hers repairing nets near the docks in Brixham, a gel who considers herself in Harry's debt. Sabrina somebody. She was happy to help Harry disappear and Miss Chase make a quiet return home."

Nick closed his eyes, trying not to picture Harriet in a dress.

"Tesoro is a huge hit with friends from my Army days. He loves to show off. I've already received a half dozen offers to buy him, some of which we might want to consider. Depending on how profitable or not your wine business is, of course." He took another sip. "Though a few more evenings with the cards in my favor, and I might just buy him outright from you and keep him for myself. The old boy is a delight."

Nick hedged. "It's early days yet." The profit from the port wine so far had exceeded that of the profit from his lands this year, but that was more an indictment of how badly the harvest had been. As cold as 1816 had been, no one'd had a good harvest. So far the money coming in from the wine would assure his tenants and flocks would be well-fed, housed, and warm for another year. Berwick, his steward, had nearly cried in relief.

Zach took a deep drink of the brandy, sighed in pleasure, and hauled himself to his feet. He withdrew an envelope from his coat pocket and tossed it on the desk. "I think it's time to revive a tradition."

Nick eyed the envelope with the same suspicion he'd had for his as-yet-untouched brandy. After a glance at Zach, he broke the wax seal and read the card. "This is an invitation. From me."

Zach clapped him on the back. "Just the sample so far. I can have the printer proceed with the rest of the order tomorrow."

Nick studied the invitation. "We haven't held the Sheffield harvest celebration since Adam died."

"It's been five years," Zach said softly. "Don't you think it's time?" He leaned one hip against the edge of the desk. "You're head of the family. It's not going to happen unless you do it."

Nick thought back to the celebrations his mother used to plan, held every autumn after the harvest work was completed. This would be the latest in the year they'd ever held one. They might as well be having an early Christmas celebration. All the tenants, servants, and their families were usually invited, as well as Zach and all the Langston progeny. Nick's five sisters, their husbands, and children usually attended, minus any who might be close to giving birth or recently having done so. All of Mother's children had been born about nine months after Adam came home on leave, so their spacing was irregular. There was a gap of eighteen years between Nick and Audrey, the oldest. She and Bettina were both married and running their own households before Nick was out of the nursery.

"I know how to plan voyages and sneak past blockades. Not organize social events. And—" He swallowed a gulp of brandy. "And I have no hostess."

Zach airily waved his hand. "The housekeeper at Langston Hall knows what is needed, as do your sisters. They love to plan parties. All you have to do is authorize the expenditures, then stand at the head of the receiving line and be charming."

Nick scowled.

"Yes, just like that." Zach tapped the tip of Nick's nose.

Nick tossed back his brandy and slammed the glass on his desk. "Fine."

Chapter 25

Two weeks later, Nick stood on the side steps of Langston Hall with his five sisters and their husbands, greeting every person who lived in Keyhaven, it seemed, and welcoming them to the festival in his garden. He had even dressed as befitted a country gentleman, wearing a dark green frock coat, buff breeches, and shoes with silver buckles, his long hair restrained with a black velvet ribbon at his nape instead of in a queue.

Audrey and Evelyn had both asked, but he refused to take out his earring. "It's just like the one Grandfather is wearing in his portrait," he reminded them. Per long-standing tradition, he and Grandfather had both received a gold earring to mark the first time they sailed around Cape Horn, albeit about forty years apart.

Nick and Zach had ridden horses from London to Langston Hall. Zach had not once complained about the slow, cold and wet journey, and rarely tried to draw Nick into conversation. Certainly did not mention the voyage from Portugal.

Nick had let Jonesy sail *Wind Dancer* back to Keyhaven from London. Maybe one day Nick would be able to step aboard again without feeling like a knife was twisting in his chest, that the ship would once more be the sanctuary it had been for him since the first time he sailed with his grandfather.

Everywhere he looked he saw Harriet. Even smelled her scent on his pillow in his bunk. He should never have let her write navigation entries. He could launder or replace the bed and bedding to banish her scent, but she'd left her indelible mark—literally—with her neat penmanship in his logbook. He'd have to start a new one with blank pages.

Canvas canopies had been set up on the lawn in case of rain, though the scudding clouds blowing inland revealed the afternoon sun as often as they blocked it. To keep everyone warm, two smaller fires were burning at strategic points in addition to the bonfire. Not one but two pigs were roasting. A quartet was playing on the back lawn—a fife, pennywhistle, and two fiddles—and a temporary dance floor had been laid on the grass. At least two dozen people were dancing a jig. Cider was flowing freely, and tables were laden with platters of food, including one table devoted entirely to apples—pies, dumplings, toffee apples, sauce, apple chutney to go with the roast pig, and a platter heaped with apple slices next to a pot of caramel sauce bubbling on a brazier.

Food and other preparations had been made in such a way that the kitchen staff and footmen were able to come out and take part. Every servant, employee, and tenant of the Sheffield holdings was out here with their families, to gawk at and thank the much-absent heir who had finally resumed a beloved tradition.

"Your mam would be proud, you bringing everyone together again like this," said Mrs. Gilmer, holding her hand up. Nick lightly grasped her gnarled fingers and dropped a kiss in the air above her knuckles.

"Thank you." Nick had to swallow a sudden lump in his throat. "I can't take credit, though. It was Uncle Zach's idea."

"Oh, he's such a scamp." Sun broke through the clouds, gilding her white hair like snow. She had lived on Langston land so long she would have been a young bride greeting his grandparents on this very spot decades ago. "She was so happy to finally have a boy after all them girls. You look just like you da, you do, tall and handsome."

To his surprise, Nick was able to smile without hesitation.

She raised a work-roughened hand to cup his cheek. It was quite a stretch for her, as the top of her head barely reached the middle of Nick's chest, her shoulders stooped.

Nick recalled how the shepherd's wife, now a widow, had often requested Nick "test" her biscuits and jam tarts when he was out exploring the fields and forested lands around Langston Hall, a boisterous child escaping his tutor. He cleared his throat. "How is your cottage? Was it snug during the storm two nights ago?"

She beamed. "Mr. Berwick sent a crew of energetic young men. Got the whole roof replaced in just one day, they did, right before the rain came. The winds blew but nary a drop came inside. Bless you."

Impulsively Nick bent to give her a quick, gentle hug. "Have to take care of our most revered residents," he said softly. And he meant it.

As he straightened, he felt the weight of all four viscounts who had preceded him, over a century of male ancestors. This time the pressure wasn't suffocating. It felt more like a comforting cloak settling around his shoulders. He wasn't a harsh taskmaster like Adam, nor was he an unpredictable pleasure-seeker like Zach, but somewhere in between their extremes. He was a Langston, damn it, however it came about. He'd fulfill the role and give what was due to the title and all it encompassed. He just wanted to have fun along the way.

He now understood why Adam had given away everything that wasn't entailed.

Because Nick inherited the title but no funds, he couldn't spend money in pleasure clubs in London, in gaming hells, or betting on boxing matches like Zach. Nick had to *do* something. Had to go earn his own liquid assets, in the form of working for the Home Office during the war, then a little importing business during peace. He liked to think he would not have become as ramshackle as Zach if he'd been able to lead a life of leisure. Thanks to the course Adam had set him on, though, Nick would never know.

Mrs. Gilmer gave Nick's cheek another pat and moved on to reminisce with Audrey and Nick's other sisters.

Other tenants like Mrs. Gilmer shared memories of previous festivals hosted by his mother and the preceding viscount, conjuring images that Nick had suppressed for years. He was finally able to see past his mother's deathbed confession and remember her as the happy hostess, laughing and chatting with her guests on these very steps, arm-in-arm with her husband if he was not at sea.

At last there was a break in the stream of people wanting Nick's attention. He took a look down the receiving line at his sisters, standing next to the best husbands their dowries could buy. Except for Caroline in the middle, of course, who'd fallen in love at seventeen with the surgeon who happened to be Grandfather's houseguest that week, who had bandaged her sprained ankle when she fell off a horse. Norton saw Nick and gave him a wave.

Nick gave him a jaunty wave back.

His sisters had lined up in family order rather than the rank they'd married into, so Evelyn, the youngest, and her earl were at the end of the line instead of the beginning. "Save the best for last," Lord Crandall had joked, before staring adoringly into Evelyn's eyes.

Nick brightened further when he saw that the next carriage to pull up in the drive bore the Penrith crest. When the footman let down the steps and opened the door, instead of the Marquess emerging, Nick's friend Alistair, Viscount Moncreiffe, unfolded his long frame and stepped out, and held his hand out to assist his wife down. The couple strolled toward the receiving line, the epitome of decorum, until Charlotte let go of Alistair to run the last few steps and throw her arms around him. "Nicky!"

Nick used her momentum to grab her and hoist her up, swinging her around in a circle, before he set her down and planted a kiss on her cheek. "Charlie! Glad you two were able to tear yourselves away to come."

"Paws off my wife," Alistair growled.

Nick held his hands up in mock surrender. Alistair hauled him in for a bear hug and a hearty slap on the back.

Nick cleared his throat when they separated. "Not well done of us," he said, tugging his waistcoat back into place. He adopted the most pretentious voice he could muster and cast a sharp glance at Charlie. "Certainly wasn't behavior expected of a future duchess."

"Oh, shut it, Nicky."

He gave her a grin and one-armed hug before relinquishing her to her husband.

"Must say my jaw hit the floor when I received your invite," Alistair said, possessively wrapping his arm around Charlie. "Wasn't sure you were even in England, let alone interested in hosting a party."

"Blame Zach. Whole thing was his idea." Speaking of, Nick hadn't seen him yet today.

"Oh," Charlie said, sounding disappointed. "I thought you might be using the occasion for something. An announcement, perhaps?" She tucked her arm through Alistair's, and they gave each other such an adoring look Nick thought he might be ill.

"No. Just an excuse for my sisters to spend my money." Which, to be fair, wasn't entirely true. Audrey had suggested additions to the housekeeper's more modest menu and had then provided the fancy provisions in the quantities necessary for such a large gathering. Evelyn and Crandall had brought the canopies. Diana's husband had sent the pigs yesterday. Bettina and her husband had shared from their apple orchard harvest. "And Zach wanted it. Which is why I don't understand why he's not here."

As if conjured, Nick saw a figure waving to him from the far side of the lawn, and recognized Zach making his way toward the party. Just past the point where Zach had appeared, the garden dropped down to the brook that marked the boundary between Nick's estate and Zach's on the other side. Half the size of Langston Hall, Zach had inherited the land from his mother's side. Nick's grandparents grew up next door to each other, so to speak, and the wooden footbridge over the brook made visiting easy.

Another carriage rolled up, and Nick was surprised to see the Sinclair crest on the door.

"Oh, good, Tony made it," Alistair said.

The footman let down the step, and Tony exited. He gave Nick a wave before assisting his wife Sylvia down, then reached in to help out another woman, this one with auburn hair whom Nick had met only once before. With a cheeky grin, Tony held up his hand again, only to have it batted away by his big brother Benjamin, the Earl of Sinclair, who emerged from the carriage last. Sinclair stumbled his first couple of steps on solid ground. The auburn-haired woman linked arms with him, and his gait steadied.

"He's walking without a cane," Nick murmured, and found himself smiling.

Charlotte looked at him sharply. "That's hardly unusual."

"Surgeons at Waterloo had planned to amputate his right leg."

"Oh my."

The two couples headed for the receiving line. Tony and Nick exchanged handshakes and hugs. "You look as fine as the day you married this rogue," Nick said, bowing and raising Sylvia's hand for a kiss above her knuckles after Tony had given him a dirty look at even a hint that Nick might try to steal a kiss.

"You're as charming as ever, Captain," Sylvia replied, laughter in her voice at the exchange between Nick and her husband.

"Guess who was visiting Lavender Hill Farm when your invitation arrived?" Tony stepped aside as Sinclair and his wife approached, the earl's strides becoming more confident the longer he was in motion.

Nick shook Sinclair's hand. "You look much improved each time I see you."

Sinclair gave a rueful chuckle. "Couldn't possibly be worse. Once again, I am obliged for the ride home you gave me."

As a captain in the army, Sinclair had disappeared in the aftermath of the Battle of Waterloo. He had limped away rather than let surgeons hack off his badly injured leg. Weeks passed and the Army had written him off as missing and presumed dead when Tony asked for help. Alistair, Nick, and his crew had found the earl holed up at a farm in Belgium, still so weak from blood loss they'd had to hoist him into the hold on a cot before they could carry him to Norton's cabin for the sail home.

Nick couldn't help glancing at the woman at Sinclair's side, confidently linking arms in such a way that he now saw was helping Sinclair stand upright. He remembered that Tony had set off on his journey that led him to Sylvia just days after Sinclair had married.

"You've met my wife, Jo." Sinclair said.

Belatedly, Nick recalled how to behave in polite company, and he bowed and kissed her hand. "Delighted to see you again, Lady Sinclair."

They chatted for several minutes, catching up. Last time they'd all been together had been at Alistair and Charlotte's wedding breakfast.

"Let me make sure I remember correctly," Charlotte said after a bit. "You were married this June."

"Yes." Sinclair wrapped one arm around Jo's shoulders.

"And you were married in August."

Tony put his arm around Sylvia's waist and nodded.

"And we were just married in October." Charlotte tugged Alistair down for a quick kiss. "So that means there should be another wedding in December." She looked at Nick expectantly.

Nick felt his face freeze in a polite smile but couldn't speak. He had no air. His chest hurt too much to breathe.

Tony took pity on him. "Alas, I think the streak is broken, Lady Moncreiffe."

Sylvia and Jo exchanged glances. "At the risk of being rude," Jo said, "I'm famished. Is that apple pie I smell?" She gave a slight tug and Sinclair gave a "what can you do?" shrug, exchanging an adoring smile with his wife before they made straight for the food tent, Sinclair's limp less noticeable with each step.

Nick almost groaned. Everywhere he looked today there were happy couples gazing adoringly into each other's eyes.

The rest of the group moved down the receiving line and Nick was finally able to draw breath. He jumped when Zach appeared at his side and thrust a glass into Nick's hand. "Cider," Zach said. "Looks like you could use the hard stuff, though."

No more carriages were arriving, and he'd already greeted everyone on the guest list he could recall. He drained half the glass in one go, wished it was brandy, and strode toward the food tents. "Nice timing. You should have been here for the receiving line."

Zach fell into step with him. "They want to see the mysterious viscount who disappears for weeks or months at a time, not the mad uncle next door."

Nick gave him the side-eye. He started to put food on a plate, decided he had little appetite, and set it down. "Surprised you arrived on foot. Thought you'd want to show off your horse."

"*Our* horse. And I figured your stables might be full." Zach gestured at the assembled guests, a sea of people on the lawn.

Nick's sisters had arrived with husbands and children, and also the requisite maids, valets, governesses, coachmen, and footmen. The arrival of Nick's friends meant even more servants, horses, and carriages. Not only would there be more people sleeping in the house tonight than in the last five years, every stall in the stables was likely occupied by now.

As Nick was thinking of a suitable reply, Zach left to greet Caroline and his other nieces. Nick selected an apple and tossed it up. Before it fell back to his palm, it was snatched out of the air. He turned his head in time to see Jonesy take a bite out of it. "All is well?"

His first mate grinned around a mouthful and nodded. "Sailed like a dream, light as a feather, right into our usual slip in the harbor." He took another bite of apple. "Goats are in the pasture with your sheep. Cat went hunting on the docks."

Behind Jonesy, Chang was filling a plate. The gunner saluted Nick with a pork chop. He wore his usual powder apron tied around his waist.

Nick acknowledged his first mate's report, then turned to Chang. "All is ready for the fireworks?"

Chang nodded. "Just wait fo' sun to go down."

Nick scanned the crowd but didn't see any others from his crew.

"Tucker and Jack went to Portsmouth, shopping for canvas and a three-pounder," Jonesy said. Before Nick could open his mouth to protest, Jonesy held up a hand. "They know you ain't likely to buy just yet. They're hoping to find bargains you can't pass up."

Nick rolled his eyes.

"The others are taking turns guarding the ship and going ashore. A little resting and recreating."

Nick gave him a pat on the back and wandered through the crowd to play host. His guests ran the gamut from farmers and shepherds in their best homespun, to servants in half a dozen different liveries, to his friends and family in the relatively relaxed attire of country gentry. He felt overdressed. He'd rather be in a peacoat and duck trousers like Chang and Jonesy.

He passed Charlotte and Sylvia deep in conversation at one of the tables and chuckled when he overheard them comparing best methods for safely traversing a beach in the dark.

At the next table, Tony patted the empty chair beside him, and Nick sat down, with Alistair across from him. "They going to join us, you think?" Nick tilted his head, indicating Lord and Lady Sinclair, who were strolling around the perimeter of the lawn.

Tony poured a glass and pushed it toward him. "Ben needs to walk a while. His leg gets stiff after too much time in a carriage."

"I'm surprised they left London at all," Nick said. "Can't have been a comfortable trip for him."

Tony grinned. "They wanted to come down to see Lulworth Cove for themselves and meet my wife's gang. Do some traveling before it gets too uncomfortable for Jo."

Nick raised his brows.

"Congratulate me. I'm going to be an uncle next summer." He seemed genuinely delighted at the prospect of never inheriting the title from his brother.

Nick and Alistair raised their glasses with Tony in a toast.

"And congratulations on getting Sylvia to pursue a safer occupation," Nick added. "Cheese-making is infinitely preferable to smuggling." He quashed any thoughts that he was being hypocritical.

Tony shook his head. "I didn't get her to do anything she didn't already want to do." He looked over his shoulder, sending a besotted smile toward his bride. "In fact, she was a little miffed that I came up with the cheese idea first, when she'd been searching for an alternative occupation for the villagers long before I stumbled into their midst."

Nick harrumphed and shifted his focus to Alistair. "Are you going to persuade Charlie to stop breaking into hotel rooms and scampering about on roofs?"

Alistair looked taken aback. "Why would I do that? I do my share of clambering about on roofs."

"You're one to take issue," Tony interjected. "You've certainly done your share of sneaking in and out of hotel rooms. And bedchambers."

"But no one was shooting at me. Worst I risked was being called out for a duel at dawn."

Alistair shook his head. "There's hardly any risk of someone shooting an astronomer with his telescope up on a roof."

"Spies, however, get shot all too frequently," Nick countered, lowering his voice. "She's already been shot once. Next time could be worse."

Tony leaned in close, avidly following the conversation.

"Yes, I know," Alistair said tersely. "I was there. I was the one who stitched her up, if you recall."

"I didn't think there would be much call for spies these days," Tony said quietly. He glanced around to see if anyone was eavesdropping on their conversation. "But your wife is one?"

"You'd be surprised at the need." Alistair sent a fond smile toward Charlotte, who waggled her fingers in a wave at him in return, still deep in conversation with Sylvia.

Alistair turned back to Nick. "I would never ask her to stop being the woman with whom I fell in love." He gave another longing look at his wife. "I do, however, insist on going with her most of the time."

Lord and Lady Sinclair strolled back to the food tent just then. Sinclair seated Jo at the table with Charlotte and Sylvia and a plate loaded with desserts from the apple table, before he joined Nick and the other men.

"She can't get enough fruit these days," Sinclair said with a proud grin. "Sends me down to the pantry in the middle of the night. Might have to start keeping a basket of apples beside the bed."

"At least she isn't involved in dangerous activities," Nick groused.

Sinclair froze in the act of pulling his chair up to the table, and exchanged glances with Tony.

Tony let out a bark of laughter.

"What?" Nick snapped, looking between the two brothers.

Tony cleared his throat. "It depends on if you consider dressing as a man and passing herself off as 'Mr. Quincy' for five years to be dangerous."

Nick gaped at Sinclair, then glanced over at Lady Sinclair, and back to the earl.

"In all fairness, she never referred to herself as Joseph or Mister," Sinclair said. "She just signed her name with the initial J, dressed the part, and let people make their own assumptions." He leaned back in his chair, his right leg stretched out, hands folded across his flat stomach.

Nick finally noticed that while Lady Sinclair's auburn hair was fashionably styled, it was not pinned up. Instead it hung down loose, so short it barely brushed her shoulders.

"She was living as a man? Until you two married?" Nick had more questions. But the answers were none of his business.

Sinclair nodded. "Quincy is the best damn secretary I've ever had."

Nick groaned and buried his face in his folded arms on the table.

"So, Nick..." Tony drawled, adding an extra syllable to his name. "What adventures have you been up to since we saw you last?"

Oh hell. Nick sat up and waved over the nearest footman, uncaring whose livery the man wore. "Bring me a bottle of rum, please." He gave the location in the cellar where he stored the good stuff.

"Yes, m'lord."

Sinclair, Tony, and Alistair scooted their chairs closer to the table and leaned in. "This ought to be good," Alistair said.

With a sigh and as few details as possible, Nick told his rapt audience about Harriet and their search for hidden treasure. By the time he finished, the bottle was empty, having been split four ways. He considered calling for another.

Alistair chuckled. "The hidden treasure turned out to be a horse named Hidden Treasure?" He laughed again.

"She climbed the rigging to work in the foretop?" Tony looked a bit green.

"Not everyone gets seasick like you." Nick patted Tony on the arm. Tony smacked him on the shoulder with the back of his hand.

"Well, now your questions about our wives make sense," Alistair said.

"The only question that remains," Sinclair said with the condescending superiority that came from having five years more maturity than the other three, "is to determine if you fell in love with the proper and demure Miss Chase you met in London, or the self-assured and independent Harry who sailed home from Portugal."

Nick suddenly had trouble breathing. Perhaps he should see Norton about it. He hadn't said he loved Harriet. Not to these men. Not to her. Not even to himself.

"I think I know the answer," Tony said much too brightly.

"I have a theory as well," Alistair chimed in.

Nick groaned and buried his face in his arms again.

"There, there, lad," Sinclair said, patting Nick's shoulder.

Nick mumbled.

"What's that?"

Nick lifted his head high enough to prop his chin on his forearm. "I said, it doesn't matter. She already told me to bugger off." He sat up, trying to save a shred of dignity. "I proposed, and she said we wouldn't suit."

"After all that you went through together?" Sinclair sounded incredulous. "On what grounds?"

Nick thought back to the wonderful, awful interlude they'd had in the hold. "All I did was say how nice it would be to come home to her when I return from voyages. Move her mother here to Langston Hall so she wouldn't be lonely while I'm gone."

Alistair made a snort of disgust. "You took her on an adventure to exotic lands, taught her how to sail, and you thought she'd then be content to sit at home in England and wait for you while you go to sea?"

"As my mother would say," Sinclair said blandly, "you're an idiot."

Nick winced. Wanting to keep Harriet safe had *seemed* reasonable. Logical.

Alistair's brows rose. "You took no for an answer? Just like that?"

"If a lady says no to a kiss, you have to respect that," Tony said. Alistair waved his hand back and forth in an "of course" gesture. "But if it's because you botched your proposal, that's another matter entirely," Tony finished.

Nick narrowed his eyes. "And you should know from botched proposals."

"Oi, I made it right!" Tony cast a glance at Sylvia, his smile turning gentle. "It just took me a second try to make sure she knew I was asking her to be my wife, not my mistress."

Gah. Nick looked over the assembled crowd. The laughing, happy crowd. Eating, dancing, chatting. Couples strolling arm in arm.

He squeezed his eyes shut. Thought about never seeing Harriet again, holding her, never hearing her laugh. There was that knife-in-the-chest sensation again.

He was confident she no longer planned to marry Sir What's-His-Name the farmer, so Nick wasn't jealous of another man. What was she going to do instead?

It didn't matter, so long as she did it with Nick. Side by side.

He sat up straight. The treasure he'd found on their voyage to Spain and Portugal wasn't the horse, or peace with his past. It was Harriet.

His chest loosened and he was finally able to inhale a deep breath. "Zach has her direction. First thing in the morning, I'll ride to Brixham and win her back." He'd go now, but the sun was already so low in the sky, it would soon be dark enough for Chang to set off fireworks. Arriving late at night covered with mud from a mad cross-country dash would not curry favor with his bride or future mother-in-law.

Alistair slapped his palm on the table. "Yes!"

"A toast!" Sinclair said.

Tony stood to grab a jug of cider from a passing footman, and stayed standing. "I saw your first mate and gunner earlier," he said, looking over the crowd toward the back lawn. "It appears another of your crew has come to the party."

Nick rose partway from his chair to have a look, expecting to see Big Jim, though he usually stayed the first night ashore in the barn with the goats, then stood so fast his chair tipped over backward.

With brown hair in a queue topped with a blue knit cap, wearing a navy peacoat and duck trousers, a large knapsack slung over one shoulder, it did appear as though another sailor had just arrived at the festival.

From the footbridge over the brook.

Heart pounding, Nick ran.

Chapter 26

Harriet climbed the rise from the brook, wooden treads set into the hillside making it obvious the path was old and oft used, and surveyed the crowd with dismay. The butler at Zach's house had only said that Mr. Langston was visiting next door and directed her to the footpath. He didn't mention the large party in progress. How was she to find Zach in this sea of people?

Maybe she'd help herself to a plate of food and warm herself by one of the fires while she searched. No one had given her a second glance. There were guests from every social strata dancing and mingling on the lawn. Even wearing sailor's garb, she blended in. She'd warm up and get a hot meal, find Zach and say goodbye, and leave. She could still walk a mile or two farther on her journey before stopping for the night.

Before she could put her plan in motion, one figure headed straight for her at a dead run. The crowd parted to allow him passage.

She froze. Should she race back down to the brook and find a hiding spot among the trees or in the treetops, or stand and prepare to fight?

The tall, broad figure thundering toward her was a blur until a last bit of setting sun broke through the clouds behind him and glinted off his gold hoop earring.

Nick.

Her breath caught.

He halted in front of her, searching her face as though to make certain of her identity, his eyes wild, his chest heaving, before he cupped her cheeks with both hands and swooped in to claim her mouth in a toe-curling kiss.

The familiar thrill coursed through her. She dropped her knapsack and kissed him back with equal abandon, letting him in as she wrapped one hand behind his neck, the other reaching in under his coat and around his waist to pull him closer. The world narrowed to the sensations of their kiss—exploring his chipped tooth with her tongue, his big hands holding her. She tugged on the ribbon tying back his hair and freed it, letting the strands fan out loose over her hand, twining her fingers in it. When he growled approvingly deep in his throat, she felt it more than heard it.

One of his hands slid down to caress the side of her neck, his thumb stroking along her jaw, the other hand sliding down to the small of her back. She felt cherished. Desired.

She wasn't sure how long the kiss went on, but gradually she became aware the hubbub of conversation had died away. The musicians stopped playing.

"Nicholas!" came one shocked female voice. "*What* are you *doing*?"

"Heard them sailing folk had odd appetites. Didn't think they'd indulge while at home, though," said another voice nearby, an older male. Other people murmured comments in a similar vein. Heat flooded Harriet's cheeks.

She broke the kiss and withdrew. Nick followed and kissed her again until she planted her palm in the center of his chest and pushed. "We're making a spectacle of ourselves," she whispered.

He slowly opened his eyes, looking a bit dazed. He licked his lips, distracting her all over again, and finally glanced around, seeing the crowd that was drawing near. He gave the musicians an imperious gesture. "Play on!"

They started another jig. Nick grabbed her hand and led her down to the brook. People could still gawk if they peered over the bank, but at least the sound of the babbling water would keep their conversation private.

At the water's edge, still holding her hand, Nick reached up with his other hand to cup her cheek and lean in for another kiss.

Her heart breaking anew, she took a step back. "Nothing has changed between us," she said in a broken whisper. She cleared her throat of the lump that had risen. "I came to say goodbye to Zach. I didn't know you'd be here."

He didn't release her. "Zach?" The shadows made it hard to read his expression, but his grip on her hand remained firm. Possessive.

She breathed deep, filling her lungs with the scent of fresh water and damp earth and courage. "When he took me home, he asked that I let him know if I was going to leave Brixham. I've signed on as a landsman on a barkentine out of Plymouth. We sail for Athens in five days. I've never been to the Mediterranean. At least, not that I was old enough to remember." She'd had trouble deciphering the little map Zach had drawn on the back of his card. Now she understood why he'd been vague about his address. If she'd known Nick lived so close, she would have written a letter instead of coming in person.

His fingers tightened on hers. "Don't go."

She shook her head. "Gabriel is back in school now. I've paid this quarter's mortgage. I should be back before the next is due and my wages will cover it. There are enough funds leftover to meet Mama and Gabriel's living expenses until then if they're frugal." She swallowed hard. "There's nothing to keep me here."

He raised their linked hands to drop a kiss on her knuckles. "Except me."

She felt the raw pain in the back of her throat that was the prelude to tears. Robins and thrushes twittered in the trees along the brook and beyond. The brook rushed on its merry way, oblivious to her tumultuous emotions. "Why are you making this difficult? We've already agreed. We won't suit."

He cupped her face with his free hand. She fought the urge to lean in, to nuzzle.

"I was wrong."

She tried not to be distracted by his callused thumb slowly sweeping across her cheek.

"It has recently been brought to my attention," he took a deep breath, "that I'm an idiot." He briefly squeezed his eyes shut. "An inept idiot."

She raised her fingers to caress the back of his hand, hardly daring to hope. "You are, but what has that to do with me?"

A fleeting grin passed over his features, both of them remembering how they had bantered this way in Portugal. He grew serious again. "I have realized the woman I fell in love with is the demure Miss Chase I met in London. The brave chit who was intimidated by me yet refused to back down. And the determined woman who wouldn't let go of the rope when dragged overboard in a storm."

Her stomach was twisting in knots, but in a good way.

"The woman who kept her wits when tied up by a highwayman. And," he took another deep breath, his shoulders rising and falling, "and the woman who overcame her fear of heights and now enjoys scampering about the foretop. Even though watching her doing so in a storm scared a decade off my life."

He let go of her to rest both hands on her shoulders, his thumbs and fingertips gently massaging as if passively touching her was insufficient contact. The growing twilight made it difficult to see his expression. She tugged on his neckcloth and he bent a little, and they rested their foreheads together.

Her breathing was ragged, but she barely heard it over her pounding heart.

"I would be an idiot to try to change you, to make you be someone you aren't." With his thumbs he stroked her neck, just below her ears. "Marry me, Harriet. Sail with me. Manage this manor and estate with me. Whatever life requires of us, so long as we do it together."

She grasped his face with both hands, frustrated she couldn't see the sincerity in his gorgeous blue eyes through the tears blurring her vision. She sniffed.

"I'll beg if I have to." He started to bend one knee.

She hauled him in for a kiss. He wrapped his arms around her and lifted her off her feet, holding her against the length of his body, and she twined her arms around his neck.

He leaned back, his head tilted. "Does this mean yes?"

"Yes," she whispered. She cleared her throat. "Yes, yes, yes!"

She was about to kiss him again when applause and cheers from above caught her attention. They both looked up. Whoever had been standing at the edge moved back out of sight so quickly, only shadows were visible.

"Um, you have a party going on."

He still had his arms wrapped around her lower back, holding her up snug against his big, masculine body. He gave her a squeeze. "Is that a double entendre?"

She chuckled. "I was referring to the large group of people gathered on your lawn. Who a few minutes ago witnessed you kiss a man. At least that's what it probably looked like to them."

"Bugger them. I'll kiss who I want." He tried to kiss her again.

She tilted back out of his reach. "Oh, really?" She arched her brows.

He nodded. "And the only person I want to kiss is you."

After another lengthy kiss, he gently set her on her feet. He looked up the path to the lawn and sighed, then quickly brightened as though just remembering something. "There are some friends here I'd like you to meet." He took her hand again, interlacing their fingers, and led her up the steps to the lawn.

The quartet was still playing for a handful of couples on the dance floor, but there was a suspicious crowding near the edge of the lawn, including his friends, all failing miserably at feigning nonchalance and disinterest.

He quickly introduced Sinclair, Alistair, Tony, and their wives.

"That was my favorite waistcoat, you know," Charlotte said, throwing her arms around Harriet. "It's so good to see you again!"

Harriet laughed and hugged her one-armed, as Nick hadn't let go. "You as well."

"It appears you were right, Charlie," Nick said. "I have an announcement to make after all."

She whooped with delight, which she quickly muffled against Alistair's sleeve.

Nick shortened his stride to match Harriet's, but she was still breathless when they climbed the steps at the side of the house. Torches had been lit and set at intervals around the lawn's perimeter to stave off the darkness, and the bonfires burned brightly. The musicians ended their piece and Nick gestured for them to rest. Conversation still buzzed. Tony put two fingers to his mouth and gave a piercing whistle.

Absolute silence fell, and all eyes were on her and Nick. Harriet gulped.

He gave her hand a reassuring squeeze.

She scanned the assembled crowd of at least two hundred people, and after a moment spotted Chang, who put his hands together and bowed, and Jonesy, who tugged his forelock. Close to them she saw Norton, who gave her a big grin. The woman with her arm tucked through his wore elegant English clothing, accessorized with a tall, jeweled comb and green lace mantilla over her black hair. Caroline.

Harriet's eyes widened when she realized nearby were four more women, each with the same distinctive black hair and blue eyes as

Nick and Zach, in their late twenties to early forties. Nick's sisters. And there was the rascal Zach himself, standing beside them, beaming at her. Harriet shook her finger at Zach in mock anger. He spread his hands in a gesture of innocence. Charlotte and the friends Nick had introduced her to stood just behind them.

"Thank you all for coming today," Nick announced in his Captain voice. "You know how much I enjoy giving long speeches, so ... I would like to introduce you, my friends and family, to Miss Harriet Chase. Soon to be my wife." He turned to her, his gaze caressing her face. "And co-captain."

She would not turn into a watering pot in front of all these people, but it was a near thing.

There were cheers and applause, startled exclamations about her gender and unusual attire, and comments in the vein of they "knew his lordship weren't kissing a man." Harriet barely heard them, as Nick held her hands in both of his and claimed her lips in a chaste kiss, publicly sealing their betrothal.

They stepped down to the grass and were immediately swarmed with well-wishers. Harriet was introduced to a dizzying array of sisters and in-laws, a white-haired stoop-shouldered lady who claimed to have known Nick since he was in leading strings, and a host of other tenants and workers.

His friends gathered round and the women gathered her up, especially Charlotte.

"But what about the fair Esmeralda at the Duck and Drake in Weymouth?" Tony teased.

Harriet put her hands on her hips, her brow arched, watching Nick's jaw move but hearing no sound emerge.

After a moment, his shoulders slumped. "At the risk of damaging my reputation, I'll let you in on a secret." He looked at each of them in turn.

Tony, Alistair, Sinclair, and their wives leaned in close, as well as Harriet.

"Esmeralda is sixty if she's a day and makes the best jam tarts in Dorset." His expression turned sober. "Apparently I remind her of her grandson who went off to war and came home in a box."

Tony's brow furrowed. "Not a mistress, then?"

"Good heavens, no." Nick looked at Harriet. "Ten years ago I was at the Duck and Drake shortly after Grandfather died. Inheriting ownership of *Wind Dancer* was small compensation for losing him, and I was ... grieving. Esmeralda took away my whisky and gave me jam tarts and tea instead."

Harriet covered her mouth with her hand, her heart swelling at the image of an adolescent Nick and a surrogate grandmother comforting one another.

"Since then, I've made a point to visit Weymouth and check on her as often as I can." His friends started to ask questions and tease him, but Nick tugged Harriet away, to the outer edge of the crowd. Her hand still tucked in his, he tilted his head back, cupped his free hand to his mouth, and over the din of the crowd shouted a phrase in Mandarin.

From the far side of the lawn, she heard an answering shout from Chang.

"A new addition to the Sheffield harvest festival tradition," Nick said, sharing a mischievous grin with her.

Moments later there was a small explosion and a bright burst of light in the sky over the manor house. More explosions ensued in rapid succession, the fireworks getting bigger, louder, and higher, with bright orange flashes and golden light. Guests gave startled shouts, applause, and laughter.

Harriet tilted her head back to enjoy the show. She didn't care that she was grinning with childish delight. Nick, soon to become her husband, stood at her side. Chang was putting on a much better exhibit than the simple fireworks traditionally set off on Guy Fawkes Day in the Brixham village square. Her heart was full. The day could not get any better.

Still holding her hand, Nick caressed her cheek, his mouth curved in a tender smile. "*Mi pequeño wren marrón*," he said softly, just before he touched his lips to hers.

Being called a little brown wren wasn't the most romantic sentiment, even though she had recently learned it was a Spanish term of endearment. Well, she did have brown hair and brown eyes. It wasn't much different from being called a little cabbage in French. But the important thing was that Nick was saying she was *his*, just as he was hers, and belonging was more important than elaborate, poetic declarations.

He leaned back far enough to gaze into her eyes. "I love you."

That simple, sincere declaration was all the romance Harriet needed from her pirate. Privateer. Honest merchantman. Whatever.

Happy tears filling her eyes, she tugged his neckcloth to bring him close. "I love you, too," she whispered as another firework burst overhead, shooting showers of sparks.

* * *

Thank you for reading *The Viscount's Hidden Treasure*, the fourth and final book in the Scandalous Ladies series. I hope you enjoyed Nick and Harriet's story!

Previous books in the series are *What An Earl Wants*, featuring Benjamin, Earl of Sinclair, and Jo Quincy; *Kiss From A Rogue*, featuring Ben's brother Tony and Sylvia; and *Confessions of A Viscount*, featuring Alistair and Charlotte. Each book can be read as a stand-alone, though most readers prefer to enjoy them in the order published.

To stay informed about upcoming releases, please visit my website: ShirleyKarrAuthor.com

Subscribers to my email list can download a free copy of my *Regency Phrasebook: A Compendium of Slang, Idioms, and Curious Phrases Commonly Found in Historical Fiction.* I only email about once per month or when I have news to share. I hate spam as much as you do!

To help other readers find my books, I'd be forever grateful if you posted a review at your favorite site to buy or discuss books. A review can be as detailed as you like or as simple as "I liked this book." Thank you!

* * *

Keep reading for a sneak peek at my next book, *My Reluctant Earl,* book one of the Brazen Bluestockings series. As a teacher at Madame Zavrina's Torquay Academy for Ladies, Harriet is officially the last heroine of the Scandalous Ladies, and unofficially the first heroine of the Brazen Bluestockings, which follows teachers and staff from the Academy.

* * *

On the terrace outside the ballroom, David, Earl of Ravencroft, paused a moment while his eyes adjusted to the faint light of a waning half-moon. There, at the back of the garden. A flash of pale-colored skirt disappearing into the gazebo. He ran down the path, keeping his footsteps light in case he had misread the situation, and peered into the gazebo.

The young woman was semi-reclining on a bench, her head lolled back, one foot on the floor, one leg stretched out on the bench. The man with the striped waistcoat had his breeches unbuttoned and was trying to raise her skirts. She roused a bit at that and feebly batted at his hands. "No. Go 'way," she slurred.

David stepped into the gazebo. "Leave her," he commanded.

Striped Waistcoat dropped the girl's skirt and glared at the intruder. "Get your own bit o' muslin. Bugger off."

"Leave now, under your own power," David said in a conversational tone as he retrieved his dagger from its hidden pocket. He held the blade up, letting moonlight glint off the sharp tip. He dropped his voice two octaves to a rumbling bass. "Or you'll leave as a eunuch."

The man squeaked—really, no other word could describe the high-pitched sound that emerged from his throat—and stumbled from the gazebo, holding up his breeches with one hand. David watched him dash down the path until he melted into the shadows near the house.

The woman was struggling to sit up. "Go 'way," she said. "I'll bite."

"I'd prefer that you didn't." David reached for her but then hesitated. "I'm going to help you stand." She didn't protest further, so he grasped her wrists and pulled her upright.

She swayed and fell against his chest. "So tired," she mumbled into his cravat, her hands grabbing his waist. "Don't un'stand."

"Let's get you back to the ballroom before anyone misses you." He wrapped an arm around her shoulders, got her moving, and steered them out to the path.

They'd walked only a few steps when she wrenched from his grasp. "Sick."

He caught her about the waist in time to keep her from pitching face-first into the rose bushes while she cast up her accounts. He held her silk shawl back, and soon he was supporting most of her weight as she hung over his arm, retching. He hoped she missed his shoes.

She groaned. Coughed and spit. And groaned again.

"Can you walk?"

She needed help to stand upright again, but then pushed away from him. She took two steps and her knees buckled.

David caught her and swung her up into his arms.

"Guess not." She patted his shoulder. "Good catch."

"You're welcome." He headed for the terrace but slowed his steps as he realized he could not possibly return her to the ballroom in her present condition. Not unless he wanted to see their engagement announcement published in *The Times* two days hence.

After some swift calculations, he swerved off the path and headed around the side of the townhouse, staying in the shadows. He paused while they were still fully in the dark. If he stepped out into the light of streetlamps and the half-moon to reach his carriage, her face would be seen.

He propped one foot on a garden bench that no doubt afforded a lovely view of the rosebushes, and supported her weight on his knee. "Please trust that I am trying to help, not make things worse."

She didn't speak but patted his shoulder again.

He tugged the delicate silk shawl with its distinctive colors and pattern from her shoulders and stuffed it into his coat pocket. Praying that she didn't have anything more to cast up, he shifted his grip, heaved her up, and settled her over his shoulder, one arm wrapped around the back of her thighs, the other holding her arm over his opposite shoulder.

She made a muffled sound that might have been an indignant protest but sounded suspiciously like a giggle. Her left arm hung down in back, occasionally bumping into him as he walked. He could swear that more than once she patted his bottom.

He strode toward his carriage as if carrying a miss over his shoulder was an everyday occurrence, ignoring the stares from passers-by and coachmen.

"My lord?" Gilroy, his footman, jumped down from the bench. He and the coachman exchanged worried glances.

"A blackguard put something in her drink." He quickly gave instructions for Gilroy to find the girl's chaperone, a matron in a purple turban with three ostrich feathers, and tell her the miss had a headache and was going home with friends. And then convey David's apologies to his sister, as her party would need to find another way home.

While the footman was gone, the coachman helped David climb into the carriage. The mysterious miss was as limp as a rag doll, incapable of sitting upright. To keep her from sliding to the floor, he settled her on his lap, her head on his shoulder.

She shivered and tried to burrow inside his coat. He mentally smacked himself. "Grab the blanket, if you please."

"Right away, my lord."

Soon the carriage blanket was draped over her and she relaxed against David with a sigh.

Gilroy poked his head in the door. "All done as you requested, my lord."

"Thank you." He'd been running through his options of what to do with her that would have the least consequence for either of them. "Take us to my Aunt Constance, please."

Moments later, the coach rocked into motion.

She struggled to sit up, frantically looking around the dark interior of the coach. "Can't b'lieve I'm being abducted," she muttered, pushing away from him.

"Appearances to the contrary," David said, tucking her back against him before she overbalanced and ended up on the floor anyway, "this is not an abduction. It's a rescue."

She snorted.

"You'll have to forgive me. I have limited experience at rescuing damsels in distress."

She giggled. "I have lim'ted esper ...exp ... I'm not used to being in distress."

"We'll just have to find our way along together, then."

To read more of *My Reluctant Earl*, check your favorite book retailer or my website: ShirleyKarrAuthor.com

Also by Shirley Karr:

Brazen Bluestockings
My Reluctant Earl
My Devoted Viscount (spring 2024)

Scandalous Ladies
What An Earl Wants
Kiss From A Rogue
Confessions of A Viscount
The Viscount's Hidden Treasure

Watch for more at ShirleyKarrAuthor.com.

ABOUT THE AUTHOR

Shirley Karr's love of all things Regency began in childhood, when her father's Air Force career took the family to England for four years. Not only did they visit historic houses, museums, and castles galore, they lived in centuries-old housing.

She currently resides in the Pacific Northwest with her husband (whom she met on a blind date and married five months later), son, and multiple four-legged family members. To unwind, she loves to make jewelry with gemstones and pearls, grow tomatoes, and go tent camping at the Oregon coast.

She's back after a fourteen-year break from writing, telling lighthearted stories of adventure and romance with a dash of spice, set in Regency England.

I love to hear from readers! Drop me a line at
Shirley@ShirleyKarrAuthor.com
Visit me on the web: ShirleyKarrAuthor.com

Follow me on social media:

Facebook: Shirley Karr Author

Instagram: Shirley Karr Author

Pinterest: Shirley Karr Author

BookBub: Shirley Karr

Goodreads: Shirley Karr